Machines and Men

For Edward John Carnell
1912–1972

Machines and Men

Keith Roberts

WILDSIDE PRESS: MMIII

Stories

Machines

Manipulation	9
Escapism	36
Boulter's Canaries	61
Sub-Lim	83
Breakdown	110

Men

Therapy 2000	133
The Deeps	154
Manscarer	174
Synth	198
The Pace That Kills	250

'Manipulation' and 'Boulter's Canaries' first appeared in *New Writings in SF 3* (Dennis Dobson, 1965), 'Escapism' in *Science Fantasy 67* (Roberts & Vinter, 1964), 'Sub-Lim' in *New Writings in SF 4* (Dennis Dobson, 1965), 'Breakdown' in *SF Impulse 8* (Roberts & Vinter, 1966), 'Therapy 2000' in *New Writings in SF 15* (Dennis Dobson, 1969), 'The Deeps' in *Orbit One* (Putnam, 1966), 'Manscarer' in *New Writings in SF 8* (Dennis Dobson, 1966), 'Synth' in *New Writings in SF 7* (Dennis Dobson, 1966), and 'The Pace that Kills' in *SF Impulse 3* (Roberts & Vinter, 1966).

Machines

Manipulation

No!

No! No! No!

I said I would never use my Power again. I won't. It's wrong and vile. I remember what I promised myself ten years ago, walking in the dark after Mother died.

It kept her alive for years. The doctors had never seen anything like it. It was her heart. . . .

God knows it was difficult. Not like this thing I want to do now. This could be so easy.

When Mother was alive I used to stay up nights, work round the clock on that feeble old heart, strengthening, renewing. I built a new valve once, piece by microscopic piece. Three days and nights that took me, working non-stop. Do you know how many cells there are in the ventricles of a human heart?

I do. . . .

Mother knew what was happening. She could feel all the little adjustments going on, the million cobweb-forces twitching between us keeping her alive. She tried to give up three times. But she couldn't die because her heart couldn't stop. And her heart couldn't stop because I was driving it.

Technically she did die once. I worked that heart for twenty hours before it would beat on its own again. They'd use an electronic pacemaker now. There was nothing of the sort then.

I was born with my Power. It didn't seem wrong to use it. I couldn't sit and let her die. I never realised though until almost the last, how she'd come to hate me. Hate my phosphorescent eyes and my million hands, tiny, invisible, never-resting hands. . . .

I pull the bedclothes over my head, trying to make the black room even darker. I dig my face in the pillow, try to shut out the deep noise of the overrun as Julie changes up after a corner. But I only succeed in muffling my ears.

Mother won in the end. She was too clever for me. If she'd cut her wrists or opened her throat it wouldn't have mattered because I'd have seamed up the wounded flesh as fast as the blade went through it. If she'd jumped from a building I'd have caught her and lowered her to the ground. But she didn't do that. All she did was swallow a hundred little white tablets.

I woke in the night. I was already inside her. I knew what was wrong. Knew she'd beaten me. I was fast enough to juggle cells as they multiplied and died, but these were molecules. The wrong sort of molecules. They came pouring and flooding through the universe of her body, changing things as they came. I could see amino acids and peptones, watch proteins building up like pearly chains against a void, but now there were too many molecules. I fought them. I was everywhere at once, grabbing them, altering them, making them harmless. But it was no use. It was like a locust plague. Like trying to catch the insects one by one in your hands and kill enough to stop the swarm, and the sky dark with them for miles. . . .

I had to walk out from inside her, leave everything still and quiet. I ran away from the house, using my feet. I never went back. Since then I've never used the Power. I won't now. I've been hungry, and not used it. Sat in a cell and unlocked and locked the door the long night through. It was only a poor steel thing, useless and simple, and I played with it, but I wouldn't help myself. My mother killed herself to get away from this . . . thing I can do. I won't ever use the Power again.

You can look up telekineticists in books. They'll tell you they are people who can move things without touching them, change physical states at a distance. They'll also tell you such beings don't exist. Well, the books are wrong.

I'm one. . . .

I ram the heels of my hands against my eyes. Peacocks flick their tails beneath the lids. The nervelights paint Julie in crazy colours, lilac and aniline red and burning green, but they can't block her out.

She's driving a wheeled rainbow. The colours lap and flow along the bodywork, stream out behind the tail. I relax the pressure and the iridescence vanishes. She is still there.

I can't help it. I have a million hands again, groping over that flying car. I'm low down in the chassis, in the springs, feeling the shocks stream into the tempered metal. Watching the curving rush of the road, looking out through the stone-guard with the white fans of the headlights in front and the geometric cliff of the rad behind me. I'm in the engine seeing in spite of blackness the clamouring ballet of pushrods and tappets. In the steering column feeling the stresses from the wheels, the countering resistance of Julie's arms. I linger at the steering rim, savouring the transition from metal to flesh where her hands are gripping it firm. . . .

I feel my pulse accelerating. That pounding, that isn't the engine. That's my heart. I go rigid, not breathing, thinking of what I'm going to do. I poise two of my hands over her wrists, others above the roaring venturis of the carbs where I can see the throttle linkages move in unison as she drives through the bends. In a second I'm going to whip her arms behind her, pinion them, open the throttles and take control. I'm going to watch her face as the silver road snakes at her and the trees, as the revs climb and the wheelrim in front of her swings to the bends. Faster, and faster, and faster . . . and when she's had enough, when she can't take any more, *I'm going to let go.* . . .

I roll out of bed and slap at the lampswitch with my hand.

My face and body are covered with sweat. I run the tap in the handbasin, put my head under it. The cold water shocks. I glare round. See double. The details of the tawdry room registering dim through flashing, white-lit trees. The noise of the engine, it's drumming in my ears. I reel about, put my hand out to the rushing macadam that is a wall. I know I've got to break this link. I concentrate, put all my being and will into it. The images I want form somehow. Putting out an oilwell fire. Reeling fuse, waiting, pressing the plunger . . . *Now* . . . a huge flash, obliterating everything.

Silence. Dimness. A little room in a cheap boarding house. Faded, striped paper. Useless gasbracket draped with cobwebs. Cracked mirror. My jacket, trousers, slung across a chair. I'm leaning against the wall trembling. I go sit on the bed. Light a cigarette, drag the smoke down deep. This is better. I'm O.K. again.

I don't think I'm just a telekineticist.

God, listen to me! *Just* a telekineticist. . . . It's true, though. I've got this other thing, E.S.P., psi factor, devil possession, I don't know what its name is. To . . . do a job, I don't even have to be there. I can walk through a city miles away, see the neon and the crowds, alley cats prowling, leaves and cigarette packets in the gutters, rain bouncing on the roads. I can watch a murder done there, or an act of love, and have to go find a nameboard to see where I've been. . . .

Distance is nothing to do with it. Near or far, it's all the same. For instance right now I know Julie's driving a car. But I don't know where. She could be a mile away. She could be in Nevada.

I think about something else, anything. I don't want to go back to Julie for both our sakes. I pull on the cigarette. I get mad. I ask myself, what do books and names matter, what the hell's a name? Nobody like me has ever existed before. I've got a wild talent.

The room is quiet as a grave. I finish one cigarette and light another from it. I still feel shaky. I get up, go to the cupboard over the washbasin. It's a flat-brown, rickety little cupboard, fluff and muck on the top of it, badly fitting doors. I scraped a bit of paint off a door once. It wasn't wooden. Made out of bits of Victorian newspapers stuck together to make a sort of cardboard. Next the cupboard there's the mirror, one corner gone, glass flecked over with greasy ginger spots. That's the sort of trash I live with. And I could have made my fortune.

I open the doors, get out a bottle of Scotch and a glass. I pour myself a treble and put the bottle back. Suddenly the room seems stuffy, full of smoke. I go to the window, undo the catch. I bang the grimy frame to free it and lever it open. Cooler air moves against my face and there's the noise of the main road just down the hill. I lean on the sill and stare at the moving reflections of the lights. The road roars like that all night long. Julie's on a road right now, driving somewhere. God knows where.

Something wakes up in my mind. It's like stepping on a dog you didn't know was there, seeing it come up at your face. It's as quick as that. For a second I'm seeing the bonnet of a speeding car, hearing an engine louder than the ones outside. I jerk back into the room in panic. The car vanishes. I realise how careful I've got to be.

I lay back on the bed with the glass in my hand. I start to make up a mental image. Something I can hang like a screen in front of the thing I don't want to see. I compose the picture all of opposites. Julie's car is rushing along doing eighty or ninety. So I take something static. A rock will do. It's a red car so we'll have a neutral, blue-grey sort of rock. The car's moving in darkness, so my rock will be in pouring sunlight. Yes, there it is, big and blue. Immensely static. Deep shadows round its base where it's embedded in the ground. It's a good sharp image; I can see the striations in the rock and the weathering, feel the sun heat striking back from it on to my face. I stand back mentally, appraise my work. Yes, that'll do, it's fine. That rock won't ever move.

The roomlight starts to annoy me, glaring in my eyes. It's a naked bulb on a flex, no shade. Yellow crab-patterns from the filament reaching across the ceiling. I put my hand out and switch it off. I don't need light any more.

I finish the whisky and go back to my rock image. I recognize it now. It's a rock I saw when I was on holiday with Bill years ago. There's that little bay behind it and the sun-haze, the twinkle of the sea. I remember that holiday well, little bits and snatches of it are so clear. How old would I have been? Nine, ten? Something like that. I try to work out how long it's been since I saw my brother. Must be all of six years. Old Bill was a good chap. Hadn't got my . . . gift, lucky blighter.

He knew about it though. That's why we're estranged. . . .

I think back to that holiday, evoke as much of it as I can. The cigarette makes a steady arc in the blackness as I draw on it, let my arm sag to one side, draw on it again. The sun-glint on the water, hot sand, the tallness of cliffs. Coolness and hardness of their great flanks turned away from the sun, suck and boom of the sea in the hidden caverns at their bases.

Julie has gone on holiday. Down to the coast with Ted to laugh and kiss and lie in the sun and show off her body. . . .

The whisky starts to take effect. I feel dopey and confused. I'd had a good thrash before I came up tonight. I'm with Bill again but he's not sitting on the rock, he's driving it. It's red, it has headlights and it roars. The road slips away behind it.

The cigarette bites into my fingers. I fling it away and lie back again. My hand throbs. But I don't bother to mend the burn. I'm glad of the pain. It keeps me within myself, lying on a bed in this rooming house, safely. I lie for an hour, watching the moon rise over the rooftops, hearing the cars on that distant road. I sleep.

It's a hollow, confused sort of dream. There's Julie, face underlit from the dash, eyes big and soft-looking in the light from the dials. The wind gusting through the lowered driving window, playing in her hair. Short hair, gay-unruly, curly, copper-brown. She's a redhead, but not green-eyed. Deep blue eyes, aquamarine. Dark now, solemn. She's concentrating on the road. She's a good driver. I can feel how good she is by the responses of the machine. She's not riding that motor, she's a part of it. The wheels, the gears, they're extensions of her body. I crane round for a look at the speedo. She's holding a steady eighty, keeping it up mile after mile. No effort. I wonder where the hell she's going in such a hurry. This wasn't scheduled . . . I wonder about the car. It isn't hers, I'm sure of that, and it couldn't belong to Ted. It's just a fine motor, not flashy, not chromy enough for Ted. Not showy enough by half.

I don't worry long; in dreams, you just accept. I watch the road whipping under the bonnet, streaming out behind the clean line of the tail. After a time I get to feel the car's stationary, the wheels just idling, keeping pace with the flying ground. Then I seem to see the whole earth rolling under those wheels, the car fixed in space but still leaping towards the rising sun. I feel myself whirling with the planet, the tug of gravity urging my body down towards the deep core. I begin to lose all sense of identity.

A road sign goes past but I'm not quick enough to read it. I move restlessly on the bed, conscious of doing wrong, too sleepy to pull out of the dream again. I start playing with the steering.

This is fun. I'm holding the car's wheel, hard, opening my grip and letting the rim slide to the bends, feeling Julie's strength take the motor round. Then grip again, relax, grip . . . if she wanted to move that wheel now she couldn't because I've got it braced; she couldn't move it a fraction. I'm stronger than she is—

Damn—

Oh, I was too late then. A hundredth of a second was all but I was still too late. I should have known, she's got such a touch . . . she felt the wrongness there in the steering column. She knew there was something. A sudden tug, unexpected, trying me out. My hands were away and gone in a flash but she felt the resistance. I saw the frown come, in the same instant I let go. She's testing again now, cautiously, little pulls one way then the other. But the wheel is free. . . .

I sit up slowly. A second ago I was nearly asleep. Now sleep is a million miles away. I was never so awake, so cold.

I . . . felt something then. Only for a moment, but it was there. A little surge of feeling, the first start of panic. *And it wasn't my fear.* . . .

I try to swallow; but my mouth, it never had any saliva. It's bone dry, desiccated, feels raw. I find the cigarettes. My hand is clumsy, spills them over the bed and across the floor. I feel for one in the dark, light it, flick the match away. I lie there with the thing in my fingers, drawing on it, seeing the glow reflect back ghost-pink off the ceiling. My body is quiet, but not my brain or my heart. The heart thuds steady, savage; I can hear the thumping in the silent room. I'm . . . intensely alive, head to toes. My body feels everything, knows everything. I can sense the earth turning again and myself spread-eagled on it inching towards the sun. . . .

That's what I meant about Mother hating me. Right at the last, when we were fighting like that, me wanting to keep her and her trying to go away and down, I felt her mind. That's how I know. The hate, it was like a bright flame scorching at me then getting dimmer, flickering, dying away. . . . No words. They're nothing. It was worse than words. Later, when the shock had gone a little, I wanted to do it again, make a contact with somebody else. But I couldn't. The telekinesis, that was no trouble ever. It refined itself and sharpened, got more and more sensitive even though I'd left it lie to rust. . . .

I know why my heart is protesting like this. It's because I realised subconsciously in that split part of a second when I was touching Julie's mind that this other thing has been grow-ing in the dark as well. I know now I can do it again. I know I'm going to be a telepath.

And they don't exist either.

I go back, deliberately this time, to the car. I feel as if I'm moving along a predestined course that can have only one end. I study Julie in microscopic detail.

She's driving slower, not much above fifty. She's still testing, veering in to the verge then back out to the cats' eyes again. Pulling and touching at that steering, trying to account for what she felt. I don't know what's in her mind. I strain to make a contact but there's nothing there. She centres the wheel and accelerates. I catch a tiny shrug, the smallest lift of an eyebrow. She's decided she dozed for a moment. She'll have to be more careful. She's been driving a long time and she's sleepier than she realised.

They weren't her thoughts, they were mine grafted on. I know when I'm in another mind; there's . . . something. Everything. Colours and textures all different. A new way of breathing, thinking. Impossible to get it into words. It's weird. You own another body, another soul. . . .

I've got to be careful here. I can't be sure, but I think she suspects me. . . . I meddled with her once you see. A long time back. It was late at night and I was drunk. She felt the incubus. I'm sure she knew it was me. It didn't do any good, and afterwards it gave me hell.

I lie there a long while trying to rest. My heart is still pounding away under the bedclothes. I move my hand down and feel it bumping at my ribs like something trying to crack out from an egg. I know, in a detached way, my body won't stand this strain for ever. Something will have to give . . . Somehow or other I've got to resolve this thing. Then I can relax.

First, I've got to beat the fear.

There are a lot of sorts of fear. I suppose one sort comes if you're on your own some place and you cut an artery and there's nobody to help and you know you've only got minutes. That's fear . . . and another sort is when there are the footsteps in the night, and the creaks and the laughing, and the branch taps the pane, insistent there behind the curtains; but there isn't any branch. . . .

I'm about to enter another mind. That's the worst fear of all. . . .

I've done it before, but only seconds at a time. And then it was bad enough. This is going to be worse than opening a private diary, packed full of things about you. Worse than looking in a mirror under a glaring light. Worse than these things, more truthful than the diary, more searching than the light. I begin to see the only thing that keeps any of us sane is that we can't communicate. Oh we can talk, write letters maybe or compose music, a poem, they're better ways of getting across, but we still have to be tuned and nobody's ever finally certain what the message is. . . . We're all in a mist, thick, like cotton-wool. We hide in it from each other, from ourselves, wrap ourselves away. Deep down we want it like that because it's for the best. . . .

But there's a devil inside us, we call it hope. That last little thing the girl let out the box, that was the worst plague of all. It's hope makes you ask the question when you already know the answer, hope makes you open that locked diary, turn on that glaring light. . . . I don't want to hope. I'm through with it, done. But I'm hoping. . . .

I try to steady my heart but my own body's out of control. I turn my ears inward, hear the blood move like water pounding through a weir. I realise I'm gasping for air and somehow make my breathing slow down.

I can see now, all my life I've been moving towards this one point. I'm going to do something now that nobody's done before. I'm going to develop, shake out my wings and soar. I'm going to do it because it has to be done. This will be a turning point in the history of the world, the first event in a new order of things. It's going to happen here, in this damp, peeling attic room. Well, a man can't always choose the place and time.

But why Julie; God, why does it have to be with Julie?

Got to stop thinking like that. I tell myself I don't matter. I'm dead, dust. . . . I try to see the bigness of what's going to happen, the panoramic significance of it. For a few moments I almost manage it. It isn't exactly like a vision; it's like standing on the edge of a great sea and hearing the bawling, confused noise of it and knowing it stretches away and away for all time. . . .

Once there was a primal cell. It hung in a void and it was complete and perfect, it *knew itself*. . . . But the cell had to split, and the halves sailed away, and there was mystery. And the mystery grew, through all the years stacked on years that we call evolution. There were people, groping in the mist, trying to know; man and woman, the woman wanting to enfold, the man wanting to lose himself, go right back down to that primal core, that oneness. That's the only peace we look for till the grave. Nothing in life but needing to join; and that's a need we share with everything that ever lived right through time. The soul passing to Nirvana, that's the state of not-being, of union with everything, ultimate rest . . . the gods will die at the Ragnarok, all things cease at Armageddon . . . not-being is fusion, fusion not-being. I see the whole shape of evolution, complexity increasing, the old cell running and jumping and crawling and slithering and oozing and flying, then gliding back, recombining into an all-seeing, all-knowing unit; the end of mystery. Here, in this dirty room in a two-bit town, that reversal is about to start. Two entities go back to oneness. The cell that split all that dumb time ago knows itself again.

This is it now. Go steady, boy. You're uplifted, outside yourself. You've left self behind. Nothing matters except that you go steady, go slow, *make your base*. . . .

I can see her face again in the light from the dash. Her eyes, mouth . . . little beauty spot on her lip, her teeth, hair curling against the collar of her windcheater. I never paid even Julie this close attention before. I feel I'm getting closer to the thing I want to do. . . .

Surprise.

I know, dimly, the way I'm going to manage the jump. How to get across into the other half of perception, the part they call telepathy. It's a sort of—twist, a piece of mental acrobatics. There's no basic difference between this and what I could do before. But I thought . . . never mind. Let it go, it doesn't matter. Sort it out later. The end counts now, not the means.

I was trying too hard before, thinking there was a difference. It's still a case of grasping something at a distance, it's just that I've never tried to hold anything as nebulous as this. Like catching a will o' the wisp. I retain the physical picture of Julie, as clear and sharp as an image in a stereoscopic film, and I keep . . . moving forward is the only way I can describe it, edging after that Jack o' lantern Thing that doesn't quite have a form. Julie's thought. . . .

I'm getting a clear picture through her eyes. That's something I never quite managed before. I realise arbitrarily how good her sight is. We watch the flick-flick-flick of the cats' eyes in the road. Our minds are very close now. She's half hypnotised by the winking studs. So am I.

Deeper again, nearer. . . . Back on the bed my body has stopped breathing. I'm almost home. Somewhere a thought forms. *'Been a long night.'* Another answers it. *'Yes, but the night is nearly done. . . .'*

Her thoughts?

No, mine. Both mine. . . . There's one of hers though. In the mist. Mist? Fog, void. Primeval. . . . It's iridescent, with a texture, a resistance of its own. Impossible to hurry here. Like swimming under water. Nightmare, seeing the thing ahead, not able to move. Don't know where I am. On the border of things physical . . . inside an atom. . . .

It's easy, at last. The thought, the thing that fills her mind; it's there right ahead, opening like a flower. I'm stationary, not pushing any more, swallowing fire that doesn't burn. . . .

A click. A lens dropping in some complex array. Final adjustment. . . .

Reflex. A leap, a gurgling flailing convulsion that takes me out of

her, body and mind, with a cold wrenching, leaves me falling, a
hundred miles up, no parachute, the ground spinning up to meet me as
I come right back down to earth—

I'm lying in the little room. There seems to be a weight on
my chest, pressing me down. My stomach is full of quicksilver
or lead; something heavy and cold and final. A taste in my
mouth, rusty, salty, like blood. Heart pounding still but
slower, heavier. All effort done.

There was feeling there. A rushing sense of love, compound
of sorrow and pain. And an image, vague at first and shaky
like something seen through water then hardening and taking
on form and colour, becoming recognisable. . . .

Ted, grinning up at me out of the depths of Julie's brain.

I hold a hand out in front of me in the darkness, slowly
clench it into a fist. I open the fingers again and see the white
half-moons on the palm darken and fill. I don't make a
sound.

I try to remember what I was thinking about a few minutes
ago. It's cloudy now and vague. I'd been going to change the
course of history, hadn't I? Achieve something of cosmic im-
portance, reverse evolution. Give God a bit of a helping hand,
solve the Mystery of Life. How completely can you fool
yourself? I'm not going to solve anything. Or achieve anything. I see I was putting off the moment when I had to poke
into Julie's mind because I was scared of what would be there.
I never wanted to change the universe. I only wanted one
thing. Julie. It's more than a want now, it's a burning, a huge
need. But I can't have her. I know that finally, from what I
saw in her mind.

I'm nothing. I never was anything. Telekinesis, that's a toy
for kids. I can see that now. We've all of us got telekinesis,
we've had it for years. We can all move things miles off, look
into closed boxes, see round corners. Well can't we? We've got
machines can do all that for us, all that and more, telekinesis
isn't new any longer. And the other thing, what good is that,
it can show me how people hate, despise. . . . I can see myself

in their minds bloated, obscene, a reflection from a Hall of Mirrors. . . . I don't want to see myself like that, painted garish colours by Julie's fear and loathing. I don't want to see her sublimated vision of Ted. I don't want anything any more.

Just that short time ago my Power was the reason for existence. Now I don't want the Power. There's nothing left. No point in going on.

I lie there a long while under the weight of that snippet of knowledge. Then, slowly at first, I begin to see the wild humour of the thing. I start to chuckle.

I roll my head backward and forward on the pillow. I can see myself now as a sort of cosmic clown, shaking my unearthly cap and bells. The image is hilarious. The laughter gets louder, bubbling out of me. I realise the noise is ringing in the little room. I try to stifle it. I hold my breath; for a time I quiver inside then I get calm again.

I still have a decision to make. It isn't the decision I thought it was though. It's something quite different.

Suddenly I remember a guy I used to know years back. Lorimer was his name, or Latimer. Yes, that was it, Eddie Latimer. Good-looking guy with a sensitive dark face and the sort of strong thin wide-knuckled hands you see on an artist or a craftsman. But he was beat, way down. He was a sculptor, or had been, and he drove a dumper for a living, and all the hate there ever was showed there in the backs of his eyes. We used to swill beer together in some town or other, I've even forgotten the name of it. And he only ever had one message for me. 'Hate' he used to say. 'Hate is O.K., it's the same as love. Insignificance, not-mattering, that's the only thing that's all-out bad. If you can't be loved son, *be hated*. . . .' He'd done some black things, had Eddie, in the name of hate. . . .

There isn't a decision any more, it's been made for me. I'd been going to use the Power for good, take a step forward that maybe folks everywhere would have learned to copy. It was a big experiment, I didn't mind being the guinea pig. But the first thing I saw embedded in Julie's mind, the image of the grinning gigolo she picked out for a mate . . . I couldn't take that, I wasn't expected to.

So it looks like this is the Will of God.

Nothing that breathes can ever really stop still, only in death. And I'm not going to kill myself. I can't stop using the Power now, I can't build for good so I'll build for evil. Just like Eddie. I can't be loved so I'll be hated. *I will not be mocked.* . . .

Now I need the stimulus of rage. I could reach into myself and milk my own adrenals, set them pumping. But I won't. I'll do it the slow way. That's better because you can feel the power inside you build up and up. That way there's a consummation.

I go back in time to just after Mother died. I parade all the empty days, the effort, the hopelessness.

Like I said, I gave up telekinesis. I owed that much to her. But I was smart. I used the other thing instead, the harmless watching ability. I'd got a plan for myself.

Right back from when I was a little kid I knew what I wanted. Money, and the power it gives you. I was going to make sure nobody would push me, work my guts out, break me like they broke Mother. I saw her get old trying to run the family, keep us fed. That's the way it is in this life. You either burn up other people or you get burned up yourself. Mother got burned up. Maybe she was happy in a way. I don't know and I don't care. All that matters is they burned her up. I had to watch it. I used to tell myself whatever else came, that wasn't going to happen to me.

The things of this world. . . . Like a mug I thought I could get them. Even without the Power. All I had to do was take a job, any job. And wait. Follow people about, the way I can. Meet their pals, listen to them talk business. Follow them into the bars, into the shut offices where the big deals are made. Overhear them planning then forestall, move out on my own.

Buy the land the Supermarket needed, snap up shares when the
price was rigged to climb. . . .

But it didn't work out.

The world's a big place. Take any city, any town. Did you
ever try watching a thousand people at once? Did you ever
try *listening* to them?

I'll tell you about it. It's like a sea. It's like a sea and you
drown. You can't take it. It's meaningless. You hear snatches,
scraps. They jazz about in your mind, just on the edge of
making sense. Then you lose the pattern and the thread and
you open out a little more and in comes a tidal wave of voices
and you drown. . . .

In the end I found out how to select. I could tune my brain
and pick up anybody anywhere and hold them like I was holding Julie. I learned a lot then. I always knew where ten notes
would make fifty or a hundred would breed a thousand. And
you know what? I didn't have those notes. Not the hundred,
not the ten. And you can't make money without money, did
anybody ever tell you that or did you find out yourself the
hard way? In the old days I'd have stood outside a bank, close
up by the night safes, and the thousand notes would have come
rustling up the chutes into my hands, but the old days were
gone. I'd given up the Power.

There was another thing. That got me worst of any.

I had a boss once. Big man. I used to call him sir. And it
was yes, sir, and no, sir, please, sir, and thank you, sir, day
after bloody day. Until I—followed him home. Saw the little
castle. Saw how the wife handled him when nobody was
around. Then I knew why he was a big man all his days.
Because he was a cringing thing all his nights. . . . And after
that the yes, sir, no, sir, it wouldn't come any more. So I got
out. . . .

I was working with a guy once on a machine. Two of us
on that one big machine all day long. He was a nice quiet guy.
I used to go and drink with him odd times. He was a nice guy.
Used to talk on soft and low about all the evil there is in the

world, about wanting to bring in some goodness when he could and live in peace. Well, one night I followed him as well. With my mind. He'd had a few drinks, I wanted to see he got home O.K., that was all. . . . But he didn't go home. He crossed over some waste lots, and prowled, and waited. He found himself a little schoolgirl, out too late alone. . . . So I moved on. Because after that I couldn't work the machine with him any more, or drink with him or treat him like a nice guy. . . .

It was always like that. And there were the little people round me pushing and scrambling, and the great gift I couldn't use, the thing I couldn't even talk about because they'd have taken me and strapped me in a cell. . . . Do you know what loneliness is, or frustration? I knew what Eddie had felt like while he worked that dumper, while those strong artist's hands of his pulled levers and twisted throttles, and the machine hauled muck from one place and tipped it in another. . . .

Then I met Julie.

I remember the first time I saw her. It was in this town, a couple of years back. I was making pin money slinging beer in one of the locals. It was summer and the air was hot and heavy and sweet. It was Festival week and the bars were full, skiffle bands playing, everybody going a bit crazy and letting down their hair. She shouldn't have noticed me. Girls like Julie just don't see the guy who hands their drinks. But she saw me. Those eyes . . . I can remember her like it was yesterday, standing laughing in the smoke and brightness. But her eyes weren't laughing. They were watching, calm and deep, and anything you wanted to believe, if you looked in those eyes, it was there. . . .

I saw her again. When I wasn't working. Maybe I was crude about it. Maybe I was brutal. She didn't care. I got myself a little joke of a car and we used to go about in it, drive somewhere and find a quiet place to have a meal or go way out in the country, just sit and listen to the trees. And she'd watch, and talk, and it was right. I knew it. Just right. Until Ted moved in.

At first I didn't believe it. I thought I knew you Julie, I really did. I tried to joke about it once, remember? Only you wouldn't laugh. You said, 'He's nice. I like him, we have fun.' And the way you accented that last word, just enough. That word went through me like a knife, just how it was supposed to. And then you watched me, carefully. You waited to see how I'd react. . . .

Even after that I kept trying to think it was some sort of game you were playing. His face started to haunt me. I can see that damned face now. Pale and triangular. Heavy-framed glasses. And that smooth dark sweep of hair over the temple. Oh don't forget the hair, the college-boy status symbol. And the eyes. Almond shaped and tilted and leering, always leering, gloating at me. Even the way he walked, that was an insult. He used to walk like an animal. Swing those thin hips somehow. I don't know how . . . there was something there that was like an animal. But that was what you wanted all along wasn't it?

Wasn't it?

He was a car salesman. When he wasn't selling cars he was driving them. Great rangy cars, the sort of machines I could have owned just by stretching out my hand. . . . They were the things you really wanted, weren't they? There was the night you let him dice me, all up the road and down. You were sitting with him and your hair was blowing and you were waving and grinning at me clattering along in my old Ford Eight. That was your big night Julie, do you remember that?

Maybe it wasn't your fault. The way I feel now I could be sorry for you. I thought there was something deeper in your mind. I thought under all the laughing you were like a kind of little waif straying about looking for something a bit better than kicks. It wasn't your fault I was wrong. . . .

I only realised after I lost out how much you'd got to mean. I couldn't see anything any more but the back streets and the rain, misery and coldness stretching to the end of time. You'd put the years and the frustrations away from me somehow. When I was with you it was like they never happened. But now all the pain was back, and I didn't know how to keep going. . . .

But from now on in, things are going to be different. To-morrow I'm going to lift myself a couple of hundred in old untraceable notes and some ready cash in silver. Then I'm going to start working on it. And by the end of the month I shall have a couple of thousand, Julie, and in two months I shall have ten, and an alibi nobody will break, not if they try for years. Then I shall have a car, just like the cars you want, and clothes like the clothes you expect to see on your men. And I shall have women and wine and there will be songs but I won't be singing them any more. And I shall go on, and go on, and I shan't ever stop. You hit the detonator, Julie, and the bomb is going off, and it's the biggest damn bomb anybody ever set off in this sweet world. It's going to be a beautiful explosion.

But there's just one thing. *You won't be there to see it.* . . .

You didn't know I could kill, did you? Neither did I, up until a few minutes ago.

The Rage!

It wants to get free now and tear and maul and run red-handed in the streets. But I'm holding it back because I've still got to be careful. Later on, when they all know there's a new god on the earth, it won't matter. . . .

I wish I could invite an audience to watch this. The world's only telekinetic engineer is about to give his first real demon-stration. I'm going to kill a false thing called Julie, because she put shame on me. And shame I will not bear. It won't be a pleasant death. It isn't supposed to be.

This has got to look like an accident. I could kill abruptly, finish her like you might dispatch a rabbit, but I don't dare. Not yet awhile. There are just a few people who suspect me. Eddie was one and there was my brother, I don't know how much they understood. . . . Somebody might see a news item

in a paper, put two and two together. They might ask themselves, what breaks a girl's neck in a speeding car then floats
out through the crashing metal unharmed . . . and they might
guess. Then the word would get out, the whisper in the dark,
mutant . . . and you'd come for me with death in your hands.
I know you humans when you're scared. . . .

I'm moving my fingers forward and back along the chassis
of Julie's car, examining every projection, every bolt. I'm
looking for a weak link, some unit I can take apart so it'll look
like it fell to bits on its own. I think of the brakes. I work my
way from the foot pedal down to the master cylinder under
the floor, along the hydraulic lines where they twist through the
chassis and out to the hubs. I don't want to touch the master
cylinder, that would look too obvious, but the unions on the
slave cylinders are a possibility. Undo one of those nuts and
the fluid would spout free when she touched the pedal, there'd
be no braking action at all. But I'm not certain she'd crash.
She's a great driver and she'd still have the handbrake and the
gears. She'd feel the sponginess in the pedal as soon as the line
started to bleed, she'd get stopped somehow. This has got to
be something that makes the motor uncontrollable the instant
it comes adrift. Like a tyre burst. I wonder about the tyres but
there's no quick way of weakening a tread.

I watch Julie's face for a moment. I get sick. I ask myself,
why did she have to choose that second to be thinking about
Ted. . . . I don't give the idea a chance to develop. How
do I know how many hours a day she spends drooling
over him? Tune in any time, the call-sign's always the
same. . . .

I move away again thinking about fire. I have a look at the
tank end of the fuel-gauge system. No chance there, the thing's
cased in too well. I could make a spark but it wouldn't touch
the vapour. And anyway petrol's queer stuff, won't always burn
just when you want. I come back along the chassis, hang in the
noisy space under the scuttle and watch the acceleration torque

tilting the engine, the roadsprings flexing in front of me. This isn't as easy as I reckoned.

The car's a huge complex machine and there's a monster riding it, soaked away in the very pores of the metal, but the monster is nearly helpless. I can't break an axle, I'm not that sort of superman. And I've realised I daren't touch Julie, the fingers would leave marks, it would look bad. . . . I'd like to get a wheel off completely but even that might not do what I want. You shed a roadwheel at ninety it isn't healthy, but your car doesn't necessarily lose balance all at once. You plane along till you slow down, then your brakedrum drops and you spin, but chances are even whether you spin off and crash or whether you just spend a kinetic fortune tearing up the road metalling. And anyway I can't get hold of the wheelnuts. You work out the trajectory of one of those nuts when the car's moving, you'll find it jumps along in a series of ellipses like a high-speed grasshopper. I can't hold a nut when it's acting like that. . . .

Something moves under my hand. I focus downwards and I have my answer. Under the bonnet the steering column ends in a bulky steering box. The roadwheel assembly connects to it via a drop-arm that's held in place by a castellated nut. I take a mental cross-section of the unit. If that nut came free nothing could stop the drop-arm riding down the splines and falling clear. You couldn't steer, Julie, with the linkage taken apart. And if you braked, with the front wheels running free. . . . There are a lot of things can go wrong with a car while you're driving. There are remedies for most of them. There's no answer to this. This is death.

I take a long breath, and hold it. Then I find the split-pin that locks the steering nut in place, compress it with my fingers, draw it through the shaft and let it fall away. I expect the nut to start twitching undone. It doesn't move. I test it. Still tight.

Back on the bed my body frowns, bites its lip. I bring more strength to bear. No use. I put out full effort for a moment, relax with a grunt. The nut stays firm.

Julie slows for an intersection and suddenly there's a lot more traffic. I see signboards but I'm too slow to read the names. I leave the car and hurry back, but I get lost in the dark. I home on Julie and get on with what I've got to do.

I use a technique I developed once to deal with things like this. Normally I can't put out much more strength at a distance than I can with my bodily hands, but this does sometimes work. I place—that's as near as I can get to describing it—I place a pair of hands on the nut and grip it tight. Then I bring another pair into play at right angles to the first. Then another pair and another until I've got the shaft surrounded by a ring of force. The leverage is the same as you get from a spider, one of those multi-armed socket spanners they use in garages. I wait, gathering strength. I twist.

A jolt from the road helps. The nut starts to turn. More than that, the drop-arm comes free on the splines. I gasp a bit and spin the nut loose. It drops off the end of the shaft, hits the road and bounds away. I'm afraid of it bouncing back and clanging against the chassis but it vanishes without a sound. That's good. . . . It's just the splines now holding the drop-arm to the box, and Julie's motoring as hard as ever. I ease the arm almost clear, nearly to the end of the splines, and hold it there. And I yell, a long noise that goes tearing down the night.

For not thine but mine . . . mine is the kingdom, and the power. . . .

Only an eighth of an inch on the splines now and the whole thing getting hard to hold. I hang on to it, strain to keep it in place while I have a last look at Julie. . . .

Julie damn you you can't do that. What are you doing—

I should have expected it. You were big and bold right up to the last minute when you knew you have to die then you remembered you were a woman and the lashes of your eyes got salty and tangled and the tears ran down to your chin but it doesn't make any difference Julie, this is the jungle and we're the animals and you lost out because I was stronger than you thought. This doesn't figure, animals don't cry. . . .

The night and space splitting apart, laughter crackling among the spheres. Julie's holding the car at ninety down a black straight and she's crying and I was going to wipe her out like she was a bug on the wall but I can't do that while I can see the tears. They remind me she's real and she can be hurt and scared and her hair smells good and her body's strong and warm. I'm doubled up on the bed and there are two vibrating arms coming out of my mind to the steering box holding the link in place and I can't think any more. I only know this is Julie, I'm killing Julie, I can't do that . . . I can't hold the hate-image while I can see the tears, it's like trying to make a picture of water and see it run shapeless and drain away. I can see the crash now, eyes widening and widening and her mouth trying to scream and the metal fingers coming jagging in, opening her body like a red-silk rose. . . .

Julie this is Alan pull in Julie get off the road get off the road get off—

I think of something and act before the thought has time to finish forming, reach up and try to sweep the plug-leads off the block, but I can't spare the power and the drop-arm jerks and I nearly lose it. I cram it at the box, trying to force it up the splines, and my body arcs off the bed but the link won't shift, I can only grip it and hold it where it is. There's something wrong, why won't the drop-arm go back on the splines . . .

No hand to spare for the ignition key. Nothing to spare. . . . My voice is yelling at Julie and there's somebody beating on the wall. I can see the window swirling about, the sky beyond it bright with the moon, shapes moving there against the stars. The shapes are in my brain.

They used to burn people at the stake for trying to do what I can do. Why can't I be like other people, they only go to bed to sleep . . .

I can't hold on too long at a distance, I never could. I'm still holding the drop-arm but now it's like it was covered with acid, eating the flesh off my hands. The strain builds faster all the time. Plot it on a graph and you'd get an asymptote, because there's a quadratic involved in the basic expression and the curve swings up from the time axis towards infinity. . . . The stupid idea churns in my head and I try and find some clothes.

There's light showing under the door, somebody trying to get into the room. My body falls against the wall, stands up breathing a gale. Why am I trying to dress, it's all hazy. . . . The bit of me that can still reason is telling me I've got to try and close the gap between self and subject. I fumble with the doorlock, the key. . . .

There are stairs in front of me. Oblongs of light from open bedroom doors. Hands grab for me and I fight them, then I'm falling, holding the drop-arm, the hallway coming up to meet me. I land with my ribs across the stair-treads and the drop-arm slips and I think Julie, you didn't have to hit me so hard, why so hard. . . . I'm standing again but there are hot wires in my body burning the flesh as I move. I'm holding the linkage, but my fingers are so weak now it's like trying to keep it together with pads of cotton-wool. Got to get closer to Julie, it sometimes helps. . . .

I fumble at the street door and it opens and there's a rush of night air. Then I'm running, with the fire banked up and crackling in my chest. You broke me up, Julie, the bones feel like they're swilling round loose inside me. . . . I stop at the corner, hang on a lamp standard, see flashes in the night the colour of spilled mercury, but the footsteps come rattling after me and I run again. Black buildings jerk past each side. I make the car park and weave across it in the moonlight and there's the old Ford by the wall. My mouth feels like it's full of blood.

The keys are in the dash and I start up, holding the drop-arm. Julie, I'm sick. Why are you doing this to me? Get off the road. . . .

I accelerate and the people who were after me get out of the way somehow. The faces loom in the headlights and swing sideways and there's the gateway and I get through it with the tyres making a noise like something's dying under the wheels. There's the main road ahead and the lights. My foot is down on the boards and the Ford is roaring and stinking and I'm praying Julie, be out there somewhere, be coming towards me from the west, don't be going the other way. . . .

I can hear the banging as the suspension bottoms. Head-lights sail at me and the cats' eyes stretch away wriggling and shining and I don't know where I am, I'm seeing through Julie's eyes again and I can't drive in six dimensions. . . . I swing to a bend and the bend isn't there, I crab back on to the real road and there's a blare of horns behind me and the long wild noise of brakes. I'm clocking sixty and the Ford's building up on a long slope and the bearings are yelling for mercy and I pray again, don't let her throw a conrod, sweet Jesus don't let her throw a conrod. . . . Two roads fork out from the windscreen and one is a hurtling ghost, but I can't shut it out. . . . I see an X-ray mess of images, the roads, the night, the drop-arm with the splined shaft locked through it. Julie, her hair, the tears. . . .

Can't see where I am . . . my side . . . got to stop, lie on the grass, vomit out all the sickness and pain. . . . I ram at the brake but the pedal feels solid and I'm in nightmare, the throttle is still pressing itself on the floor . . . I kill the ignition but the key twists again under my fingers and the silencer bellows and the engine comes back to life and I feel like I'm choking, can't get any air. I yell, *Julie.* . . .

And it's like the sun came to meet me, putting out golden arms.

The images she sends, I can't take them in. She's so happy, she splashes them out like a kid playing with water. She asks me, *Couldn't you tell? Couldn't you tell when you saw my eyes?* I should have known. There were a thousand things should have told me. . . . When I felt her in the car, nobody could drive like that and be a part of the cogs and gears unless they were like me. I'm not alone any more. . . .

She makes a sea and it's golden and she wants me to go into it and sink down in the quiet and the cool to where the light's

2

half blue and half gold but I can't go into the sea because of the drag-link. . . . I try to tell her about the steering, but she swamps me. She sends laughter and it bursts inside me like the sun exploded. I've got my hands over my face trying to stop the brightness and the wheel is moving on its own and Julie's playing with me like a kitten with a ball of wool. . . . She sends the Ted image again and something comes jumping after it and catches it and Ted shrivels like a worm under a burning-glass. She knew there was somebody like herself and she thought it was me, but she wasn't sure and she had to be careful. . . . She used him to make me react, but I wouldn't move, I just let her go. . . . She left him and went home and begged her father's car and drove and drove to get back to me because she had to know for sure. And she felt me in the controls and she was happy, then she lost me and she started to cry because she thought I'd gone away. . . .

But I hadn't gone away, I was down there at the steering box getting ready to kill. . . . Julie, the steering box, get off the road. . . .

She asks me, what? What was that? Then there's a gasp and a scorch of rage and I know she's found the linkage and both our minds are down there holding it on the box, and she's trying to brake. . . .

The hands come off the Ford's wheel and I grab it and there are two roads, jazzing and swinging. I drive for the straight and then I know I'm wrong and there's a bend in front and I'm not going to take the bend. The car's bonnet dips under the brakes and she starts to swing and the trees are coming, growing out of the night, and Julie screams and the drop-arm falls off the box . . . .

Time, it's slowed right down. I shall have time to tell you about death. . . .

I feel the Ford bounce across the studs in the middle of the road, see the surprised headlights as the oncoming traffic tries to get out of the way. I miss the first lights, but the second pair swing out to meet me and I know this is it. And I realise the Power that was given to us, it was too much for us to bear.

The load was too heavy, we had to set it down. I'm sorry, Julie, I didn't want to make you cry. . . .

The thing that's going to kill me is close now, turning out to meet the Ford. The headlights glare but I can see between them and underneath. The light from a following car strikes through under the wheels and I see the useless steering link hanging down, dragging along the road.

There won't be time after all. I have half a second left to laugh. . . .

Escapism

Ever been hit in the chest by a two thousand foot film spool? I have. That's how I met Dave Curtis.

It wasn't pleasant. Being clobbered by the spool I mean, not meeting Dave. I was walking along Wickenford High Street one Saturday morning in May. Wickenford is a quiet little town in the chalk downs of the West Country. It's a pleasant enough place to be at any time of the year, and with the sky blue and the sun shining I was feeling full of the joys of spring. I hadn't even noticed I was passing the front of the Coliseum. Suddenly there was a crash from somewhere and a yell, a noise of old hinges giving way to an invincible force and I had a glimpse of a black disc about eighteen inches in diameter spinning at my face. Then I was lying flat with a huge stinging in my chest where the spoolrims had caught me and another in the back of my head where I'd cracked my skull on the path. Something prognathous in shirtsleeves leaped across my reoriented angle of vision (it nearly stamped on my hand). Then Dave was leaning over me. He asked me something but I didn't quite catch the sense of it. At first his face seemed to loom and recede, then things steadied and I sat up. He put his arm under my elbow and I was hauled to my feet, a bit wobbly but more or less intact. I started trying to fumble under my shirt to find out the depth of the grooves across my breastbone. Dave said, 'Frightfully sorry, just one of those things. It was a film spool.'

I said, 'Thanks, I know what it was.' I looked across the street. The spool was still moving, unravelling celluloid surprises as it went. Prognathous fielded it at the Town Hall steps. Dave passed a hand across his face like a man suddenly weary. He said, 'You don't look too well, old chap. Come and have a quick one on the firm.'

That seemed a good idea to me as well. We extricated ourselves from the little knot of people that had gathered and worked our way through the traffic, piling up nicely now, and into the saloon of the Old White Hart just across the street. Half a pint of beer later I was feeling better and Dave was explaining he was the chief operator at the Coliseum, Wickenford's one cinema and surely the most misnamed building in town. He said he couldn't help feeling personally to blame for the accident. I wasn't too concerned with moral responsibilities, I was more interested in exactly how a loaded spool happened to be flying at head height across the pavement. Dave explained. The mechanics of the paradox were simple. 'Pongo,' said Dave, '*Alias Bugdust*' . . . and here he raised his voice to a parade-ground roar and glared out of the window, and Pongo, or Bugdust, trotting back with his arms full of several hundred unravelled feet of 'Love Among the Palms', grinned an unhappy, twitching sort of grin and vanished up the stairs by the Coliseum paybox. 'Pongo,' went on Dave in a more reasonable tone, 'being the sort of lad he is, has only one way of rewinding.' He gestured graphically. 'Place a full spool on one side, an empty one on the other, and crank like the hammers of Hell.' Apparently this time the junior had forgotten to locknut the idling spool onto its shaft, with the result that the thing had passed him on the bench at about a thousand r.p.m., leaped through the open door, gained more acceleration on the way down the stairs, smashed the street door apart and bounded into the Great Outside. The rest I already knew. 'Damned sorry old man,' said Dave again. 'I mean, you might have been killed."

I agreed there had been a possibility.

One beer tended to lead to another and it was nearly twelve before Dave left to salvage what he could of the unfortunate reel. I went across to the Coliseum with him, not having anything better to do, and stood talking while he spliced and swore and made veecuts by the dozen. Finally we screened the result. All considered, it didn't look too bad. The copy had been in a fairly appalling condition to start with; as Dave remarked, half the street sweepings of Wickenford wouldn't have made a sight of difference to it. He was more concerned about the effects of gritty stock on his machines.

The mechs were years out of date; Simplex heads, Western bases, Ross arcs, they looked like ancient mechanical patchworks. But they had the sleek air that comes from careful handling, the spoolboxes were polished, the driptrays scoured and gleaming. That was Dave's way with mechanical things, he had a feeling for them. He'd spend hours fitting a new intermittent sprocket for one of those old nags, fetching the shaft down with metal polish to get it just exactly right. He loved machines. 'Anything dumb,' he said once, 'that can't defend itself.' Dave was a great guy, it's a pity he's dead. Leastways I think he's dead. It's rather a matter of viewpoint.

He didn't look like a chief operator, if there's a way for chief operators to look. He was burly and tall, somewhere over six feet, he was blond, he had very bright blue eyes and wore a neatly trimmed beard. That and his imposingly hooked nose gave him a vaguely piratical air; somehow wherever he was he never seemed to fit his surroundings entirely. It was as if he'd been born too early or a long time too late.

I had a lot of things in common with him. I'd been in films myself once, on the production side. I finished the hard way; I fell out with a dishy little production secretary who could pull too many strings and I was fired within the month. After that I moved about from job to job, never stopping anywhere too long because show biz had got into my blood and everything else bored me. I finally stopped bouncing in Wickenford, though what I was doing there doesn't concern the story.

Dave had had a chequered career as well. Merchant seaman, bit-actor, garage mechanic, salesman, he'd tried his hand at most things. He'd learned to handle thirty-five millimetre projection gear on camp cinemas in the RAF, and when he'd blown into Wickenford five years earlier with only a drop-head Morris Eight and a tea-chest full of books to his name and found the local fleapit needed a chief he'd just stepped in. As he said, he spent his days making dreams for himself and his nights doing it for other people. For some men it would have been a lonely life but it suited his odd temperament ideally. He was in the part of the country he liked best, he had a good pad and a steady job, he wasn't rich but he could afford petrol and beer and that was about all he needed.

I ought to explain about the West Country. He had a feeling that of all the places he'd seen the West of England was somehow the least changed. He was looking for something, he himself was not sure what, and he felt nearer to it here than anywhere else. He had strange fancies about the chalk hills. They intrigued him; I remember once when we were walking on the downs near the sea he stopped and asked me whether I was afraid of waking them. He said we were moving on their backs like fleas on a whale. I asked him what he was talking about and he laughed and said they'd been asleep too long, we didn't mean anything to them now. That was typical of Dave; he was a mystical creature, made all of opposites. He moved in his own paths, I haven't fully understood him yet.

The friendship went well right from its inauspicious start and after a week or so I'd got into the habit of going round to Dave's place on his nights off duty or meeting him in the Old White Hart for a jug of beer and a chat. When he was running the show on his own and he had a programme change I'd go up to the box and plate off reels for him, drag the cans downstairs ready for Transport. That way we'd still have time for a pint before they closed.

I'd known him just over a year when the train of events started that was eventually to part us in a strange way. I remember the evening well. I'd gone over to the Old White Hart; it was a fine night, too warm to stay indoors, and beside myself there were only two or three people in the bar. The door stood open, martins were circling and in the fading light the old High Street looked more like a stage set than ever. Across the road was the Coliseum; I could see the brightness of the undercanopy strips, up on the roof the yellow rectangle of the box door. The noise of the mechs just carried to the pub, and a ghost of sound from the monitor speaker. A Western was running and I could hear the occasional ricochet of a bullet, the tinny clatter of hooves. Once Pongo's low-skulled head became visible, silhouetted against the light as he leaned on the parapet overlooking the street and indulged in an illicit fag. Dave usually came over about nine, when they got onto the last run of the feature, but this time he was late. It was nearly half past before he showed up. I was trying to decide whether to have another drink or go over the road and see what was keeping him when he came in the door. I ordered two beers, rolled a cigarette and lit it. He drank absently, frowning and looking out the door into the night. Very obviously he had something on his mind. I said, 'What's up, Dave, Pongo dropped the middle out of a reel again?'

He looked vaguely surprised, then laughed. 'No, he hasn't done that for over a week now. I don't know what's happened to the lad, he's nearly efficient. Bill . . .'

'What?'

He pursed his lips. 'What do you know about stereo projection?'

I shrugged. 'A bit. Probably not as much as you.'

He inclined his head toward a corner table. 'Let's go sit. I want to talk about stereo.'

It was my turn to be surprised. Normally he was a bar drinker. He used to say the stuff wouldn't drain down right unless he was standing. I followed him to the table. He got out a packet of cigarettes and lit one, still with the far-away look in his eyes. He said, 'Shoot. Tell me about stereo.'

I couldn't see why he'd asked me because he knew at least as much about the subject as I did. But I knew enough about him to play along with his mood. Something was worrying him, this was his way of getting round to it. I talked.

I suppose most people know the idea behind the original stereo experiments. We get three dimensional vision from the fact that as our eyes are a few inches apart, each retina receives a slightly different image of anything we look at. The brain translates the differences into terms of depth. If two images are presented to the spectator in such a way that each eye sees only the picture intended for it, the brain can be fooled into taking the parallax effects for real depth. That's exactly what happens in a 3D movie; the chair comes out of the screen right at your head.

Getting the images proved simple. Two cameras were used, rigged so that the distance between the lenses corresponded to the space between a pair of human eyes. Putting the results onto a screen was even easier; the two copies were projected simultaneously by the left and right machines working as a pair. The motors had to be interlocked of course, either mechanically or electrically, to keep the mechs in frame sync, but that was technology, it didn't affect the principle. The stumbling block was the reseparation of the images. Unless each eye of each spectator got the picture intended for it the result was just a blur. In the crude three-dee they had in the twenties the images were tinted red and green and the audience wore red and green glasses. Later techniques made use of polaroid screens, allowing films to be shot in full colour, but glasses were still essential and that was where the whole thing fell through. It was fine for a gimmick but that was all; people just didn't like sitting with a pair of cardboard specs on their nose. So commercially three-dee was a lame duck.

That was about as far as I could go. When I'd run down Dave sat and brooded with his tankard in his hand. Then he said, 'Fine. Now how about three-dee without specs?'

I described the system the Russians first demonstrated in

Moscow. That worked without glasses, the trick was in the screen itself. They'd managed to produce a prismatic surface that reflected different images to each eye. But I'd read that in the cinema where it was demonstrated the seats were arranged on certain optical lines and to keep the illusion you had to hold your head almost completely still. So that hadn't been commercial either.

Dave nodded, twirling the glass. 'So far so good. Now tell me about three-dee without specs, without a kinky screen.'

I laughed. 'You're making your orders rapidly taller. You can play about with split lenses and so on till you're blue in the face but you won't get true stereo. You might manage some crafty illusions with perspective shifts on twin images but you're lacking two basic essentials. First, the original left and right eye negs. Second, the means of splitting the picture elements on the retinas themselves. That's a physiological must and to do it you need glasses. I'd say anything else is impossible. A one-eyed camera can't see stereo any more than a one-eyed man.'

He looked serious. 'I'd say so too. That's why I'd like you to see some. Full three-dee without specs, on an ordinary screen, through an ordinary lens, from one projector running as far as I can tell a completely standard thirty-five mil. print. Coming across?'

Like Hell I was. I dumped the glasses on the counter and followed him out the door. I said, 'Dave, my son, if the heat hasn't addled your tiny mind we have a fortune in our grasp.'

He was dour about it. 'We'll see, shall we?' That was all I could get out of him.

We thumped up the stairs to the box. The last reel was on when we arrived, and the Queen was laced ready to run. Dave checked the incoming mech, ran the leader down to the three frame, reset the carbons and dropped the mirrorshield. Then he came and leaned against the back wall of the projection room, talked over the monitor noise and the clatter from B machine. 'Been running rushes every night now for nearly a week. Some film company or other. Don't know where they're shooting.'

I was incredulous. 'Rushes? Here?' Units on location often use a local cinema like that but in my experience it had generally been a circuit house, an ABC or an Odeon, certainly not a crummy joint like the old Col. I couldn't understand it.

Dave looked sardonic. 'This is our one little moment of glory. Why they come here, I do not know. They've got some sort of agreement with old Watts, that's all I can tell you. I don't know how much they're paying him but when they're up here they fling money about like the proverbial water.'

I said, 'These rushes . . . they're the three-dee you were on about?'

He said, 'They are.' He snapped his fingures. 'Dust-sheets, Pongo.' Each night he swathed those old beaten-up mechs like they were babies. That was typical of him.

I walked forward to B machine, saw ten minutes on the takeoff spindle and went back to Dave. 'Has Watts seen this stuff?'

'Not to my knowledge. You know what he is.'

I did know, every well. The old manager had never forgotten the happy plushy days of the music halls. The Coliseum was a sad comedown for him; he hated the place, and every night he drowned its image conscientiously in gin. By ten thirty he could be relied on to be, if not pickled, at least well on the way; the cinema was usually put to bed by Dave and an elderly doorman. If we'd opened up after hours as a strip club Watts wouldn't have cared. Not that such a thing would have gone over in Wickenford . . .

I said, 'When do these folk arrive?'

Dave shrugged. 'On the dot. You'll see.'

The last five minutes of film were running. I offered to take dimmer and non-sync for the closedown and Dave looked relieved. 'That means we can ditch Pongo. Thank God . . . he's a lovely lad but after ten he gives me the creeping horrors.'

The lad in question came back into the box, draped the dust-sheets over the firebucket brackets and relapsed into rigor mortis. Dave cracked his fingers again, pointed to the door and where Pongo had been, was a space. Dave laughed. 'So far I've run all the stuff on my own. I tip him a quid from the perks. He hasn't worked out what it's for yet; he thinks I like him, bless him.' He looked into the spoolbox, wound up the carbons, walked round to A machine. 'Stand by,' said Dave.

He tabbed for the end of the feature, started up again and swung into the Queen trailer. I brought in floats and house-lights, started the non-sync and we had a dozen bars of play-out. Then Dave zeroed the fader. The Coliseum was empty already, and deader than a mausoleum at midnight. I peered down through the port to the brown vagueness of the tabs. I heard the boys arrive.

They came up the stairs at the double, chattering like so many parrots, and erupted into the projection room. There were around half a dozen of them, and as far as I could tell they all looked exactly alike. They wore dark suits, they had crewcuts that cropped the hair almost completely away, they sported heavy-framed glasses of the junior exec. pattern. They looked like film men or admen. They didn't talk like either.

Now I'd been around studios for a year or two and I thought I'd picked up most of the jargon of the film world but these boys' chatter sounded half Dutch to me. They clus-tered round Dave, waving their arms and giggling and talking nineteen to the dozen but I just couldn't make sense of it. I distinctly heard one of them say something about Solidos, and another made a crack about chronoshifting that brought a twitter of laughter from the whole gang. I stood over by the dimmer board trying to work out what the Hell was chrono-shifting, then I caught Dave's eye and he shook his head slightly so I didn't say anything. I elbowed my way out to the rewind room and clapped a spool onto one of the takeups. Dave followed me carrying a thousand foot can. I heard the visitors crowding back down to the auditorium. I opened my mouth to ask what was going on and Dave stopped me with a raised hand. 'This,' he said, 'is nothing. We can talk later.' He took a cardboard box down from the top of the cupboard and got out a waxer. Obviously it didn't belong to the Col, they hadn't seen a new copy since pictures started to talk. I expect he'd scrounged it from somewhere just for the rushes. It was the sort of thing he would do.

He adjusted the lavender strips above the stock and I ran it on slowly. There seemed to be about eight hundred feet; damned good shooting if that was a day's work. Halfway through I stopped and had a look at the print. It was colour, and it seemed normal enough. It had an emulsion coat both sides but that on its own was nothing extraordinary. I said, 'No circus tricks tonight, Dave. This is a common or garden mute print.'

He shrugged. He said, 'I can't splice this stuff. Amylacetate won't touch it and Tricoid runs off like water so it isn't nitrate base and it isn't tri-acetate. I found that out the first night trying to put a leader on it. They said not to bother. They said not to do this either but the Hell with it, I'm not running green stock on those nags without wax.'

Two of the boys hung round till we'd finished treating the print. Then we shoved them downstairs. ('Chinks,' Dave said decidedly on the way back up to the box.) I laced A machine, which had the steadier crossbox, and Dave carboned up again and struck the arc. He checked the gates, turned the motor over, gave me the sort of look that told me I was going to get the fright of my life and started up. I snapped out the overhead light, went round to the other operating port and looked down at the screen.

Only there wasn't a screen.

I yelped something, I don't know what, and grabbed at the wall in front of me. For a second I thought I was going to fall straight down into an expanse of sunlit sea. I was suspended over the water, the waves were sparkling in green and blue, I could see little crests of foam forming and breaking and sliding away. This wasn't stereo; it was like the auditorium had vanished, and the box was afloat. There was no sound track but it wasn't necessary. I could hear the surge and chuckle of that ocean in my mind. I could smell the sweet wind moving over it towards the land.

Dave was looking at me across the back of B machine. I straightened up to say something, changed my mind and bent to the port again. I couldn't afford to miss any of this. I was watching a technological miracle, and I knew it.

The ships came on in line abreast, dipping in the swell; and they had masts and yards like nothing afloat, they weren't ships of this age. Sails bellied and flapped, long pennants dropped to flirt with the sea and rose again with their tips dark with salt. I looked down on the decks; the standing rigging seemed to move past a few feet from my face. There was an air of excitement and adventure; I saw men talking animatedly, pointing to the loom of the coast. The sun winked on swordhilts and pistols, burned whitely on lace. Subjectively I could feel that sun on the back of my neck. The viewpoint sank till the hulls towered over me. I saw little details; the decorated mouths of cannon, run out and primed; cracks and weathering on a painted bulwark; weed clinging to the bottom sheathing. Then the vessels were past, heading in toward the land.

A bay opened out ahead. There were houses in the distance. Their roofs seemed to huddle together. The ships passed a headland and the sails emptied one by one as the cliffs took their wind. The hulls rolled awkwardly, sidling in like a troupe of clumsy wooden ducks. I saw the burst of smoke as a cannon was fired, imagined the sound booming across the water. There was a cut, and I was watching from the quay. Boats were being launched and folk were running about. The vessels edged forward under shortened sail. I felt I was being jostled by the crowd. Children were pointing and staring. I saw a mounted man riding away from the water; another waved a musket and shouted something at the people. The leading ship was close now; I saw a rope thrown and caught. Another cannon went off; a group of brightly dressed men appeared in her waist. I screwed up my eyes to try and make out their faces and town, quay and water vanished in brightness. I blinked; Dave closed the dowser and I was staring into a dark auditorium. I heard the tail of the film crackle through the firetrap. Then the cleaners' lights came on and I could see the dinginess of the screen, the open girders in the roof of the Coliseum. Down below the little men were leaving their seats and hurrying up the hall.

Dave shut off the mech and the fireshutter clanged, the sprockets ticked into silence. I frowned across the top of the lamphouse and when I spoke I know my voice wasn't much more than a whisper. 'Dave,' I said, 'What the Hell have we got here?'

He shook his head. 'I don't know, Bill. And if you could tell me . . . I'd reckon you were a good bloke.'

They came for the print within seconds; Dave said they only ever ran the stuff through once. One of the little people shoved something into his hand and he looked momentarily surprised, then they were gone and we had the Coliseum to ourselves.

We shut up shop. Somehow the place seemed . . . empty. Drained out. I can't quite describe it; a cinema after the show has finished is always spooky but this was different. It was as if something real had happened inside the walls and the real thing was done and there was nothing left but mortar and bricks and steel. We walked round mechanically to the carpark and got into the Morris. Dave started up and drove to his digs. He only spoke once on the way. He said, 'And this has been happening every night for a week.'

I could see why he'd been worried.

We talked for hours, while the street lamps went out and the crickets started their symphony and stopped again. We brewed endless cups of coffee, smoked cigarette after cigarette. We argued till the dawn was trailing grey rags in the sky and we were no wiser. I was half ready to believe I'd had some sort of hallucination. Dave cured me of that. He laughed suddenly and groped in his pocket. His hand came out holding four crisp notes. Fivers. Ten pounds for each of us. He threw my half across to me and I sat and felt my mouth sag open; it was an effort to haul it shut again. He said, 'No gags, Bill. These are for real.'

Perhaps you'll understand my state of mind better when I say that that gross tip meant next to nothing. I was too wrapped up in what I'd seen. I said, 'Look, Dave, this sounds stupid but I still can't take it in, did that . . . image come out of that machine? I mean, I was there but . . .' My voice trailed off. I didn't know how to finish the thought.

He nodded. 'Right through the lens William, the same as any picture. If you stick your hand in the beam you get a shadow. Only the shadow is a solid, it cuts out in depth as well . . . I tried it the first time I ran stuff for them. It looks damned odd, I can tell you.'

The hardest thing was to decide on a course of action. We both felt we ought to do something, but what? I knew this thing just couldn't have happened, if any firm or motion picture company had got hold of a process as revolutionary as that it would have been tested behind locked doors, not rushed casually in a two-bit cinema in a little country town. I said over and over, 'It's just bloody daft. Turn it about, look at it every which way, it doesn't make sense. There's something here that's outside my experience. I can't even start guessing what it is.'

We adjourned at five in the morning and I at least had to face a day's work. I don't know how I got through it. I snapped at the boss and swore at the secretary; somehow beside what I had seen everything else was too trivial for words. All I wanted was to be in on the process helping develop it, use it. A technique like that had no limitations; at least none that I could see.

The next night they brought sound.

I spotted the combined print as soon as I started running it on. The track wasn't optical, nor did it look like any magnetic stripe I'd ever seen. It was silvery, with queer shadings in it that altered and shifted as it caught the light. At some angles it was as if the frequencies were visible as striations, at others it was blank. Dave fingered the copy and shook his head over it. He said, 'I can't run this, boys. We've got optical gates.'

One of the little men sneered and brought out an object that looked like a contact mike without a lead. He walked through into the box and clapped the thing on the p.e. housing of A projector. He said, 'Run sound, man.' And all I know is, after that sound came through the speakers . . .

I waited till Dave was ready to open up then I scrammed down the stairs. I was going to take this one from inside.

I opened the stalls doors and walked into a grass field. I scuffed my feet to feel the blades move against my shoes. There was no grass of course, it was part of the illusion. I could feel the threadbare texture of the carpet but it didn't help. My eyes told me I was in a field.

I groped forward to a seat and eased myself down into it. I looked right and left but there were no walls, just blue distances. I wanted to walk down the hall and touch the screen but illogically I daren't move. It seemed I would have to push my way through a column of armed men.

They came on steadily, feet swishing in the grass. The sound seemed to move with them. They carried swords and home-made pikes; behind them children and dogs skirmished about, an old man pushed a rickety cart. Its wheels squeaked abominably. The group passed stolidly and the scene dissolved to show another column and another, moving along rutted lanes or over the backs of the downs. Some men came openly, riding horses and waving crude banners, some skulked in by twos and threes keeping to the shelter of the hedges, but they were all converging on the little town I'd seen the night before. They flocked in by the hundred; it looked like a countryside on the move. Shouts were exchanged; 'he' had landed, 'he' would lead them. Who 'he' was, I had no idea.

The end of the reel took me by surprise again. The film ran through and I was back in the Coliseum gazing at the empty screen. Dave closed the housetabs. The motor clanked in the stillness.

I got up and plunged out to the front of the theatre but I was too late. The little men were piling into a car like so many reversed Jack-in-the boxes. The car started up and shot away leaving me standing there like a fool. Across the road the Town Hall was bright in the moonlight. A policeman was working his beat, checking the fronts of the High Street shops. For a crazy moment I wanted to run over to him and ask him if he didn't know a war had started.

The next night we showed a flashback to the disembarkation. It was a queer affair. A handful of men left the ships and walked up into the town. They moved in a silence so deep I could hear the chink of their sword-hilts, the scraping of their shoes on the cobbles. The crowds parted to let them through. Ruddy-faced men stared blankly; the sun beat down on the old buildings; a woman stood in a cottage doorway and twined her hands nervously in her apron. It seemed that I myself moved between mute lines of people, neither hostile nor friendly. I felt sweat start out on my face. Eyes seemed to bore into my back.

The strangers nailed up a proclamation. Each stroke of the hammer raised a clapping echo from the house-fronts opposite. The people crowded forward, still quiet. I heard muttering as the news was passed from mouth to mouth from the few who could read. The officers watched anxiously from the windows of an inn. Then someone shouted, and cheering spread out along alleys and streets till the whole town was in uproar. It was a terrific sequence.

When the reel ended the letdown was still as acute; this time though I was quicker off the mark. I intercepted the little men as they scurried out. I caught the last one as he was pushing his way through the door and literally spun him back into the stalls. I said desperately, 'Look, I'm sorry but the Stereo, the

Solido, whatever you call it ... How does it work? I've been
in the film game, I thought I knew all the answers, but this ...
I've never seen anything like ...'

He looked up at me as if I'd just stepped out of a sewer. He
said, 'Yammer-yammer-yammer. Always yammer. Like,
making too much wind with the mouth, Daddy-O'. He
shoved me in the chest and I was startled enough to let him go.
Next second he was away with the rest of them.

I suppose I shouldn't have been surprised. After all, film
boys are film boys the world over ...

The following night's reel took the action a stage forward.
That prying camera was everywhere. Normal spatial restrictions didn't seem to affect it. It hovered a hundred yards in
the air, floated through walls, into closed rooms. This footage
had been edited; there was a sardonic montage contrasting the
actions of leaders and followers. Here the young prince, as I
was beginning to think of him, lifted a wineglass to his mouth
and drank; here a square-built, brown-faced man methodically lashed a scythe to a pole, while another hauled an old
rusty sword from a trunk and began to work its edge. A
blacksmith forged an axe amid a shower of sparks; the prince
laughed, showing lines of strong white teeth; a pike slashed
into a straw-filled dummy and sent it spinning. A group of
men rode across a field, framed in the fresh green of oak leaves;
a squirrel skittered along a branch; a soldier was dragged from
his horse. Steel flashed; there was a quick sound of dying. The
squirrel scolded; the prince reached for a decanter. A man
strutted with the soldier's hat on his head, and waved a
stained sword ...

By this time the thing had grown on me till I could think
of very little else. For me, nights were the only reality; that
precious ten minutes when I stood in the Coliseum and Dave
struck up and trimmed the arc and the people in the film
started to breathe again. I watched the growth of the revolution. The rabble became an army, ragged and vast, flaunting its
home-made banners and chanting, artillery at its head and

horses, and men flocking across the fields to join it. I cheered mentally as old wooden towns fell to it, or opened their barricades with shouts and the noise of bells. The shouts began to make sense. 'Monmouth' . . . The name floated on the air. 'Monmouth . . . Monmouth and the King . . .'

I took a morning off work and spent it in the local library. They didn't have much of a reference section but there was a *Britannica* and that was all I needed. I read how the Duke of Monmouth, the last of the Stuarts, left exile in France to raise the West against his uncle, James the Second of England. I read how he quartered the country, through Dorset to Somerset, down to Cornwall and back, skirmishing with the Royalist troops, raising men and arms all the way. After that I felt sick because I knew what was going to happen.

I saw his last battle the same night. It went according to the book. After a series of reverses, James in far-off London raised an army big enough to squash the rebellion. A night of early July, 1685, found the King's men under Lord Feversham camped a bare mile or so from the forces of the 'Protestant Duke'. Monmouth, urged by his advisers, decided on a sur-prise attack. The men who reccied the ground between him and the Royal troops reported it clear. It wasn't clear. A great ditch ran across right in the line of Monmouth's cavalry. The *Britannica* had hinted at betrayal; Monmouth wasn't be-trayed, at least not in the normal sense of the term. The boys who did the sortie were scared and drunk, nobody got within half a mile of the enemy lines.

They mounted the attack in the dawn, as the sky was lightening to grey. The dew was rough on the grass, some-where a solitary bird was piping. The jingle of harness, the champ of a bit carried for yards. The lines of horsemen passed pale as ghosts and behind them were the men of the West, silent and dour, holding up a forest of pikes.

The charge went in and the horses crashed over the ditch screaming and threshing. Men writhed in the mud; there were cries from the other camp, the flash of a musket, the dim rumble of the discharge. Then the sun was streaming low across the grass, horses and men kicking in the land-drain and the squadrons behind backing and piling up, gathering into knots and floundering across, rushing onto Sedgemore Field....

They didn't have a chance. Monmouth bolted and the rest was a rout. The film makers wasted no stock on the phoney Pretender. They held the camera on the battle.

I'd seen good filming. I'd seen *All Quiet* and *Gone With The Wind*, the Odessa steps massacre and the fall of Babylon from *Intolerance*, but I'd seen nothing like this. It was the details that got me. A man loping for cover, sweating and grinning with his hands full of his own entrails. Severed flesh on the grass. A soldier's arm stripped by a swordcut. I saw a horse take a pike head in the nostril, saw its face turn to smashed bone. I saw something else too, as Monmouth's men rose to receive the Royal cavalry. That upset me worst of all.

Five minutes later it was over. A riderless horse moved past the camera cropping grass. Smoke drifted slowly. There was a noise of birds, mixed with the baby-voices of dying men. The reel ended.

I went up to the box. Dave was walking round methodically snapping off mains. A projector was ticking as it cooled. I stood and looked at the machine that had made the miracle. I said, 'Dave, that was Sedgemoor.'

He got the dustsheet down, flung one end across the back of the mech and twitched a fold over the top spool-box. He said, 'Yes, I know.'

I tucked the sheet round the lamphouse tail, reached up and closed the flue vent. A flake of ash drifted down. I put my hands on the lamphouse and felt the animal warmth radiating out. I said, 'You don't get me. I don't mean that was a film of Sedgemoor. I mean that was it. The real thing. It wasn't any film.'

He stayed still for a moment, looking at the wall. Then he shook his head. 'You're round the twist, Bill. You don't know what you're saying.'

I followed him through the door and down the stairs. The lights were out in the lobby. Somewhere I could still hear the horse scream as the pike went home. It was like a tinny echo, grating on the nerves. But there was nothing in the Coliseum now, and the people had gone. I said, 'Dave, I only know what I know.'

He started to chain the doors.

I said, 'Look, the photography. If it is photography. The Solido. That's impossible. We both know it. And the acting. Nobody acted like that, ever. Olivier got closest but it wasn't the same. They weren't actors. It's all impossible, why stick at this?'

He looked at me. He was in silhouette, I couldn't see the expression on his face. He said inconsequentially, 'That was the time to live, Bill. No main roads, no housing estates. America a pirate's Eldorado, London a town out of fairy tales. It was quite a time.'

We walked up the road to the car. I said, 'What are we going to do about it, Dave? We've got to do something.'

He nodded. He said, 'That's it, William. We've got to do something. We're crazy as coots, but we can't leave it like this.'

.   .   .

We marched up to the reception desk of the Green Dragon. I was lagging behind a little because in the clear light of morning the whole thing seemed too mad for words. There was nobody about. Dave rang the bell and nothing happened. We stood looking at each other in the lavender-smelling quietness. He shrugged. He said, 'If they're staying anywhere in the district they'll be here. It's the last chance anyway, we've been everywhere else.'

There was a stupendous crash.

Plaster fell from the ceiling, dust rose in clouds. Overhead a lighting fitting swung and tinkled. I stared at it, looked round and found I was alone. I just caught sight of Dave's heels vanishing up the stairs. I ran after him. It seemed the only thing to do.

Upstairs the dust hung in a greyish cloud. There was a babel of voices. An old lady in a floral dressing gown loped past. I ask you, a dressing gown at twelve a.m. . . . . I rounded a corner and ran full tilt into a redfaced man with a huge moustache. He vanished behind me, shouting for someone called Robinson. I caught up with Dave at the end of the passage. He was wrenching at a door-handle. From behind the panels came high-pitched shouts. I'd heard that squeaky intonation before. Dave backed away and slammed into the door with his shoulder. It opened abruptly and we fell through it together.

The dust was thickest of all. It was moving in whorls, sparkling in the light from the windows. There were vague shadows flitting about; in the centre of the room stood a great bulk of machinery, indistinct, haloed with blue flashings. It was like somebody had dropped a printing press in the little room. The floor was bowed where its weight was depressing the beams. Dave pulled up short. He bellowed, 'What the Hell goes on?'

There was silence. The little men stopped gyrating, the machine spun and twinkled. Dave walked forward deliberately and picked up one of the boys by his lapels. He didn't seem to put any effort into it. He said easily, 'I asked you what the Hell is going on. And what is this machine?'

The dust started to settle in a pale film. I closed the door behind me and leaned on it. Footsteps clumped past in the corridor; a voice shouted something about 'Up on the first floor.' I heard the distant clanging of a fire engine.

A vein bulged on Dave's forehead and he shook his victim like a doll. The little man gurgled; his toes scraped desperately at the carpet. I started to get really scared. Dave said, 'How does a Solido work? Who are you people? *What is this machine?*'

Somebody sniggered. A voice said, 'Like it's played through, fellers. They dig us.'

And they were all talking at once.

'So Holman the Fourth he sends for Ferdie, he says Ferdie son and colleague, get me the works. Don't tell me your li'l old troubles, Ferdie, get the works. And when Holman the Fourth talks like that there's a screamstick on the end of every word and things move man, they move . . .'

'So we set up the chronochain plenty fast and we scram. Because when Holman wants the works, things move . . .'

' "I don't buy this crap about temporal interference," says Holman, "Jeep back to the twentieth, rush your footage in some crazy joint where they don't dig you. We'll pay the fine," says Holman, "we'll pay plenty. But get the works." '

'You can't chrono a whole Realization Unit,' babbled one of the Chinks. ' 'Cause the energy displacement expoes up to a star-and-space type freightage charge and Holman, he'll stand an interference fine but he can't stand a freight charge like that . . ."

The door started to bulge and I found I was holding it shut. I also found I was covered with little bodies, all shoving the door via myself. It was like being at the bottom of a collapsed rugger scrum. The machine started to emit a roaring note and somebody yelled, 'Hold 'em, man, hold that door, she's displacing . . .' I got a glimpse of the thing fading out like a trick shot in a movie. Soon it was nothing but a lilac and gold outline that the sunlight couldn't touch. Then that vanished; there was a 'plink', a sense of relieved pressure. The floor-beams groaned and eased back to their normal height.

The door snapped open and I was staring at the top button of a blue uniform. The uniform was on the biggest firechief I'd ever seen. He glared round the room. I found my voice somehow. I said, 'Er . . . can I help you?'

He squinted at me as if he'd just caught me redhanded setting light to Buckingham Palace. 'Some damn fool let off a bomb somewhere. You people see anything?'

I shook my head, grinning inanely. 'Not a thing. Now officer, if you wouldn't mind . . . we've got a . . . script conference going on here, we've been interrupted enough as it is . . .' I occluded him with the door before he could see the shattered catch.

I sat down in the nearest chair and found I was a hero. They had a good bar up there and after I'd shifted a couple of double Scotches I was able to take a calmer view of things. I said, 'Two questions. Or rather three. First, what was it? Second, where did it come from? Third, *where did it go* . . .? '

Dave took over. He looked a bit dazed but his voice was steady enough. 'That, Bill, was a chrono generator. They set up a string of them, spaced half a century or so apart, then step back down them to where they want to go. Right?'

The little men chirruped agreement.

'But some fool,' said Dave heavily, 'parked the nearest stage a little too close to home, temporally speaking. Because when Holman says move they move, and they didn't have time to get organised properly. Right?'

It was beginning to make a crazy sort of sense but I was still half baffled. 'So where did the thing come from?'

'It didn't *come* from anywhere,' said Dave. 'Today just caught up with it, is all.' He sat down too, and reached for a drink.

Jointly we seemed to have made the grade as far as the boys were concerned. They even introduced themselves; Duesey and Smart and Snow and Hope and Thankless, or something like that. Nicknames or Christian names, I don't know. A lot of the ways of twenty-third-century admen are still beyond me. Analysing their gabble, they had had a commission to reel in a piece of Old England for the makers of Kaufman Wonder-Slugs. What they are, or will be, I have no idea . . . And Holman, the mighty Fourth, had promised a rolling of heads if the Solidoreels weren't on his desk by the Junequarter following. (The names of the months are changed of course in the twenty-third century; or perhaps you know). They'd chosen the Monmouth rebellion, and by God they'd *got* the Monmouth rebellion, and everything had been running super-Duesey until the generator had allowed itself to be caught up with and we had turned up to pull the twenty-third century fat out of a particularly hot fire. And that, with un-avoidable gaps and omissions, brought us up to date. 'Holman don't care,' said one of the Chinks, Snow I think it was, or it might have been Thankless. 'Holman wants the action. He don't care we can only shoot ancient-type Solidos, he wants the action. And Holman gets what he wants.'

That I could believe . . .

There wasn't much more to it. We all had some more drinks and we praised their filming, and they praised our projection, and nobody got very far with the why and how. I did find out they had some sort of statute about time travel, or chrono-shifting as they preferred to call it; they weren't supposed to materialise any of their gear later than the eighteenth century or earlier than the twenty-second because of the danger of effecting a technology jump that was outside the calendar of human development. There were pretty steep fines for break-ing regs; a hundred doz of credits was mentioned as a possible settlement for using the Coliseum if they were ever found out. I didn't know how much that was but it seemed a Hell of a lot. After that there were more rounds of the hard stuff, we toasted them and they toasted us, and when you're celebrating the displacement of a chrono generator you're apt to drink pretty deep. Half an hour of it and I was fuzzy at the edges, an hour and I was out in space. They'd laced the whisky with some-thing called 'Rocket Flip' that they'd brought down the ages for a contingency like this and that stuff wasn't a drink, it was hydrogen warfare in a glass.

There was only one advantage to it. You didn't get a hangover.

*   *   *

I woke on the bed in my flat. The sun was low, I guessed the time to be nearly nine. I got up and found a bottle of Rocket Flip on the table beside me. After I'd poured it down the sink I hunted round for the letter from Dave that I knew would be there. I found it on the table in the living-room and opened it knowing more or less what I was going to read.

It looked as if I was going to have to run the last rush at the Coliseum that night; Dave would be indisposed.

I got down to the theatre about twenty after ten and finished the show with Pongo. After he'd gone and the people were out Snow brought me the reel and I waxed and laced, trimmed the arc and started the machine and watched the end of the story. I saw the tarpots bubble on Poole foreshore, saw them bring the salt for the quarterings, so much for each traitor. Jefferies hung his court with red and washed the West in blood.

I shall always remember the last shot of the film. At sunset, a cart rumbled into a village. As it moved down the street people came out the houses and followed it. First there were a dozen, then a score, then a hundred or more, all walking in absolute silence. And they stood in silence and watched while soldiers lifted down the tarred quarters of men and nailed them on the door of the church. So King James's justice was done, and the slack drums beat, the broken staves and banners sank in mud. And the camera planed up from the smoking land, music swelled sullen and deep and the thing was over.

Snow fetched the reel and clapped me on the back, gave me fifty English pounds and scurried out of my life and times.

Dave? He was a great guy. He just didn't belong to the twentieth century though. He was looking for something broader than we could offer, a mystery he thought he could solve in the West. Like he said in his letter, he didn't want to live in a land that was nothing but pink houses and soap coupons. He rode back with the boys to take those final shots, then they carried him farther off again to where he wanted to be. That was some lift to thumb, I couldn't have done it. But Dave did; he thanked them and waved and walked away from the chrono, into the past.

I keep wondering if there was any way I could have stopped him. I tell myself if I'd warned him of what I'd seen in the film of Sedgemoor he might have changed his mind. But I don't see that I could have altered anything. What he did was already written, and what has to be has to be.

There was a shot of the rebels as the cavalry was coming down on them. A quick track along the lines of faces showing the tension there, the sweat, the bitten lips; and among them, quite unmistakably, was Dave. I saw him go under, offering his pike up to a grinning mounted man. . . .

I'm still in Wickenford. As a matter of fact, I run the show at the Coliseum. The screen is just a screen, and the mechs are just mechs, and the place is getting really haggard now; I think it will close soon and where it stood there will be an aridness of shops and flats. The monster that sits in the corner of your living-room has taken the audiences from the little halls; the old Col is no use any more except to lovers when its raining. It's dreary and dark and full of cobwebs and Keystone ghosts and the smell of gas. But I keep it going because I've had a change of heart and I'd like to see Dave again even if he does have to die at Sedgemoor. And you never know, three hundred years from now Holman the Fourth might bang his desk and yell get me the action, and Snow and the boys might just come back.

Boulter's Canaries

I've known Alec Boulter for years. He's always been a damned clever chap. He keeps a rein on his imagination now though. Once he almost got too clever to live.

Boulter is an engineer by profession, but he can find his way about in electronics as well as anyone. He's a skilled turner and fitter and if I also mention that he writes and paints and has an interest in the occult you'll begin to see what a way-out character he is.

He's never made a great deal of money of course. This is the Age of Specialisation. The trend nowadays is for people to know more and more about less and less. There aren't any openings in commerce, or for that matter in science or the arts, for an unpredictable combination of mechanic and mystic. I sometimes feel Boulter should have been born back in the Renaissance. Da Vinci would probably have understood him.

At the time I'm thinking about he was taking an interest in amateur movies. I'd done a little work on it myself; nothing great, but better than the baby-on-the-lawn stuff you usually see. When Boulter started to dabble I sat back and waited for something remarkable. It was not long in coming.

He handicapped himself by choosing to work with sixteen millimetre stock. That isn't really an amateur gauge at all. Boulter wanted quality though, and in those days the standard of processing was a lot lower than it is now. If you'd told us for instance that medium-price equipment would ever give tolerable results from a striped eight-mil print we'd have laughed at you. But the cost of processing the wide-gauge stuff was high and it curtailed Boulter's activities more than somewhat.

He was never interested in plain movies. He shot sound right from the start. I remember the first recorder he ever owned used paper tape. Fantastic to think how primitive we were, and it was only a handful of years ago. He soon graduated and had one of the first Ferrograph decks to come out. Later he used an Emi, then a Ferrograph stereo. After that he built some machines of his own. For location work he rigged up a deck that would run from his station wagon. The results were first rate.

We travelled round a lot covering subjects that took his fancy. He tried all sorts of things from regattas to car auctions. He picked up a couple of awards at Edinburgh, but he was never really concerned with things like that. He went off on a new tack.

I went over to his place one day and found him with a collection of textbooks, some Ordnance Survey sheets and an A.A. guide. As soon as he saw me he said, 'Ever heard of Frey Abbey, Glyn?'

I nodded. 'Vaguely. Up north somewhere, isn't it?'

'Yes. I make it a hundred and twenty from us, give or take a few miles. What do you know about it?'

'Not much. Wasn't there some talk about poltergeist activity?'

He laughed. ' "Some talk" runs to about twelve volumes. By all accounts it's one of the most haunted spots in the country.'

I said, 'I'm not really with it. What if it is?'

He slapped the books decisively. 'It's interesting. I'm going there. Want a run up?'

'It's a bit of a distance. I'm easy though, I'll come if you like. What are you going to do up there?'

He said, 'Take pictures of ghosts.'

I laughed, then I saw he was serious. I said, 'How are you going to set about it?'

'I dunno. I expect something will suggest itself. Have a look at these.' He handed me some photographs.

I thumbed through them, I said, 'I don't suppose they're yours?'

'No, they belong to Kevin Hooker. You know, that chap at the film society. Thin, wears glasses. He was at Frey last week. Thought he'd try his hand.'

I said, 'Well, tell him before he tries it again, to get a new camera.'

He said, 'There's nothing wrong with his camera. It's a Rollei, and he can use it. These are control shots from the same neg. They're rather interesting. He took them in between the others; one shot of the ruins, then one a quarter of a mile away, then another of the ruins. And so on.'

I went through the prints again, more carefully. There was very little left of the Abbey. Just a few stones and some hillocks in a field. Boulter said, 'They dismantled the original building in the seventeenth century. I suppose they were tired of the manifestations. A very learned Prior tried his hand at exorcism. He was buried a week later. It's all in the book here. It isn't very pretty.''

I frowned. Each shot of the ruins bore queer blemishes. The black patches seemed to have no relation to the field of the camera. They looked as if they were poised here and there over the remains of the walls. Apart from the spots print quality was excellent and there was evidently nothing wrong with the check negatives at all. I said, 'Why did he do these other prints, Alec?'

'It's an old trick,' Boulter said. 'Nobody can take pictures at Frey. He knew about it. That's why he had a go.'

I said, 'You mean this has happened before?'

'Every time.'

I said, 'That's fantastic!'

'Yes, I know. That's why I'm going.'

I began to get interested. 'But you're doing movies. Has that been tried before?'

'Couldn't say. There's a first time for everything.'

We drove up the following weekend. On the way he expounded his theories. 'It's been said there's a poltergeist up there. I don't hold with that. The site has been deserted for centuries. It isn't in the nature of poltergeists to hang about after the humans have gone. If people knew more about them they wouldn't quote them so readily.'

'How can you tell what isn't in a deserted place?' I said. I was having some odd thoughts about things that are only there when you are not. Boulter snorted. 'To my way of thinking a poltergeist isn't a ghost at all. Not in the classic sense of the term. It's a sort of energy projection. In every well-documented haunting you'll find there's a child or an adolescent concerned somewhere. The thing follows them around from place to place. Eventually the manifestations just fade away. There's never any purposive quality about them. I don't think a poltergeist has an existence apart from the mind that creates it. They say it feeds, taps off energy. I don't go along with that. I think it's telekinesis tarted up with a new name.'

When he talks like that you believe him. I said, 'So what are these things at Frey?'

'Don't really know. My guess is Elementals.'

'What are they when they're at home?'

'Nobody can say. It's more a proposition than a definition. I suppose you could describe them as Nature Spirits. The psychical research folk pass them off by saying they're spirits that have never inhabited a human form. A sort of raw energy that has always existed.'

'Is that feasible?'

'You define feasibility and I'll answer you.'

I said, 'That puts me off somehow. I was hoping for a

diabolic twist. You know, the House of the Lord being taken over by the Great Enemy.'

He smiled. 'Don't bring God into it, it makes things too complicated.'

We found the place without any trouble. We stopped in the nearby village, had a couple of drinks and a snack at the local pub and managed to fix up some accommodation for the night. Then we went up to the Abbey.

I was not over-impressed. There was very little to see. We walked along the old foundations and climbed a few of the grass-covered remnants of walls. We had brought no gear. Boulter planned to make an early start in the morning. We worked out the best site for the camera and paced the distance to where we could leave the van to make sure our recorder feed would reach. Then Alec took out his cigarettes and we lit up. I stood with my shoulders hunched against the evening wind. I said, 'The only trouble is we shall be shooting blind.'

'What?'

I said, 'We shan't know if we've got any woozlums until the stock comes back from processing.'

Boulter said, 'Eh? No, we shan't.' He seemed to be pre-occupied. After a moment he said, 'You'd expect to hear something somewhere, wouldn't you?'

'What sort of thing?'

He gestured vaguely at the hills, the darkening sky. 'I don't know. A lark. Some bird or other. There isn't a thing, Glyn. Hadn't you noticed?'

I had sensed something, or a lack of something. I listened carefully. Apart from our voices there was not the slightest sound. The wind moved against my face, but even that seemed to be silent. It was as if some deadening layer insulated the spot, cutting it off from the rest of the countryside. I looked round at the barren land, the moors rising behind us. Way off the lights of the village were beginning to twinkle. Boulter said, 'You'd expect a lark at least.'

'Too late in the year for them,' I said.

3

He shrugged. 'Maybe. Anyway, let's try something.' He turned and walked away. I followed and he waved me back. 'Stay there for a minute, Glyn.' He moved a few more paces then stopped and turned. He said, 'Does my voice sound all right?'

It certainly did not. I said, 'You're faint. Sounds as if you're talking through felt.'

He nodded as if the words merely confirmed his suspicions. He walked another ten yards and the effect was increased. It built up rapidly with distance. At fifty yards I could see his mouth moving and knew he was shouting but not a scratch of voice reached me. The place was as dead as an anechoic chamber. I made wash-out movements with my hands and pointed to the road. It was getting dark rapidly and I didn't fancy the spot after night had fallen. He joined me at the gate. 'That's the funniest damn thing,' he said, 'I bet if you charted the dB drop you'd end up with an exponential curve. Queerest acoustic I ever came across.'

I agreed that something was certainly odd. I hoped it was only the acoustic.

Next morning was fresh and blowy. We set up the camera on the spot we had chosen, a hummock of grass from which it could command most of the ruins. Then I brought the recorder from the van. I placed the mike a few feet from the camera and went back to check for wind noise. The deck speaker was dead. I tested the connections. They seemed perfectly all right. I called over to Boulter. Either the dead effect had lessened or the darkness of the previous night had made it seem worse than it was. I said, 'The recorder won't work, Alec. Can't quite see why.'

He came over with the look on his face that he reserves for special problems. He tinkered for a time, starting and stopping the motors. They ran readily enough. Then he fetched his Avo from the car. He tested systematically, sat back and shook his head. 'It should be O.K., Glyn. Try it again.'

I turned up the audio gain to bring the windboom through the deck speaker. There was nothing doing. Boulter looked baffled. I'd never seen him licked before, and this was his own machine. Then he said, 'Fair enough, Glyn, take it back to the van, will you? Don't disconnect though. Just put it in the back. I want you to record "Mary had a little lamb." Over there somewhere.' He pointed towards the village.

I knew better than to argue. Boulter never does anything without a reason. I got the stuff back into the brake, turned round in the gateway and drove off. A quarter of a mile away the machine functioned perfectly. It gave me quite a shock. I started to experiment. I fixed the mike through the window, turned up the recording gain and drove back towards the ruins. At two hundred and fifty yards the windrush from the monitor faltered. At two hundred there was nothing. I repeated the test to make sure then went back and told Alec. He shrugged. 'That's it for the moment, then. We can't run a mike lead all that distance. We shall have to think of something else.'

I said, 'Do you think there's something we can record?'

He answered ambiguously. 'I know there's something we can't.'

He took a few shots of the ruins with me walking about demarcating the lines of the old walls. We left it at that until the afternoon, when we repeated the experiment. We drove back on Sunday after a last look round, and he dispatched the neg for processing as soon as he could.

The results were disappointing. There were some peculiarities; once the whole field fogged for no reason that we could discover and there were several patches where the focus seemed to have gone haywire. Most of the stuff, though, was quite normal. I shrugged. 'Well, at least we've exploded the myth. You can take pictures at Frey. I suppose that wraps it up.'

Boulter shook his head. 'You've forgotten the recorder that wouldn't record. There's something there all right, Glyn. I'm going up again next weekend. Give it another whirl.'

As it happened I couldn't go with him that time. He made two more pilgrimages on his own. He rang me about a month after our first trip. He sounded excited. He said, 'I've got something damn queer, Glyn; can you come round?'

I went over. He had converted his lounge into quite a reasonable viewing theatre, with projector and room lights controlled from a desk within arm's reach of one of the easy chairs. The mech was running when I walked in. He switched off immediately, unlaced and set it to rewind. He said, 'I'd like to go through this from the start. I think you'll find it's worth it.'

I noticed a bottle of Scotch and some glasses on the occasional table. I nodded at them. 'What are you celebrating?'

He said, 'Breakthrough. We'll have a drink first. I'd like to put you in the picture. What you see will mean more.' The leader started to flack-flack round on the top spool of the projector and he touched the console in front of him to stop the motor. I sat down. I said, 'What have you been playing with?'

He poured drinks. 'Filters,' he said, 'Cheers, by the way. All the best. I tried various stocks first. I was thinking about infra-red or something like that. I used the filters as a last resort. The answer's easy, Glyn; polarisation.'

'What does that do?'

'Makes 'em visible. Well, it makes something visible anyhow. I don't quite know what. I just put a polaroid screen over the lens. I rather think it's more effective at some angles than others but I couldn't be sure. Anyway, it's pretty good.' He got up and relaced the projector then came round and started up. He said, 'See what you think.'

The room lights went out. On the screen appeared a clock-face. It was mounted on a blackboard and underneath was a slip bearing the date. Boulter is nothing if not methodical. He said, 'I knew the filter worked because I'd tried it the week before. I used the clock because I had some idea of establishing a cycle of activity. As things turned out there was no real need for it. You'll see why. The camera was focused on the datum board right the way through. That's why the ruins are a bit off.'

The clock read eleven fifteen. A couple of minutes of film went through with nothing untoward, then Boulter touched my arm. He said, 'Look at that, then.'

In the field behind the clock a shape had appeared. It was totally lacking in definition. Its edges seemed to pulsate and waver. It looked exactly like positive fogging except that it moved slowly, creeping across the grass from the right hand to the centre of the screen. It paused at the bottom of one of the ruined walls. Boulter leaned forward slightly and I guessed something remarkable was coming. The shape stayed where it was for a moment, throbbing slightly; then it *climbed. . . .*

I said, 'Good God, Alec, it's—'

'Following the contour of that wall. Exactly. And if you can tell me any camera fault that would give an effect like that I'd be fascinated, if ungrateful.'

I shook my head. 'You're safe enough, Alec. This beats me.'

When the thing reached the top of the wall it was joined by a second appearance that also entered from the right. Woozlum number two moved a lot more rapidly and seemed to blend with the first. Then they separated and both left the support and floated towards the camera, expanding as they came into star or octopus shapes with wispy arms of blackish fog. I drew in my breath sharply and the screen went blank. Boulter laughed. 'At that point I stopped the test. I couldn't know what I was getting of course. That was a set five-minute run. I did two tests half an hour apart. Here's the second one now.'

This time only one of the shapes was visible. It seemed to be moving across the top of a wall. After a time it floated vertically off screen. The last two minutes of the film were uneventful. Boulter stopped the machine.

I said, 'Activity's pretty constant then. What the hell are these things, Alec?'

The room lights came on and I blinked. Boulter took out his cigarettes, lit one and threw me the packet. He said, 'They aren't physical in the sense that we understand it of course. We're not photographing anything there, just a hole into which the camera cannot see. Why it should affect film stock that way and not the human retina is anybody's guess. But as for activity, have a look at this.' He started up again.

This time the hands of the clock were moving visibly round the dial. I said, 'Stop action. What's the time lag?'

'Minute intervals between frames. The maximum I could get. I made up a unit for it. It seemed the best way to get a cross-section of a weekend at Frey.'

There was a lot of fast, dark movement all over the place. After a moment or two the picture faded out. That was nightfall of course; half a minute at this speed represented twelve hours of real time. In the darkness the things were still visible, surrounded by faint haloes that the daylight scenes had concealed. As far as I could see there was no cessation of activity. I said, 'Busy little chaps, aren't they?'

Boulter said, 'Yes, aren't they just? Sunday was even better. This is it coming up now.'

The first acceleration was to one frame per thirty seconds, the next to one frame per fifteen. At that speed the movements were most effective. The things seemed to dart and flit about, perching here and there to preen their vague outlines on the tops of the old walls. That was when I coined the phrase by which we came to know them. I said, 'Christ, they hop around like ruddy canaries.' Alec chuckled. 'They're a new breed. Boulter's canaries. Sounds good, doesn't it?'

The slow test continued. I watched it, fascinated, while Boulter explained his next steps. He had left the camera running while he tried a new experiment. He had set up the tapedeck again and fixed round it a frame of chicken wire which had been earthed to a perforated copper rod filled with brine. With the aid of the contraption he had managed to record a test tape. He stopped the projector, crossed to the deck in the corner of the room and started it up. His voice came through the playback scratchily, as if from a fifty-year-old recording. He said, 'I think that must have annoyed them.'

'Why?'

'I tried shooting again that evening. See what they did.'

He switched on the projector once more. The shapes appeared. This time they engaged in what seemed to be purposive movement. From the walls they launched themselves into the air and each one floated directly towards the camera, spreading into the tentaculate shape I had already seen. Up close each filled the field before fading behind or through the lens to make way for the next. After a time the screen went blank. Boulter switched off and the main lights came on. He said, 'Well, there you have it. How long they played goose and fox I don't know. I packed up and came home.'

We discussed the whole business far into the night. Boulter was keen on the theory of some localised electro-magnetic disturbance and outlined a few ideas for learning more about it. I wasn't so sure I wanted to know. I hadn't minded the things as they flitted about, but that progression of grabbing shapes was another matter altogether. There was too much deliberation in it. Boulter scoffed at the idea of danger. 'There can't be sentience in the way we understand it,' he explained. 'Any more than there can be a brain in the Northern Lights. The thing is, we can attract them. We should be able to go on from there without too much trouble.'

I shook my head. I'd been doing some reading of my own. 'The old abbot tried some independent research. He didn't live five days. And there was a monk too. He had himself locked in a haunted cell all night as an act of faith. He wore half an inch off his fingers scratching to get out. They found him stiff in the morning.'

'I think you're flapping a bit, Glyn,' Boulter said. 'I'm as

ready as the next to admit the possibility of paranormal
happenings, but in this case we're not dealing with anything
as complex as that. After all we're getting the history of Frey
at secondhand through a fog of ignorance and superstition.
Any queer things can probably be attributed one per cent to
the canaries and ninety-nine per cent to auto-suggestion, self-
hypnosis, call it what you will. This is an electro-magnetic
disturbance of some kind. The behaviour of the tape recorder
proves it. It's localised and it has some damned interesting
characteristics. For instance, this crawling up the stones. You
can't rule out the possibility of a static effect there. If you
saw a balloon roll up my arm and had no knowledge of
electricity you'd take me for a magician.' He laughed. 'Old
Ronnie—you know him, he gave that lecture at the club once
—he was on the phone from the lab just before you came. I
told him it was a new optical effect we were trying out. He
offered me a hundred quid on the spot for the lens we were
using.'

We arranged to go to Frey again during the coming
weekend. I had a touching faith in Boulter's ability to assess
the situation. If I'd had less faith then I'd have fewer grey
hairs now. The matter stayed on my mind through the week.
I suppose *Aves Boulterii* had taken a good hold on both of us.

This time we only set up the recorder. We ran some tests
with the deck protected by its odd-looking cage, then
Boulter fixed the mike in a parabolic reflector on a tripod.
Why he does these things I can't say, but he seems to have a
knack of divining the best approach to fundamental research.
I watched the recording gain and he moved the prab slowly,
scanning the grass area of the foundations. He'd taken the
trouble to calibrate the mike support so he knew exactly
where to aim. We had no luck with the first sweep and he
went off and set up numbered posts at measured distances
from the tripod. By sighting on these he could get an even
better range. He explained he was trying to pick up at about

four feet from the ground, the average of the apparent height of the canaries. He started to move the reflector bowl again. He said, 'I've even been wondering whether we've been getting real or virtual images. This should answer that at least.'

I was about to ask him how he could be sure the canaries emitted anything when the gain meter twitched. I caught his arm and he looked down. The prab was pointing at the highest of the walls, just where we'd seen most of the effects. I put the cans on but there was nothing to hear. The meter zeroed and I reached up and caught hold of the prab handgrip, wobbling the bowl to get back into focus. We held the emission for half a minute before it faded. Boulter resighted the prab on the base of the wall and we picked up something else immediately. I shoved the ear-phones back and said, 'What is it, Alec? I can't hear anything.'

Boulter frowned. He was trying to juggle the reflector and keep one eye on the recording meter. He said, 'Run tape, Glyn. Fifteen i.p.s. I think we shall need it. It can't be subsonic if you can follow it with a bowl as small as this. Must be high frequency. There's a devil of an amplitude though. Ouch, look at that needle kick. No wonder our ears got screwed up.'

We recorded for about ten minutes then we ran out of responses. I shut down and Boulter locked the prab and got out the cigarettes. I was none too happy. I said, 'I suppose we've annoyed the things again now.' I looked back at the ruins, brown in the sunlight. There was nothing to see. Boulter laughed. 'I shouldn't concern yourself too much. There isn't anything to worry about.'

There was a sharp clang and the tripod fell over on the grass. He moved faster than I'd ever seen him. I was sitting near the little knoll on which we'd first placed the camera and he flung himself flat beside me. He said, 'Get down, Glyn.'

'What the—?'

He shoved me in the chest and I got down anyway. He glared round. He said, 'Some bastard's taking pot shots at us.'

'What?'

He said, 'Look at that thing. If he'd hit the prab I should have been really pleased.' He pointed at the tripod and I saw a bright mark where something had glanced off the mounting just beneath the panning head. Below it on the wood was a long furrow. I stared incredulously. I said, 'Well, if that was a shot it came from straight above us.'

We both looked up; one of those stupid involuntary actions. The sky was empty of course. We stayed where we were. The tension began to mount. After all, it was a queer situation. The two of us lying there, the deserted moors round about the ruins, the bright car in the distance; and an invisible marksman, apparently aerial, waiting for another chance. After a while Boulter got up. He frowned at me then walked away and stood looking round the horizon with his hands on his hips. Then he called. His voice had the faded quality we had noticed on that first evening. He said, 'Come on, Glyn. You look a bit of a nit down there.'

I sat up carefully. 'And you'll look a bigger one if our sporting friend has another go.'

He laughed, throwing his head back as if I'd made a huge joke. He said, 'Nobody shoots at people on the open moor these days, Glyn. This is the twentieth century.'

I picked up the tripod and fingered the mark on the wood. I still had a nasty feeling that there was something at my back. 'Then what made this?' I said.

He shrugged. 'It must have been a solitary hailstone.' And that was as far as he would commit himself.

We packed up the gear soon afterwards. I for one had rather lost heart in the project. We drove back to the village and had a meal. Then, surprisingly, Boulter decided to move south that night. I didn't argue with him. I'd seen enough of Frey for one week at least.

We got back in the small hours and I stayed overnight at Alec's place. By the time I got down next morning he'd had breakfast and was already tinkering about in the workshop.

He had a variable-speed deck there and it was on that we first heard the sounds.

I was still eating when he came and dragged me out to listen. He'd worked out the frequency of the emissions; they ranged from fifteen to twenty k/cs. He switched on and turned up the playback gain. The wall speaker began to pipe. It was a queer sound, undulating and quavery. It was like a choir of singers poking around after top C and not quite getting there. Yet not human singers. It upset me more than the visual record had done, but Alec was alight with enthusiasm. He tried to talk me into going to Frey with him again. He had some things he would like to try out.

I refused. My nerves were beginning to get ragged. I said, 'In any case I'm tied up next weekend.'

He laughed. 'Who said anything about the weekend? I'm going back tonight.'

I gave him a short run-down on my views about the proposition. He tried to get me to change my mind, but he was talking to the Rock of Gibraltar. I left him shortly afterwards still raving about his way-out ideas. Apparently he wanted to communicate with the canaries. He managed that of course though not quite in the way he had thought.

It was midweek when I heard from him. I thought his voice sounded strained on the telephone. He was rather mysterious, just asked me if I'd like to come round and see something remarkable. I said sure, whenever he liked. He said a curious thing before he rang off. 'Come when you're ready, Glyn; I don't think there's any risk.'

I put the phone down and stood looking at it. Risk? I didn't like the sound of that. What risk, and why tonight? I shrugged. Boulter was always devious and infrequently incomprehensible. I reached for my jacket.

I was standing by the door of my flat looking round before I turned off the light when there was a crash of glass from the bathroom. I hurried in thinking a cat or something had got through the window. There was nothing. At first I couldn't account for the noise, then I saw my shaving mirror was smashed. The fragments were scattered all over the place. None was larger than a pea. I picked one up and examined it, feeling at a loss. As I stood there the door of the wall cupboard opened and bottles and shaving brushes began to fly at my head. I backed out, slammed the door of the flat and hared to the car.

It was a bad night, cold and spitting with rain. I peered through the screen looking for Boulter's drive. I swung up to the house and turned off the engine. In that second there was a sharp 'ding' and the car rocked on its springs. I sat still and any hope I might have had left me. That had happened twice on the journey. Both times there had been a vehicle in front of me and I'd attributed it to a flung stone. I remembered the attack on the mike tripod at Frey. They'd got my number then, whatever 'they' were. Something told me Boulter was faring no better. I touched the doorhandle and it was yanked out of my hand as something threw the car door open. I ran for the house, hunching my shoulders against the rain.

Boulter let me in. He was smoking when he came to the door and I noticed he had not shaved. He wasted no time in preliminaries. He said, 'Dump your coat and come through, Glyn. This is worth seeing but I don't know how long we've got.' As I followed him down the hall I saw a ridge appear in the carpet. It ran rapidly away to the end of the corridor. He opened the door of the lounge and a directory flew from the phone table. He fielded it as it passed his head and slammed it back down. He said, 'Circus tricks. Don't let 'em throw you.' I followed him and he closed the door after me. Instantly a thunderous knocking began. I saw the door panels jump with the force of it. He yelled, 'Oh, shut up. I'm talking.' The noise subsided.

I sat down before I fell. I said, 'So we were attacked that day, weren't we?'

He looked up from lacing the projector. 'Only indirectly.'

'Then I've just been indirectly attacked again,' I said.

He looked incredulous. 'You?'

'Well, the car. It's got a damn great dent over the wind-screen. And despite your well-known cynicism my flat has been taken over by a poltergeist. As I see, you've got one here as well.'

He said, 'It was only to be expected. There's no danger. You're better off here anyway; I'm insured.'

I wondered what he was talking about. Then I saw he had the camera and the mike set up facing the tall windows. I said, 'Alec, what the hell are you playing at?'

He finished with the projector, came round and stubbed his cigarette. He lit another and sat down. He said, 'No in-terruptions, Glyn. You can ask questions later. I want to fill in the background as quickly as I can. I went back to Frey last Sunday as I said I would. This film was shot on Monday. I only got the results tonight. I shall have to get you to help me run them.

'As I said, I wanted to set up a system of communication. I'd changed my ideas about non-sentience, by the way, after our last trip. I reasoned it thus. The canaries—I'll call them that for want of a better term—emit frequencies of up to twenty-thousand cycles. Not sound as we understand it, but it can be rendered as such. That's enough for present purposes. Also they seemed to be attracted by any electro-magnetic distur-bance in their area. I decided to have a chat with them.'

'How in Hell?'

'Comparatively simple. I set up a signal generator. I shot twenty k/cs at them with a Morse key.'

I stared at him. I was beginning to see the reason for all the upset. I said, 'You prize bloody clown, you've finished the pair of us.'

He shook his head impatiently. 'I don't think so. As I was saying, I signalled to them. I sent arithmetic progressions first, one, two, three and so on, then some geometric sets, squares and cubes over short series of numbers.'

Despite my shock I was interested. 'How did you check results?'

He started the projector. I saw he had set up the datum board again, this time with a panel in which numbers could be shown. He said, 'This was before I signalled at all. As you can see one of the things is in field.'

The screen went blank and he shut down for a moment. He said, 'Can you handle the recorder, Glyn? I should wheel it across to the chair. Then you can see the screen.'

I did as he asked. When I was settled again with the deck at my elbow he said, 'O.K., switch on will you? This is an edited transcript of course. I slowed the emissions as I did the first set, and re-recorded them.' In the speaker I heard his voice, over-laid with what we had come to know as Frey distortion. It said, 'Camera running. First series transmitted. Additive progression in ones.'

The embryonic voices began to pipe and flutter. The projector started up, showing the visual he had taken at the same time. The slowed sound bore no direct relation to the picture of course but the film confirmed what the track had already suggested. The things were present in great numbers. They seemed to be agitated and were drifting rapidly up and down the low hummocks of stone. I left the recorder running and Boulter switched the mech in and out to keep roughly in sync with the tracks. After each transmission from the generator he had started the recorder, changed the number on the datum board and filmed a set period of fifteen minutes in slow action. It became evident that the canaries had been greatly excited by the signals. Their movements became quicker and quicker and soon developed into that floating projection towards the source of their annoyance that we had seen before. This time the movement was too fast for the camera. Boulter reached back and slowed the projector. We watched the jellyfish shapes jerk towards us, hover and vanish. Boulter laughed. 'Not very pretty at close quarters, are they?' I shuddered and agreed.

He sat back. He said, 'By the time I reached the ninth test—that's it coming up now, stop a minute will you and I'll get back in sync—by the time I got to that, which was the end of the series, things had really hotted up.' He speeded the projector again, got the number nine on the screen and nodded to me to start up the sound. He said, 'This was the cubic progression. Bit of a bore; in case you hadn't worked it out it goes two, eight, five hundred and twelve.' His voice echoed him from the tapedeck. 'Ninth test, a cubic progression from two. Partially completed.' 'I stopped at about two hundred in the third figure. I had to; they knocked the generator about fifty feet. I took this immediately afterwards.'

The projector showed a flashing whirl of dark movement. The corresponding sound was eerie. It was as if hundreds of the things were present, piping and fluting for all they were worth. There was another noise as well, one that I hadn't heard before. It was much lower than the normal emission, sounding by comparison almost husky; a chittery, whirring sound with a gibbering quality to it that started my scalp prickling again. Boulter said, 'The canaries, very cross indeed.' The film record ended and he switched off the machine and brought the room lights up to a glow. I shut down the playback and was glad enough to do so. There was silence between us for a moment. I was still trying to digest what I'd seen and heard.

I said, 'That's it then, Alec. You've stirred a hornet's nest this time, no mistake. It was them that knocked the mike down that day. They did it to the signal generator on Monday.' My voice rose slightly. 'And better than that. They've followed you home. And all you had to do was ring me and they had me too. They've got the pair of us taped!'

He nodded sombrely. Something scratched at the door. I didn't feel like opening it. He said, 'Sorry about all this, Glyn. They do appear to have extended their operations. I should have listened to you earlier on.'

I got out a cigarette. I felt I needed it. The middle of the room was bright enough, but round the walls the shadows seemed to crawl together, thickening and darkening. I stared at the evidence of twentieth-century know-how; the tapedeck, the projector, the camera and mikestand. I felt I was in some sort of dream. But it was all true enough. I said hollowly, 'If ever men were haunted, we are.'

He was quiet for a space. Then he said, 'Yes, unfortunately that is true.'

I was dazed. I said, 'Well, what are you going to do, Alec? And furthermore, why the hell did you drag me over here? Or ring in the first place? It's your mess. You said on the phone there was no danger.—'

He said, 'Yes, I know what I told you, Glyn. I still believe that. In a way I have to. You must too.'

'But what are you going to do?'

He got up and bent over the tapedeck. He spun the reels forward then stopped and switched to playback. The speaker began to emit a steady, high-pitched note. He said, 'Four thousand cycles. At this speed they won't react.'

I experienced a sinking feeling. I said, 'Look, this isn't a suicide pact. What the hell?'

'They're angry, Glyn,' he said. 'They resent disturbance. Maybe they don't like the idea of anyone having any real understanding of them. But there's just one hope. That they're not mad with us. And to my way of thinking there's only one method of finding out. They've tracked something they resent to this room. We must find the depth and direction of that resentment. I've no doubt they could kill us if they wished. If they do, too bad. I don't think they will. If they spare us; well, we shall be able to sleep easy again. This is the only way.'

I reached out to grab his wrist, but I was too late. He had already taken the speed control up. The note rose, turned to a whisper and vanished into supersonics. I tried to reach the recorder and he pushed me away. I said, 'You're bloody mad.' I grappled with him and tripped. We both went sprawling. Then it happened.

The door and the windows resounded to a series of cracking blows. Then the latch burst and the door crashed open. The windows, frames and glass, exploded inwards in a shower of fragments. I saw the recorder jump in the air and poise impossibly on one corner, and as it hung there the deck dented in half a dozen places as if from the blows of huge, invisible beaks. I just had time to see the camera toppling and the bowl of the prab flying towards me, then there was a flash and an electric fizzing and the lights went out. I lay in the darkness with a crashing and snapping going on round me as if a pack of gorillas was loose in the room, taking it apart. The air seemed thick and pressure waves like those from explosions pushed at my eardrums. I heard Boulter's voice saying faintly, 'Don't move. Don't try to stand, don't go for the door. Don't get in their way.' I did as I was told. I don't think I could have moved far anyway. I was paralysed with fright.

The destruction seemed to go on for an hour though it was probably over in five minutes. Then the noise began to die down. My eyes had got accustomed to the darkness and I saw the curtains flow out over the ruined windows, jumping and flicking as a host of invisible somethings shouldered them aside. Silence fell, and the drapes stopped moving. Boulter stood up. I saw him silhouetted against the light from the windows. He said calmly. 'Well, that's that. Somewhere I should have some fusewire . . . .'

Later, after we had cleared up the mess of glass and dural that had been a tapedeck, a camera and a microphone, he condescended to explain why we were still alive.

'I had it more or less worked out after that incident with the prab. These things are sentient, and they're damned easily aggravated. But they've got their limitations. I suppose any intelligence must have with the exception of the Prime Mover itself. For instance, they could have stopped operations a lot more easily by going for us that morning. We were standing there, we were easy meat. But somehow they couldn't accept our brand of radiation as a motivating agent.

They simply flew at the thing they could detect. In that case the mike. Later, the signal generator. Now of course they've cleared the lot. Pity about that, there was some good equipment there. But it was machines, Glyn; machines every time. In all the centuries they've lived, and nobody will ever tell their age, they've never come to terms with the human brain. Maybe they did at one time, and they've forgotten. I just don't know.

'I don't know if they understand progressions either, or if their reaction was simply to sonar emission. It's a pity; I'd like to know more but I don't fancy setting up the gear again, even if I could afford it. Next time they might twig us . . .'

I must say that was one sentiment with which I could most heartily agree.

As far as I was concerned that was the end of the matter. I've never gone back to Frey, and don't intend to. I would be safe enough of course as long as I did nothing but sit and look. But I know what's there, you see. I just don't fancy the idea any more.

As far as I know Boulter forgot the whole thing within a week. He likes to move on and try out new ideas. A short time ago he heard about the startling experiments with laser light emissions that are being done in the States, and right now he's trying to think up a substitute for synthetic ruby so that he can build a gun of his own. I'm all for it; after what he played with at Frey Abbey, death-rays seem positively homely.

Sub-Lim

Look Doc don't bother with intros there isn't time. I'm Johnny Harper, I'm a guy who makes films, that'll do. Doc, I'm in bad trouble. I got something stuck down inside my head and I got to get it out. Can you fix that for me, Doc? Have you got a machine can reach into a guy's brain and find a thing that shouldn't be there and snap it out by the roots, have you got a machine can do that? . . .

I'm not crazy, honest to God I know what I'm saying, you've got to help. Look, I'll give you the whole story from when it started then you'll know I'm not crazy, you'll know what to do. . . .

Have you got a girl can take shorthand? Well get this down yourself then. Don't argue man, get a pad or something and get this down, it's the most important thing you ever heard. Get a name first. Freddy Keeler. Take that down right now, he's the guy that matters. It all started with Freddy, blast his Goddam soul. . . .

He's studio projectionist, shows all the rushes. Well that's part of his job, the rest's secret. I'm telling you about it so you'll know what to do with Freddy——

What? What studio? Oh God—— No Doc, I'm sorry, I guess I didn't say. Hill Studio, the people who make the Little Andy films. You know Little Andy, everybody knows Little

Andy . . . you don't see television? Then I'll tell you, you're the luckiest guy alive.

Hill Studio's the biggest thing in the business. Six months ago we were broke. Bust, flat, finished. We'd fired off all our staff, all we had left were the two partners, J. B. March and Jeff Holroyd, and little Freddy and Connie the secretary, Connie the lion I called her. And me stooging round with a director's ticket and nothing to direct. Just five of us and the red light was burning for everybody and I was plenty worried, the state the trade was in ex-directors were going to be a drug on the market.

We'd started up along with ten hundred other little units about the time commercial television got going and we'd outlasted most of the rest. J.B. was smart, he saw to it right from the start we'd got more than one string to our bow, we did animated cartoon, we did stop-frame and special effects and we'd got a good name for live action. When the big slump happened we carried on making films for the Far East and Germany, then we began to feel the pinch and we had to start laying people off. A year ago we'd got fifty staff, then it came down to twenty, then ten, then like I said it was just a handful of us hanging on the best way we could. I knew the axe was going to swing again soon and Connie wasn't taking enough out the firm to make it worth firing her, and anyway you got to keep a smart-looking popsy in the front office because the rest of the boys expect it, so I knew it was Freddy or me that had to go.

I went along to see J.B. I didn't get on too good with Jeff, he was a sort of emotional type, always getting worked up, but I got on fine with J.B., you knew where you were with him. Arguing with him was like playing Russian Roulette with half the chambers loaded but if you knew how to sort of smooth him along you were O.K. I went into his office, I said, 'J.B., I'm worried about old Freddy. You know he's a great guy, but I'm sort of worried about him.'

He looked at me like he'd heard it before. He said, 'So you want him out, Johnny.'

I lit a cigarette. I said. 'Projectionist's not much good with no films to show.'

J.B. got nasty. 'Director's no better off with none to direct.' I could see this was one of his bad mornings, he'd been married a few years and there weren't any kids and some days his wife gave him hell, you know how it goes. I said, 'I'll put it to him nice, J.B. He won't hardly feel a thing.'

He shrugged. 'O.K., Johnny, but do it nice, you know? He's a nice little guy, I like Freddy a lot.'

I said, 'I promise you my face will be wet with tears.' I made for the door and J.B. called me back. He said, 'Funny thing Johnny, he draws pictures. You ever see one of his pictures?'

I didn't get it. 'So what, what's that, J.B.?'

He said, 'Get him to draw you one. Did one for me, they're pretty good. I was thinking we could use them but . . . that's the way it goes.'

The idea struck me funny. 'What does he draw, Snow White and the Dwarfs? Or is it grown-up stuff for the lavatory wall?'

He glared at me. 'Just get him to draw. And don't push too hard Johnny, could be he's more use than you.'

I got out.

After that I had to play it safe, so I ran Freddy down in the pub where he got his lunch. He was standing up at the bar when I went in, he was scoffing a sandwich and a pint of beer. He's a little guy Doc, sort of thin on top, fiftyish, wears hornrim glasses. Nothing to look at. I went up and clapped him on the back, I said, 'Hello, Freddy, what's new?'

He looked at me like he was going to choke. I reckon he knew why I was there. He said, 'You want to see me, Mr. Harper?'

I whistled up a beer for myself and paid for another for him. I said, 'I do, Freddy, I do. I want to sort of have a quick talk. 'Things aren't too good, Freddy, but believe me they could be worse, they could be a lot worse.' I got hold of his arm and steered him to a table. God I get tired of soft-talking punks like Freddy, when a guy's through he's through, that's all he needs to know. But I did it slow, the J.B. way. I said, 'The boss tells me you're a bit of an artist, Freddy boy. I didn't know.' I figured from that I could get round to the fact that he was soon going to need a spare profession.

He shook his head. He said no he wasn't an artist, he couldn't draw worth a damn. He just made images.

Doc, cinema operators are a funny lot. They stand all their lives watching films through a little square of glass, after a time it gets them so they're no good for nothing else. They're queer Doc, they get things on the brain. All sorts of things. Freddy had spent years watching Images flicker about and jump up and down, he'd got to think Images all day and all night long. . . .

No don't get me wrong, not pictures, *Images.* That was how he explained it to me, he said a film director, say Hitchcock, anybody you want to name, is always worrying consciously or subconsciously about Images, trying to get some shape on the screen that'll help the actors along, make you *feel* what's going on. He said that was what a good film was, not a lot of shots of actors and such, but a set of Images that made you feel what you were supposed to. He said it was done with the picture composition and the lighting and everything. And he said for instance, if you saw every thriller ever made and studied them all over and over you could work out a shape from all the Images all the directors had ever used, and the shape would sort of represent fear, all on its own. He said if you drew it and showed it to a guy he'd get scared to death and he wouldn't know why. He said if the Image was right it would sort of lock onto his mind and make him feel whatever it meant. He said it was possible to make an Image for every emotion, every one in the book, once you'd got the hang of drawing them.

You know I thought that was pretty smart. Coming from a guy like Freddy it was a pretty smart idea. It was crazy but it got me interested. It even took my mind off why I was there. I said, 'Freddy, I can see you've been doing some solid thinking.' I grinned. I said, 'Just for kicks, can you draw these Images or is it still in the theory stage?'

He sort of stared at me. He said, 'Oh no, Mr. Harper, I can draw them all right. It took me years to find them all out, but I can draw them now. Any sort of Image you want.'

That wasn't what I'd expected. I stopped laughing and wondered just how nutty he was anyway. I said, 'Er . . . yeah. Look these Images, Freddy, they take long to do?'

He shook his head. 'It's dead quick. Easy when you know how.'

I said, 'O.K., Freddy, I'll try you out. You make me one of them. Let's have that fear thing to start with, you scare me to death.'

He got a pen out of his pocket and smoothed a paper napkin. He started to draw. The ink ran in blots, when he'd finished it just looked a mess. I said, 'Sorry, Freddy, I must be thick-skinned. Doesn't do a thing for me.'

He was very eager. 'Give it a chance, Mr. Harper, sometimes they have to sort of grow on you. You keep looking at it, you'll feel what it means. Honest, Mr. Harper.'

Well what the Hell, I was humouring the guy, wasn't I? I picked the thing up and leaned back in my chair and held it up in front of my face. I stared at it for maybe five seconds and then——

I was on my feet and the napkin was screwed up and thrown in an ashtray and I couldn't remember doing it. I was trembling, I said, 'Christ in Heaven . . .' Then things came back into focus a bit and I saw a couple of guys staring at me and I sat down again, but I was still feeling pretty bad. I said, 'O.K., Freddy, what's the gag?'

He looked worried. He said, 'I'm sorry, Mr. Harper, I really am . . . it gets you, don't it? I can't see 'em myself, they won't work for me, but I know what they do, I should have told you.'

I lit a cigarette. I needed it. I said, 'I asked you, what's the gag?'

'No gag, sir, honest. It's the drawing. It's a sort of trick.'

I shook my head. 'You're a liar. That's crazy.'

He reached for the napkin. 'Honest, Mr. Harper, it's in the d——'

I knocked his hand away. I didn't want that napkin unrolled again. I said, 'All right Freddy, so I buy it. Can you do it every time?'

He sort of smirked. Like a guy who's spent twenty years on some damn fool model boat, showing it off and getting praised. He said, 'Every time, Mr. Harper. You say what you want, I'll make you an Image.'

I said, 'Happiness, Freddy. Can you make an Image can make me laugh?'

He picked the pen up again and started to draw, and the result of that was on the way back to the studio I had to stop every twenty yards or so and wipe my eyes. People must have thought I was crazy.

In the end of course I didn't fire him, I wish to God I had. . . .

I sat in my office all the rest of that day smoking and thinking about what I'd seen. I knew I was on to the biggest thing in showbiz, but I couldn't see a way to use it. You couldn't make a film just of Images, nobody would watch it. And even if they did, if they got what I'd got they wouldn't be back for any more. Freddy's gimmick was the smartest thing I'd seen but it didn't help Hill Studios out of the mire one little bit.

You know how it is when you've got something in the back of your mind but it just won't form out? I kept thinking there was some way we could use this crazy talent. I got high that night because I knew unless I came up with a dilly of an idea we wouldn't last the month, and it didn't seem I'd got an idea in my head. I got back to my flat about midnight, I lay on the divan and kicked my shoes off and put the light out and in time the room stopped revolving and I dozed. Next thing I knew it was dawn and I was sitting up shouting Hallelujah. I'd solved it and there wasn't much standing between me and my first million.

I got up and hunted out a drawing-board and some instruments. I was trained as a draughtsman once Doc, I can set an idea down on paper so it'll work. I made myself some coffee to clear my head, then I started to draw and by mid-morning I'd got all I wanted, I fetched the car and drove down to the studio like hell.

I walked in on J.B., he was dictating to Connie. Jeff wasn't around. I banged my stuff on the desk. I said, 'J.B., this will not wait.'

He started to get wound up. 'I've been waiting since nine this bloody morning, where the hell you been—and get that crap off my desk and get out, I'm busy——'

I held the door open. I said, 'Connie, suddenly you remembered you just had to powder your nose.' She looked at me like she'd get a kick out of putting arsenic in my soup but she scrammed. J.B. got up. He was real mad. He said, 'By Christ, Johnny, but this has to be so very good.'

'It is good. Now look at these J.B., and knock it off, I've just made us a million apiece. . . .'

'What in hell are they?'

I said, 'Drawings for God's sake, mods to a projector. Sub-lim——'

I guess he'd got a right to blow his top because up to that time sub-lim was a dirty joke. He yelled at me. 'What we going to say then, you got it scripted? How about "buy our films" or "best British studio", that's a good slogan, Johnny, that's great. Now this is just about the craziest way you ever lost a job——'

I just yelled louder. Beat him down. 'We don't *say* anything for Chrissake, we use *Freddy's Images*. . . .'

He stopped dead with his mouth open and his finger still waving round at me. He said, 'What? Johnny, what did you say?'

I said, 'I looked at his stuff like you told me. It took an hour to get it out of my system. If I'm not careful I can still remember it.'

He said, 'Yeah. Yeah, I know.' He sat down and pulled one of the drawings across the desk. He said, 'What's this, Johnny?'

Do you know about sub-lim, Doc? There was a big row about it four, five years back. Somebody said it was unethical. That was a joke because it never worked anyway, they didn't use it right.

Look I'd better tell you about this, you've got to get the picture. The ad boys worked it out that if you took a word, say a product name, and flashed it on a screen too fast for the eye to pick it up the guy on the receiving end wouldn't know he was being pressurised but he'd get the message anyway, sub-liminally. The idea was great, trouble was getting a thing on the screen and off again quick enough. They tried it, tried it on television. I know because I damn well saw it. Doc, film speed through a projector gate is twenty-four frames a second, twenty-five for television to help the scanning. And that isn't fast enough. They'd overprinted single frames and you could read them as they went through, it wasn't sub-lim at all.

My idea got round all that. What I'd designed was a second optical system with a film gate and all that we could strap alongside the projector mute head. I hadn't sorted all the details, but I knew what I wanted and I knew it would work. There was a second intermittent movement geared to a stop-frame assembly, cans to hold a spare film roll . . . and behind the gate, try to see this Doc, behind the gate a lamp housing with an electronic flash. You know you can get those things to fire down to thousandths of a second? Using the rig we could pump in rogue pictures whenever we wanted and nobody would be any the wiser. And we didn't have any junky product-names to play with, we had Freddy's Images. I wish I could draw one for you Doc, but Freddy's the only guy can do that. I can't even remember what they look like, all I know is if they say laugh you laugh, and if they say cry, by God you cry. . . .

When I'd done, J.B. just sat and looked at the drawings. Then he said, 'It's great, Johnny. The greatest thing ever. For cinema. But television?'

I was prancing round the office, I couldn't keep still. I said, 'Why not the little screens, J.B., don't electrons move fast enough no more? Strap a unit on the telecine gear, rig a prism behind the lens, slam the Images straight through the camera. . . .'

He licked his lips. He said, 'They wouldn't touch it. They wouldn't dare.'

I walked back to him and put the palms of my hands on the desk and stared him in the eyes. I said, 'We make up a pilot. We get some of the boys down to see it. We run it with sub-lim. The Images tell 'em they love it. They tell them how much to pay. How much do we want to make apiece J.B., got any ideas?'

And that's how Little Andy was born. . . .

You don't know who Little Andy is do you, Doc? Oh yeah, I forgot, you don't see the Lantern. But, Doc, if you did it wouldn't make no difference. *Nobody* knows who Little Andy is. They just know they love him, that's all. Is he a puppet? They don't know. Is he a real live actor? They don't know. Is he a cartoon? They don't know, Doc, but they laugh when Little Andy laughs, they cry when Little Andy cries. He's all that matters, they *know* he's real. The Images tell them, that's sub-lim. . . .

I started on my prototype that same day. I got in a couple of guys I needed, I had to promise them plenty. I didn't know where the money was coming from and I didn't care. That was J.B.'s worry, I had troubles of my own.

We only had one projector in the place then, the Kalee Twelve in the viewing theatre. I planned to use that for the experimental hookup. I scrounged a lens and we fitted a bracket to carry it just above the mute gate. The stop-frame unit wasn't so easy, we had to rob a linetest camera and adapt the parts to fit. I'd intended to run it from the mech but when we got down to it breaking into the geartrain was a major job, so we settled for a spare motor strapped up behind the top spoolbox and rigged a flexible link to the camera drive. The flash was no problem, one of the boys built up a unit and we made a housing out of tinplate and hitched it on behind our auxiliary head. Then we made up the cans to hold the filmstrip and it all looked a crazy mess but mechanically it was O.K.

Freddy hung round all the time, fussing like an old hen. I told him we wanted to try out his Images just for kicks, he was pleased as hell. I set him onto producing a range of stuff to cover every emotion I could think of, all the subtle things like worry and hope. And I got him to grade them down a bit. The thing he'd shown me, that had upset me plenty. I didn't want to frighten people to death, just glue 'em to the screens. He brought the work in the morning after I asked him. I looked through it and it was great. I took time out to set up one of the rostrum cameras and get the whole lot on film. I did my own processing. I didn't want any little prying eyes seeing what we were doing till we were ready to hit the market.

When we'd got the sub-lim head built we started on the control system for it. I'd had a hell of an idea for that. Problem was to inject the Images just where they were needed to back up the action. For a time I thought we were going to have to do it manually then I realised I was crazy, all we needed was a split roller somewhere on the film track and metallic flashes on the master print to trigger our relays. We fixed the roller, then we rigged a solenoid on the stop-frame trigger, keyed it to a microswitch and we were home and dry. Bridge the roller with a wet finger and the spare cross turned, the flash went off behind it; each cue on the master roll would bring a new frame into the sub-lim gate, each frame would register on the screen as a split-second rogue image. All we needed now was a pilot film to cook.

J.B. had been working on that while I was playing with the mech. Don't ask me how he talked Jeff into trebling the overdraft, but he did it somehow; when J.B. starts operating stones have haemorrhages. Hill Studios was back on its feet and we'd got a staff of nearly twenty again. He'd dreamed up Little Andy himself and written the pilot script. We got a combined print a week after the projector was fixed and I got busy on it, making a sort of trackreading of the action and marking the frames where I wanted a sub-lim pulse to help the audience get the message. The emotion sequence was pretty simple; J.B. had scripted to keep it that way. The opening of the reel was happy, there was a middle section that needed a sad treatment, then there were a series of gags, then things went happy again for the fadeout. I cued for fifty or sixty frames of each Image, trying to grade the timing so the effect would come on the audience gradually, then build up. While I was working on the print J.B. started eating carpet, the bank balance was getting redder and redder and he was scared the labs were going to clamp down on processing; if that happened, we were through. I told him there wasn't a thing to worry about, if we wanted a bigger loan all we had to do was get the bank boys round, show them a film and load the cans to make 'em love us, but there wasn't time for playing games like that. J.B. wanted results on the pilot and he wanted them fast.

The cutting took a while because the system was still crude. Like I said, it was only rigged to give one flash per frame so if I wanted fifty Images to register that meant fifty frames on the sub-lim roll and fifty cues on the master. I finished in the end, I took the crazy-looking reel through to Freddy and watched him lace the cans and run a final check to see the roller was bridging O.K. Then I went and told J.B. we were set to blast. We ran the first test just two months after I walked into his office with those drawings.

We jammed a couple of dozen people into the viewing theatre, cameramen, secretaries, everybody we could lay hold of. Jeff was there, he hated the whole idea but J.B. had soft-talked him into coming along. And Connie, she was still giving me the freeze treatment every chance she got. That was a pity, because she was a great girl. Connie the cat, Connie the little lion . . . that was what she reminded me of Doc, a lion. Tawny hair and tawny eyes, and she walked like she knew what she was worth.

J.B. had decided we'd show the pilot twice. The first time it would go through straight, with no sub-lim, so we could get the normal reaction. Then we'd run it again with hot cans. That meant the test rig would be circuited, pumping Freddy's Images at the audience. We'd developed a new slang, that was what we meant when we talked about hot cans. . . . J.B. gave a talkdown, saying we were going to see the same thing twice, then he buzzed Freddy and the mech started and the lights went out. The main title came on the screen.

I tell you Doc, that picture stank. It didn't raise a grin. When the lights came on at the end even the secretaries were yawning, and J.B. was looking like thunder. Nobody ever got round to telling him when a story stank, he always had to find out for himself. Freddy rewound and laced, I gave him the thumbs-up through the port and we started over.

For a minute nothing happened. The film was just like it was before. I felt the bottom was dropping out of my stomach, I stood at the back wondering if the flash was triggering or if I'd got a break in the roller circuit. Then slowly I realised something. I was feeling good.

Doc I tell you, it was crazy. I just felt great. Little Andy was great, the world was great, J.B. was a great boss, Connie was a great guy, everything was fine. I wondered was I going scatty, then I got it.

This was the happy section. . . .

I couldn't help myself. I was in that rotten little film, following it like it was the best thing that ever hit the screen. When Little Andy was scared, I couldn't breathe. When he came out on top of a gag, I wanted to cheer. We got to the sad sequence and one of the girls started in crying like she'd never leave off. It curled 'em up, Doc, it laid 'em in the aisles. There never was a film like that, not ever before.

Came the funnies, I started to giggle. Wasn't a thing I could do. It was just . . . well, the world was so crazy, you know, there was nothing to do but laugh . . . I'd got my arm round Connie, she was rolling her head on my shoulder and howling, we couldn't have hated each other if we'd tried. She kept pointing at the screen and trying to say something, then she'd sort of choke and start laughing all over again. Up in front J.B. was banging the chair arms and throwing his head back and having hysterics at his own junk. There was no fighting it, you had to go. I'd never seen anything like it. Then there was the happy section at the end and the lights came up and we felt great, just great. . . .

That was the only time I watched a Little Andy show with hot cans. Doc, it *is* great. It's great for the jaybirds, but if you can sort of think, you know what I mean . . . afterwards, it's like you went down on your knees and bayed the moon. . . .

I guess Connie was the first to come round. I was still hanging on to her, she looked up at me. She said, 'Johnny, did you . . .' She giggled and crammed a hand over her mouth. Controlled herself. She said, 'Did you . . . do whatever that was?'

'I did.'

She said, 'It's . . . great. Just great.' She wiped her eyes. Poor old Connie, she was in a hell of a mess with the tears and all. She said, 'You're worth a million pounds.' I fixed a date with her that night, told her we'd paint the town. The way she was feeling she couldn't have said no to a thing, and I don't miss a chance like that.

I told Freddy the show had gone over fine. It was queer, the look he gave me. Like the whole world was a party and he hadn't got an invite. You see he was the only one couldn't get a lift from the Images, they wouldn't work for him. I said he was a great guy, to keep right on at the job, I'd see J.B. about getting him a raise. He said, 'Thanks, Mr. Harper, sir, thanks very much indeed. . . .' You know Doc, he sounded like he *meant* it. . . .

I took Connie round the swank bars. I threw the money about. Money didn't matter, the more I thought about sub-lim the more loot I could see rolling in. I got stinking drunk Doc, I'll tell you. . . .

She got the whole story out of me. Oh, it was a question here, a touch there, I gabbled it all out because I thought it didn't matter, she couldn't understand what the cans were or how we hotted them. She understood enough though. She understood Hill Studios had got something nobody on God's sweet earth could refuse to buy, that we could write our own cheques from here on in and that I was the key man in the whole shebang. The way she played up to me I felt a mile high.

I tried to be sort of modest, you know? I told her about Freddy, I said, 'Honest to God, the little guy's the one that matters. He's the only one can make the Images. I can use 'em, but Freddy has to draw them. . . .'

We were alone in a quiet bar, the lights were low. She said, 'What are you doing about him, Johnny?'

I hooted. 'Do? Raise him. Raise him fifty a week, a hundred. Yeah, give him a hundred a week. Worth every penny.'

She banged her cigarette in the tray and glared at me, she said, 'What are you doing, Johnny, you gone crazy?'

'What? Now, honey . . .'

She said, 'Did you tell him? Did you talk crazy money like that?'

I kind of touched her hair. I said, 'What in hell's that scent?'

She got mad. She said, 'Listen Johnny, tell me what you said. You say a thing like that to him?'

'Course not, but what the hell, we got to keep him. . . .'

She said, 'So you play to lose. A hundred a week, Johnny, what'll he do? What would you do, go down the road and get two? You put a price on him, he knows what he's worth. . . .'

'Well, what the hell——'

She crossed her long legs and there was a sort of frothing of lace. She said, 'Raise him a quid. And pat his head every Friday. That way he *knows* he's nothing but an op.'

It took a time to sink in because I was plenty stewed, then I started to giggle. I said, 'Connie, my pet, who has the brains. . . .' She said primly, 'Me, Johnny. Tell you what. Pay me the hundred a week, I'll use them all the time.'

I looked her up and down a long, long while, and those tawny eyes, it was like they were saying things. You know, all sorts of things. I said, 'Connie, I might just do that. . . .'

We got out to the car and she sort of slid down in the seat and she didn't care about her skirt. She said, 'Johnny . . .'

'What?'

She found my hand in the half-dark. She said sleepily, 'Going to be a big man. Going to the top.'

I said, 'Could be.'

She was sort of close. She said, 'Johnny, take me along. You can do it if you want. . . .'

We stayed in the car a good while, and it was great.

It's a long way to the top, Doc, a damn long way. I got Connie moved out of the main office, made her my personal secretary. I got a girl to work under her, so she'd have nothing to do but polish her nails. Then I had to fix up to manufacture the sub-lim adaptations. We wouldn't just need units for our own gear, we'd need them to supply to anybody that bought our films. Before production could start there had to be a prototype, so we tore the test rig apart and rebuilt it in a single housing so it looked like something that might work. We had trouble ironing out all the bugs, because the end-product would have to fit half a dozen different types of mech

4

and telecine gear. Right in the middle of things, as though we didn't have trouble enough, we had trouble with Jeff. Like I said, he wouldn't stand for sub-lim. J.B. tried to get me to fix a reel just for Jeff to see but he was too smart, one time with hot cans had been enough, he wouldn't watch any more. There was a big row. I was in on it. Jeff shot his mouth off for maybe an hour, not even J.B. could get a word in. He sort of raved about morality and warping people's minds and a lot of crap like that. J.B. tried to tell him we were in too deep, we couldn't pull back, but that didn't make no difference to Jeff. He was like that when he got an idea in his head. I told Connie afterwards. I was telling Connie nearly everything.

I was too mad to keep still, I sort of paced up and down the office while I was talking. I said, 'It's like he's got a complex, you know, like the captain going down with the boat. Wants us all to pack up and go home, says he's not putting his name on anything that's got sub-lim mixed up in it. And you know Jeff, once he gets a thing in his head he won't shift.'

Connie laughed at that, she thought it was pretty funny. She said, 'Jeff's a nice guy, it's just he's got a bit old. Sort of set in his ways. I'll be sorry to see him out to grass, but maybe it's time.' I asked her who was going to put Jeff out and when, she just purred and used those cat-eyes on me, and the eyes said you wait and see. . . .

I had a call from J.B. that night. You could tell he was mad on the phone. He'd had Jeff round to his place, tried to gin him into saying yes. Sub-lim hadn't worked neither did the gin, I could have told him he was wasting his time. He asked me what I thought, I said I didn't know. He said he wanted to see me, said to get round there fast. I asked could I bring Connie and make it a party, he said the hell with that, to come on my own and make it fast. I put the phone down. I'd never heard him so set, and when J.B. gets set on something better get out of his way, brother. I got the Jag out and went over to his house, a week later I was partner in Hill Studios.

Jeff took it bad. He resigned on the spot, and we found him

his coat and told him we hoped he'd keep in touch, then I shook hands with J.B. and we were all set to go. I moved into Jeff's office. It was about ten times bigger than mine and it had a carpet. I'd never had an office with a carpet, it was a pity I didn't have time to admire it.

Connie spent about ten minutes showing me how pleased she was and that bucked me up a lot, because what with the work and the trouble with Jeff I hadn't seen much of her for weeks. Well, she'd asked for the top, and that was where we were headed. I told her to get lost for a few hours, I'd got work to do. I sent for Freddy. Next problem was to get the television boys to see things our way. I needed some more Images.

We got the circus down from Town and showed them the pilot with hot cans. There wasn't any argument, they signed us up for a series of fifty and that was the end of our money worries. The studio was in an old house that stood in its own grounds and we bought what extra land we needed, shoved bulldozers through everything on it and started putting up a couple of sound stages. J.B. bought a dozen writers, he knows when he's licked, and we started vetting the first scripts and fixing production schedules. And I raised Freddy another pound; that made him the best-paid op in the business.

I passed out most of the routine work. I'd got a team building a new control system; instead of the pulses we planned to use low frequency signals on the track itself, that way we could programme the gear to insert patterns of any number of flashes off one frame. It made life easier and it also meant our control was better, we could play an emotion up or down, hold it at a pitch, peak it just at the right time. It all depends on the Image strength Doc, the number of flashes a second, the duration of the pulses. We can trim it just how we like. I tell you, Little Andy is nothing. We don't need the film, we could make you writhe just looking at an empty screen. The Video's only the excuse for what happens to you. . . .

Biggest headache was getting the sub-lim units installed at the transmitter end. We licked the problem eventually. We made up a film about sub-lim, what it was, how it worked, and the Images that went with it told you it was great, you had to buy it. You know how we used that film Doc, you can work it out for yourself . . . anybody didn't like the idea, we just got them down to the studios, showed them our movie. Every independent telecine is wearing cans now, every machine. And they can do anything you want. They're still showing Little Andy, all they've done is make us a nation of saps; that's nothing, they haven't even started. What say we wanted a change of government, or to kick all the foreigners out of the country or set up pelota as the national game. Do you see what this thing is, Doc? We could do it, all it needs is the film and the Images that make you *know* it's true. . . . That's why I came to you Doc, that's why I want out, but now I don't think there's time. . . .

After the first show was telecast J.B. went wild. The papers were full of Little Andy; the cheap dailies got it straight away, but inside the month the great nationals were giving the junk spread after spread. I guess people all over the world started wondering what the hell had bitten us. By the time the second film was ready I'd named Connie as dialogue director and she'd had her physique splashed across every paper in the country. I guess I should have worried more, but there wasn't time; the place was like a madhouse most of the day, workmen tearing down walls, installing gear, units shooting scenes in every damn corner they could find. I got to my office one morning, couldn't get in the door for cables. And somebody had got a pneumatic drill going just outside, you couldn't think. I grabbed Connie and got out, went and found a quiet bar where we could talk. She said J.B. had got an idea for a new series, he wanted to start work on it right away.

That got me. I was the guy who should be told a thing like that, not Connie. I said, 'The hell with it, he can't start anything else. We haven't got the space or the time, we haven't got the staff. We shall need the new stages for Little Andy, we can't start something fresh.'

She sort of looked at her nails. She said, 'Fact is, Johnny, we've got more space. We bought Orbit Films a week ago. The whole lot, stages, everything.'

I couldn't wait to get back to Hill. We managed to stop the building boys long enough to talk. J.B. tried to calm me down. Sure we'd expanded, sure I hadn't been told, hadn't I got enough worries on the technical side anyhow? Each man to his job, that was what J.B. said. He said not to worry, there was enough profit for everybody. He said within twelve months we'd have sub-lim cans on every telecine in the country, in two years we'd have the whole world. The hell with that. I said, 'Look J.B., let's take this slow. They find us out, they find out what we're doing, they'll hang us off the trees right there in the road. . . . Let's make films,' I said to him. 'Let's stick at that. I'm a film man. I don't want to own a planet. . . .'

But I couldn't get through to him. He just slapped me on the back and said not to worry, he'd look after everything. I tried Connie afterwards, she blew cold. 'O.K. Johnny,' she said, 'play it your way. I don't care.'

That hurt because you know, Doc, she was a great girl, she'd got way under my skin. Wasn't supposed to happen but it had. Somehow I'd done the lot for Connie, if she didn't care it made the whole thing sort of empty. I said to her we'd get out, go someplace and enjoy ourselves, we didn't have to work no more. She wouldn't answer me direct, just shrugged and said she'd see. I hadn't had a drink for months, but I went on the beer that night. I couldn't see my way round anything, somehow it had all got too big.

I had a call next morning from a guy I know, a newsman. It was late, about ten-thirty, but I was still shaving. I got to the phone, I said, 'Hello, Eddie, what's the trouble?'

He didn't waste time being civil. 'You bastards got something over there that's sending the country crazy, Johnny, what the hell you doing?'

I said, 'What's the matter Eddie, don't you like Little Andy?'

The phone made a noise. It said, 'I don't see Little Andy. I been wearing dark glasses for a month . . . what're you doing, Johnny, what in hell goes on?'

'Well you know, pal, just making fi——'

He said, 'J.B. was in here yesterday. Got a newsflash for us. If you don't know, you better had . . . he said he'd sold a new series, reckons it'll make Little Andy look like feed for the chickens. And I know he hasn't sold a thing, Johnny, he wants us to run the story but hell we can't do a thing like that. . . .'

I finished shaving fast as I could and bolted for the studio. All that soft talk, he'd been working over my head all the time. I parked the Jag and half ran to his office. I kept thinking, supposing for kicks he wanted to start World War Three. Supposing he gave out in the Press, the Russians didn't like Little Andy. Just you think about that Doc, just you try that for size. . . .

I went in. I said, 'What the hell J.B., you gone off your rocker? This crap you gave out about the new series, you can't do that. . . .'

He was sitting at his desk. He looked me up and down. He said, 'Johnny, it's done.'

I started to swear. I was the guy that mattered in that firm, I was the one had done all the donkeywork. I said, 'You can't do this, J.B. It's just you and me, and I'm not having you do this. . . .'

I hadn't seen Connie. She was sort of behind me. She came forward purring. She said, 'We can, Johnny. Sorry.'

I got it. Oh, but I got it all. And I knew I couldn't fight the both of them. I couldn't fight Connie. I thought of all the time she'd been playing about with me, she'd been hating my guts. I said, 'Great. Just great. The new Mrs. March, I presume? Or won't you bother. . . .'

She said, 'You've got to understand, Johnny, it's just one of those things.'

I said, 'Yeah, one of those things.' I put my face about six inches from hers. I said, 'It's true love at last, it always finds its little old way. What's the matter, Connie, can't you resist the smell of his breath——'

I saw the swipe on the way and ducked. I didn't miss with my backhand. I'm like that Doc, somebody takes a swing at me I swing right back. . . . I felt good for about half a second, then it was like the ceiling fell on me, I didn't know J.B. was that tough. . . . He hit me again right where it hurts, and I was on my knees on the carpet and it was like I'd swallowed a ball of something red-hot, it was stuck right in my throat. . . . When I could see again, he was standing in front of me dialling the police.

She took the handset off him and threw it on the cradle. She said, 'Forget it, J.B., he's through.'

He hauled me up. He was still plenty mad. He said, 'Throw the bastard through the door.'

She said, 'No, leave him. Let him go. He don't matter, let him stick around. You want to stick around, Johnny, see the fun?'

I got hold of the edge of the desk, that meant I could stay on my feet. I didn't answer. She said, 'Come on Johnny, I want you to stay, you're a useful guy. Just one thing, you may have to move your office, but stay around, we'd miss you if you went.'

I tried to talk. I was so mad the words wouldn't come, it was like talking through felt. I said, 'Anything more, Miss Connie?'

She grinned at me. She only used one side of her mouth. Her hair had half come out the clips and the bruise was already showing on her cheek. She picked her bag off the desk, opened it, threw down a couple of coins. She said, 'Get me some cigarettes, Johnny. It seems I run right out. . . .'

So I got out of my office. I had to because J.B. was building a new place for her and there was going to be a projection room so she could watch rushes without getting up from her desk. The box-suite cut my room in half. I moved downstairs.

For what it mattered I was still a partner, I wasn't leaving. I knew that was what they wanted, that was the way we ditched Jeff. I wasn't going out like that.

Nobody came near me, because the whole place knew how things stood. I bought in a couple of crates of Scotch and had a sort of lost ten days. I could look out the windows, see the stages going up, all the activity, I could hear Movieolas running all over the building, the whole damn place was jumping, but I didn't belong any more. Everybody was riding the same wagon except me, I'd been kicked over the tailboard. I heard them installing the mechs for Connie. J.B. put in a pair of new Kalees because she'd said she liked the colour of the finish. . . . They were right over my head, when they were running they shook the walls. Freddy would come in about ten and warm them over, and they'd show rushes three, four, maybe half a dozen times a day. And I sat and soaked whisky and listened to the projectors and thought about Connie and what she'd done. . . .

I felt pretty bad for a time, then I got over that and started getting wild. I didn't care no more about Little Andy sending the world crazy, I could only think about Connie. Nobody tears me down like that and gets away with it Doc, but nobody . . .

It took me days to think of it. If I hadn't pickled my brains I'd have worked it out straight away.

I laid in enough money to cover the deal I was going to make. Then I waited. Five-thirty that night I heard the studio packing up and going home. I left it a few minutes then I went and got the Jag, gunned it down the drive to the road. There was a bus stop a couple of hundred yards away from the gates. Freddy was waiting. It was raining, he looked like a little rat standing there with his collar turned up and the water running out of his hair. I did a skid stop and opened the car door. 'Come on Freddy,' I said, 'you've got a lift.'

For a minute I thought he was going to turn me down, he sort of looked round like he might make a run for it but there was no place to run. He got in the car. He said, 'Very nice of you, Mr. Harper. Very much obliged.'

I got to his place ten minutes later. He lived in a scrappy little terrace over on the other side of town. I got out of the car. There was one streetlamp alight, the housefronts were shining with wet. Freddy tried to nip past and I got hold of his coat. I said, 'Just a minute Freddy, want a talk with you.'

He stood there looking at me. He said, 'Yes Mr. Harper. I thought you did.' I waited. The rain beat on the pavements. He said, 'You better come in.'

He opened the door with a latchkey. The hall was dark, there was a sort of sour smell. Somebody called from upstairs, 'Freddy, is that you? Who you got with you, Freddy?'

He put a light on. He said, 'She's bedridden, Mr. Harper. Can't get about no more.' He shouted back. 'All right Mother, only Mr. Harper from the studio. Shan't be long.' He opened a door. 'In here, Mr. Harper. Isn't very warm, I'll get the old fire on in a jiff.'

I said, 'The hell with it, doesn't matter.' I followed him into the room. There was an old table, high-backed chairs set round it. Faded floral paper. A big print on the chimney breast that showed all Wren's buildings in one engraved heap. Freddy turned back to face me. He said, 'Mustn't be too long, Mr. Harper, she gets worried.'

I lit a cigarette. 'This won't take long, Freddy. This won't take no time at all. You remember I helped you out once?'

He sort of stood and pulled his lip.

I said, 'You were for the chop, Freddy, I kept you on. Remember?'

'Yes, Mr. Harper, yes, I do. . . .'

I said, 'Right then, you know what they say. One good turn . . . you're going to make me an Image.'

He said, 'Eh?'

I said, 'Special sort of Image, Freddy. A love charm. A simple. An Image for love, can you do that Freddy?'

He swallowed. He said, 'I don't know. I haven't ever tried.'

I said, 'You're going to try now. And you're going to succeed. There's an Image for everything, Freddy, you said so yourself.'

He said, 'Mr. Harper, Mr. Harper sir . . . who's it for?'

I started to laugh. I said, 'The mechs in the new suite Freddy, the new Kalees. They got cans on?'

He jumped like I'd stung him. He said, 'I couldn't do it, Mr. Harper. Not for a thousand quid I couldn't. . . .'

I got hold of him. Like I told you Doc, he's a little guy. . . I backed him against the wall, I said, 'Don't play games, little man, I don't have the time. . . .' I got my free hand in my pocket, took out a wad of notes. I rammed them under his nose. I said, 'A straight thousand, Freddy, no questions, no tax. You can get out, go any place you want. You'll do it, little man.' I banged him against the wall, made his teeth rattle. I said, 'A love charm. For the one and only Connie, for the little lion. Come on, Freddy, I'll break your back. . . .'

Some expression went across his face, like a fool I thought it was fear. He said, 'All right Mr. Harper, let go, I can't get my breath. . . .'

I stepped back. I said, 'Attaboy, Fred.' You can buy anybody any time, Doc, you just gotta be sure you're paying the highest . . . I slung the wad down on the table. I said, 'Get the stuff to me tomorrow Freddy, I'll love you like a son. Don't let me down.' I went out and left him staring at the notes.

He brought me the drawing next day and I looked at it just long enough to make sure it was the real thing. I couldn't do anything about it till the evening. When the studio had emptied I set up one of the rostrums and filmed the Image. I developed the neg and printed enough frames for both mechs. Then I went up to the new suite and laced the Kalees. I set the heads for independent running, maximum saturation. From then on, Doc, everything she saw she'd see with hot cans. . . .

I sat in my office next day and laughed every time the mechs started up. I knew each time the crosses turned Images were stabbing into Connie's brain like hypo shots.

It didn't take hardly any time. I met her in the corridor and her eyes were wild and she glared at me, and I stared right back and I knew. . . .

I took her home that night. We walked into my flat just the time the Little Andy show was starting up, all the suckers in the country crowding round their sets. She took her coat off and she was shaking. Her eyes were crazy like an animal and the tears were running down her throat, but her hands couldn't stop unfastening her skirt. 'You bastard,' she said. Over and over. 'You bastard.' Doc, it was great. The little lion had an itch, and Johnny Harper was the only guy in the whole sweet world could do anything about it. I sat on the bed, then I lay on it, and laughed myself sick.

And then I made her crawl. . . .

God, that little bastard Freddy, he'd got it worked out right from the start. He was twenty moves in front of me all the way. . . .

Doc what's the matter, I thought you were smart. Freddy, he'd got nothing. He'd go home nights, look at the picture of all Wren's buildings, sit and watch the fire. See to his old mum, wipe her mouth, feed her meat broth. . . . He was through Doc, he was a little old guy nobody could use. No front-office girls for Freddy. No Connie, not ever. Until I made my move. The Images wouldn't work for him, there was no way he could get her, I put her right in his lap. She had to get free of me, he was the only guy could fix it. He knew she'd go to him, he knew she'd pay plenty. *But she wouldn't pay in cash.* . . .

What? How could she get free? Wake up Doc, do I have to spell it out for you. . . . She couldn't get the Image out of her head once the cans had driven it in, she was tied to me till I passed my check. That's what she got Freddy to fix, he made me an Image as well. *My Image was death.* . . .

I . . . I only got it once. Up in the main theatre, I saw a print this morning, the cans were hot. Somehow I knew as soon as the mech started, I tried to look away from the screen but I wasn't quick enough. It only needed the once, it must have been a masterpiece. I expect it was, Doc, it was a labour of love. . . .

Doc, I've got an itch now, I know what it's like. . . . I didn't know how I was going to do it till I bought the razor. I'm trying to keep my hands off it Doc, I'm scared, I don't want to go this way. Yeah, you'd better get on the phone, get the boys in with the jacket. . . . But Doc, don't put me out, if you do I won't wake up, my body's programmed . . . get moving man, for the sake of God. . . .

The razor. Can't . . . put it down. Don't try to take it off me Doc, I could kill you, don't try and come too near. . . . Doc, don't watch Little Andy. Find Freddy Keeler, break his back for me. . . .

It's . . . like there was a magnet in my wrist, pulling. That's where the itch is, Doc, it's in my wrist right down near the bone. I can scratch it with this, I've got to do it, got to scratch, and scratch. . . .

Doc, don't, don't be crazy, I told you——

Don't——

God. . . .

God Doc, I'm . . . sorry, didn't mean to . . . clout you like that, couldn't help. . . . Doc, look I . . . done it, I had to. It was easy, going through the tendons was like cutting straw . . . it's better now Doc, the itching's gone away. . . .

Messing the carpet a bit, Doc, sorry. . . . God listen, you can hear the blood sort of whistling. . . . I . . . thought about it, what it'd be like, didn't . . . think of that. . . .

Doc I'm scared, I want Connie. . . . Try and listen, you gotta find her, look after her. . . . She didn't know what she was starting, he'll . . . do it again, sell her to somebody else, and she'll buy off and then he'll sell her, again and again, he'll break her Doc, she won't walk proud no more. . . . He's the most dangerous guy in the world, we made him that way. . . . Doc, this is sub-lim, you see what it can do. . . .

Funny. Like I can feel all the blood I got go rushing down my arm. Is that for real Doc, is that what happens——

Don't feel too good. Can't see . . . shoulder's hurting, guess I better . . . sit down . . .

Sort of want to cry, but maybe better make a . . . gag instead. . . . *Roll credits and fade to black.* . . . *Doc this is it I don't want to go*——

Connie darling please I never . . .

never . . .

meant . . .

Breakdown

I knew I'd got trouble when I saw old Billy Caswell driving in.

My name's Fredericks. Bill Fredericks. I run a garage in a little town called King's Warrington. Warrington isn't much of a place; you might have passed through it sometime on a trip across the Midlands but if you have I doubt if you'd remember it. There's nothing much there but we don't think it's too bad; we get along in our own queer sort of way.

I've owned Turnpike Garage a good few years now. Ever since Pop died. I've had my smooth times and I've had my rough but by and large it's a fair sort of living. I try and turn out a good job; and that's more than you can say for a lot of the motor business these days. I know it's my racket and all that but I still don't like the way things are heading. We're a replacement trade now whether you like it or not; all this taking bits off the shelf, slapping 'em in and handing the can back to the makers, it isn't my idea of engineering. Never has been, never will be.

That's what causes most of my headaches. I could have a nice easy life if I wanted, believe you me, but it isn't my way. It wasn't Pop's either. I reckon we were both as thickheaded as the other. But the thing was, Pop had a sort of name in the district. If you'd got something with wheels inside it and it wouldn't run you took it along to Old Man Fredericks. And somehow or other the bloody thing would run. Mangles, sewing machines, vintage typewriters; he never could turn a job away, whatever it was. I remember one time he rebuilt Stoughton village clock. That was just after the war, it hadn't worked in years but things had been let to slide. Well, Pop took a fancy one night to make it go. And he did. God alone knows how old it was; it hadn't got a screw or a bolt in the whole frame, everything was rammed together with bits and pieces of wedges. Pop fixed it; he took it apart and he put it back together, just like it had been. No fancy stuff, no welding or bolting or anything like that; just the wedges, the same way it was built. The parts that were rotten, eaten through with rust, he forged new ones to replace 'em. It took him months, and I don't think he ever got properly paid. But that didn't matter to Pop once he got the bit between his teeth. That was the way he was.

When I got myself sorted out and took the business over the first thing I told everybody was there was going to be a different system. My word yes. No more of the village blacksmith stuff; I was an auto engineer, I'd trained as an auto engineer and cars were all I was going to work on. I gave it out round Warrington we were a repair shop now, not a tinkers and tailors and candlestick makers. (Pop had made those too in his time.) I behaved like a right so-and-so to start with but I couldn't make it stick. There were Pop's old cronies, with their old cars that Pop had kept running for years, and the local kids with their first Rubys and Morris Eights; there always seemed to be a solid reason for messing with an old crock and not charging the earth. I knew things were getting on top of me when I got landed with a grandfather clock that belonged to an old biddy called Hollis down in the village. It had shown the phases of the sun and moon once and the state of some far-off tide. It was really my wife's fault I'd got lumbered; I told her one night, 'Sheila,' I said, 'that heap of junk's going straight back where it came from. I'm not putting a screwdriver on it, what the hell do they think I am?' She didn't answer, not directly; but it was still the end of Frederick's Modern Carwash and Comfort Station.

Billy was one of the clients Pop had looked after; I inherited him along with things like leaks in the roof. He was a nice old boy, lived along at the other end of the village. Widower, cottage with a garden full of roses, brewed his own wine, read a lot and generally pottered. Oh, he collected pipes too. He'd been something in insurance, I don't quite know what; I don't think he was too badly off, he'd got a good pension coming in, but these are expensive times for anybody. He'd got this big old heap of a car; she'd been a good motor in her day, but she was shot. Tired out. Maybe you didn't know cars can get tired like their owners, just want to lay down and die. Take it from me, they can.

I'd tried a few times to get him to trade her in for something nearer his weight but he wouldn't have any. He always kept her smart, I'll grant him that; she'd trundle through the village a couple of times a week on his shopping round, Sundays she'd wheeze up to the golf course and back and that was about the extent of her travels. He reckoned she'd see him out, there wasn't any sense chopping and changing at his time of life.

Now Billy was about the most unpractical man I ever met. As far as I was concerned that was his major trouble; a dozen times he'd pulled critical bits off that motor looking for some imaginary knock or squeak and it was me that had to go up and repair the bomb damage. He took the steering box adrift once, tightened it back up with the cross-shaft all adrift; that time he nearly did join the angel band.

Anyway when I saw him coming in I heaved a long deep sigh and considered for a minute taking refuge in the john while the boy got rid of him. But that was only putting off the evil hour, I had to cope with him sooner or later. I went out to him. 'Morning, Billy,' I said. 'How's the roses?'

The roses were fine. He was fine, the motor was fine. Running as well as she ever had. Everything was great.

I started to get fidgety. I'd got a heavy day ahead, I couldn't

spend half the morning chewing the fat with elderly gentlemen. He'd got something on his mind of course. I took him
back to the office, sat while he filled a meerschaum and puffed
the thing alight. Half a dozen matches later he got round to
what was bothering him. Could I slow his car down a bit? She
was running too well, he wasn't as young as he used to be.
Couldn't stand the pace.

I let my chair down sort of gentle onto its all four legs and
stared at him. I thought he was kidding; but he was straight as
a die.

Now I've been asked to do some funny things in my time.
I've had sick motors brought in, dead motors, motors in every
state of natural and unnatural collapse; I've put the go back
into everything from roller skates to musical boxes, I've
worked in petrol, I've worked in diesel, I've worked in steam.
But never, not before or since, have I been asked to do a thing
like that.

To slow something down.

I took a cigarette out and lit up, watching Billy under my
eyebrows. 'Look, Mr. Caswell,' I said, 'I'm just not sure I'm
with you. What exactly's wrong with your motor?'

He got a bit annoyed at that. Fanned the air with his pipe-
stem and jetted a rank cloud of smoke. 'That's just it,' he said.
'Just what I'm trying to get across.' He puffed again, vigorously. '*There's nothing wrong*, Bill. Nothing at all. She's just
going too well, that's all. I want you to slow her down.'

We didn't seem to be getting very far. 'Look Billy,' I said,
'better put me in the picture a bit. When did she start . . . er
. . . running well?'

'Oh,' he said, 'quite suddenly. After that little chap fixed
her up. Don't know what he did, haven't got a clue. But it's
too much for me . . .'

'What little chap?'

'Had a bit o' trouble the other night,' he said. 'Forgot to say.
Coming back from Bampton I was, been over to see m' sister.
Always go once a month. Lives on her own. Expects it . . .'

I steered him back as gently as I could. 'Billy the . . . er . . . car . . .'

'Mmm,' he said. Puffing hard. 'Comin' to that. Well, it was lateish. Round about eleven. Never late back from the sister's. Not as young as we used to be y'know. . . .'

I sighed again and let him get on with it in his own way.

It seemed a couple of miles out of Warrington he'd broken down. Sounded like a plain petrol shortage to me. He'd had that happen before. He was insistent he'd nearly got a full tank. He'd filled up at Turnpike the day before. 'O.K.,' I said. 'So it was a blockage maybe. What'd you do?'

'Well, I thought of ringing you. But it meant walking into Warrington of course. "No," I thought, "can't be dragging the chap out all hours. Have a look at it m'self." '

I shuddered. I'd have much preferred to be dragged out.

It had been raining steadily. He played round under the bonnet for half an hour without getting anywhere. Then the chap, whoever he might have been, had come along. 'Little chappie,' said Billy. 'Shorter than me.' He was a bare five-six himself.

'What'd he do?'

'Ah, now that's the funny part. Damn all as far as I could tell. Only took a minute. He took the torch, d'ye see, and asked me to sit inside out of the wet. Nice of him. Then he said. . . . I remember just what he said, sounded foreign . . . "Is right," he said, "I have completed." '

'Had he . . . completed?'

'Oh yes.' Billy beamed at me. 'Very well too, very well indeed. But my word, the drive home. I didn't think I was going to get there. Just like a racing car. You know, one of these Jaguars . . .'

I had a quick vision of Billy trying to come to terms with an XK, and shoved it to the back of my mind.

'Well,' I said. 'Sounds a bit queer all round from what you say. Got me foxed. You say it's still . . . er . . . doing it?'

'Oh, yes. I drove down very carefully. "I'll take this to Mr. Fredericks," I said to m'self. "Only thing to do . . ." '

I got up. The sooner I sorted the old boy out the sooner I could get on with some paying jobs. 'Well,' I said, 'better have a look, Mr. Caswell. Don't expect it's anything much.'

'You drive,' he said. 'And be careful. Oh, my word . . .'

I got into the car and hitched the seat back three or four notches. Billy climbed in the other side. I started her. She fired on the first spark. Certainly ran better than I remembered. Looked as if I'd got some competition in the district. I dropped into second and let the clutch out.

Next thing I remember was the blur of the pumps going past. My lad shouted something, God knows what. That old wreck had gone off like a freshly scalded cat. Left two long black snakes of rubber across the forecourt.

I managed to haul up just before the main road. I sat and looked at Billy for a minute then I got out. The only thing in my mind was I the victim of a singularly complicated gag in some candid camera show. I yanked the bonnet open. I don't know quite what I was expecting to see. XK unit maybe. There wasn't one. Just the old weary straight six, leaking oil a little at the seams. The unit ticked away quietly. I pulled at the throttle linkage. It bellowed like a tank.

I got in again and drove, very carefully. I'd never had power like that under my foot before and I've driven some hairy motors. I headed away from King's Warrington. About three miles out there is a stretch of dual carriageway. It leads up over a pretty hefty hill, a long pull of a mile or more. Beacon Hill we call it. As I hit the bottom a Zodiac passed me at the run. I tapped the throttle. It felt like I'd been kicked in the back.

I passed the Ford in about a hundred yards. The surprised blur of the driver's face just registered. Near the top of the hill an MGB was doing stern battle with an Alvis. I blew for room and hummed by the pair of them.

Over the top of the Beacon the road narrows and there's

half a dozen tightish bends. I started to slow for them. Halfway through the first corner the seat of my pants was telling me I was wasting time. The motor was going round on rails.

I started to get the feel of her. I'd forgotten Billy; I think he was just sitting there paralysed. The car was clocking nearly eighty when I came out of the last of the bends and she didn't sound strained. Engine note was high, way over peak revs, but that was all. I wondered vaguely what was keeping her from flying apart. Somehow I knew she just wouldn't.

I put twenty miles behind me before I turned back. Regretfully. I was on a good stretch of road. I decided to find out what she'd really do.

I'd flicked by the patrol car before I even saw the flasher on the roof. Or rather I'd seen it but it hadn't registered. By the time I was wise to them the boys were in full cry astern. A long way astern admittedly but coming on well. I remembered belatedly the latest Governmental lunacy; we live, breathe and have our being in the shadow of a blanket limit.

There wasn't really any answer. Except one. I put my foot down, the heap responded; a scandalously short time later I was back on Turnpike forecourt. I'd been round the houses a bit first of course. There was no sign of the prowl car. I drove into the workshop just to be on the safe side, parked at the back and let Billy out. It was only when I saw his face I remembered I hadn't the faintest idea what I'd been playing with.

I had time then to be scared.

I took him home. In one of the garage cars. I can't remember how I passed the thing off, I wasn't listening to myself at the time. I got away eventually. When I got back the car was sitting grinning at me in the daft way these things have. All set to go again.

I couldn't touch her till the evening. We had a hell of a day. At six I phoned Sheila to tell her I was going to be late. There was a little café just down the road, I used it sometimes when I was working on through. I went across for a meal. I didn't sit over it. I just had to get to grips with that insane motor.

I was forestalled again. When I got back in sight of the garage I groaned. Two cars sat on the forecourt. One racing-green Mark Two Spitfire. One blue-lamp-embellished Wolseley.

I might have known the boys would be around.

The Spitfire was a slight problem too. The bird was one Philadelphia Prescott. I knew her father pretty well. Only chap I've ever seen loading sacks of meat offal in a Rolls Bentley. I think he was in glue; whatever it was, his top tax rate was fifteen bob in the pound. Fond daughter was just back from Switzerland, been spending a few weeks with friends. The car was her mother's bright idea. Philadelphia wanted a Stage Two tune. Now you take one of those little bundles of fun, smack on a high-compression head, spatter the block with goodies and she'll knock a hole in a hundred and twenty. Phil thought that might be amusing. I'd already had words with her Dad about the sort of things that would happen to me if I obliged.

She was going over well with the patrol boys. She sat in the Spit in dark glasses, skinny sweater and eighteen inches of skirt and they'd got her pretty well surrounded. All two of them. They didn't waste quite so much of their excess charm on me. They wanted to know, to the point and in a word, who'd been ruddy well mucking about.

Now I don't know why if anything funny happens within twenty miles of Turnpike people come straight round and lay it at my door but that's the way it goes. I told them no, I hadn't got any specials in. What, do a ton and a half down Beacon Hill? I wouldn't dream of it. They'd better have a look round, if they could find anything that'd touch the half of that I'd like to see it. What was I supposed to have been driving?

They exchanged funny looks. That seemed to be a major problem.

There are such things as registration numbers. I was a bit worried about that. As it turned out I had a right to be. They walked straight across the workshop floor to Billy's jalopy, stood looking at it. I went over with them. Philadelphia followed us in for kicks.

'You know,' I said, 'I'd clean forgotten this one. Gave her a decoke last week, she might do a couple of ton on the straight. Hop in, I'll give you a burn.' I leaned in and switched on. Pulled the choke and started up. 'Got a bit of a blow in the exhaust,' I said, 'but it doesn't seem to hold her back. Haven't finished the tune yet but she's better than she was. Used to be a bit sticky over a hundred and fifty. No git-up-and-go.'

For a nasty minute I thought they were going to take me up on the offer of a run. I opened the bonnet. 'I thought I might have to plane the head,' I said, 'but we got by without.' I peered inside, wits maybe sharpened a little by crisis, and saw something I hadn't noticed before. Along the offside of the block, under the inlet manifold, ran a thin bar of metal. It had a sort of dull silver glint to it and at one end was a rounded housing that looked as if it might about hold an ignition coil. I certainly hadn't put it there; it didn't look like any part of any engine I'd ever seen. 'That's the secret of course,' I said. I pointed to it. 'The Fredericks Accelerator. Fitted in a flash, no bolts, no drilling. Guarantees a genuine two hundred. Saves on the juice too. We haven't ironed all the bugs out yet but we're hoping for the land speed record later on. We're working up to it; standing mile, stuff like that. Nothing too spectacular. You know.'

The driver—Pete Timms, his name was—shoved his hat up on the back of his head. 'Look, Bill,' he said, 'have you been bloody well playing about or haven't you? Were you up on Beacon this morning or not?'

I looked annoyed. 'I just told you, didn't I?' I banged the side of the car's bonnet. It rattled dismally. 'Gotta test out somewhere fellers, have a heart . . .'

We walked back toward the door. On the way he told me a few things. Like what happens to people with multiple endorsements and how they deal with falsification of number-plates and stuff like that. Interesting. It's nice to be in; I always like hearing about other people's jobs.

I watched them prowl off. Phil watched too, thoughtfully. 'Bill,' she said finally, 'you were joking with them, weren't you?'

'What?' I said. 'Me, joke? You never heard me do a thing like that now did you? Be fair . . .'

She gave me a dirty look. 'That's Mr. Caswell's old car,' she said. 'And you can make it do two hundred. But you won't do a single thing for me.'

I thought of a funny little remark Sheila had made a few days back. She's broadminded, as broadminded as they come, but I suppose everybody's got their limits. 'You missed a right little giggle,' I said. 'Archimedes Fredericks rushing forth from his place of gainful employment, naked save for oilstains, shouting Eureka . . .'

'Bill,' she said, 'if I brought the motor in toward the end of the week——'

'I'd send it straight back again. Phil, we are just too busy. It isn't the sort of job you can do in a hurry——'

'You've been talking to my father,' she said. 'I know what's going on.'

'Move that lamp will you?' I said. 'I want this motor over the pit.'

She kicked the handlamp cable away disconsolately, hands rammed in the pockets of her skirt.

I started Billy's jalopy and drove forward carefully. Got the lamp and climbed down underneath. I don't know what I was looking for. Sticky bombs maybe. Anyway, there weren't any. I got back out. We had an Alpine GT in for decoke and general service; Philadelphia was sitting on the bonnet swinging her legs. 'Where were they?' she asked interestedly.

'Where were what?'

'The oilstains.'

'Look Phil,' I said, 'I've got a hell of a lot to do. Go home, will you? Curl up with a good book.'

She slid off the Alpine, brushed at her skirt and looked haughty. 'I'll take it to old Charlie,' she said viciously. 'He'll do it for me. I'll see you still get the blame.'

The workshop door banged behind her. I heard her rev the Spit and drive away.

I don't like chucking people out but I wasn't going to start playing with that thing on Billy's car while she was anywhere in range. I went over to the toolbench, fetched a screwdriver. Held my breath and pushed the blade between the block and the bar of metal. Nothing exploded. The goody came away easily; seemed it was fixed by magnetic clamps. I started the motor again, revved her. She clattered.

If that heap got above fifty it would be by the grace of a following tornado.

I took the bar back to the bench and stood and looked at it. I tapped it. It rang with a faint, bell-like note. I examined it inch by inch, one end to the other. The metal wasn't like anything I'd ever seen. It looked nearly like pewter only it was about ten times too light. I nipped one end in the big vice. Nothing happened. I squeezed some more. Steel would have bruised; a dural tube would have flattened. The whatever-it-was did neither. I had the feeling it would cut grooves in the vice jaws first.

I didn't clout it with a lumphammer but I suppose I did things damn near as silly. I put a pair of Stilsens on the coil part and tried to unscrew it. There was nothing to undo. I tried drilling. The bit skidded, didn't leave a mark. It didn't mind neat acid or a torch. The torch heated it up a bit but it didn't discolour.

Just for a laugh I clamped it alongside the block of the Alpine. When I revved the tacho needle hit the stop that fast I was surprised it didn't wrap itself round it like a coilspring. I didn't try to drive that one.

I put the widget back on the bench and lit a cigarette. It was late, nearly dark; I'd been playing with the thing for hours. And I was hopping mad. I'd never been defeated by a chunk of metal before. This oddment had me on my knees.

I never lock the front doors when I'm working. I've got pretty good ears, I can always tell if somebody's mooching about. This particular customer managed to cross a crowded workshop in the dark without making a squeak. First I knew was when he coughed by my elbow. Sort of a polite throat-clearing noise.

I don't know why I was expecting something like that but it didn't come as any particular shock. I turned round slowly and looked him up and down. It didn't take long; like Billy had said, he was very short. Nearly a midget. He was wearing a dark suit, trilby pulled well down; he had a little bland round face, tiny feet and hands. Looked like a bank clerk who'd lost his way. Except there was something . . . I don't know, something not quite right about him somewhere. Like he'd just got dressed up in the clothes and they fitted where they touched. He looked . . . wrong, is all I can say. Out of place in an offbeat sort of way.

'Wishing forgiveness,' he said, 'for intrusion maybe inopportune.'

I looked at the widget lying on the bench then back to him. 'Is this,' I said, 'your idea of a joke?'

He looked concerned. 'Comprehension is difficult,' he said after a bit of a pause. 'No joking was required.'

'That's all right,' I said. 'No joking was achieved. This is yours, isn't it?'

He frowned. As if he was trying to come to some epoch-making decision. 'No', he said finally. 'Not being mine . . .'

'You put it there though.' I was starting to get annoyed over again. 'On my customer's car.'

He nodded at that, looking more worried than ever. 'Not requiring offensiveness,' he said. 'Considerable apologies.'

Now here's a funny thing. There I was at night on my own

with this character; he was certainly a mile from being normal, for all I knew he was crazy as a coot but do you know, I liked him. Something instinctive, no reason for it. He was standing twiddling his thumbs and looking at the widget like he was ready to burst into tears. I thought perhaps it wasn't his after all, I'd just confused him. Maybe there were two foreign midgets wandering round Turnpike and only one of them was a mechanical genius. 'Look,' I said, 'it's late and I'm not open for business. What's your problem?'

'Not wishing offensiveness,' he said. 'Firmly regretful . . .' He looked round the shop a bit helplessly. 'This is for mechanicals?' he said. 'A place of working and repairs?'

'Look,' I said, 'have you broken down? If so, what in and where?'

'Ah . . .' He pulled at his lip and frowned. 'A vehicle, yes,' he said. 'Most malfunctioning.' He seemed to have trouble with the hard vowels, like Mr. Jorrocks. 'Requiring mechanicals,' he said. 'Assistance very grateful. Please . . ?'

I'll admit I was about ready to shy a spanner at his head. I'd had a long hard day; I'd got a problem that frightened me cold, something I couldn't even get to grips with let alone crack, and here was this little wog mumbling and bumbling and spraying his much apologies right left and centre. Where he'd broken down I didn't know; what the trouble was I didn't know. I was considering advising him to try in hell but like I said I'm just as thickheaded as Pop was. His vehicle was most malfunctioning. Requiring mechanicals. Well, Pop never turned a job away. And he never refused to go out to somebody in trouble, not in all the years I knew him. It wasn't my place to start.

'All right,' I said. 'I'll have a look. You far up the road? Far enough to take a car?'

The look he gave me, I don't think I shall ever forget it. Sort of pure gratitude. Childish. Like a kid who's just been given a huge new present, something he'd never even guessed about. People just don't look at other people like that. Not unless they want to be misunderstood.

I got my jacket and backed the pickup onto the apron. Locked the doors and left the lights burning. He sat in the cab, all tensed up on the edge of the seat. 'Where is it?' I said. 'Where'd you leave your car?'

He looked confused.

'Right, or left?' I said. 'Which way?'

'Forward,' he said. 'Forward to here.' Holding up his right hand.

I turned right on the road.

We climbed Beacon Hill. It was a fine night. Warm, with a high full moon. Either side of the road the woods looked like black velvet. There wasn't much traffic; moths scuttered through the headlight beams, once an owl dipped across in front of us. I was wondering how far this character proposed to take me when he touched my shoulder.

There's a layby at the top of the hill. I pulled into it expecting to see a stranded motor. There was nothing. I turned to him but he was already out of the truck, hopping from one foot to the other and waving me.

I keep a bit of hose in the dash cubby. Loaded, you know. Not that I'm essentially a suspicious type but I do get called out on some funny jobs at some funny times and you can't be too careful. I took it out and slipped it in my pocket. But I didn't need it. I never needed it, not with him.

He was looking panicky again. When I got out he pulled my arm. 'Having the mechanicals,' he said. 'To repair . . .'

I presumed he meant my toolkit.

I squinted at him. 'Where is it?' I said. 'Where's your car?'

He pointed to the woods.

I shook my head. 'No thanks friend,' I said. 'Not in there. Just what's the ruddy game anyway?'

I thought he was going to get down on his knees. 'Please,' he said, 'for assistance. Is being no other. Great trouble . . .'

'Yeah,' I said. 'Great trouble. Not for me though.' I started to walk back to the pickup.

He just stood there looking miserable. Shoulders drooping,

like Chaplin playing a sad scene. And of all things, wringing his hands. People don't wring their hands except on the stage. Then, you laugh.

I opened the truck door and got in. Switched the ignition on, turned it off again and groped in the cubby for the torch. 'All right,' I said, 'let's get on with it shall we? Before I change my mind?'

He bounced off into the undergrowth like a puppy.

I made heavy going of it. The bushes were waist high in places and well laced with nettles. If I hadn't had a crazy day already I wouldn't have kept going. As it was, well . . . I've never decided whether I'm glad I went along or not.

Right at the top of the hill was a sort of clearing. There was a depression in the ground, a little dell. Screened round with the bushes, maybe a quarter mile from the road. Not the sort of place a picnic party would get to. Or anybody else for that matter. Maybe keepers or bailiffs. If there were any.

In the clearing was the vehicle.

I stood and looked at it. I walked round it. Then I stood and stared again. And now maybe you're in for a let-down; because I'm not going to tell you what I saw. I'm not even going to describe it. I don't think I could, not adequately; and if I tried you'd say I needed putting away.

I felt I was crazy myself. I sat on a little bank and grinned and lit a fag and laughed. While he waited there at my elbow and dithered and wrung his silly little hands.

This was the machine he wanted me to repair.

There was an . . . opening into it. He got hold of me again finally and pulled me toward it. I was still dazed. I didn't argue. I walked forward and put my foot on the sill of the . . . door, port, you choose a word. As I touched it the whole thing reacted. Trembled, sort of shook like a leaf in the breeze. Shivered, like it was alive. As though it could feel me, and see.

Don't get me wrong. It was a machine all right. It was a machine like half a thousand great watches all ticking and whirring one inside the other. It was a machine that quivered and trembled and maybe sang a little; I don't know, my ears were buzzing anyway. It was a machine made of gold and steel and rubies and pulsing light.

It was beautiful.

He was showing me what I had to do. Twittering, touching and pointing. I couldn't make sense of the things he was handling. There was no sense. Not my sort of sense anyway. There were ingots and rods, crystals and carved shapes, lumps and chunks of preciousness. I remember I started to sweat just looking at them. 'You're crazy,' I said. 'I can't do work like this. None of us can . . .'

But there he was still touching and pointing, smoothing at the bits with his little pale paws, showing me that and this. Cracks and discolourings, this to be renewed, that to be turned and milled, made good. There'd been a smash-up somewhere you see. In some part that never broke, couldn't break. I nearly started to see the funny side. We've got machines that can't break too. Rolls-Royce halfshafts, they never crack. But there's a funny story about one all the same. I expect you know it.

I hauled all the spare metal and broken bits up together. There was an armful. Some of the shapes were too heavy, some were too light. I backed out of the . . . thing, the machine, with him following me. Bouncing along, holding the torch. Halfway back to the truck he dropped it, left me floundering in the dark. I rammed my head against a tree. I knew what he was now. Or rather what he wasn't. It didn't stop me swearing blue fire at him.

Walking blind in a dark wood, it's bad to hear breathing in front of you. Worse to trip over something soft that squeaks. I went down in a heap, with a musical clanking. The thing wriggled and heaved. It had fur, or hair. I shoved myself away, violently.

'If you do that again,' said Philadelphia furiously, 'I'll yell the bloody place down . . .'

'Oh my God,' I said. 'What the hell are you doing here?'

'Look who's asking,' she said bitterly. There was a scrabbling and a torch came on. Hers. 'Phil,' I said, 'are you hurt?'

'Oh no . . .' She was scraping at twigs in her hair. 'You only jump on me with half a ton of blasted scrap iron first. You are a rotten swine Bill, there wasn't any need for that . . .'

'Look girl,' I said, 'this isn't funny. For God's sake clear off. Go home . . .'

'Try again,' she said. 'I don't know what you're up to Bill Fredericks, but whatever it is I'm up to it as well . . .'

I gave in. I was too tired to argue. This just made disaster complete.

We heaved the junk in the pickup and the Spitfire convoyed me back down. I drove into the shop, locked the doors and started one of the lathes. I didn't have too clear an idea what I expected to do. I just had this thought of maybe a jury rig, a lashup. Something that might just get him . . . home. I started working.

Pop trained me on a lathe. And he was good. He'd do things with a four-inch Myford most people wouldn't try with an engineering works backing them. I wanted him there then. Badly.

I tapped threads through stuff that looked like luminous ruby. Twisted Mobius strips and weird shapes, welded them and riveted, annealed. I turned square shafts from gold. Yes, turned 'em, with the work in the toolrest and the tool in the chuck. All the time with the little creature pawing and touching, explaining. He knew what he wanted, to the last detail. It's just he wasn't . . . mechanical. Phil made coffee, cup after cup of it; I banged and swore and sweated.

Dawn was in the sky before I'd finished. Or I thought I'd finished. I looked at my customer. And he nodded his head. Slowly, up and down, up and down. Yes, it was done. It was good.

I shoved the bits into a heap and stared at them. I don't know; somehow I had this feeling what I'd done wasn't . . . engineering. Not what we mean by engineering. I can't explain this too well; but once I helped an artist character knock up some stuff out of old junk he'd found, old gear-wheels and rods and bars. He was staying in the village, I gave him the run of the shop. I've seen his work in the papers since, some of it fetches good money. I got the same feeling then, watching him hammer his scrap iron and burnish and weld. He had a sort of feeling for the stuff he was using, for the metal. It wasn't art, not how I think of art anyway; and it certainly wasn't engineering. Just a new . . . activity. This was the same.

Maybe they know about that sort of thing where my customer hailed from. Maybe they don't think like we do in little tight compartments, everything neat and labelled and in its place; maybe if we told how we put art on one side and the sciences on the other, they wouldn't understand. Because when they want to fly they don't set to and build a plane, they make a wish. And the wish gets clad in metal and jewels, and it flies. I don't know, it's just a feeling I've got. I'd like to know more, sometime. Maybe I will.

I'm not making too much sense there. I didn't make much sense at the time. I was too damn tired.

We loaded the gear back in the truck and covered it with a square of tarp. Drove up to Beacon and lugged it through the woods. And I got it hooked together, and the inside of that golden scraptip looked just the same as it had before I started. Only it was finished now. Ready to go.

My customer was . . . well, I suppose you might say pleased. Then we got to the awkward bit. He couldn't pay.

You see he hadn't brought his trade goods with him.

Phil took hold of my arm. I could feel her shivering. He waved at us and gave us his much thankings again. The port slid closed and the . . . vehicle moved away. With a flash and a bound, a soundless jolt that sort of seared the eardrums. Rose like a dream till it was a spot of light that turned and dwindled, streaked away to nothing, winked and went out. And there were the silent woods, the silent iron-grey sky.

I don't know what I felt like. I'd seen something that night that none of us ever saw before; maybe we'll never see it again. Something that outclassed anything we've ever done like an ocean liner outclasses a dugout canoe. And I'd let it go.

So what was I supposed to do? Clip him over the ear, tie him up, drag him off, send for the Civil Defence? I told myself, it was late and he'd broken down and he was a long, long way from home. He was in trouble, with a machine. He came along to Turnpike; and I did him a middling fair job.

We walked back the way we'd come. Phil was looking tired and white. 'I'm sorry,' she said. 'There's going to be trouble over this, isn't there?'

'Yes,' I said, 'I think maybe there is.' She didn't speak again and neither did I. I was too busy thinking.

It's logical when you work it out.

Say you're an . . . observer. Anthropologist might be a better word. You've trained for the job, spent years graduating, turning yourself into a specialist. Learning more and more about less and less. And you get sent out on a tour. There's nothing much to it. People think it's a glamorous sort of job but it isn't. It's run-of-the-mill stuff mostly; you've got reports to file, data to send back for evaluation. In between you while the time away thinking what you're going to do on your next furlough. The tales you'll tell, the back pay you'll draw and spend. It's easy, nearly boring. You can't go wrong.

Only one day something does go wrong. Maybe there's a crack and a sputtering, a hatful of yellow sparks. A part breaks that can't break, a wheel busts that was built to run for ever. And down you come. You're stranded, in enemy ground. With a broken-down machine. What can you do? Nothing. You're not a scientist, you're not a practical engineer. You opted for the humanities, remember? That's why you're here.

You sit and brood and think. You can't yell for help because help's too far away. And you can't advertise. There's a big black book somewhere that lays it all on the line, tell you what'll happen if you ever break the rules.

So you get an idea. It's a crazy way-out chance but it's the best you can think of. You take a piece out of your machine. A neat little widget that messes with gravity, plays about with mass, cancels friction. You go sit by a road and wait. You fix it on an old busted-down car.

Why'd you do it? Because you know sometime that . . . part, that widget, is going to get to an engineer. Somebody who'll know it for what it is. Or isn't. Is he going to be the right sort of engineer? Is he going to help you, get you away? You don't know. That's the chance you take.

And it pays off.

Well that's the way I see it anyhow. Maybe there's other explanations. I expect there are. Maybe I was conned somehow. But I say this. If I was conned, then it wasn't by the sons of men. I'm an engineer; I might not be too bright but I know enough for that.

When I got back to the garage the widget had gone. I hadn't seen the little guy take it. I shrugged it off. Or tried to. I reckoned I'd run into what people call Dramatic Inevitability.

There was trouble, of a sort; not exactly the sort I was expecting.

I spun Sheila a yarn, I think she swallowed it. You can't ever be too sure about that of course; but she didn't make a big production out of it and that was all I was asking. I do a lot of breakdowns and crashes for the police anyway, it wasn't the first time I'd been out all night and I don't expect it'll be the last. How Philadelphia got away with her evening on the tiles I couldn't say. I didn't enquire.

I didn't see her for a month. In its way that was a pleasant relief. I'd half forgotten the whole crazy business when I ran into her again. Nearly literally.

I was fetching a Mark Ten in for servicing. I was coming down over Beacon Hill, moving well. And I was passed. The thing that went by was squatting down between its wheels and travelling like a dark green streak. I put my toe on the floor but there wasn't a chance, by the time I was off the

5

Beacon the motor was nearly out of sight. When I got back to Turnpike it was sitting on the forecourt with Phil narrowing her eyes and daring me to say just one word. I thought of a lot; but they all stuck on the way up. Because if I grass, so will she; and I can just imagine her old man's face while I try to explain how I spent the night in Beacon Woods with his daughter helping patch up a fl—— no thanks, not for Fredericks.

The thing that's sitting under her bonnet? She tells me the power's wearing thin. I can't say I'm sorry. I don't think anyway even if I could get it back from her it would be any good to us. If there was a hope of our understanding, it wouldn't have been left here. Like the man says somewhere, when its time to steamboat we'll steamboat. Not before.

There's just one other thing. If in the next few months your XKE happens to be buzzed by a pint-sized scrap of a racing-green Spitfire, don't bother to try a dice. You wouldn't get anywhere; and death lasts a bloody long time.

Men

Therapy 2000

It was the earplugs that started the trouble. Or rather the absence of earplugs, the difficulties Travers encountered trying to purchase such an antique and potentially unsociable commodity. Although he had of course prepared a cover story; in fact he had four, each vaguely less credible than the last. But not even as a laboratory technician conducting experiments in a new and highly secret project concerned with sonic warfare was he successful. Earplugs were not to be had.

Once implanted though, the notion wouldn't leave him. He developed the reprehensible habit of stuffing his ears with assorted scraps of paper, tissue, anything that lay to hand. He considered the Sound-absorbing properties of a wide range of substances. Hot wax at one time seemed a possibility; but there was no way of controlling its runniness. Working on one's own perhaps, one's head turned thus, sideways on the table . . . His one experiment was a messy failure. Wax was definitely out; but other things, equally definitely, were in.

He became absentminded. His vagueness manifested itself in increasingly painful attempts to ram further objects into ears already stuffed to capacity. The trouble was of course, the whole trouble was, that nothing *lasted*. A few minutes, perhaps only seconds, of delirious numbness, the total lack of auditory sensation; then Sound would once more begin to seep and creep in at the edges, through the interstices of the wadding; and there were the devils again, albeit muted, hoofing and pounding inside his skull.

He developed a new theory, one that despite scientific implausibility he was unable to drive from his mind. In essence, it was that the plugs *soaked up* noise, became soggy with din and therefore permeable. His fresh preoccupation dictated rapid, frenetic changing of plugs and alternation of materials. Ceramics were in now, and well greased hand-carved wood. These latter masterpieces he lay regularly in the sink, ostensibly to drain.

This was Travers' life. At dawn, with the Dicky Dobson Rise and Glow Show, he obediently rose. Two hours later— two hours of Sporting Roundup, and the Humming Hill-billies, and Keeling Cocos Walker and his Set and the News in Brief and Howdy Again Folks and all the rest—the interblock tube disgorged him at his place of work, the forty-storey highrise topped, as a cake is topped with icing, by the two floors and mezzanine annexe of Maschler-Crombie-Cohen Associates. There it was his pleasure to paste up an endless flow of newssheet small ads, juggling objects as disparate as hormone cream and harmonicas into proper relationships with the fat-face type, the bursting stars and dollar signs that since time immemorial had been deemed fitting to proclaim their excellence.

'Pasteup man'—the ad game, for decades now merely the poor relation of the PR industry and one of the more conservative of professions, still attached such antique labels to its minions. In fact Travers used a Grant and Digby, a bulky combination of epidiascope and dyeline printer that enabled images to be enlarged, reduced, squeezed, expanded and jazzed up at pleasure before being fixed by the simple pressure of a button. It was a nice machine; some illusion almost of privacy might be gained once Travers had involved himself in the intricacies of its various folding black plastic hoods. Though even there, of course, the office din penetrated. No video, naturally; but the wallspeakers belched forth for the stipulated Union minimum of six and one-quarter hours a day, their repetitions interlaced with the irate shouts of the studio manager pursuing this or that vanished example of still life: and of course each artist had his own Mintran propped beside him so that at any one instant the total effect might be enriched by tinny renderings of subjects as far removed as Puccini and mid-twentieth-century Progressive Jazz.

At sixteen hundred hours Travers tubed homeward to begin his long evening of leisure. The tubecars were all fitted with Trivee now; he wondered how the youngsters had ever sustained their short journeys without it. He himself, he had decided, was no longer young. He could remember tubecars without Trivee, and many other things; after all he had given twelve years of his working life now to the Grant and Digby. Once indeed while shaving—the twenty-first century, in other respects the acme of technological perfection, had not as yet universally disposed of the human whisker—he discovered a single fairly long white hair. He told Deidre about it that night; but she merely laughed at him in the cool slow way she had, and told him how little age mattered to real men and women, and kissed him and ran away to throw a pebble in the sea.

This was Travers' life in the evenings. The tubecar dropped him again at the foot of his own Elbee. Then he would ride the elevator—they were talking about Trivee for elevators too now, he'd read—past floor after shouting floor to his own room on the forty-third. Though the phrase 'own room' struck him from time to time as curious. If by some mischance he happened to find himself one day not in Room 633 but in another of the eight hundred-odd cream-and-floral plastic boxes that comprised the Living Block, how, he wondered, would he divine that the cell was not his own, his private, personal and totally secure fragment of twenty-first century culture? From little marks perhaps, dents, scuffings on the walls where from time to time he had hurled objects in those

fits of childish pique that seemed to be becoming more frequent with him. The missiles of course provoked no reaction;
so Sound-soaked were the walls that one crash more or less had
become as nothing between friends. So Travers' boots, the
condiments from his meagre eats cupboard and occasionally
Travers himself, were projected against yielding, translucent
walls of rose-budded plastic behind which shadows that were
human and shadows that were electronic bawled and strutted
throughout the livelong day. And through all but a fragment
of the livelong night.

But how precious that remaining fragment! Travers had
long since counted the number and decided on the exact dis-
position of the Trivee sets within his immediate range of
hearing. Basically, he was surrounded. Above and below,
naturally; and on two sides. The third side of the room, the
corridor partition, though by no means impervious, provided
the nearest approach to a dead area. The fourth side was the
party-wall of a toilet. There was no window. Rooms with
windows were expensive; eighty dollars a week against the
mere fifty Travers paid for his pad. Not that the absence of a
view perturbed him unduly. He was, or had become, impervious to views. He had not, unfortunately, become impervious to Sound; an outside wall would have afforded him
another slight zone of quiet, rendered less multidirectional the
continuous assault on his senses.

Travers lived what amounted to his life in the three hours
between the Wee Small Show (that came after the Late Show
and the Late Late Show) and the dawn chorus of the inimitable
Dicky Dobson. At one time, the gap in transmission had lasted
four hours. Before that, four and a half. Travers had watched
its remorseless closing with terror and dismay, rather as a
primitive man might observe, frowning, the inexorable
swallowing of the sun during an eclipse. Once indeed the gap
had been reduced to a mere two hours; but (possibly for the
first time) God had come to Travers' aid. Not admittedly in

His own person but through the offices of Walk-In-Light, that immensely powerful body with cells in every country of the globe. Travers heard the announcement perforce, one evening; in accordance with the illimitable possibilities of mathematics, three neighbouring Trivees had at last become tuned to the same channel and the results penetrated the latest version of the Travers Sanity Protector with tolerable ease. The declaration was made by the Chairman of Walk-In-Light in person; at megadollar expense, he reported proudly, the Corporation had negotiated one hour's Silence per day, for meditation and for prayer. Presumably there was an outcry; but Walk-In-Light were rich, very rich indeed, and the ban had held. Travers, in gratitude and curiosity, had even sent for their pamphlet, *Salvation*; it came in a manilla-tinted plastic envelope on which a naked man and woman, both tastefully sexless, held up arms to an engulfing orange sun. Travers was intrigued; not so much, admittedly, by the prospect of Immortal Friendship as by the soundproofed Chapels of the order, where meditation time could be purchased on a ticket-and-rota basis. But enrolment and subscription fees were high, out of the question for Travers with his mere $200 a week, and he had had reluctantly to shelve the dream.

His other dream—the important dream—remained.

He called her Deidre. Or rather by mutual consent they had decided her name was Deidre. She laughing and golden, flicking her golden hair. She was his one vice, hope and recreation.

He didn't know, or couldn't remember, how Deidre had come into being. Born of childish fancies perhaps, those stories children tell themselves at night beneath the bedclothes; but Deidre was not a night-shape, a succubus. She was real and vivid, real as any woman, more real than some; she got the blues and headcolds and PMT and once she cut herself and bled, she'd have her quiet moods and reflective moods and there was one special kittenish mood where nothing he said was right and nothing he did was right and he'd get mad,

knowing she didn't mean it but thinking she didn't realise how
Time was slipping and fleeting. Then they'd fight or she'd just
sit quiet and watch him, her face calm and frozen and in pain;
and next day would be hell. Hell at the office, hell inside the
projector where images of her swam bright and golden-brown
and sea-blue, distracting spots before his eyes. Next day and
next night, till the last Trivee flicked off and she'd come
running to him, a little girl, out of cool dusk or dawn, and say
how long it had been, how it had been so long. Then she'd
tell him about her day and what she'd done, the clothes she'd
made—she was brilliant at making things, clothes, homes,
happiness, anything—and ask him how it had been, how
things had gone with him. And it would come pouring out,
the frustration, the hopelessness, the endless grey and bright-
vivid din in the endless grey and bright-vivid city, the human
hive of Nothingness. Then she'd hold him in her arms, head
pushed hard against her breasts, and croon and laugh and make
him forget and he'd lose himself in the warmness of her and
sleep to wake, and sleep again.

That Deidre was real was his own private and carefully-con-
sidered conclusion. Somewhere, somehow, a spatial, a temporal
link had gone bust, he'd come half-way across into another
reality, the only reality that held any meaning for him.
A time link, almost certainly; for the things Deidre showed,
the places they roamed, couldn't exist. Not now, not any
more.

Did she invent the places, to please him? He'd asked her
often enough. But she only laughed then, invariably, and
teased him, and wouldn't say. He'd thought for a time she was
keeping something from him, some lonely secret that once
unlocked might plunge them both back to the limbo of night
and day. But there was nothing; she told him that once,
honestly and simply, hands round his hands, blue eyes searching his, flicking forward and back in those little shifts and
changes of direction that were so much a part of her. When
she spoke like that, with calmness and assurance, there was no

doubting her. In that voice, and with that manner, she had told him there was indeed a God.

Being real brought its drawbacks. For who could tell in what of a hundred, a thousand ways, Travers might harm his girl? Something done or said, unknowing, in the day, some curious link forged that might . . . what? Destroy, poison somehow all that was lovely and real? With the knowledge, Travers experienced a huge reaction. For months afterwards, nothing was too good for Deidre. And Deidre was so deliciously, so easily capable of being spoiled. For this she took, accepted, with that same naïve—not naïve, that wasn't the word, nor childish nor simple either—that same delight, that revelling in things physical, that characterised all she did. 'Look after me,' she would say. 'Wrap me up. Make me feel all warm and yummy.' These things he did, rejoicing yet still afraid; that one day, one day . . .

'Tosh.'

Diedre was sitting on a beach. Her favourite beach. The curve of sand, white where the sun had dried it, cream-brown where the retreating tide uncovered it, stretched to a high hill, a green headland crowned by a clump of wind-swept trees. Beyond the headland were others, pillars of rock that marched in stately progression, sunlight misty on their faces, to the bright haze of the horizon.

'Boo,' said Deidre. Then once more taking his hands, 'Dear, *I love you*. Can't you see—oh I can't explain, I'm no good with words. But can't you see that's all that matters?'

He wouldn't answer, not then. He was wrapped in thought. Till she scooped up sand to flick at him, and ran away, plunged into the sea. And they came back, to the hut by the beach—it was the hut this time, not the cottage. She had a cottage too with white walls soaked in sunlight and hung with brass and copper pots and pans and a great hearth with inglenooks and deep, deep creamy-white sheepskins for rugs. They would pile the skins and make love on them, in the dancing leaping shifting light of the flames. Afterwards was when he could most look after her. Coffee simmered on the hearth; he would take a cup to her and lift her, still wrapped in the fleeces, hold her while she nuzzled and drank. And she would half wake up, or barely wake up at all, lie tousled and golden and supple, the flamelight on her face, eyes shut, making the warm-cat noises in her throat, smiling maliciously to tease him; then want to go back to bed, and do it again, and sleep, sleep wonderfully. And he would brush her hair, long silky hair she'd grown for him, and she would purr some more and call him childish names and coming from her the brown warm syllables didn't sound wrong. Then at last they would hurry and scramble, both afraid of Time, like kids caught at a cookie-jar more than responsible, responding Adults; and she would hold him again, briefly, and kiss him once more and—

How did she leave him?

He didn't know.

But the cream walls of the cubicle were alive with light, and beyond them the familiar hated voices hammered.

'*Wakey-wakey, Rise and Glow; it's the Dicky Dobson Show . . .*'

While Deidre faded, wraithlike and sad, into mists.

But the days; the long, pointless, Sound-filled days! The hours stretched it seemed interminably until he could call her again. Sleep, for Travers, was impossible against the din; and tranquillisers were equally denied him. Once, drugged, he had tried to summon Deidre and she could not or would not come; she had been just a darkness in the dark, a silhouette that cried and cried as a bird might cry, paled and thinned to vanish into another dawn. Hence, he had never touched the stuff again. Hence, the games with the plugs.

Deidre disapproved of them when he told her, bit her lip and frowned. She would not tell him why; he sensed the hurt and worry, and felt lost, and a whole irreplaceable hour passed before they were themselves again. After that he said nothing more to her. He had never, as far as he could remember, kept a secret from her before.

Three days later he found out, in part, why she had been concerned. He developed an abscess.

It was very painful. To be more precise, it was as if a small blazing sun had become locked irrevocably and agonisingly on to his jaw. Sleep with it was out of the question; though he sensed the hands of Deidre, the soul and life-force of Deidre, striving to reach him through the blanket of pain. He shouted and cried, banged his head, fainted perhaps; in the morning, at first light or before—before, even, the Dicky Dobson Show —he was forced to seek his doctor.

Four agonising hours before his appointment. He videoed his studio manager, who laughed at his face then asked if it would help if he cried and when Travers, wordless, shook his head, laughed a good bit more. By then Travers had become grotesque, the pus bursting and squeezing into new pockets, causing fresh inflammation. Though with the increased swelling the pain was mercifully eased. The spiritual pain was worse now; the knowledge of wrongness and stupidity, of having somehow, through what he had done, hurt Deidre. He needed urgently to see her, explain, hold her in his arms. But that was impossible. Instead, there was Doctor Rees.

The doctor was annoyed. With, Travers suspected, good reason. For the Foreign Bodies Doctor Rees accused him of inserting into his ears—some scraps and oddments were apparently retrieved—were the primary cause of suffering; and Travers' suffering was the primary cause of the doctor wasting his time. Travers was upset. He liked Doctor Rees; or more exactly he tried to like him, conscientiously and seriously. Yet it was difficult; for the doctor had a Trivee clamped to his desk and while he worked and diagnosed Kandinsky—for the fifth time that week, Travers had counted—fought again his classic fifteen rounds with Bleeding Billy Cheshire. Shafts of colour played across the desk-top, and there was Sound. Travers was developing, he decided, a retentive memory. He had the frantic commentary by heart, nearly word for word;

he found himself correspondingly more ready to twitch at every Covering Up, every barrage of Leftsandrightstothe-body, every Scarlet Niagara.

But the doctor was talking.

He was a bland young man with a paunch. And unbeliev-ably, quite extraordinarily, spotty. Secretly, Travers blamed that on the Trivee. It was another of his theories, equally un-scientific; that continued Sound, aimed largely at the head, must in time be absorbed till the tissues, becoming as one might say waterlogged, rejected each new assault of breves and semi-breves, each shockwave of octaves and dissonances. Doctor Rees' face sweated Sound, through the entire audio spectrum; forty hz to fifteen thousand, with traces of twentieth harmonic discernible only by oscilloscope. The Harmonic, or Unhar-monic, Theory of Pustules . . .

Travers really must pay attention. He was being sent to a Specialist, he understood, because this must stop. Yes, he nodded, yes; he understood and did agree. They had dressed his face for him; it felt clean and comfortable. He would do anything, anything at all; for his own good, he appreciated that. Or there would be real trouble; and Travers, uncon-sciously and a trifle mysteriously, would be in it.

He told Deidre, that night. She had half a hundred ques-tions for him; about the doctor, and what he had said and done, and the Specialist Travers was to see. What sort of Specialist?

Travers blushed, feeling foolish. He had been too nervous to ask.

But he thought once more what he had thought many times before, what a splendid nurse Deidre would have made. He saw her in a cool ward, white and starched and tall, with a headdress like a great crisp linen butterfly. He woke for once refreshed; and the image sustained him through his hours at Maschler-Crombie.

In the evening though, there was trouble again.

He had wanted to call Deidre early. Really early, just for

once. Because there was so much to say again, about his short, tumultuous day. He'd heard—just heard mind you, it was only in the wind—about a new position going at Maschler. An upstairs job. He'd asked his studio manager and Rawlinson hadn't refused, definitely hadn't refused. Hummed and hawed maybe and glared over his glasses tops and doubted this and doubted that, but he hadn't said no, not outright. There were fifty dollars a week in the change, the chance of an outside room. Travers felt nearly faint at the thought. An outside room, with all the privileges it entailed; a whole wall, one complete side of his existence, free from din! In his mind's eye he already saw the room, himself sitting at the window; a summer night maybe, with the millions on millions of winking jewel-lights that were the city shimmering and crawling, a living map spread out far below . . . After that the reality of Pad 633 was hard to take. Particularly now that he had been forbidden his secret vice. He sat and brooded in the brightness and yammering din, hands cupped to the sides of his head; lay down on his pallet, tossed, got up, made coffee, drank it, lay down again, sat. The hands of the wallclock crawled with impossible slowness, marking the seconds and minutes sullenly; as if even the clock wished to deprive him of that interlude of peace still so achingly far away.

Towards twenty hundred hours a curious mood took possession of him. For the first time, perhaps, in years, he found himself questioning why he, Travers, must be singled out for such bizarre misadventures. The affair of the plugs, for instance; thinking back, reconstructing his every action, he could find no flaw in logic, no point at which one might say 'Here, Travers went off the rails.' No, he had done what he had done out of a need; a quirk perhaps, but basic necessity to him as an individual. Then he took to wondering if there had ever been a time—in the Cambrian for instance, or the lazy, lagoon-haunted Devonian—when there had been Quiet. If there was in fact any place now (apart from those priceless

Chapels that had made the fortunes of Walk-In-Light) where
Quietness might be said, even briefly, to prevail. Certainly not
in what remained of the countryside. He had scraped and
saved years enough to buy his one brief vacation away from
the city, but it had been pointless. Everywhere, every few
yards it seemed, in those carefully-preserved fields, on fragments of beach, in the hills that at one point defined the city's
limits, they had set up comfort posts; the tourists, wandering
aimless and a little scared, clustered round them plugging in
earphones, handsets, recharging the accumulators of Mintrans,
drawing a precious ambrosia of Sound into their very souls.
There had been nothing for him there. None of those empty
beaches of his, or Deidre's dreams, no sighing of wind in
grass, plash and chatter of waves and rock and sand . . .

He found himself, against his will and better judgment and
much to his surprise, using his vidphone. The directory numbers flicked past green and vivid as he spun through the lists.
He found what he was looking for, dialled Post Office,
Central Tower, gulped twice and made his complaint as
clearly and concisely as he could.

The gentleman who faced him from the small, fizzing
screen was sympathetic. Yes, yes, excess of Sound, very
regrettable; each citizen was of course strictly controlled, was
given a decibel rating in exact accordance with his status; was
Travers *sure* local db regulations were being abused?

Travers was sure.

Then, said his new friend and benefactor, action would be
taken. Immediately. Central Engineers combed the city constantly in search of defaulters; a van was on call in the locality,
was in fact already on the way. Not to worry, Mr. Travers;
just sit tight, and wait for the light . . . With an impersonal,
professional grin the complaints clerk erased himself.

I've done it now, thought Travers, with a mixture of terror
and exultation. *Deidre, I've really done it now . . .*

But what if . . . suppose, hope against hope . . . suppose
something was actually *done*? Travers imagined, or tried to

imagine, Silence. Spreading like a balm, like the stately ripples on a pool, from his cubicle, through and across the building. He gave himself up to dreaming. He saw himself the patriarch, the archpriest, of a new faith. What if, from its tiny beginning, that faith was to continue to grow? Through the city, the country; leaping seas maybe, to span the world. The vision was giddying and immense. Silence; a new creed gathering hundreds, thousands, millions perhaps of converts. How large a box, he wondered, would be needed to ensure total Quiet? Walls a yard thick, a hundred yards, half a mile? Money would be no object. He saw the treelined roads that would radiate from the shrine, the traffic on them crawling and muted. He saw the place with inner vividness, the white square sun-drenched block of its walls. Inside, an eternity of Quiet. With Deidrie . . .

The caller telltale above the door winked insistently, an angry red eye.

How long had he been engrossed? Minutes only; but even Sound had temporarily faded from him. He drifted to the door, dreamlike still in his new and temporary exaltation.

There were two engineers. And a vast amount of apparatus, meters, bowl-shaped direction finders, trolleys replete with controls and dials, a microphone on a collapsible stand, its head flattened and jointed like a shining chromium snake. They plugged in this and tested that, logged the time, reported back to headquarters, checked Travers' name and Identicode; consulted sheafs of tables and notes, produced from somewhere a huge plan of the Elbee—they were it seemed wonderfully well equipped—and at last were ready to begin.

Travers prayed, silently.

The microphone head turned questing, while the dial needles swung and quivered. Lights flashed off and on; Travers felt sweat break out on his forehead and beneath his arms.

The microphone was snuffling at the ceiling now.

'Negative,' said the Post Office man. 'Two point eight (something or others) inside max.'

They pointed the little machine at the floor.

'Negative there,' said the operator, recalibrating. 'Five off zero reading.'

But the screaming and yelling, the music, the rhythms that mixed and madly overlapped, the brilliant, endless din; this was *negative*? The microphone was deaf, or not adjusted. They were cheating him.

'Look, mister,' said the Post Office man. 'You got us on a kind of bum call here.'

'Wait a minute . . .'

Fresh hope.

The mike head was pointing at a corner of the floor. Almost, to Travers, it seemed to be quivering. As if scenting a victim.

'We've got a nine five over there,' said the operator. 'O.K., mister, you got a case.'

Direction-finders were put into operation. Dials consulted, the plan spread out on Travers' pallet.

'That's the guy,' said the Post Office man, pointing. 'Name of Lupcheck. That's an eighty dollar fine. O.K., Mr. Travers, thanks for calling us. Can't have people getting all upset by racket. Not good for the system.'

And with a final scurrying of leads and flexes, a vanishing of shining, incomprehensible objects into boxes, they were gone.

Travers wrung his hands.

Lupcheck . . . He knew Lupcheck, well enough. And Lupcheck knew Travers, their paths had crossed once before. Lupcheck drove a crane at the local hypermart; a bulky, bright blue affair that raced continuously, with pneumatic hissings and snorts, along the complication of rails suspended above the acre and a half of displayed wares. Grapefruit, canned goods, toilet packs and MinTrans, artificial flowers, eggboxes and cheese, each and every conceivable commodity was seized by Lupcheck from its warehouse rack, flung to its allotted place as the dumps dwindled under the feverish, picking hands of the Consumers. Often Travers had admired his dexterity with the crane; till one day some complicated event took place that left a Consumer buffeted and hatless and spilled banana clumps and tinned Sevilles and marmalade pots and cereals across the floor. The Consumer shouted something angrily at the roof, and was answered, and kept on shouting, till Lupcheck swung down—he had a little spidery unexpected ladder that extended from the side of the crane. Lupcheck was not tall; but he was very broad, and sported orange-grey hair that grew in erratic tufts across his wide skull and thick, reddish forearms. His fists were large, with knuckles that were seamed and cracked; one swipe from one fist and the Consumer's spectacles were terribly embedded in the side of his face, and blood was dripping and splashing in big round gobs on to the floor, and the Consumer was crying while Lupcheck climbed, still annoyed and grumbling, back to his machine. And Travers walked quickly to the exit, feeling ill and not wanting the things he had bought, wondering with a sort of sick amazement why he had never realised before the full destructive power of the ball of bone at the end of a human arm.

Travers was afraid of Lupcheck. Now he had cost him eighty dollars.

Some time after the decibel hunters had gone, one might or might not have detected a small reduction in the overall uproar from the Trivees. Travers passed a restless night, too miserable for sleep, unable to summon Deidre. As always, disbelief came with the cessation of the din. It was like trying to remember pain; it seemed inconceivable that the Elbee had not always been wrapped in a breathing quiet. Lights flicked off in the surrounding cubicles till Travers lay staring into velvet dark. In the dark, he cursed himself bitterly. What a little thing it seemed after all, this simple matter of Sound! For no reason at all, or hardly any reason, he had jeopardised the coming morning. And denied himself Deidre, and hurt her; he had no doubt of that. He composed himself for sleep with a species of desperation; but dawn inched up, and Dicky Dobson burst into his daily cacophony, while Travers still lay red-eyed and restless. Now, horrors yawned; for if he avoided Lupcheck, this was in any case the Day of the Specialist.

Lupcheck caught him in the elevator.

Travers thumbed the controls in panic but the other was too fast for him. He rammed a shoulder at the door as it was wheezing shut; the mechanism whistled peevishly, slid open and closed again with Lupcheck inside. The elevator started its smooth descent.

Lupcheck twisted his fingers in the front of Travers' clothing, lifted him to his toes and pushed him against the side of the car. Travers wheezed, staring into bulging pale-blue eyes. As had happened before, he felt curiously detached; a part of his brain realised that Lupcheck was genuinely angry and puzzled over it while his eyes recorded the coarse texture of the other's skin, the networks of tiny branching veins, the individual tousled hairs of the thick brows, some reddish, some white, some grey. A tiny muscle twitched at the corner of Lupcheck's mouth and Travers wondered for an instant of time whether the crane operator might not be as unhappy as he. Then the rage came, swimming and cold. It dictated that Travers should drive his knee into Lupcheck's groin, bring down a disabling fist on the junction between nose and eyes. What he had seen in the hypermart held him back. Lupcheck was invincible; there would be other blows, like the blows of a great salty hammer, too terrible to be borne; and things breaking inside Travers' mouth, he could see the blood already and feel the pain. So he hung limp while Lupcheck banged him at the side of the elevator again, and growled and promised and swore.

Whatever happened now Deidre would be angry. Angry at his cowardice, angry if he fought and was uselessly hurt. So Travers had to hear the things Lupcheck said, and make the undertakings Lupcheck required, and scuttle away, when Lupcheck finally released him, grateful and reprieved. The rage still seethed and boiled; it wouldn't leave him now, he knew, till Deidre had suffered for it. As ever, against his will. But suffer she must; if for no other reason, for the folly and incompetence of God.

The rage buoyed Travers on his way to Hospital Block. He had been there once before, years ago, and dimly remembered the way. He shoved along crowded underpasses echoing with the high-pitched clatter of Travellators, the heavier thunder of streetcars. Trivees, set here and there in walls and roofs, competed with the din. Interspersed with them were talking posters and advertisements, round the borders of which blue and pink and scarlet, white and yellow flame-shapes and tartan-patterns raced. Hospital Block was well sign-posted. It seemed to extend electronic nerve-fibres into the underpasses; soon Travers found himself confronted by the conflicting possibilities of Path, Ear, Nose and Throat, Ophthalmic, Geriatric, Cancer and half a dozen more ominously-labelled departments. The light-trails—follow the Red and Blue—also flashed, confusingly. He went wrong twice, backtracked, found his way eventually to a Travellator that wound smoothly up a steepening incline, deposited him in the reception area of the place.

This too he remembered. The endless concrete walls, the hard white glare of lighting from many troughs; and the din. Loudhailers, aimed in all directions, rasped strings of Identicode numbers, referring Outpatients to any of a score of gates and elevators. In line after line of frontless, unpainted cubicles, cases deemed unworthy of admission to the maze above were treated by frantically-rushing white-coated staff; beyond was Casualty Section, hectic with the influx of an entire city. Ambulances, delivered at intervals of seconds from a range of entry lifts, disgorged stretchers and walking injured; more staff, nurses and orderlies, swarmed round them. There was a constant clanging of alarm bells, a clash and rattle of trolleys. In one place Travers saw the wreckage of a vehicle, transported in the maw of a huge recovery truck, decanted with scant ceremony on to a sloping slipway. Men scuttled forward, one lugging the cylinders of an antique oxy-acetyline cutter. The victims would presumably be extracted on the spot, like fresh bright herrings from a can. Travers shuddered and turned away, presented his Identitag to the impersonal scrutiny of an Appointments Monitor. The machine blinked, ticked rapidly and rewarded him with a punched and coded card. He hurried on, jostled now, deciphering his instructions as he went.

Within the Block proper the din was if anything worse. There were wards, full of noise, bright-glimpsed as he hurried past; corridors echoing with the mechanical clatter of trolleys and utensils. He was harried and buffeted, directed from point to point. At length, high in the building, the wall codings began to make sense. He found his corridor, counted off doors, presented the card to a scanner and was mechanically admitted to a featureless, carpeted ante-room.

At least it was quieter here. A solitary Trivee played, its Sound muted. A receptionist—human at last—took over the direction of Travers' affairs. He was told to sit and wait, given a plastic-leaved magazine to thumb. He read, automatically, words that made no sense. And prayed for Deidre. At other times, other great crises in his life, the technique had worked. He closed his eyes, concentrated. Forced back the light that filtered through the lids, forced back the Sound.

'Mr. Travers . . .'

Travers looked up with a start at the testy repetition. Again, he was off on the wrong foot. Now he had annoyed the Specialist.

He was ushered to an inner office. Here, at last, was Quiet. A Quiet so intense the whick-whick, the slow whirr and rustle of the ceiling-mounted fan sounded loud. The Specialist consulted a plastic-covered folder of notes, frowned, clucked and shook his head. Then he steepled his fingers, regarding Travers morosely over their tips as he talked.

The great man made his points carefully, occasionally

tapping the desk top for greater emphasis. First, Travers must realise the considerable problem he and others like him posed to a modern society; a society, the Specialist stressed, organised on sound historical principles for the greatest good of the greatest number of its members. He repeated, in effect, the admonitions of Doctor Rees; while Travers nodded dumbly, wishing to be no inconvenience. Only wanting, were the truth to be known, to escape once more into his desert of Sound.

But that, it seemed, was not to be. For the Specialist was still talking, questioning and probing now, insistently. The direction of the questioning was strange. Things from Travers' childhood, remote events to be dredged up and re-examined and puzzled over. Travers answered the questions, reticent at first then more eager, till at last the whole grief came blubbering and boiling from him, the Need, the great Need of his soul, for Quiet. The notion of the Shrine.

Travers stopped, appalled. But the Specialist was beaming now, urging him to continue. The Specialist himself understood Travers' problem; he really understood. As for a solution; why, within this modern society, in this best of all possible worlds, anything could be achieved. And the Need was after all very simple to fulfil. The answer? No mile-thick pill-boxes, no apparatus, no romantic, unattainable dreams . . .

Travers blinked as the full beauty of the solution dawned on him. So simple, so sublimely simple, simple as Relativity, simple as all truly great and original ideas . . . It would mean of course the sacrifice of his new position, the end of the day-old dream of an outside room; but his mind glowed already with the other, greater possibilities. Happiness, total and complete; for him, and for Deidre. He saw himself already, breaking the wonderful news; of Time, Time unlimited. Time for them to be together. The world faded; he saw nothing but the bright and perfect future. He nodded, feverish, voiceless in his impatience, eager only to sign the forms the Specialist proffered him, and begin.

He was conducted to yet another room. Aseptic this time, white and gleaming. The nurse who readied him was brown-skinned and supple. Like Deidre, almost; with silky hair, a wave of it he was sure, hidden by her neat white cap. But she shoved and pushed at him indifferently, as if he were a carcass, a simple hunk of meat unworthy of human consideration. Her eyes, when they once met his, seemed full of a bored contempt; then he saw the Mintran speaker in her ear, the spidery flex running into the collar of her uniform, and was able to return the stare from the height of a loftier indifference.

The local took effect immediately, an icy numbness spreading from jaw to neck and temples. He was led to a chair that moulded itself to him as he sat, reclined and tilted at the touch of innumerable shining levers. A lamp was switched on, planet-bright and close; he felt the momentary pulse of heat from it on cheeks and nose before a cloth was laid neatly over his eyes. His head was turned; fingers probed his dead cheeks, dimpling.

The instruments made little sounds. Ringings, and clinks. Then closer squeaks and gratings, once a crunch; then nothing. Nothing at all.

The cloth was withdrawn; and Travers stared round dazed. The nightmare was ended; cleanly and neatly, in a mere instant of time. No more Dicky Dobson now, no more Rise and Glow; no more Travellators, no more Mintrans, no more traffic, no more people; nothing. So perfect was the technique, they had assured him, that his balance would be unimpaired; just a simple matter of excision, removal of tiny bones that worked in sequences of other tiny bones, alignments functioning with jewel-precision to transmit hell from the four quarters of the globe to the inside of his skull . . .

The faces were mouthing at him now. Nurse, anaesthetist, surgeon; praise or curses, congratulations or contempt. He smiled back, euphorically. He neither knew nor cared.

And there was the silent city, outside. The silent tubecars and the silent Travellators, the silent people and the silent vehicles.

A million silent windows, eyes of cubicles that housed a million silent Trivees. Somewhere Lupcheck drove his silent crane, mimed his silent rage; poor stupid defeated Lupcheck, who now didn't matter at all.

Work was out of the question for today. Travers threaded his way home carefully, watchful for the dizziness they had warned him might possibly occur for a time. He elevated to his room, slid the silent doorpanel closed. Beyond the walls, as ever, electronic patterns danced. He smiled at them too, a smile of benediction.

He undressed slowly, now with all the Time in the world. The worry of the night, the strain of the day, had exhausted him. He curled up on the pallet, pulled the covers round himself and fell almost instantly asleep.

The beach flicked on. And there was Deidre running, running as she had never run before. He ran too, feeling his feet stumble in the sunwarmed sand, arms outstretched. He tried to hug her, but she pushed him away. He saw then, bewildered, the sheen of tears on chin and throat; and her eyes, the terrible accusation there. She fell to her knees, holding her throat and rocking with misery, asking again and again the same silent question, *why, why,* till understanding came at last.

Deidre was dumb.

The Deeps

It was bound to happen. For generations, the chain reaction of population explosion had been going on and on. While medical skill grew, while longevity increased nearly beyond belief, humankind everywhere bred and bred and bred. Houses, estates, factories to serve the vast new economies spread and sprawled, twitching out across good land and bad, climbing mountains, suffocating rivers. Town touched town, touched town; the pink octopus tentacles of houses grew and thickened as the machines graded and scraped and hammered. Green belts and parks vanished, fields were swallowed overnight. Here and there voices were raised; the voices of economists, scientists, philosophers, even at last theologians. But they were swamped in the great universal cry.

Give us room . . . The shout went up night and day from a hundred million throats, the slogan blared from loudspeakers, blazed from hoardings as political parties jockeyed for power. Increasingly, room was what they promised. Room for more houses, more estates, room to rear new families that cried in their turn for room and still more room . . .

All over the world countrysides vanished, eaten. Wars flared as nations bit at each other's borders, but still the Cities grew. The huge estates were searched, forced to yield their last acres, their secret gardens. And all for nothing, it seemed, because still the cry was heard for room. Skyscrapers soared, fifty stories, seventy, a hundred, and it was not enough. The Cities bulged outward, noisy with music and the sound of human life. A hundred yards thick they were and blaring with light, complex with stack on twinkling stack of avenues. Raucous, Technicolored, sleepless. Everywhere, they reached the sea.

And they could not stop. The pressure, the need for room, pushed them out again. The houses sank like silver bells into blueness and quiet, and at last there was room enough.

. . .

Mary Franklin sat in the living area of her bungalow, knitting quiet for once in her lap, and tried to watch the telscreen at the other side of the room. Across her line of sight Jen passed scuttling, bare feet scuffing the carpet, the straps of her lung flapping round her shoulders. Across and back, then across again, frantic now, going to a party at the Belmonts on the other side of town, and late. Mary raised her eyes to heaven, represented temporarily by a curved steel shell. She concentrated on the screen where a demonstrator, in vivid colour, divulged to her audience the inner secrets of a variant of crawfish mayonnaise. Jen yelped something inaudible from the bedroom, thumped the wall. (Why . . .?) She padded across again and back. Mary raised her voice suddenly.

'Jen . . .?'

Thump. Mumble.

'*Jen!*'

'Mummy, I can't find my . . .' Indistinguishable.

'Jen, you're not to be late. No more than nine, understand?'

'Yes . . .'

'And for *land's* sake child, *put something on . . .*'

'Yes, Mummy . . .' That in a high voice, wearily. And almost instantly the roar of the sealock. Mary got up in quick rage, walked halfway to the radio gear, changed her mind, went back to her chair. Jen, she knew well enough, would conveniently have forgotten her phone-leads.

She kicked the channel switch irritably in passing; the picture on the wallscreen jumped and altered. The set began to disgorge a Western; Mary lay back, eyes nearly shut, half her mind in the ancient film and half on the blueness overhead. The endless blue.

Jen, defiantly bare, hung twenty feet above the hemispherical roof of her home. Bubbles from her breathing rose in a series of shimmering, dimly seen sickles to the Surface overhead. As always, the sea had made her forget her compulsion to hurry; she began to paddle slowly, feet in their long fins catching and driving back wedges of water. As she moved she looked below her, at the lines of domes with their neat, almost suburban gardens of waving weed. She saw the misty squares of their windows, the brighter greeny-blue globes of the streetlighting swung from thin wires above the ocean bed. Warnings were hung on long streamers of wires for swimmers; there were well-marked lanes, corresponding to the streets of the city complexes Jen barely remembered, but many people ignored them. And most of the children. Technically she was out of bounds now, gliding along like this only a few feet from Surface.

Visibility was good tonight; onshore winds could kick up a smother that lasted for days, but there had been nearly a week of calm. Jen could make out through the almost haze-free water the faint shimmer where the engineers, her father among them, were working on the new extension to the theatre and civic centre. When it was finished, the installation would be the pride of Settlement Eighty, the town its inhabitants called Oceanville. There were a dozen other Oceanvilles scattered up and down this one stretch of coast, hundreds possibly in all the seas of the world. She shivered slightly although the water was not cold.

Beyond the lights, beyond where the divers floated round the tall steel skeletons, were long sloping stretches where the town buildings petered out and the coral and sand of the inshore waters gave place to the silt of real ocean. There was a graveyard, tiny as yet, where a few bodies lay in their metal cans; beyond again, past grey dunes where the light faded imperceptibly to navy blue and black, were the Deeps. Above anything else Jen liked to go to the new buildings, sit on one of the girders, look down into the vagueness that was the proper sea, bottomless and immense. Just stare, and listen, and wait. She would go there tonight maybe, after the party.

She let herself relax, holding air in her lungs to increase buoyancy. Her body floated upward, legs and arms slack; Surface appeared above her, a faintly luminous upside-down plain. Points of light sparkled where the moon-track refracted into the depths. Jen wagged lazily with her flippers, once, twice; her body broke the Surface and she felt herself lifted by the slight action of the waves.

She looked round. The sea was flatly calm, dark at the horizon, glinting with bluish swirls of phosphorescence round her shoulders and neck. When she looked closely, she could see the organisms that made the light floating in it like grains of brightness. Way off was the orange cloud reflection over the land, where the universal Cities bawled and yammered. Jen lay still, supported by the water. Once she would have pulled her mask aside, breathed in the wet salt of ordinary air. Now she felt no desire to do so. She turned slowly, treading water, took a last look at the moon, and dived. Her heels stirred up a momentary flash of light. Once below she moved powerfully, stroking with her arms. She arrowed down to West Terrace where the Belmonts had their dome. The party would be in full swing already; she was missing good dancing time.

Hours later, Mary prodded one of her rare cigarettes from the wall dispenser. She frowned a little, drawing in smoke and letting it dribble from her nostrils. She lay back and watched the fumes being sucked toward the ceiling vent. The telscreen was off; the last badman had bitten the dust and she had grown tired of watching. The bungalow seemed very quiet;

the buzz of the air conditioning plant sounded unusually loud, as did the recurring clink-thump of the refrigerator solenoids from the kitchen.

She stood uncertainly, fingered her throat, took a step, paused. She went to the alcove by the kitchen that housed the radio link and telephone. Beside the handset the dome metering equipment chuckled faintly. Inside the grey housings striped discs spun, needles wavered against their dials. Force of habit made her check the readings. All normal, of course . . . She touched the phone, pulled at her lip with her teeth, made herself take her hand away. A quarter of an hour, that was nothing. When she was dancing Jen forgot the time. They all did. She would be home in a few minutes, by nine-thirty at the latest. She knew exactly how long to outstay an order . . . Mary went back to the living area, turned the telscreen on, clicked the channel switch to five. While the set was warming she walked through to David's cubicle, peered in. He was asleep, hair tousled on the pillow.

Nine-fifty.

Mary got up again, walked to the window in the curved wall. She drew the curtains back, looked across the street at the neighbouring houses visible through the faint residual haze. A little fear stirred somewhere at the back of her mind, throbbed, stilled itself again. She wondered, fear of what? Accidents maybe; they happened, even in the best-run towns. Jack—but it wasn't that. She laughed at herself quietly, trying to shrug away her fit of nerves.

These late shifts of her husband's were a curse but there was no help for them; the new building was going ahead fast and as engineering controller for the sector Jack had to be almost constantly on site. She told herself, physically her husband was not far away. She could ring him if she had to. How far off was the new complex, a hundred and fifty yards, two hundred? No distance, by terrestrial standards . . . But here under the sea, just how far was a hundred yards? Could be a life-time, or an epoch. She grimaced. That was what the fear was about, what the . . . throb . . . tried to tell her maybe. That under the sea, patterns and values could change ineradicably.

She sat down, crossed her knees, laid her head against the back of the chair. After a few moments she picked up the abandoned knitting and stared at it. She was making a sweater, though there was no point in the exercise. The domes were air-conditioned and sea temperature only varied a few degrees through the year; nobody needed sweaters down here and the yarn was expensive, it came from Surface and all Surface things were dear. But it was something to do, it kept her hands busy. Above all, it was a link with the past.

Ten o'clock.

The face of the clock was round and sea-blue, the hands plain white needles. They moved in one-minute jerks; Mary imagined that she could see the tiny quiver that preceded each jump. She stubbed out the cigarette. The party would be long finished now, the dancers dispersed.

Dancers? She shook her head. She could remember the dancing in the Cities, the pulsing rhythms, frenetic jerking. That pattern, like everything else, had changed. She remembered the first time she had heard what they called sea-jazz, the shock it had given her. Jen had a player in her bedroom, it wailed and bumped half the night, but the rhythms, the melodies, were like nothing she had ever heard landside. The music howled and dragged, the beats developed timings that defied notation, had in them something of the slow surge of the tides. It was music for swimming to.

The Belmonts had a dance floor but it was outside, in the sea. Airposts surrounded it, and speaker casings; round them the kids would swirl like pale flakes among the hordes of fish that always seemed to be attracted. 'But Mummy,' Jen would say if she protested. 'You just don't *gel*, you're not *wavy*. . .' It was all part of the new phraseology; the boy down the block, Kev Hartford wasn't it, he *gelled* for Jen, he was a *wave*; but the lad from the airplant, Cy Scheinger who had visited once or twice, was out of favour. He was *neapy*, a *scorp*. (Scorpion fish?) The sea, and thoughts of the sea, pervaded their whole lives now even to the language they spoke. Which was natural, and as it should be . . .

Why did we call her Jennifer? Why, of all the names we could have used? The Jennifer was a sea-thing, and accursed . . .

It was no use. Mary killed the sound from the screen, walked back to the phone, lifted the handset and dialled. She listened to the clicking of the exchange relays, the faint purr-purr at the other end of the line. An age, and the receiver was lifted.

'Ye-es?' The slight coo in the voice, unmistakable even through the surging distortion of the sea. The Belmonts were just a little conscious of their status; Alan Belmont was fisheries manager for the area. Mary licked her lips. 'Hello? Hello, Anne, this is Mary. Mary Franklin . . . What? Yes, fine thank you . . . Anne . . . is Jen still at your place by any chance? I told her nine, she's late, I wondered if . . .'

Anne Belmont sounded vaguely surprised. 'My dear, I shooed them off positively hours ago. Well, an hour . . . Hold the line . . .'

Unidentifiable human sounds. Someone calling faintly. The wash . . . crash . . . of the sea.

'Hello?'

'Yes . . .'

'Just before nine,' said the phone. 'We sent them all off, there's no one here now . . . You say she's not back?'

'No,' said Mary. 'No, she's not.' Her knuckles had whitened on the handset.

The phone clucked. 'My dear, they're all the same; ours are hopeless, time means *nothing*, absolutely *nothing* . . . But I'm quite *sure* you needn't worry, she'll be along any moment. Perhaps she's with that *Cy* boy, whatever his name is . . . yes . . .'

Ice along the spine, moving out like fingers that gripped and clutched. 'Thank you,' said Mary. 'No, no, of course

not. Yes, I'll let you know . . . Yes, goodbye Anne . . .'
She laid the handset on its cradle, stood looking at it, not
knowing what to do. The sea pushed at the dome gently,
slurringly.

A quarter after ten.

Mary stood very still in the middle of the living area, lips
pursed. She had called the airworks; Cy was off duty, could
not be traced. And two or three neighbours and friends. No
Jen. She could not ring Jack at the construction office, not
again. Down here you helped your husband, pulled your
weight. You didn't run panicking at every little thing . . . The
trembling had started, in her legs; she rubbed her thighs un-
consciously through her dress. She touched the hair pinned
into a chignon at the nape of her neck. In front of her, on the
sill of the window, a plaster foal pranced, hooves outlined
against greenness. The greenness was the sea.

Decision. She pulled at her hair, shook it free round her
shoulders. She unsnapped the clasp at her neck, wriggled her
dress up over her head. Beneath it she wore the conventional
blue leotard of a married woman. She plucked automatically
at the high line of the legs, kicked her sandals off, crossed to
the equipment locker. She came back with her sea gear, lung,
mask and flippers. She dressed quickly, fastening the broad
straps round her waist and between her legs, the lighter
shoulder harness that held the meter panel across her chest.
Habit again made her check the dials, valve air, slap the red
cancellator-tab on her shoulder. That was another safety factor;
if for any reason air stopped flowing from the pack and that
tab was not touched, a built-in radio beacon would arrow
town guards down to the wearer.

She looked in at David again, satisfied herself he was still
sleeping. She walked to the sealock, stopped on the way to see
herself in the half-length mirror. She was heavier now, her
hips had broadened and there were maybe faint worry lines
round her mouth. But her hair was brown and soft; landside
she would still be a desirable woman.

6

She looked round the dome slowly, seeming to see familiar things in a new light that was bright and strange. The bungalow was double-skinned, the inner ceiling finished in octagonal plates of white and pale blue plastic. The half-round shape, dictated by considerations of pressure, had the secondary advantage of enclosing the greatest possible volume of space; deep-pile carpets covered the floors, the furniture was low and streamlined, easy to live with. The telscreen was tucked neatly into an alcove; to each side of it were wall tanks with fish and anemones. Through a half-open door she could see the kitchen. It was miniaturised but well equipped, with plenty of stainless steel like the galley of a ship.

The whole bungalow was as safe as it was functional. In the unlikely event of a fracture in the pressure shell, the second skin would hold the sea while instantaneous warnings were flashed to a central exchange, ensuring help within minutes. Not that anything could or would go wrong of course, the whole system was too carefully worked out for that. People had been living undersea for years now, and fatalities were far fewer than on the overcrowded land.

Mary grimaced, stepped through into the lock and closed the inner hatch. The ceiling lamp came on; she pressed the filler control, heard the hiss as air was expelled through the outlet valves.

She squatted in rising water to work the straps of the flippers over her heels, straightened up. The coolness touched her hips; she pushed her hair back, spat in the mask and rinsed it, pressed the transparent visor onto her face. The plastic was self-adhesive, moulded to her skull contour; it fitted from forehead to chin. She palmed the earphones into place, reached under her arm for her mike leads, flicked the tags onto the magnetic contacts in her throat. The compartment filled, water rising greenly over her head. As the pressure equalised, the outer segment of wall slid aside automatically, letting in the hazy glow of the street lighting. Mary kicked away and floated up from the dome, sensing the old lift as the sea shucked off her weight. Her hair swirled across her eyes gracefully, like fronds of black fern.

She swam slowly across the town. To each side, lines of round-topped buildings marched out of the haze. Some of the houses were still new and bright with their coated steel skins, others had grown a rich waving cover of algae. In the main street the shop windows were brightly lit; the plate-glass ports displayed seafoods set on white dishes garnished with fronds of weed; there were aqualungs and radiophones, Surface ware of all sorts, clothes and books, records, dolls, toys. Here the ocean floor had been cleared to the rock that underlay the sand; overhead were slim arches to which were moored the sledges of out-of-towners, the fish herders and oceanographers whose work took them to lonely domes scattered over the bed of the sea. There were lights on the gantries; each globe hung glaring in greenness, surrounded by a flickering cloud of tiny fish like moths round a terrestrial lamp. Over everything was an air of peace; the dreamy peace of dusk on an ancient, unspoiled Earth.

There were few human swimmers about, but here and there, careering over the roofs of buildings, Mary caught sight of glistening shapes. Dolphins—they had been quick to discover the sea-floor communities and take advantage of them. Many families, in fact, kept one or more of them as semi-permanent pets, became very attached to them. Other creatures occasionally troubled the townships—sharks, rays, the odd squid. But the repellants carried by the swimmers in their harness had been developed to a stage where there was little to fear. The town guards could be relied on to harpoon or shoo off any of the big fellows who hung around too close or too long, though in the main there was little to attract predators.

Disposal of garbage was rigidly controlled; locking offal into the sea was about the worst crime in the book, it could result in being sent landside. The 'monsters of the deep', in so far as they existed, tended to avoid the colonies. They disliked the brightness and noise, the bustle, the thud of many vibrations criss-crossing in the water. As Jack never tired of pointing out, life down here was as safe or safer than on land.

Mary doubled back, passing the king-size domes that held the town distillation plant. The per capita consumption of fresh water was fifty percent higher for Sea People than for Terrestrials. Frequent bathing was necessary to remove ingrained salt from the skin; supplying salt-free water was one of the biggest problems of the ocean-floor settlements. Beyond the distillery was the airworks. The electrolysers reached halfway to the Surface, each mass of tubes contained in an insulating shell of helium. The current for the oxygen separation came from strategically sited tidal generating stations up and down the coast. Many domes were already on tap from the plant; eventually they would all avail themselves of the new municipal service, though they would retain their own gear as a fail-safe in case of emergency.

Mary swam round the huge stacks, peering into locked shadows, calling softly through her mask. 'Jen . . . Jen . . .' The harness pack radiated the word into the water, farther than a human voice could reach in air, but there was no answer. She clung to a steel stay twenty feet above the seabed. Bubbles curled up from her in a shimmering stream as she tried to quiet her breathing. A group of children went by, out late and swimming fast; she heard their chattering, realised with a cold shock how similar it was to the noises of a fish herd in the hydrophones. She shivered. Thoughts like that had been plaguing her for months now, maybe years. She called urgently, but the child-shoal swerved aside, accelerating and vanishing in the gloom. There was quiet; beside her the great cans vibrated, the sensation more felt than heard. The stay seemed to buzz in her fingers.

She let go quickly, because electrolyser stacks cannot make any sound. She concentrated. That deep, thudding boom . . . Was it her heart, or just fear, or was there something . . . something else . . . No, it was gone. Slipped over the edge of perception, into silence. She started to swim again, thoughts

churning confusedly. She remembered a conversation she had
had with her husband weeks back. They had been lying abed
after his shift had done; the house was silent, or as silent
as it could get. Just the airplant, buzzing in the dark . . .

She had spoken to blackness. 'Jack,' she said, wondering
at herself, 'the Deeps. Have you heard what they've been saying about them—that they talk?'

'I've heard a lot of rubbish.'

She said, 'They talk. That's what the kids say. Jen . . . she
says she's heard it a . . . thing, I don't know what. A calling.
Jack, be serious, listen to me . . .'

'I am serious,' he said. 'Completely. Mary, there's nothing
in the Deeps except one hell of a lot of water, at one hell of a
pressure. Oh, there could be a slip somewhere, volcanic
activity maybe, a long way down, that would send up pressure
waves, you might be able to feel them, but that's all. I'm an
engineer, I've been working with the sea more years than I
want to think about, now take my word, I *know*. This . . . thing,
it's a fad with the kids. You get little gangs floating out there
waiting for revelations, I've seen 'em. I don't know where it
started but it's just a craze, it'll die off when something new
comes along . . .'

She was quiet, thinking of all the towns stretching through
the warm seas of the world, all along the Continental shelves.
The domes were snug and secure, automated; nothing could
go wrong. But what if . . . what if there was an enemy, something more insidious than pressure? Something in people, in
me she told herself, or in Jen. Something working outward
from the roots of the brain . . . She said abruptly, 'Jack, how
can you be so damn sure you're always right?'

The bed creaked as he moved. 'You going Continental on
me, Mary?'

She did not answer. His hand reached the contacts on her
throat, stroked. 'You know what I told you. What we agreed
when they put these in. Once down, always down.' He
paused. Then, softly, 'What's for us on land?'

She lay remembering the lowness of the roofed City streets, the flaring miles of fluorescent strip, the crushing sense of over-contact. Hive phobia of a crowded planet.

He could play her mind, he always could. 'Listen,' he said. 'You can still hear it deep down. The roaring. Escalators, pedivators. Traffic. Dancehalls. Wallscreens all yelling, fighting one against another. Buy this. Buy that. Vote for freedom. Use our toothpaste. Don't copulate . . . Just remember it, Mary. Markets. Moviehouses. The whole heaped-up, tipped-up jumble we made for ourselves. Is that a thing to go back to? Take the kids to? Well is it?'

No answer. He carried on talking. The old vision. 'Down here we've got peace. We've got security. Well, as much security as people can find anywhere. And more important, we've got a democracy. A real practical working democracy, maybe for the first time ever. Down here your neighbour's house is always open because that's the way it has to be. We can't afford to fight each other, the sea takes care of that. And the sea's forever.

'So we've got unity, and drive. Right now maybe you reckon there's a lot of us but I say we're still villages, settlements. We're dependent on Surface, we still buy down supplies. But it won't always be like that. I can see whole nations and tribes of us scattered over the oceans, everywhere in the world. Right down into the Deeps. We'll be independent. We'll draw everything we need straight out of the sea: Gold, tin, lead, copper, uranium, you name it you'll find it's right here in the sea. Billions of tons of it, waiting to be used. In a small way we've started already. The land's old, burned out. Let the Continentals keep it . . .' He chuckled. 'Tell you what, we'll pop up one day, in a thousand years maybe, for a little trade. Find they've gone. All of them. Blown each other apart, starved, lit out for the planets, anywhere. We wouldn't know. If the whole world burned up, how should we tell? We shouldn't care . . .'

She was making patterns in blackness, drawing on the

pillow with one finger. Biting her lip. He touched her hair; his hand found the pendant warmth of a breast and she moved irritably, twisting away from him. 'I was thinking,' she said, 'about the kids. All the kids we've got down here—'

'All the kids,' he said tiredly. 'Mary, all the kids have *changed*. Adapted to their surroundings, now that's the most natural thing. We'd be having to worry if it wasn't happening. This environment, after all it's alien. Outside racial experience. In a sense this life of ours is being lived on a new planet. We must expect new skills, new adaptations, and they'll show in the children quicker because the children have known nothing else. That's the way it has to be, that way's right. This has taken a long time coming out in you, Mary, can't you see what's happening?'

'I can,' she said bitterly. 'Can you?'

'Mary, listen here a minute . . .'

She felt that obscurely he was still hedging. His mind maybe would automatically reject anything that could not be measured and calibrated. She wanted to scream; the confidence, the know-how, suddenly it all seemed so much smugness. The sea was infinite, from it could come an infinity of fears. She said, 'We all . . . they say we all came from the sea. Well, couldn't we . . . regress, you know, sort of slip back . . .'

He clicked on the bedside light. 'Mary, do you have any clear idea what you're saying?'

She nodded vigorously, trying to make him understand. 'I thought it all through, Jack. I mean about birds losing their wings and seals—didn't seals go back into the sea, degenerate somehow? And now us, the children, they . . . swim like fish, more and more like fish . . .'

'But hell,' he said, 'Mary, do you know how *long* a thing like that takes? A biological degeneration? How many millions of . . . Oh look, Mary, look here. A million years. That's how long we've been around, give or take a few thousand. And that's nothing, nothing at all. It isn't . . . that.' He snapped his fingers. 'You're thinking on the fine scale, the historical scale. All that time, that million years, wasn't enough for us to lose our little toes. Look, the Earth's a day old. Took twenty-four hours to evolve, go through all the cycles of life and get to us. You know what we are, what all our history is? The last tick of the clock . . . That's how long evolution takes, it's a very big thing . . .'

But it was no use, she'd heard it all before. 'Maybe it won't be like that this time,' she said. 'We . . . evolved that quick, at the end. Maybe we'll go back now just as fast . . .'

'It isn't anything to do with it,' he said. 'Nothing at all.'

She said desperately, 'We were so smart, Jack, getting out like this, living in the sea. Making a new world. But maybe . . . couldn't that somehow be what the sea really wanted, all along? What we were *meant* to do? Oh, I know this sounds crazy but believe me when I see the kids . . . Jen slipped the other day, in the kitchen. When she tried to get up, I think she tried to turn like she was swimming—she forgot she was in air . . . And David, he swims just like a little shrimp . . . When I see things like that I think . . . Oh, I don't know what I think sometimes—maybe we're not . . . pioneers at all. This thing about the Deeps, they say they call, pull . . . Maybe we're just sort of being sucked back, that's where we belong . . .'

He was angry, finally. 'All right. So this craziness is all true. We've got a racial memory in our brains; in our nervous systems. We remember the beginnings of life all those years back, so many years we can't even count the thousands. Well then, we're home already, Mary. Right where we are, this is where life started. In the shallows, swilling in the sunlight. Not in the Deeps. It moved down there, same time some of it spread onto land. There's nothing can call us from there. We don't belong there, never did.'

She was quivering a little, looking at the pillow, seeing the texture of it. Every strand in the weave of the cloth. 'I wanted to stay human,' she said. 'That was all. Just to stay human, and the kids . . .'

He touched her. 'You're human,' he said. 'You're all right.'
She wouldn't look at him. 'I think,' she said, 'I think now
... I'd take the Cities. Jack ...'

He didn't answer, and she knew the expression on his face
without looking. Something inside her seemed to twist and
become cold. He would do anything for her maybe, except
that. He would not go landside, not now. The empires, the
herds and tribes of the sea, they were in his brain, they called
too. The dream was too strong, he couldn't let it go.

He pushed the clothes back and swung his legs off the bed.
She heard the little swish as he picked up a robe. 'Mary,' he
said, 'why don't you get a little checkup? You're run down, it's
my fault. I should have realised ... Too much time on your
own, you don't get about. Not any more. Maybe you should
have a trip landside. Go and see your folks. Tell you what—I'll
get a couple of days leave, we'll have a run up to Seventy-five,
take the kids, how's that? They've got the new theatre up there,
whole pile of junk. Sound okay?'

She didn't answer. 'I'll have a talk with Jen,' she said. 'I'll do
it tomorrow. This is silliness, it can be stopped ...' He walked
out, turned on a light. Started tinkering in the kitchen. He
brought her back coffee laced with rum. She pulled a bed-
jacket over her shoulders, sat drinking, hands gripped
round the warmth of the cup. Feeling the trembling still deep
in her body, hearing the buzz of the airplant, imagining the
silly, silly meters checking and recording. Pressure, humidity,
oxy-level, all the things that didn't matter. While Jack sat
and watched her, smoked and smiled and did not understand ...

Mary swam the length of the town again, moving slowly,
watching to right and left at the domes nestling in shadow,
their windows like square bright eyes. The sea was darker
now; in the real world above, the moon was setting. Surface
was just visible as a greyish sheen; tall weed fronds were
silhouetted against it, leaning majestically to the current like

trees bowed by an endless wind. The tide was setting out, toward the Deeps.

After that talk with her husband, her restlessness had become worse. Quite suddenly it seemed the whole furnishing of the dome was oppressive, stultifying. The curtains had come down, the glinting blue fabric with its faint interlapping tidal patterns had been put away. Mary had hung new yellow cloth, sun-yellow, printed with designs of buds and flowering trees. She had banished the spiny amber-spotted shells and the urchin lamps, Jen's untidy collection of sea bed fossils, even the cushion covers on which she herself had once worked swirling Minoan patterns of weed and octopi. In their places were landside things, figurines of horses and kittens, panting china dogs. Creatures long vanished now but that reminded her of Earth and the way humans lived once on a time.

Every ornament, every yard of cloth, had had to be bought from Surface; the cost had been enormous but once started Mary had seemed unable to stop. Jack had raised his eyebrows but said nothing; Jen had protested more noisily.

Things had reached crisis pitch the day Mary found, in the wall tank in Jen's room, a piece of old human skull, coral-crusted, put there as a home for crabs. She had slapped her daughter for that, a thing she had never done before, and emptied tank and contents through the lock. Jen had fled squalling, into the sea, and not come home for hours. After that Mary spent a week scraping the whole top of the dome, polishing away the velvet coat of sea-growth till the plastic-covered panels gleamed like new; but it seemed the more she did, the more she tried to banish the presence of the sea from her home, the more the sea invaded. At night, lying quiet, she imagined she could feel the slow push of the wave force against the bungalow, tilting it this way and that, slow, slow, this way . . . then that . . .

She drove herself across to West Terrace, built slightly higher than the rest of town on a curving ridge of rock. Nearly to the Belmonts' dome and back, calling all the way. Jen was not in town; or if she was, she refused to answer. Mary's face was wet now inside the mask and her lungs were labouring. Thoughts tumbled in her mind. Nitrogen narcosis . . . no longer possible, the lungs delivered an oxy-helium mix. Oxygen intoxication then, the thing they used to call rapture of the depths; that could make you throw your mask off, breathe water and die. But it was nearly unheard-of. Low down on Mary's back, and on Jen's, were other contacts. They led to cells deep in the body that metered the blood itself, tasting it for oxy-content. The lungs were self-compensating. Pack failure? Crazy, the gulp-bottle on Jen's belt would give her twenty minutes' breathing. And the beacon, there was the beacon. But beacons could go out . . .

Mary doubled, swerving under the rigging of the street lamps. Across to where she could see the divers working on the new building complex. The bodies hung round the curving ribs, tiny with distance, silver as fish under the glare of the lamps; below, the windows of the construction office just showed in the gloom. Soon she would call Jack, she would have to . . . She felt the fear again, like a coldness round her heart. There was only one place she had not been. She began to swim purposefully away from the town and its lights, towards the Deeps.

Just beyond the domes the sea bed fell away in a series of troughs, miles long and wide. Unseen, their contours could still appal the mind. This was the frontier, the last frontier maybe on the planet. She passed over the graveyard, trying not to see the frail crosses sticking up from the silt, name tags fluttering in the current like grey leaves. Out to where the last light faded, and beyond . . .

She was in a void, bottomless, pit-black. Above her a vagueness that was just one shade less dark than darkness itself. Not light; some trailing ghost maybe, that light had left behind it. Mary drove deeper, hopelessly, feeling pressure begin to squeeze her body like cold hands. She was panting, though there was no sound of it in her ears; her breathing alone could not activate the throat mike. She called again; her voice was a vibrating thread, nearly lost in immensity.

And there was something, a blemish in the gulf. Tiny, nearly invisible, its shape so vague it mocked the retinas. Mary swam, hair flowing; there was a longness, a paleness, like a body caught and floating on some denser stratum of the sea. Deep down, far below . . .

'*Jen!*'

Mary kicked out, desperate now, her movements losing smoothness and coordination. Fighting the pressure was like butting at a wall; she imagined her whole body shrinking, condensing, becoming tiny as a fish.

'JEN!'

She'd reached the thing, she was stretching for it with her hands, when it moved. Eeled away, rolled . . . She saw the bright cloud of breathing suddenly released, the fins threshing. Heard her daughter chuckling in her earphones.

Fear turned to anger. Mary arced in the water. 'Jen, get back this *instant* . . .' She grabbed again and the girl eluded her, quick as a fish. 'Mummy, *listen*. . .' The voice bubbled through the sea. 'It's loud tonight, *listen* . . .'

Mary opened her mouth to yell again, and stopped. The noise . . . *was there a noise?*

She listened, straining. Found herself not breathing. It was impossible; no outside sound could come through her blocked ears. Nonetheless, it came. There, and again . . . A thudding, but not a thudding. Some pressure, like a concussion against the brain. Immeasurably slow and powerful and somehow *ancient* . . . Pulsing with her heart, fading, swelling back to touch her body. Earthquake or volcano, she had no idea. Nor did she care. Somehow it was sufficient that the sensation, the not-sound, was there. This was something immemorial, eternal. The true, dark, jet-blue voice of the sea . . .

Woman and girl hung a little apart, bodies vaguely glowing motes against a hugeness of water. Mary felt she could lie all night, not speaking, just soaking in the strangeness that seemed to fill her by rich stages from feet to head. Hearing rhythms that were not rhythms, that blended and crossed, melding each into each like the sounds of the sea-jazz. Soothing, calming, somehow *warm* . . .

She could hear Jen calling but the voice was unimportant, remote. It was only when the girl swam to her, grabbed her shoulders and pointed at the gauges between her breasts that she withdrew from the half-trance. The thing below still called and thudded; Mary turned reluctantly, found Jen's hand in her own. She let herself float, Jen kicking slowly and laughing again delightedly, chuckling into her earphones. Their hair, swirling, touched and mingled; Mary looked back and down and knew suddenly her inner battle was over.

The sound, the thing she had heard or felt, there was no fear in it. Just a promise, weird and huge. The Sea People would go on now, pushing their domes lower and lower into night, fighting pressure and cold until all the seas of all the world were truly full; and the future, whatever it might be, would care for itself. Maybe one day the technicians would make a miracle and then they would flood the domes and the sea would be theirs to breathe. She tried to imagine Jen with the bright feathers of gills floating from her neck. She tightened her grip on her daughter's hand and allowed herself to be towed, softly, through the darkness.

Manscarer

By dawn most of the spectators are in their places in the stands
and already making a din that is causing Roley Stratford to
rage and fume. This the plebs will never understand; that the
true introduction to the coming spectacle is Silence. One
cannot play Silence, the primordial entity; so there is nothing
to which to listen, and the people are not quiet.

Roley has dressed for the occasion as a British admiral of
the early nineteenth century; his white breeches are soiled with
grass stains where he has helped one of the working parties
make last-minute adjustments to the great shanks of *Manscarer*
lying along the clifftop. Jed Burrows, A.D.C. for the day,
fusses behind his temporary chief, carrying the bottle of rum
Roley has declared indispensable to the period flavour. He also
started out with a brass telescope and an astrolabe, but the
latter was left behind as too unwieldy. The telescope he still
carries, tucked in the crook of his blue-uniformed arm.

The dawn wind is cool; Jed shivers a little, stepping from
one foot to the other as the shade of Nelson harangues the
Leader of the orchestra. A minor difficulty has arisen; the
contract clearly specifies a thirty-minute overture before the
Pomp and Circumstance extracts that will herald the Assembly,
but only part of the band awnings has arrived in time. A
harassed group of City engineers is still at work erecting the
rest, manhandling the awkward lengths of billowing pre-

formed plastic. Leader, Strings and Woodwind are prepared to play in the open air; the Brass Section, keen Union men one and all, are not. The boys claim it will chap their lips. Somewhat obscurely, Percussion and Effects are backing the argument. Jed tires of the row and wanders off, leaving the rum placed on a conspicuous outcrop of rock. Part of the Book calls for volleys of Verey lights; he will have ample warning of the start.

Most of the Colony are scattered round the concrete pads on which *Manscarer* will take shape, by the grace of God and in spite of the force of gravity. The working teams lounge on the grass, still keeping roughly in position; here and there a bottle is raised in greeting to Jed as he paces solemnly the dural beams of the Crow. As he walks he rehearses again in his mind the complex stages of Assembly. The first members, once socketed into their pads, will serve as derricks for the raising of the greater beams, the weighted and counterbalanced shafts that will set the head of the sculpture in huge and complicated motion. The beak itself, the *corvus*, lies along the clifftop like an old-time ploughshare monstrously overlarge. There could be trouble with the placing of the assembly; it is heavy, very heavy, and the triplefold tackles that will bear its weight are none too hefty for the job. The answer would have been a flying crane, but Roley refuses to countenance the use of such an apparatus. The machine would spoil the form of *Manscarer* at a critical moment, and its din would drown the orchestra.

Jed checks the donkey engine that will make the great pulls. Steam is already raised—steam and steam only has been deemed fit by Roley for his masterpiece—and Bil-Bil and Tam are fretting over their gauges. On the roof of the engine shed Reggy Glassbrook, nimble and hairy, sits grinning like an ape. He is the Colony's steeplejack; he will be first into the rigging today, handling the split-second alignments as the beams sail to their positions, sure-footed and quick as one of Meg's pet geckos. As far as Jed is concerned he will be welcome to the job; the A.D.C. has no head for heights, and from the feet of the *Scarer* to his main goosenecks will be all of ninety feet.

A hundred yards beyond the donkey shack a gully running to the cliff edge makes a shallow windbreak. Crouched in its lee, Bunny, Whore Nonpareil and the Witch of Endor eat alternate sandwiches of crab and caviare and serve passers-by with Hock from a Georgian coffeepot. At their feet a coffee machine heated by a small spirit lamp glugs and burbles to itself. 'What are we, girls?' shouts Jed. 'Artists or engineers?' The gag, in the new 'flat humour' favoured by the Colony, raises a chorus of unanswers, nods and headshakes and somewhat glazed morning-after grinnings. Jed looks up, visualising the great blue negative the sky will make round the whirling bars of *Manscarer*. Pushes his telescope more firmly under his arm, touches his hat and moves on.

Artists or engineers? As an artist Roley called for underpinnings to reach down unseen into the cliff, a hundred and fifty feet to sea level. Through them *Manscarer* would have grown from earth's roots, sweeping up, continuing the lines of stress inherent in the bulging stone, shackling the ground firmly to the sky; but the City engineers refused him more than twenty feet, just enough to hold the ponderous swirling of the tophammer. It will serve though; *Manscarer* will peck and thunder, nibbling perhaps at his own sinews and feet to fall one day in glorious dissolution into the water. Perhaps before that the Colony will hold a ritual destruction; there will be more stands and more admission charges and more selling of high-priced ice cream. And the South Sector Symphonic again, if it can be arranged.

Symphonic . . . Jed, a quarter of a mile from the podium, can still hear in the breaks of the wind the evidence of Roley's apoplexy. The Overture was timed to start as the sun's disc broke clear of the sea; but the daystar has lifted now his own diameter from the horizon, and not a brass bleat has been heard from the pack of them. The occasion is ruined before it begins. Jed mounts a hillock of grass to gain a view of the distant stands. The State Police are having a mite of trouble keeping order over there; he marks a dozen separate and complicated scuffles taking place on the grass in front of the awnings. Programmes are being fluttered and some sort of organised chanting has started. He sees a man running, another being belaboured by a mounted Cossack. He swears at the risk to the Colony's precious horses.

He looks along the coast. Symphonies are playing already, the mute works the plebs refuse to hear. The notes are of lilac and seething pale blue, touched with the thin glittering of sunlight. Far below at the feet of the cliffs are the crawling lace curtains of the tide. Jed turns away slightly giddy. The Assembly teams are standing now, chafing their hands and flapping their arms across and back against their shoulders. The jeans and reefer jackets of the men amount almost to a uniform, but no two girls are dressed alike. Jed sees a fine Firebird swirling in a mist of fluorescent nylon; nearer are a Pompadour, a Puck, a shivery paint job all black and white zebra stripes. Meg Tranter is dolled up in ancient half-burned newsprint, the textured leaves flapping round arms and knees. She carries a placard with the legend *Zeitgeist 1960*. That too is 'flat' humour; she is explaining to the plebs what they lack the mental equipment ever to understand.

Between the Assembly site and the nearest of the terracings a collection of Colony possessions has been set up on display. Armoured and well-guarded cases hold stacks of old books; dogs and beribboned goats are being paraded and Piggy and The Rat are doing a brisk trade in genuine hand-executed Seascapes. There is a constant coming and going from the ranks of sightseers. In the City, Colony artifacts fetch quaint prices; through them Jed's folk are self-supporting in theory at least. Jed wipes his face and looks farther along the cliffs. Way off and blue with distance he can see the City's impossible side, like the edge of a hundred-yard thick carpet pulled across the land. The structure covers all England with its grinding weight and sameness. In its catacombs, trapped in the miles on honey-combed miles of chambers and passages, men can live and die, if they are born poor enough, without seeing the sun. The tiny open spaces round the coasts, full of the mad artifacts of the Colonies, provide a relief from Sameness that the people come trooping year after year to see. Without them, populations might run shrieking mad themselves. Artists are a therapeutic force now, recognised and protected by Government; the lunacy of the few safeguards the sanity of the many.

A bang-crock; the report and its echo lift a paperchase of gulls from beneath Jed's feet. He watches them soaring out under the glowing ball of the signal. Shreds of music reach him; at long last, the Overture has begun. He paces back methodically, lips pursed, keeping in character as he walks the quarterdeck of the cliff. From the tail of his eye he sees Reggy, stripped now to shorts and sleeveless leather jerkin, springing and posturing on the roof of his little shed. Someone runs to Jed and presents him with chipolatas on sticks and a stuffed olive. He munches as he walks, savouring the Surreal delicacy of the gesture, climbs the rostrum where Roley dances in a furor of creativity and apprehension. A speaking trumpet is gripped in his hand; the fingers that hold it are white-knuckled with strain.

The music climbs towards its first climax. 'Lifting teams,' bellows Roley. 'Teams, *ha—ul*. . . .' A jet of steam rises from the donkey-hut; oddly assorted groups of Colonists, drilled to perfection, scurry across the grass, taking up the slack in the controlling tackles. The spars of the lowest Configuration rise with surprising speed, waver and . . . *bang-bang* . . . thump down, dead on beat, into their sockets. The thing is done, like a conjuring trick out on the grass. *Fortissimo* from the huge gaggle of musicians, a half-heard firework gasp from the crowd and then cheering while Roley waves his arms again leaping up and down and damn-blasting the plebs, lilac in the face with rage. The gestures are eloquent, even effective; the little blue-dressed figure, capering mad as a clockwork monkey, quietens the crowd. The occasion after all is a solemn one; the plebs, who have fought for tickets, are duly impressed. They are witnessing a demonstration of an artform in which Roley alone excels; the erection, to music, of a supermobile. Uncomprehending, they still stand in stark awe of lunacy. That after all is what they have paid good money to see.

The Interval. After an hour's work the main spars stand supported by their guys like the disfigured kingpoles of a Big Top. Smaller secondary beams, feathered with bright lapping sheets of metal, already spin and dip, humming in the wind; the goosenecks that will take the great spars of the main assembly are in place, and the lifting tackles. The donkey-hut becomes obscured by steam as Tam blows pressure from his waiting boiler; on the roof, Reggy, still sweating from his exertions and wrapped in a hand-woven poncho, holds court before an admiring half-circle of Colonists. Roley, squatting on the edge of his rostrum, waves brief encouragement before readdressing himself to his bottle of Captain Cat (home brewed in the Colony). Below him, musicians lounge on the grass; mush-sellers circulate between them bearing aloft feathery *incubi* of green and pink candyfloss. The machines of aerial observers, newsmen and photographers, hang racketing round the struts of the mobile, some dangerously close to the guys; people from the ground teams are waving their arms, trying to shoo them back.

The sun is hotter now; Jed mops his face with a bright bandanna. Beyond the half-completed *Manscarer* other mobiles loom; Jed, watching, sees *Fandancer* bow herself, making for an instant with her wobbling slats the outline of a hip, the big thrust of trochanter and the muscled curve below, before collapsing into Motion. One of Roley's most ingenious creations that, though maybe lacking a little in overall strength. Bil-Bil and Tam approve of her, and that isn't always a good sign. She was a bitch on the drawing board, and a bitch to put together as well. Her Assembly was a near-fiasco; it took weeks of patient adjusting and rebalancing before she condescended to shimmy in the airs of Heaven. Behind her are other sculptures, more distant still; Jed sees the flash and swoop of *Halycon*, *Manscarer's* forerunner, before his beams, flattening freakishly, lose themselves beneath a swell of grass. He looks up again lovingly at the new Structure, shielding his eyes against the sun, watching the lazily turning plates of dark blue and deathly-iridescent violet. The mobile has already a drama that the others lack.

Manscarer is a crow, or the bones of one; a vast ghost that once complete will thunder and peck along the cliff-top, the bird at last turned hunter and revenger of dead fields. Or so runs the Manifesto. Jed doubts if one in a hundred of the gaping Cityfolk have taken the trouble to read it; it would mean little enough to them if they did.

Jed moves to the hourglass strapped on the side of the rostrum. The last few grains of sand are funnelling down. He raises his arm, palm flat, and there is a scramble as the orchestra runs for its instruments. Reggy erupts from the poncho; Roley raises his baton, and construction begins again with a quiet passage in which Reggy, balanced and slowly revolving in the blue, delicately attaches the featherings of the upper rings. While he works, the hundred-foot linked shafts of the main assembly are cleared for lifting.

The secondary Configurations are nearly complete now; hawsers run from them to anchor points in the grass. Others are ready for the main beams. *Manscarer*, unshackled, would rampage across a three-hundred-yard circle, tearing and clucking at the grass; before the last of the ropes are slipped bandstand and engine house will be evacuated. Jed leaves the podium, where Roley still conducts in a berserk frenzy, runs to his prearranged position on the tackles. Every pair of hands the Colony can muster will be needed for the coming operation.

Hawsers snake upwards to humming tightness as Tam, the winch control levers in his hands, leans from the window of his shack. The music drives towards its great central theme; a shout, a heavier thundering from the engine shed, and the *corvus* lifts clear of the grass, twenty feet long, glinting with a vicious rose-and-black shimmer. Reggy balances on the skull plates, sticky-footed. A medley of orders bellowed through the music, wiry strumming as the beams snub at their restraining tackles and on the beat the whole assembly soars, weaving impatiently as the feathered tail plates feel the breeze. Jed loops his downhaul round a bollard, leans back as the creaking rope takes the strain. The beams swing higher, clang against the central masts to drop with a crash, sockets trued over the projecting goosenecks; the *corvus* falls and rises, dipping as it tastes the wind.

Triumph, and disaster. Somewhere in the rigging a shackle parts with a hard snap. Tackles come down flailing. The beams swing, driven by the wind, shearing the remaining cables. *Manscarer* rotates, unpredictable now and weighing tons, the focus of a widening circle of unhappiness. Jed sees a block swinging in decapitating arcs, falls flat and rolls on his back to watch the huge overhead clicking of violet bones. A dozen people skid past, drawn by their rope, chirping out a birdcage panic; a Cavalier's hat bowls across the ground, on edge like a little feathered wheel. The wind gusts; the *corvus* casts out far across the sea, swings back to rake screeching flinders from the awnings of the bandstand, tangles massively with the roof of the engine shed. Steam explodes outwards, gusting across to where the orchestra, on hands and knees, scuttles for its collective life. The beak, checked by the obstruction of the donkey shed, wavers and dips again to strike at the main struts, down which Reggy is still scurrying from danger. Another peck, a fleshy concussion, a shrill falling scream; a surprised gob of blood splashes across Jed's wrist from where Reggy, suitably scared, sails overhead, filling the close sky with legs and arms. He bounces against the cliff edge to fall again to the blue and white impatience of the water, his plunging splash lost far below in the morning noise of the sea. After him a French Horn, disembodied from its master, bounds disconsolately like a Surreal yellow snail.

Jed crawls to the cliff edge in the sunlight, and thoughtfully adds his quota of moisture to the ocean.

The flooring of the house is of polished yellow wood, broken by platforms and steps into various levels. Sunlight lies across it in calm rectangles. Round the dark blue walls white alcoves, circular-topped, house ancient ship models and tropical shells; handrails of copper and mahogany echo the nautical flavour. The end wall of the building is of glass; through it, distantly, can be seen the ocean. To one side of the living space stands a bright red twentieth-century M.G., her nose butted into a recess in the floor; in the centre of the room is a table covered with a spotless linen cloth. A silver breakfast service adds a last note of elegance.

Above the carport in the wall the curtains of a sleeping alcove are drawn back to reveal a plain divan covered by a heap of bright-coloured scatter cushions. From the alcove, close under the oddly pitched roof, a thick white-painted beam spans the room. Jed stands beneath it, feet with their buckled shoes in a patch of sunlight, hand on the hilt of his sword. 'That's my beam,' he says crossly. 'Just you get off it, this minute.'

The girl above him makes no movement, staring down with eyes wide with fright as those of a tarsier. 'That's my beam,' says Jed more carefully. 'Nobody can sit up there, except me.'

Silence.

'I'll run you through without mercy,' declares the admiral, exposing six glittering inches of the swordblade.

There is no reaction.

'I'll do terrible things. I'll keelhaul you and flog you through the fleet. I'll throw you to the fishes. . . .'

The girl grips the beam a little harder with her jean-clad legs, twining her bare ankles beneath it.

Jed looks thoughtful, pushes the sword back into its scabbard, walks to the table and wields a silver pot. Steam rises fragrantly. He adds sugar and milk, stirs carefully and picks up the cup in its saucer, turning as he does so to look back at the roof. 'If they made coffee in Heaven,' he calls, 'and tea in Hell, I'd take my turn at the stoking.' The hot drink soothes, steadying the shaking of his hands. He sits down, studies the table and selects a round of toast. He butters it and spoons a blob of marmalade on to his plate. 'After breakfast,' he says to the silence, 'I'll stop being an admiral. Is that what you want?'

A headshaking from the girl on the beam.

'Polly,' says the retiring Captain Hardy, 'if you won't come down I really shall knock you off. I shall do it with a broom.'

There is no response except a tensing of the legs. Polly indicates her determination to stay on the beam until killed. Jed fixes her again with a contemplative eye. 'I was sick this morning,' he says. 'I did it in the sea. Were you there when Reggy was pecked?'

A nodding. A violent reaction for Polly.

Jed pauses, the toast halfway to his mouth. 'He was killed,' he says, unnecessarily. 'Is that why you got up there?'

The nodding again.

'Were you frightened?'

Headshaking. No, no . . .

'I've decided,' says Jed. 'I won't knock you down after all. Instead I shall just wait till you get tired and fall off.' He lifts the pot again. 'Polly, you do make lovely tea.' He finishes the cup, lays down his toast and walks forward to grip the girl's dangling feet. On the ankles are faint brown watermarks. He pushes the toes under his chin, leans his forehead against the cool frontal curving of the shins. 'Poll,' he says, 'you've got mucky feet.' Then looking up, 'You are a funny girl . . .'

The Colony, cowed by death, keep to their separate homes; Roley to his bleak little sixteenth-century pub, Piggy and the Rat to their queer thatched tower room, darkly glowing with light from fishtanks and crystal globes, Meg and the Witch of Endor to their clifftop bunker full of juju dolls and scuttling lizards and the apparatus of magic. Visitors poke and pry, disappointed at the lack of activity and at missing the morning's disaster. They traipse through Polly's fragile house, empty now, leaving its doors ajar to gusts of sunlight; but nobody comes near Jed's home. He would almost welcome interference. He lounges against the rear wheel of the M.G., a cushion at his back, his legs stretched out along the planking of the floor. He is reading from an ancient copy of the *Ingoldsby Legends*; from time to time he glances up half-aggravatedly from the verse to the *succubus* still straddling the beam. A mile away *Manscarer* spins angrily, clashing and banging in the circle he has cleared. His noise fills the peninsula on which the Colony lies, penetrates bumblingly through the glazed wall of the room.

At lunchtime Jed leaves, to be away from Polly's eyes. He hunts out sketchbook and pastels on the way, and lets the outer door slam. It is only then the girl becomes active. She slides off the beam in frenzied haste, scurrying with the nervous violence of an ant as she clears the table, washes, cooks. When Jed returns she is back on her perch. He looks a little disappointed; he had hoped to find his house no longer haunted. But the dinner simmering in the oven is very good.

Jed eats the meal in silence, carries the dishes and plates to the kitchen alcove and washes them, stacking them carefully in their racks. He clears the rest of the table, shakes the cloth outside the back door and folds it. By the time he has finished Polly has at least changed her attitude, she is riding the beam sidesaddle. It is a hopeful sign; perhaps at last the strain is telling. Jed stands underneath her again, looking up. 'I could pull you off quite easily now,' he says. 'You wouldn't be able to hang on at all.' She bites her lip, knowing he will do no such thing.

He scratches his head, badly worried. 'You're Making a Protest, aren't you?'

The girl nods.

'What's it about?'

No answer.

'Something's upset you terribly,' says the erstwhile admiral. 'It was to do with Reggy, but it wasn't him being

killed. I don't know what it is. Couldn't you write it down?'
Negative. A large tear escapes from the corner of Polly's
eye and runs down her cheek. She ignores it till it reaches her
lip; then she fields it with the pointed tip of her tongue.

Jed fetches the sketchbook from where he flung it down
carelessly, and holds it up. He says a little helplessly, 'These are
for you.' Polly grabs with surprising speed, like a monkey
stealing a banana. The drawings are of *Manscarer*, his postur-
ings and violent movements under the yellow searchlight-
stabbings of sunlight. Polly clutches the book to her chest,
rocking and crooning, burying her nose in the pages to catch
the sweet scent of new fixative. She is still holding it when Jed
leaves to drink five evening pints of beer at the Lobster Pot
and tell Roly his beam has been invaded by a woman. A
runner is instantly despatched to take Polly a little hat, a copy
of the Rieu *Odyssey* and a picture book of sailing ships to look
at if she gets bored. Meg wants to send a gecko as well but Jed
says no. Polly is a little afraid of them, and it wouldn't be fair.

When he returns, the peninsula is blue with summer dusk
and the last grasshoppers in the universe are making the night
shrill with their churring. He decides he can't face supper;
he undresses in the dark, lies down and feels the bed swaying
slightly from side to side. As long as he doesn't roll over
violently he will be all right. An hour later a sudden thump
wakes him from a doze. Muffled sounds follow at intervals as
Polly pads about doing God only knows what. Jed draws himself up against the wall, waiting. He feels his heart, accelerating,
bump faintly against the insides of his ribs; quick prickling
sensations move across his skin. It seems an age before Poll
swings up the ladder to the alcove. She moves a little stiffly, still
suffering from her day of abstinence.

She wriggles her jeans off before sliding on to the divan. To
Jed she feels soft and cool, a life-size doll.

The two figures swim in a morning dazzle of sunlight, seeing the cliffs rise giddily in the troughs between the waves.

Above them the head of *Manscarer* appears once, violet and sullen, withdraws itself instantly with the ease and quick grace of a snake. The creaking of the slats carries down to the water.

Jed hangs on to a rock, seeing the long fringes of weed wash and swirl on the tide, watching the tiny close sunburnings reflect from water and bursting foam. The situation is baffling. Polly has him completely in her grasp now; he owes her a breakfast, a dinner and a night in bed, and he wants them all again. The whole affair is difficult in the extreme.

Reggy, swilling palely while the sea gurgles in his ruined side, can do nothing but nod his head up and down in agreement.

Among the bushes scattered in the little gully lights play and flash, now here, now gone; wayward gleams follow the voices of Oberon and Puck. Farther up the cliff Bil-Bil and Tam, the engineers, sit at a console alive with whirling tape-spools, setting the words of the Dream spinning and fluting through the sky. The Colony listens sleepy with poetry, clustered in the summer night. *Manscarer* swirls and clacks, gaunt and small on the skyline; but he is forgotten.

Polly, sitting crosslegged just behind Jed, pulls glassblades miserably, chewing them and spitting them away. By Act Three she can no longer control the tensions inside her. She puts her head back and shrieks, rendingly. Then again, and again. The *son et lumière* is disrupted, for ever.

The Colony panics. Dumb things that scream are bad; like the stuffed fox in the poem barking, the oak walking for love. Polly isn't a deaf-mute; it's just that two years ago she decided she had nothing else interesting to say and vowed never to speak again. But it's difficult to remember that now she's been quiet so long. A confused battle starts in the gully, figures tumbling over each other and hitting out in alarm while Polly eels about between them still making sounds like a steam carousel. The play shuts down; Bil-Bil and Tam squeak miserably, enveloped by tape. Piggy finally catches the culprit by the heel and pins her while The Rat, never far away from trouble, kisses her to make her stop. Polly is unco-operative. Meg yelps, kicked firmly in the crotch; The Rat claps his hands to an eye jabbed by a hard little elbow. The Witch of Endor joins battle decisively; she administers three sound thumps before Jed, raging, starts to hit her back. The skirmishing subsides; there is a silence, broken by the sea noise far below and the unhappy grunting of The Rat.

Roley Stratford mounts a rock and windmills his long arms against the sky. 'It's hopeless,' he booms, furiously. 'We can't hear plays if people have to scream. Polly, will you be quiet? And not start any more fights?'

Polly, still struggling, shakes her head violently and gulps. Jed claps his hand across her mouth, terrified in case she starts being ghastly again. She instantly bites his thumb. He swears, and calls up to the rock. 'She says no. . . .'

The Witch of Endor mutters something about 'nasty little freemartin'. The words come out slightly thick; she is trying to cope with a split lip. Jed, one arm round Polly, raises his free fist. The Witch ducks prudently, wriggling back out of reach. Roley jumps up and down on his rock. 'Then it's a trial. . . .' He raises his arms dramatically, fists clenched. 'A *tri-al*. . . .'

The shout, taken up by the Colony, becomes a chant. Figures surge round Polly and Jed, hoisting them to their feet; The Witch is propelled after them up the incline of the gully. Bil-Bil and Tam desert their tangled console, infected by the general enthusiasm.

'A *trial* . . . it's a *trial*. . . .'

Heavy Dutch oil lamps hanging from the rafters light the bars of the Lobster Pot with a soft brilliance. Beneath them the Colony is present in full strength, banging its tankards on the white-scrubbed tables and yelling for proceedings to begin. Roley, the Chief Justice, hammers louder on the counter top in front of him with the scarred and knotted shillelagh that is his staff of office. The Court Peculiar is convened; mine host calls for witnesses.

The Witch of Endor is shoved forward, willowy in an ankle-length dress of scrubbed hessian. Finding herself the centre of attention, she sticks out her chest importantly. 'I got smacked in the teeth. . . .' She waves a bright-splotched hankie. 'I'm a witness . . .'

'Polly didn't do that!'

'Shame!'

'She did!'

'She didn't. It was Jed. . . .'

'Well it was all her fault. . . .'

'It wasn't!'

'Was!'

'You always want to bully her!'

'I *don't*! She started it!'

'*Shame!*'

The shillelagh beats half-moons into the counter top. 'Polly,' says the Judge. '*Did* you start it? Whatever it was?'

Polly, sitting on Jed's knee, jiggled happily and nods.

'What did you do?'

'*Nothing*. . . .'

'She *did*. . . .'

'It was The Rat kissing her. She didn't like it. . . .'

'That wasn't the start . . .'

'Well that was when she hit him in the eye . . .'

Roley hammers again for order. 'Did you mind him kissing you, Polly?'

Polly shakes her head.

'It wasn't that then,' says the Judge decisively. 'Now, is there an Indictment?'

'Tam's got it. . . .' Tam is driven into the open, protesting. He stammers badly; his olive-skinned woman's face is suffused with embarrassment.

'That P-Polly did wilfully d-d-disrupt a performance of Sh-Shakespeare. And upset J-Jed getting his b-breakfast for him, and his d-d-dinner. . . .'

'And she went to bed with him. . . .'

'That doesn't matter. . . .'

'It does. It ought to be included anyway. . . .'

The Rat has hauled a chair into a window recess; enthroned on its temporary eminence he feels secure. His one serviceable eye leers horribly. '*She was a virgin too.* . . .'

'She wasn't. . . .'

'She *was*. . . .'

'She couldn't have been. . . .'

Roley whirls the shillelagh. 'This might be *very important*. . . . Were you a virgin, Polly?'

Polly blushes, and hides her face against Jed's shoulder. The Colony, impressed, makes a concerted 'aaahhhh' noise, like a crowd of plebs when a rocket explodes. The Rat hiccups inconsequentially. 'C–c'n I have s'more beer, somebody. . . .'

A jug is handed up to him. It gets well swigged-from on the way. He pours what is left into his pot, mumbling to himself. Roley clears his throat. 'The Indictment is very confused,' he says, 'but evidently the whole affair's to do with Jed. That's the first point. . . .'

'She just wants him to do something back. . . .'

'Well he won't. . . .'

'He will. He'll do anything now, look at his face. . . .'

The counter top suffers again. 'It's to do with Jed,' says Roley loudly. 'And it's also to do with Reggy, because it started when he was killed. It started with the beam in Jed's house, that should have been in the Indictment. Right?'

Polly, nodding, seems to be trying to shake her head off her shoulders.

'Then we're getting somewhere,' says the Judge, very satisfied. He swigs violently from a quart pewter mug. His neck muscles writhe in the lamplight as he swallows.

'We'd get on quicker if she'd *talk*,' says the Witch of Endor, glaring. 'I think it's just *stupid*. . . .'

'*It isn't!*'

'IT IS!'

Proceedings instantly threaten to degenerate into another

brawl. Splinters fly from the counter top as the Judge calls the court to order. '*I think*,' says the Witch primly as soon as she can make herself heard, 'she should be *made* to talk.' She tosses her wild yellow hair. 'We should push spills under her finger-nails and light them. It would be quite proper.'

Polly clenches her hands protectively and starts to shiver.

'It seems to me,' says Roley reprovingly, 'that all in all you've rather got it in for the defendant.'

'*I haven't*.' Then, sullenly, 'All right, I suppose I have. I think she's an ungrateful little beast.'

'Why?'

' 'Cos I sent her a picture book,' howls the witch, dancing with sudden temper. 'An' all I got back was a slosh in the chops. . . .'

'And I rule that *irrelevant*. . . .'

The Rat, very drunk, starts to interrupt, sees the shillelagh poised to hurl at his head and subsides.

'Irrelevant,' says Roley again, to clinch the matter. He glares round him. 'All right. We've got the Indictment, or most of it; we need a Defence. Polly can't tell us why she started to be difficult. That's annoying, but it just can't be helped. So does anybody else know?'

'Yes,' says Jed quietly. 'I do.'

A hush, in which the shrilling of the grasshoppers sounds very loud. Polly turns startled to peer into Jed's face. He puts her aside, carefully, and stands up. He's wishing belatedly he'd worn his uniform and turned the proceedings into a Court Martial. Lacking lapels, he hooks his thumbs in his belt. 'Mr. Chief Justice,' he says. 'Ladies and gentlemen. This, I believe, is what she means. No more mobiles should be built. Further-more, the figures already erected should be knocked down as soon as possible. Further——'

A gale of disagreement. Jed, shouted down, starts to jump about and wave his arms, mouth popping shut and open use-lessly. Polly, looking desperate, sees above her a heavy beam. She is on the table instantly, and jumping for it. Roley howls his alarm; the Witch, quicker off the mark than the rest, dives at her, wrapping her arms round Polly's knees. A swaying confusion; Jed, leaping to the rescue, skids and vanishes under a scuffling pile of bodies; beer is spilled noisily; The Rat, whirling his pot in his excitement, falls headlong from his perch. Order is finally restored, and Polly restrained; but not before Piggy has been knocked half silly by a brickbat, and Meg and the Witch have had their heads banged together for punching. Roley returns to his position of authority, breathing a little heavily.

'Now then,' he says, surveying the court. 'I built these mobiles.' As he speaks he bangs with the handle of the shillelagh, emphasising each word. 'I gave 'em the best years of me wanin' youth. *I* want to know why Jed says to scrap 'em; so the rest of you, *SHARRAP!*' The head of the club, whirling, inflicts a final wound on the counter; Roley bows with great gravity to Jed. 'Mr. Burrows, if you would proceed. . . .'

'It isn't only the mobiles,' says Jed quickly. He feels oddly certain of his words. 'It's everything we do. The horseriding and the archery and reading Shakespeare in the dark and holding seances, and building all those castles about the place and knocking 'em down again like the last time we had a Mediaeval War. Piggy and The Rat must stop painting their pictures and put all their fish back in the sea, and Meg must burn her jujus, and you must stop pretending to be a sort of man who doesn't exist any more, Roley, and so must I. We must destroy the Colony, we must burn it. That's what we must do.'

In the awed silence, the Judge turns to Polly. He asks gently, '*Is* that what you meant?'

She nods again slowly, tears glistening in her eyes.

Nobody else seems able to speak. Roley says carefully, 'Why, Poll? Just because Reggy was killed?'

'No.' Jed is still quite sure of himself. 'Reggy's to do with it, but he isn't the reason. He just brought things to a head. You see they'd never murdered any of us before.'

'Who?'

'The plebs. Oh, Christ, it's so obvious. . . .' He stares round at faces changing from anger to puzzlement. 'We've failed, can't anybody else see that except Polly? All of us, in all the Colonies. When they let us come out here and gave us land and money to spend, and people to help us do every crazy thing that came into our heads, when we took their terms, that was when we failed. We let ourselves down, we sold our birthright. *And theirs*. . . .

'We were too dangerous to them scattered about anywhere and everywhere all over the City. We couldn't be pushed about and led by the nose and hammered into the same shape as everybody else. When the trivvyscreens yelled at us we threw things at them, and when the plebs put us in jail for it we sat and laughed because we knew what they didn't, that we were the makers of dreams. The movers and shapers of the world, or something like that. There's a poem about it somewhere. But we took their terms; and now we aren't artists any more. We don't deserve the name.'

He waves a hand angrily at his surroundings; the stone, the warm wood, the pools of light from the old lamps. 'Polly is telling us, all this is acting and pointless make-believe. That our lives are more sterile than the lives of the people we're supposed to despise.' He raises a declamatory finger. 'We let them short circuit us. We let them put us where they could see us and count us, where they could come every day to laugh and know they were safe from us and all the nasty things that happen when people start to think. They made us into State-licenced buffoons; and we fell off the thin edge, the tightrope between creativity and dilettantism, between free thought and aimless posturing for applause. That's why we lost, and how; and that's why we've got to stop now, before we burn ourselves up any further. If we . . . etiolate right out of existence there's no hope left. Not for anybody.' He swings slightly, and returns Roley's bow. 'Sir,' he says, 'I believe I have done. . . .'

The Witch of Endor, sitting rather dazedly on the floor,

dabs at her lip with the hankie and frowns at the fresh mark
it leaves. 'Well, all right,' she says. 'All right. But you haven't
said anything new, have you? I mean, we all felt like that. Sort
of empty inside, pointless. Only we didn't talk about it. We
knew we'd been had all right, all of us.' She looks at the faces
behind her, then back to Jed. 'It didn't need saying. But what
I want to know is this. Suppose we do what you want, set
fire to everything and smash it all up. They'll only build it for
us again tomorrow. It won't prove anything. It'll just give
them some fresh kicks, won't it? And what else *can* we do?'

Everybody looks at Polly, including Jed. She brushes one
eyelid with the back of a finger, and gulps. Jed frowns, pulls
at his lip with his teeth. 'There's a lot more in this,' he says.
'But I don't rightly know how to get to it.' Polly's eyes lock
on to his and the frown becomes deeper. 'I think,' he says, 'I
think . . . we must leave the Colony. Go back into the City,
where we came from.'

Silence intensifies. Only Meg can find a voice. It sounds
scratchy and thin.

'*Why* . . .?'

'Because . . . I don't know. Because I think'—again watching Polly—'because they *need* us. The plebs. They don't know
it; but in a funny sort of way the . . . uncertainty . . . matters
to them. Not knowing where we are, where we shall pop up
next, the crazy things we shall do. They need people who've
made lunacy a profession; and that's us. Without us, they'll
forget they're living in Hell; they'll just sludge down into a
sort of great doughy mass, and forget how to think, and how
to eat, and one day they'll forget how to breathe. I think
we've got to help them . . . keeps things stirred. Like worms
tunnelling through earth, letting the air in. Us. The sub-
versives. The Unsavoury Elements, the won't-do-gooders and
won't-stay-putters. And I think we've got to do this even if it
hurts because it's important to them as well. Because we might
not like it, and we might refuse to face it, but in the long term
the plebs are what matters to us more than anything else.

7

Once we all opted for the Humanities. Well, there they are.
The proper study of mankind. The plebs. *Man.* . . .'

Polly's lips move, echoing the words; he catches her eye
again and she nods, positively and sorrowfully.

The Witch says very quietly, 'What about the sea?'

'We shan't see it any more.'

'Birds?'

'Not for us. Soon there won't be any anyway. The City will
spread over the Colony holdings as soon as we go and that'll
be the end.'

'No houses of our own?' That from Meg, in a squeak.

Jed shakes his head. 'No houses. Just miniflats in the levels,
the same as everybody else.'

'Sculpting?'

'Mobiles?'

'None. There won't be any room.'

'The sky?'

'We shall see it when we get a Liftpass. Like all the others.'

'We shall go mad . . .'

Jed nods. 'Yes, I think some of us will. But properly mad.
Effectively mad. Not like this. This is just . . . keeping up
appearances.'

Slowly at first, the idea catches on. 'I've had a monkey on
my back for years,' says the Witch. 'Here's where I shuck him
right the hell off. . . . .'

'Jujus,' says Meg, brightening. 'New ones of all the Con-
trollers. We shall be outlawed. Sent to jail again.'

'Shot at on sight!'

'Brainwashing!'

'Trepanning!'

'Leucotomy! Loads of fun!'

'But we shan't give up . . .'

'Menacing letters in the news sheets!'

'Secret societies!'

'Things ticking in ventshafts!'

'Reign of terror!'

'Popping out all over!'
'Everything breaking up!'
'Arson!'
'Murder!'
'Incest!'
'Rape!'
'Secret printing presses!'
'Forbidden plays!'
'Subversive novels!'
'Art galleries in all the sewer flats!'
'Passwords!'
'Cloaks and daggers!'
'*Orgies!*'
Roley jumps on to his mangled counter, brandishing a bottle.
'Illicit stills!'
'Moonshining!'
'The plebs can't do this to us!'
'We demand our rights!'
'Summary execution!'
'Imprisonment without trial!'
'Curtailment of free speech!'
'*We'll start tonight . . .!*'
The Colony, transformed on the instant to a mob, surges for the doors. Shouts rise outside; voices call for torches, levers, fire. There are smashings and bangings in the night.

Jed doesn't run with the others. He stands in the doorway of the little phoney pub, slightly staggered at the revolution he has started. Flames are already springing up from a dozen points in the blackness as homes and artifacts begin to burn. Meg runs past screaming, hair blowing in the wind, a blazing brand shedding a bright trail of sparks. Jed turns back, rubbing his face, and sees he isn't alone. He walks across to where Polly is waiting, puts an arm round her shoulders and gives her a little shake. She watches up at him steadily. He says, 'I didn't finish, did I? I still didn't go down all the way, to what you're really trying to do.'

She gives him no help.

'I'm still trying to think,' he says. He looks over her brown hair at the beams of the pub, the high nicotine-glazed ceiling. An extra-loud crash comes from outside; smoke begins to drift thin and acrid across the bar. 'They're all drunk now,' he says. 'They'll be sorry for this in the morning. When they see the houses burned down, and all the things destroyed.'

He swallows, and purses his lips. 'I think,' he says, 'I think . . . there was a painter once called Van Rijn. He was famous, and rich, and he had a wife and I suppose he loved her. Then everything went wrong. His wife died and he lost his house and his money and his patrons forgot about him. Everything he had was taken away. And so . . . he started painting again. He made a portrait, *The Man in the Golden Helmet*. And then more. And more. And more. . . .'

Polly watches mistily, lips slightly parted.

'I think,' says Jed, 'if there's a Thing you can call by the name of Art, if it isn't all just a delusion . . . then the roots of the Thing have to reach right down, into bitterness and darkness. Somehow it needs them, it's like a . . . swelling, a wanting to live where there's nothing but death, a needing the sky when there's no sky left to see. It's a . . . longing, an anger. That's what you've let loose; because after tonight, when there's nothing left but the City, there'll be Art again. Something locked away and suffocated, growing, not seeing the sun. Like a . . . great flower in a box, thrusting and pushing and pushing till one day it bursts the seams . . . Is that what you really wanted, Polly? Just for there to be Art again? Am I right now?'

Polly hugs him suddenly, kissing and nibbling at his neck.

He lifts her head, tugging gently at her hair. 'In the City,' he says. 'Will you talk?'

She shakes her head, slowly.

'Funnyface,' he says. 'Funnyface. . . .' He holds her against him, tightly.

In the night are pink blossomings of fire. The explosions carve out the cliff edges, altering land that is soon to vanish. In their light the mobiles flail, fall with thunderings and scrapings and long-drawn bell notes into the sea. Ploughshares and vanes, wings and sinews and metal feathers clanking and toppling; *Goliath, Civil War, Cutty Sark, Juliet, The Ant, Titania, Excalibur, Fandancer, Halycon* . . . and *Manscarer*, hugest and last. The procession of Colonists winds between the ruins, tired now, ragged and smoke-blackened and feverish-eyed. Leading them as they turn towards the distant loom of the City is a tiny red car. Its driver sports the sword and froggings, the buckles and epaulettes, the full panoply of a British admiral; beside him a slighter shadow topped by a bonnet of gull feathers clutches a picture book of sailing ships. Behind, Meg carries boxes of scuttling animals, the Witch of Endor leads prancing dogs and a goat. The cavalcade, improvised banners swirling, fades in distance; and in time the last tarara-rat-tan of a drum is gone.

The dawn wind drones up from the sea. But the wind is alone.

Synth

The apartment was small, as all twenty-second-century apartments had perforce to be, and looked out from its fifty-storey height over the panorama of roofs and canyons that was the latter-day London. On one near roof a spark of colour lodged against a grey mansard showed where a solitary sunbather took advantage of the lull between dawn and First Shift; the rest of the buildings were deserted, stark and detailed in the still light. The geometric wilderness stretched to horizon haze; Earth once had many things to show more fair.

The windows of the flatlet boasted movable frames, a rare anachronism these days; the casements stood ajar admitting the nearly smokeless morning air. On the sill beyond, sparrows chattered. With all England a built-over mass of concrete and steel these creatures, most unattractive of birds, had managed to survive.

At the windows, arms folded and frowning faintly, stood a girl. She was tall and delicately proportioned, with the rare swaying curve to the back that gives a woman's body litheness. She wore a short belted robe of white towelling; her yellow-brown hair, still tousled from sleep, hung across her eyes. The eyes were long-tailed, and combined with the sleek angle of the jaw to produce that facial type sometimes described by the fanciful as catlike. The girl was still enough not to disturb the birds; if their noise penetrated her consciousness, she gave no sign of it.

Her attention seemed totally drawn to the sunbather. As she watched the figure on the roof it sat up, waved an arm at the distant window of the flat. She acknowledged the gesture with the tiniest inclination of her head then turned away, still frowning slightly, face otherwise expressionless. She started, silently, to fix her bed. As she moved her feet whispered against concrete, raising faint moth-sounds from its bareness.

The flat was unusual in other respects apart from its lack of furnishing. No pictures relieved the walls, the little tri-dee epics that had recently become the rage in Town; and there was no calorie box, the omnipresent chute through which CentSup and their subsidiaries delivered packaged meals to half the country. The lack of eating arrangements was in fact complete; not even an ancient infra-red grill was in evidence, and the wall cupboards lining the kitchenette alcove were empty of glass and plasticware.

The girl swung the coverlet across the bed and folded the top sheet back against the starkness of the pillow. She crossed the room to the shower, shrugged off the housecoat and bathed, soaping herself vigorously. Hot air hoses, sliding from the ceiling, dried her; she stepped out, dressed carefully in a white *cheongsam* and sat at a wall mirror to work some tidiness into her hair. By the time she was finished the sparrows had done with their squabbling and flown, and traffic sounds were floating up to the room from the sprawling city below.

She palmed a switch. The first of the day's news bulletins began to unroll itself, the letters of the announcements standing out in startling colour from the wall trivvyscreen. The girl watched a time impassively; then the switch was flicked again, the images vanished in a quick electronic popping. She pulled from under the bed a plastic grip; rummaging inside, she produced an old book. Very old it must have been, for its binding was of leather. She opened it to a mark, tucked the bookmark inside the cover, and began to read.

When her wrist chrono gave her a quarter of ten she stood up, flicking at the slight creases in her dress. The book was restored to its place of concealment; she picked up handbag and gloves, stared a last time round the apartment. She walked across and closed the windows then stepped through the door, hearing the lock wards shuffle to a fresh configuration behind her. At the end of the corridor was a vaclift. She entered it and was whirled down in a matter of seconds to the level of the street.

She touched her wrist to call a cab. The vehicle waited bumbling and fizzing, tapping its antennae impatiently while she eased herself into the passenger cubicle. She spoke her destination to the intercom, leaned back to let the seat cushioning take the acceleration. The car picked up the control rails buried in the road surface, U-turned, and swooped for the first intersect a couple of hundred yards ahead.

The journey through London's confusion of traffic took some time. The cab finally slowed to a stop and she got out, feeding a token absently to the extruded box of the Autoconductor. She stood in bright sunlight, looking round slowly. In front of her was a plaza. In its centre, beside the darkened swaths of the cabways, fountains played; around them a considerable crowd had already collected. Over the people rose a huge pale block of building, more than classically severe in design, with square windows set in geometric rows. On its forehead the place wore like a caste-mark a colossal statue, a triumph of the rediscovered Cubist movement; Justice, holding aloft a golden sword and scales, proclaimed the New Bailey, greatest criminal court in the land. The girl's destination was nearer, on her side of the square. Similarly vast and white, but unornamented; the Supreme Court of Judicature, hub of the country's administration of civil law. She squared her shoulders, a tiny reflexive gesture, and began to walk towards it, heels tinkling on the bright hardness of the pathway.

For a moment she was unobserved; then the people saw her.

Shouting began; cameras were lifted, splashing back on their users her image in cubes of coloured gel; she saw a trivvyrig airborne and swooping, blunt nose aimed at her head. The crowd broke, beginning to run. State Troopers reached her first, formed round her a phalanx that butted its way through the jostling of the mob. There was much noise. More Troopers, arms linked in the old fashion, made a path for her to the entrance of the building; she stepped through the doors into a further tumult. Reporters boiled about, shouting questions and waving microphones; trivvyrigs darted from every side. She closed her mind to the uproar; her guards hurried her across the entrance hall and into a lift that spun her up into the high precincts of the place.

She sat in a small room, grey-painted, plain except for the grille of an airvent placed behind the solitary desk. At the desk, a woman regarded her sharply before consulting the lit panel in front of her and a sheaf of forms.

'Name?'

'Megan Wingrove.' The girl's voice was soft, with a trace of huskiness.

The other tapped a stylus irritably on a plastic sheet. 'Identification, please.'

'I'm sorry. M.E.G. one nine, stroke zero two.'

All this was formality. 'Tag?'

Megan searched quickly in her handbag, lifted the little metallic disc and held it forward. The other sniffed. 'Put it on please. You know the rules.'

'I'm sorry,' said the girl again. She slipped the dogtag on to her wrist, tightening the thong.

'Your place of manufacture?'

'Birmingham.'

'Year?'

'Two one seven two.'

'Thank you.' The stylus pointed. 'Wait in the next room, will you? You'll be told when your case opens.'

'Thank you . . .' Megan rose self-consciously, hips swaying

a trifle, walked through the white-painted door. Beyond was a line of chairs; she sat down, fingers playing with the lace at her wrist, eyes on the ceiling indicator as she waited her turn.

The case of Davenport *v*. Davenport would have raised enough dust to satisfy even the trivvy magnates without the astounding disclosure by Mrs. Ira Amanda Davenport of the nature of the offence allegedly committed by her husband. For a famous painter, a delineator of the crowned and uncrowned heads of royalty, a master of egg tempera and chocolate boxes, to be involved in divorce proceedings was spectacular stuff; for the other woman to be named openly was better; but—and the full impact only hit an astounded newsworld after urgent consultations with the staff of the reconstituted Somerset House—for the Party Cited, Megan Wingrove, M.E.G. 19/02, to be a *Synth* . . . why, that was past all belief. The Davenport mansion, a steel and chromium pile located not far from the Haymarket on Level Three, was besieged *instanter*; but nothing more was forthcoming. Ira of course had long since taken herself off to the home of understanding friends and Henry Aloysius Davenport, A.R.C.A., R.A., eschewed comment; or rather his lawyer eschewed comment, Mr. Davenport himself being unavailable to the public gaze. In lieu of hard news, the rumours grew; so fast and so far that Lord Chief Justice Hayward in his opening remarks for the case felt in duty bound to dispel some at least of the fog surrounding the affair.

'I think it only proper,' said the Judge, 'before beginning an investigation of the business before us, to present to the court several aspects of the matter which may in the somewhat unfortunate enthusiasm shown by the . . . ah . . . popular organs, have become distorted; and to disabuse the minds of all present of certain irrelevancies which would appear to have attached themselves to it.

'There is no question of the responsibility of the Synthetic, Megan Wingrove, in the eyes of the law. The charge preferred by plaintiff against her husband Mr. Henry Aloysius Davenport is of mental cruelty, and is acceptable under the appropriate section of the Divorce Amendment Act of 1992 and subsequent Acts. In so far as the compliance of the said Megan Wingrove is concerned, the court must decide during and pursuant to this hearing what proportion of blame is to be attached.

'These facts I expect to be firmly borne in mind by you all, and wish specifically to bring them to the attention of counsels for the plaintiff and for the defendant. Gentlemen, am I understood?'

Mr. Neville Martensson, for the plaintiff, and Mr. Richard Blakeney, K.C., for the defendant, bowed in unison.

'Very well,' said the Lord Chief Justice. 'Then I feel we may begin. . . .'

Megan, sitting unobtrusively to one side of the court, had let her attention wander. She'd seen the interior of the great hall often enough on the trivvyscreens, one channel was permanently reserved for its proceedings; but she had never before set foot in it, not even in the public galleries. She looked round at them now, at the long lines of faces, many of them turned towards her. Below, the floor of the court was dominated by the Judge's bench and the jury box; British justice still insisted on leaving the ultimate authority in the hands of amateurs. Facing each other across a floor of pale orange wood were the desks of the opposing counsels; beyond them was the railed-off body of the court where witnesses and the more favoured of the audience waited expectantly. Imitation sunlight, generated by lines of high-powered lamps, flooded through clerestory windows; the whole effect was bright, almost gay. It reminded Megan of a stage set rather than a place for the sober dispensing of justice. In a sense of course it was a set; the trivvyrigs were everywhere, whirring and humming, swooping on their near-invisible supports of telescoping rods. She could see their operators, intent behind a long glass panel set just beneath the roof.

She was recalled to the business in hand by Mr. Martensson rising to open for the plaintiff. The counsel was a short, square man, inclined to dumpiness, with pale eyes and a small red vee of a mouth that he kept tightly pursed imparting to his face an oddly prim expression. He stated his case briskly; he had a habit while talking of rubbing his hands over and over in a faintly sinister way, as if washing with invisible soap. Megan watched him, fascinated.

The facts of the matter were relatively simple. For some time Henry Davenport had been proclaimed among the top social set at least as the country's leading portrait painter. Five years previously he had married Ira, *née* Stowey, in one of the season's biggest weddings. Eighteen months later and several million dollars richer he had ordered from the Birmingham branch of InterNatMech (Great Britain) a Synthetic for general duties in the house as servant, maid-of-all-work and companion to his wife during his frequent and lengthy lecture tours abroad. The early evidence was rapidly dealt with; an official of InterNatMech confirmed the sale and delivery, while various other interested parties testified to the life of amity hitherto led by the Davenports. Martensson made his points quickly, wasting no words, and there were no interruptions from the defence.

Some months after the arrival of the Synth the first signs of friction had begun to appear. Henry it seemed had started to spend more and more time with his synthetic servant, preferring Meg's company to that of his lawful spouse. Many nights the two passed companionably by the romantic light of a fire, sitting chatting and reading poetry. The remonstrances of the unhappy Mrs. Davenport had fallen on deaf ears; then had come the evening of July 14, just three months ago now, and the great Incident. At this point counsel for the plaintiff called Mrs. Davenport to the stand; and the Lord Chief Justice, with a fine sense of timing, adjourned the court for lunch.

'Mrs. Davenport,' said Martensson, resuming his case in an air of hushed expectancy, 'perhaps you would like to tell me in your own words exactly what happened on that occasion?'

Ira, a rather overweight blonde from whom the best efforts of prosthetic makeup technicians had been unable to remove a faintly overblown air, sniffed and touched her nostrils with a balled-up handkerchief. 'It was . . . very terrible,' she said in a low voice. 'I . . . I shall never forget it, not to my dying day. . . .'

'Yes. Do please go on.'

'I . . . knew there was something wrong. As soon as I entered the house. I'd been staying with friends, I'd returned unexpectedly. The . . . atmosphere, I've always been most sensitive to atmosphere. Acutely sensitive. The . . . house was silent. Quiet as a g-grave. I . . . I was concerned, I didn't put on any lights. You see I knew something was terribly wrong . . . I went to my husband's room. He was not there. I . . . didn't know what to do . . .'

'Did you think of calling the police?'

'I . . . the scandal, the outrage. . . . We . . . had a position, Mr. Martensson. You understand . . .'

'Quite, quite,' said the counsel sympathetically. 'What did you in fact do, Mrs. Davenport?'

Henry Davenport, dapper, bearded, and clad in one of his famous cherry-coloured suits, began to exhibit strong signs of distress. He fidgeted in his seat, casting anxious glances at his counsel. The symptoms were not overlooked; a trivvyrig glided to him quietly, transfixing the artist with the cold eye of its lens. Richard Blakeney seemed blissfully unaware of the byplay; he persisted in his attempts to balance a stylus on the tip of one finger.

'I . . . waited,' said Ira. 'I daren't even . . . call out. I was having a terrible thought. I don't know what put it into my head. I . . . went to . . . that creature's room.' She indicated Megan with a flick of one varnished nail. 'I . . . I opened the door. Quietly, so as not to disturb . . . it. If it was sleeping . . .'

'And was it sleeping, Mrs. Davenport?'

'It was not. It was . . . lying on the bed. *With my husband. . . .*'

Excited hubbub from the court. The Judge rapped peremptorily for order.

'And what did you do then?'

'I . . . I screamed. I think I screamed. The shock, the outrage . . . frankly I can't remember. . . .'

Richard gave up his operations with the stylus and narrowed his eyes at the witness. Across the court Megan sat watching quietly, hands lying in her lap.

Martensson prompted smoothly. 'What happened then, Mrs. Davenport? Try to tell the court.'

'The . . . thing, the Synth . . . sat up. Its blouse was unbuttoned down the front, I saw that clearly. And my husband . . .' Ira put a hand to her forehead. 'The rest's gone. Just a blank. I'm sorry.'

'That's quite all right,' said Mr. Martensson. 'As the court appreciates, the whole affair was a great shock to you. I don't think I have any more questions for the moment.'

Richard Blakeney jackknifed himself to his feet. 'Permission to examine the witness, M'Lord?'

'Granted.'

The counsel approached the stand, leaned against it while he contemplated the ceiling of the courtroom. In physical appearance he was Martensson's complete opposite. He was tall and thin, inclined almost to droopiness; his face, with the wide mouth and long, half-veiled eyes, was that of a ballet dancer. His opponent, outwardly cocksure, watched him speculatively. The brain behind that sleepy mask had cost more cases than Martensson cared to remember.

Richard's eyes, roving quietly, stopped at Megan. He smiled, while she stared back uncertainly. He scratched an ear, harrumphed a couple of times, and turned at last to the witness. 'Er . . . good afternoon, Mrs. Davenport. . . .'

Titters of amusement. Judge Hayward rapped for order. Ira stared at the K.C., truculent and a little tear-stained.

'Er . . . yes,' said Richard. 'Mrs. Davenport, have you ever been in a court of law before?'

'Objection!' Martensson bounced to his feet. 'The question is irrelevant. Counsel is trying to intimidate the witness.'

The Lord Chief Justice raised enquiring eyebrows at Blakeney. Richard looked vaguely troubled. 'On the contrary, M'Lord,' he said. 'The question was designed to assist Mrs. Davenport. I was about to remark that witness need have no cause for concern as long as she answers clearly and concisely what is asked her.'

Judge Hayward looked annoyed. 'Well, Mr. Martensson?'

'Objection withdrawn. . . .' Martensson sat back sulkily. Richard clucked at him faintly; he always liked to score a quick first point off his opponent. He turned back to the witness. 'Mrs. Davenport, on the night you described, the night of July fourteen, you claim to have been thrown into a state of shock by the discovery of your husband and Miss Wingrove together. Yet you noticed one apparently minor detail with great clarity; the unbuttoned blouse of Miss Wingrove. Is this not remarkable?'

'I . . . no. The little things, the d-details . . . they stand in one's mind. They're often the only things one does remember. . . .'

'Yes,' said Richard. 'Quite, quite. . . . Now the blouse you say was dishevelled. To what extent, Mrs. Davenport?'

'I . . . I told you. It was undone. . . .'

'Were the girl's breasts uncovered?'

'I . . . don't know.'

'Come, Mrs. Davenport, you saw this with great clarity. It was the one detail that burned itself, as it were, on your mind. Were her breasts exposed?'

'I . . .'

'*Were they*, Mrs. Davenport?'

'No,' said the woman sullenly. 'They were covered when she got up. But they hadn't been, they hadn't been. . . .'

'That, Mrs. Davenport, is an assumption that I think is unwarrantable. Are you in a position to prove your assertion?'

'Well . . . use your imagination. It was *obvious* what had been going on. . . .'

'With your imagination already working at capacity,' said Richard sweetly, 'any attempts on my part would I feel be superfluous.'

'Objection! Counsel is intimidating the witness. His last remark constitutes an open accusation of false testimony.'

'That, M'Lord,' said Richard, 'was nothing of the sort. I merely wished to establish the degree of dishevelment noticed by the witness, and to point out that what had happened prior to her entering the room can scarcely be known to her now. Or maybe it can. You claim you are a Sensitive, Mrs. Davenport. Do you perhaps possess second sight as well?'

'*Objection!* . . .'

'Question withdrawn,' said the counsel, hearing ripples of laughter in the audience. 'Now to proceed, Mrs. Davenport. Did you on entering your maid's room notice any other signs of disorder? Apart from the blouse which we seem to have established was only slightly disarranged?'

'She was lying in an abandoned attitude,' snarled the witness. 'Her thighs were exposed. . . .'

'Her thighs were exposed,' said Richard pensively. He stared round at a vista of thighs, all bared in accordance with the dictates of fashion. Mrs. Davenport, dressed herself in the season's highest mode, reddened and twitched her skirt across her knees. Richard smiled. 'Is it your opinion then,' he asked pleasantly, 'that bared legs are an infallible sign of depravity?'

'*Objection!* . . .'

'To ease the mind of my learned colleague,' said Blakeney, 'I will not press the witness to answer that question. Now Mrs. Davenport, before we leave this apparently delicate subject, were there any other signs of dishevelment noted by you? So

far we have I think one slightly untidy blouse. Hardly con-
clusive proof of adultery, you must admit. . . .'

'His hair,' said Ira, groping. 'My husband's hair. It was all
. . . disarranged. All over his face. . . .'

'To what cause do you ascribe that?'

'She . . . it . . . had been stroking it. Running its f-fingers
through it. A *machine*! . . .' She shuddered, chewing at her lip.

Richard smiled again benignly. 'Mrs. Davenport,' he said,
'not a hundred yards from this building is an establishment,
often frequented by myself, where the payment of a small sum
secures certain services. A machine will wash and shave me;
it will shampoo my hair; and to my shame be it admitted, *it
will massage my scalp*. Twice a week I return to my Gomorrah;
I luxuriate in blackest sin, shoulder to shoulder frequently with
highly placed and respected officers of this city, while a machine
strokes my hair. . . .' He walked off quietly. Half way to his
seat he shook his head sorrowfully. 'She stroked his hair,' he
said, as if to himself. '*Stroked his hair*. . . .'

He reached his desk and turned, waiting for the amusement
to die down. 'On a point of information, Mrs. Davenport,' he
said, 'far from losing coherence, you would appear on the
occasion under discussion to have been remarkably . . . er
. . . fluent.' He drew from his pocket a slip of paper, squinted
at it painfully. 'Did you not call your husband . . . "a lecher, a
louse, a two-bit fornicator" . . . You also said, unless my information is incorrect, "You crafty little bastard, I'll get a hundred thousand a year for this. . . ." The rest is written down,
M'Lord. I'd like to pass it to you for perusal. . . .'

Laughter broke in a wave.

Before releasing his victim Richard asked permission to
recall Mrs. Davenport during his defence. The matter was
protested vigorously by Martensson; but the counsel for the
plaintiff was overruled by the Lord Chief Justice. Blakeney sat
down reasonably satisfied.

Other evidence followed; the testimony of the State
Troopers called to the house by the distracted Mrs. Davenport,

statements from a doctor and a psychiatrist and from the officer in charge of the Sector Station where Megan had temporarily been lodged. Martensson had a solid case, and he made the most of it; Richard, sitting dreamily toying with the stylus, watched the black clouds gather.

'And there can be little doubt,' said the counsel for the plaintiff, winding up his attack on the second day, 'that Henry Davenport did in fact inflict the severest mental pain on his wife. By introducing into his hitherto happy establishment the person of the Synthetic Megan Wingrove he deliberately instituted a situation intolerable to his partner; its culmination, and his disgraceful and abnormal conduct, you have already heard described. I can only ask you, ladies and gentlemen of the jury, to recommend the strongest measures in dealing with this affair; an affair that has already cost an innocent woman more than money can repay in terms of suffering and very real grief.'

He turned triumphantly to the bench. 'M'Lord,' he said, 'the case for the plaintiff rests. . . .'

Court was adjourned for the remainder of the day.

On the third morning Blakeney opened for the defendant.

'The court cannot fail to have noticed,' he said, 'that despite the injunctions given at the start of these proceedings learned counsel for the plaintiff has seen fit to base his case totally on the affair of Megan Wingrove; he has sought to prove, unsuccessfully I might add, that an illicit relationship did exist and that adultery did in fact take place. The defence feels compelled to answer and finally demolish these charges. We shall show beyond reasonable doubt that such a state of affairs did not and could not exist; and we shall prove beyond all question that the accusations that have brought us here are at best the imaginings of an overwrought and highly-strung woman, and at worst deliberate machinations dictated by vindictiveness and avarice. M'Lord, have I your permission to proceed?'

Judge Hayward nodded after a moment's consideration. 'Yes, Mr. Blakeney, you have.'

'Thank you, M'Lord,' said Richard easily. 'Then for my first witness I wish to call Mr. Pieter van Mechelren, President of InterNatMech, Amsterdam.'

A buzz of speculation. The parent company of InterNat-Mech was world-famous; it held exclusive rights of all processes connected with the production of Synths, and was one of the wealthiest business houses in Europe. To get their President on the case in person Blakeney had evidently been pulling some very powerful strings.

The man who took the stand was burly and dark-haired; his eyes were big and brown in a plump, smooth-skinned face. He looked like a moderately successful market gardener. Richard knew better.

The counsel opened smartly. 'Your name is Pieter van Mechelren?'

'It is.' The voice was deep, with a faint guttural trace of accent.

'And you are the President of InterNatMech of Holland?'

'Yes.'

'Would you describe yourself as qualified to give opinions on the characteristics and inherent capabilities of the beings known as Synthetics?'

Pieter grinned slowly. 'Jus' about, I reckon.'

Richard consulted his notes. 'I believe you do yourself an injustice,' he said. 'You hold degrees in biochemistry, physics, and physiology, you are an honorary member of the Royal Society and the Royal Institution, of the Dutch Society of Physiomechanics and of the American Institute of Bioengineering. You hold a chair in Cybernetics at the University of Gröningen; and you are generally accepted to be the world's leading authority on all phases of the construction and operation of Synths. Am I not correct?'

Van Mechelren wagged his hands deprecatingly. 'There are maybe some diff'rent opinions on that.'

Richard smiled. 'I think yours, Mr. van Mechelren, will satisfy this court.' He indicated Megan, sitting a few yards from him. 'Tell me, did your firm market the figure you see here?'

'Yes, indirectly. She was produced under licence about three years back by InterNatMech Great Britain, at their installation in Birmingham.'

'I see. Now Mr. van Mechelren, you've heard the evidence already given in court. What is your professional opinion of it with regard to your product?'

'Wi' regard to our product?' Pieter spread thick-fingered hands. 'A load of hossfeathers, a'm afraid.'

There were sniggers.

Richard nodded. 'I see. Now before coming down to detail, perhaps you'd give the court a brief outline of the nature of Synthetic humans. A short history of their development if you like. I want everybody here to be fully conversant with the subject.'

Pieter shrugged. 'Would tak' a bit of time. Is a big subject.'

'Briefly then.'

'Briefly? Well, I try. . . .' The Dutchman frowned thoughtfully. 'Th' idea of a Synth is mebbe ver' old. After all the Cretans had a guy called Talos, used to frighten the hell out of 'em 'cause he was made of brass. There is no time in the history of the race when we've bin without a robot of some kind. Something . . . automatic, something ticking, turning, singing. . . .' He rocked his hands, miming the actions of machinery. 'Engines that could go where we could not, because we were too big or too small; taste fire that was too warm for us, ice that was too cold; think faster, move faster, fly in the air, burrow through the sea. . . . Always machines, better an' better, more and more perfect robots for us to use. Only robot isn' a good name for the li'l girl here. Name comes from two hundred years back, an old Czech play. Robot, mechanical worker. She isn' mechanical. She's a Synth. . . .'

'How long have Synths themselves been in existence?'

Van Mechelren shrugged his broad shoulders. 'Long, long time. Sometimes a' like to think, ever' machine we ever made, that was a part of them. Hundreds o' years they took, bein' born. A' could give names, you know; Holstein, Rigby, Capotek; but they don' mean nothing. Is no . . . date, no time you can set down and say *dere*, th' first Synth. They jus' came along, was a continuous process. Of . . . growth, development; a li'l bit here, another there. . . . Go back two centuries, there were computers. These were some of the' ancestors. . . .'

Richard nodded. 'But computers were, and occasionally still are, bulky affairs. How did they develop into the figure we see in front of us?'

'By simplification,' said the Dutchman. 'By the transistor supplanting the valve, being supplanted in its turn; always simpler, easier, quicker. That way we always grow up, we get smart. Like the petrol engine. Was a hell of a thing. Wit' diesel, easier. Turbines; nothin' to 'em. One day, who can say? Antigrav; nothin' to that at-all. Li'l guy wit' moons an' stars on his hat wave a wand, *presto* . . . right back to de start for us.'

He held up a sleeve. 'Look. Once was glass an' metal. To make' a computer then, a brain, needed all steel an' wire. Now see, I tak' two threads. From my jacket will do fine. So I treat dem, so . . . . Now I pass through a current. In the threads, a change. Their resistance alters. To a further current, it will be greater. This is the start. This is memory.

'The li'l girl there, she has a head of cottonwool. Or what you call the stuff, candyfloss. . . . But ver' special candyfloss. The Wolfenden cerebral matrix, developed in this country fifty years ago. Intelligence; memory, extrapolation, decision, you know what it is? A function of number of cells, hookups between 'em. Nothin' difficult. So you spin a wire, ver' fine, put him in a resistant jacket. Then a thousand, just alike. A million. Ten million. Hook 'em up sideways, crossways, ever' way. You put a microscope on a Wolfenden matrix, you got chicken wire. Thousands, thousands o' layers, all balled together. There's your brain. It gets easy, it gets small. You mak' the body the same way; legs, arms, the muscles there, all easy, all small. It tak's years; but you keep tryin', you get there. You make a figure, a woman. You got a Synth. . . .'

'Well, it still sounds a very complicated process to me.'

'To understand is simple,' said the Dutchman, wagging his head. 'But to make . . in truth, it is not easy. Not easy at all.'

'Now this girl,' said Richard, 'with her rather pretty candyfloss brain. What drives her, what makes her move?'

'Same as makes you an' me move,' said van Mechelren. 'She's a mass o' muscle, tendon, all packed in. Only she don' eat for energy, she gets her push-an'-pull another way. She synthesizes, from sunlight.'

'Like a plant, in other words?'

'Yah, so. But better'n a plant. A plant's imperfect, needs th' soil. A plant *converts*, she *collects*. A walkin' solar battery, she is. The skin, the hair. . . . She loves the sun, she'll bathe there all day long. She don' need no food. She don' stick her feet in de earth for salt.'

'So Synthetic figures are in fact dependent on the sun for their energy.'

'Ah, you see. Ideally, yes. But you shut one in a box she'll get sleepy soon, curl up. Go dormant. In a room, a city, is the same. So she can recharge other ways, if she needs. Sometimes at night, when she sleeps.'

'Tell us about this business of a sleeping period, Mr. van Mechelren. Is it important it coincides so closely with the human cycle?'

'No, not at all. Same way it don' matter she got two arms, two legs, or ten. We could build 'em any way we like. But people jus' prefer having things around that act like them, look like them. Nest o' wires an' eyes sits up an' says Daddy, they get worried. Is crazy but is true. So . . . things like dat.' He waved his hand at Megan, a queer, sharp little gesture that attracted her eyes instantly, and grinned. 'We prefer 'em that way too. . . .'

'How many Synths are produced in the course of a year?'

Van Mechelren frowned. 'Oh . . . two, three dozen at th' outside. No more.'

'Then the population of these people is in fact quite small.'

'Ver' small. After all, they come a bit expensive.'

'Of course. I think the popular idea is of some sort of assembly line. This is incorrect.'

'*Ya.* . . .' Pieter scowled. 'Popular idea, I seen that. Here an assembly line, there another. De hands go on, plonk . . . de heads, bonk . . . like makin' automobiles. Is not like that at all. Is like a . . . hospital, more. A' wish you could see. Jus' one we work on, at a time. And careful, so careful. . . . This mus' be right, an' that; no flaws, not anywhere. Otherwise she jus' don' go. . . . Even the skin, the flesh. Grown so carefully. . . . Is a ver' long job.'

'*Grown*, you say?'

'Ya. Grown.' The Dutchman's eyes glittered with amusement. 'Is a hydrocarbon base, long-chain molecules. It grows. . . .'

'I see. Well, you make these people sound very human. *Are* they human, Mr. van Mechelren?'

'Ach, no. Never. Wit' humans . . . they get sick, they die sometime. They get mean, hell, sometimes they have a war. They have laws for each other, an' courts to try mak' 'em work.' He glanced round humorously. 'Wit' these people, never. They don' need no laws. They don' get mad, cut each other up. They know only one thing. Obey a human, when he talks. That's what we teach 'em, right from the start. Is a machine that drips it into 'em, ever' fibre of the brain, till they can't forget, not ever. They're not human, for damn sure. Not robot either. They're Synths. . . .'

'Thank you,' said Richard. 'Now you've heard already, in the course of these proceedings, various allegations levelled at the . . . ah . . . Synthetic, Megan Wingrove. How do you rate them, technically and professionally?'

'Like a' said. Hossfeathers.' Pieter started to grin. 'Why don' they sue de sideboard for sittin' there? Or arrest the trivvybox for attempted rape? Man, I never heard one thing the half as crazy. . . .'

'It is impossible then for a Synth to behave in such a way as to bring mental suffering to a human? Or to connive at such behaviour?'

'Is crazy. The human suffers, the fault is in dem. Maybe it hurts 'em to see the sun come up, they want the world to be dark. Is not the fault of de sun. . . . You know sometimes a' think,' said van Mechelren, 'a' like to get hold of a few of these humans. We put 'em through the mill, tie 'em on our squeakbox a couple of days, they better for it. One hell of a sight.'

'Yes, quite. Now returning to details, we've heard an accusation of immorality levelled against Megan Wingrove. How do you react to this?'

Van Mechelren reacted by rumbling with laughter. 'Man,' he said, 'how's she goin' to be immoral? What wit'?'

'I'm asking you that, sir.'

'There is no way,' said the Dutchman quietly. 'No way at all.'

'In fact you are unable to take the charge seriously.'

'I tak' it serious all right,' said Pieter darkly. 'But not like that. I think somewhere . . . is a bad smell of fish.'

At this point counsel for the plaintiff ejaculated something angrily. The doubts as to what Mr. Martensson actually said were never finally resolved; but a reporter sitting close behind his desk claimed, possibly with more optimism then accuracy, that the remark terminated with the phrase *Venus aversa*. It was enough to send a generation of newshounds scurrying for Sir Richard Burton and the *Kama Sutra*; the results of their investigations were spectacular to say the least.

The Dutchman's evidence closed the session for the morning and Blakeney promptly requested, and was granted, a recess till the following day. As soon as he was released from the stand van Mechelren walked over to where Megan was sitting by herself. He hooked a chair from beside the wall and squatted across it, arms on the backrest, chin on his hands. 'Hey magnificent,' he said, grinning. 'How's ever' li'l spurwheel?'

She looked at him startled, then began to grin back. It was the first time she'd smiled in court. A moment later Mr. Martensson, clearing the papers from his desk, glanced up and scowled. Richard, van Mechelren, and the Synth were in earnest consultation; he saw Megan lift a slim leg, tapping the knee and rotating the ankle as she made some little complaint about the joint.

'Hey, look,' said the Dutchman, still grinning, 'a' tell you what. If you can stand to watch a fat man eat, I tak' you both to lunch. O.K.?' They left with the girl shortly afterwards, van Mechelren with one hand dropped protectingly on her shoulder.

'And I wish it to be clearly understood,' said the Lord Chief Justice acidly when opening the fourth day's hearing, 'that in the event of a further outbursting of such offensive speculation, I shall order the court cleared and complete these investigations *in camera*. I trust the public, and those members of the press most guilty of this gross breach of privilege, will take due and solemn warning. Now Mr. Blakeney, are you ready to resume your case?'

For the moment Richard had no more questions for van Mechelren; the Dutchman was handed over to Mr. Martensson for cross-examination.

'I'm sure,' said the counsel for the plaintiff, opening sweetly, 'we all appreciated Mr. van Mechelren's exposition of yesterday, enlivened as it was with what I believe our Transatlantic cousins were once disposed to term crackerbarrel philosophy.'

A ripple of laughter. Martensson rode above it. 'There are, however, one or two points that I think could be elucidated. Mr. van Mechelren'—he hooked his thumbs in his lapels, a time-worn gesture—'you mentioned . . . ah . . . recharging as a process sometimes necessary to the Synths produced by your company. Will you elaborate on the system?'

'Certainly.' The Dutchman steepled his fingers. 'The charging is carried out from a standard wall socket an' supplements the main photosynthetic system of chemical energy storage. Reaction between ionised cells of the deep dermal layers an'——'

'A wall *socket*, you say?' Counsel interrupted, rotating sharply on his heel. 'I take it, then, that some form of... ah... socket exists on the body of the Synthetic?'

Van Mechelren began to smile. 'That is so. Normally, th' orifice is kept shut by a sphincter, a ... ring muscle, I think you say.' He clenched his fist. 'See, so. Lowering of th' energy level in the lumbar cortex allows relaxation of the sphincter prior to insertion of the coupling. So. . . .' His fingers parted, forming a circle.

'I see.' Counsel appeared to be biting his words into fragments, and spitting them at the witness like small explosive bullets. 'And where, Mr. van Mechelren, is this ... orifice, and its attendant muscular configuration, situated?'

The Dutchman wagged expressive shoulders. 'Wherever's convenient. Could be practic'lly anywhere; could be in the groin or hip, or the side of the thoracic cage. Sometimes in th' throat, the knee . . .'

'In the case of the Synthetic under discussion, where is the apparatus sited?'

A moment of intense silence in the court. Van Mechelren's grin became fractionally broader. 'In the right ankle,' he said, and added under his breath, '*you dirty li'l man. . . .*'

A sudden gusting of laughter from the public benches, quelled angrily by the Lord Chief Justice.

Martensson, rattled, wouldn't relinquish his bone. 'Mr. van Mechelren, would you describe to the court the exact steps by which recharging is carried out?'

The grin didn't leave the Dutchman's face, but his eyes became pure frost. 'No,' he said, with ominous gentleness. 'A' would not.'

'But I'm afraid I must insist that you do.'

'Mr. Martensson,' said van Mechelren easily, 'how exac'ly does your wife shave the hair from beneath her arms?'

Uproar, silenced loudly from the bench. 'The witness,' said Judge Hayward severely, 'will refrain from insolence towards the officers of the court. And he will confine himself to answering the questions put by counsel.'

Van Mechelren inclined his head gravely.

'Objection!'

Richard was on his feet, staring angrily at Martensson. 'M'Lord, the defence expresses its concern at the direction and tone of counsel's questioning. So far his remarks have contained nothing but pointless and embarrassing innuendo.'

The Lord Chief Justice peered over his spectacles to where Megan watched back wide-eyed. 'The matter of embarrassment,' he observed, 'seems to me to be infinitely debatable. As to the direction of questioning, the court agrees that little profitable result is to be expected. Can counsel justify his mode of approach?'

Martensson smiled nastily. 'It is not our wish, M'Lord, unduly to . . . ah . . . embarrass counsel's witnesses. I am prepared therefore to withdraw my last question.'

The Judge nodded. 'Very well. Proceed.'

The mouth of the counsel for the plaintiff was compressed into a vicious little vee. 'Mr. van Mechelren, before you step down I would like confirmation of one further point. You gave it as your opinion that . . . ah . . . biological gratification of a human male by a Synthetic is an impossibility.'

'A' did.'

'And that was in fact, and remains, your considered opinion? On that you are prepared publicly to stake your professional reputation?'

Van Mechelren's eyebrows contracted to a wary scowl. 'In de present circumstances,' he said after a moment's pause, 'yes.'

Martensson pounced. 'I did not ask you to devise circumstances, Mr. van Mechelren, I asked a general question and require a general answer.'

'Wit' one of our li'l people,' said Pieter steadily, 'it would be out of the question.'

'Then the matter is after all an impossibility. You stand by your previous remark.'

'You'd have to build a special figure,' said the Dutchman thoughtfully. 'Ver' special. . . .'

'But InterNatMech never have?'

'No.'

'Then I repeat and I stress, Mr. van Mechelren, the thing is an impossibility. You seem well versed in prevarication, sir, but we must have you stand by something. Will you stand by that?'

'Nothin's impossible,' admitted van Mechelren. Then suddenly the grin was back. 'But hell, man,' he said. 'We never bin asked. . . .'

Martensson turned savagely to the bench. 'M'Lord, I ask the court to note that despite Mr. van Mechelren's evident technological prowess his bias in this matter is such as to make him a hostile witness.'

Judge Hayward regarded the counsel for the plaintiff mildly. 'The fact is noted, Mr. Martensson,' he said. 'I would have thought that it was self-evident. . . .'

There were titters of amusement.

Richard returned from the lunchtime recess with a long face. Certain enquiries he'd instituted had produced depressing answers. He arrived back at court early, tracked down an elusive Pieter van Mechelren with whom truth to tell he'd spent a good proportion of the previous evening in moody drinking. He ran the Dutchman to earth in a side room where Megan, refreshed after her first good night's sleep in weeks, was vainly trying to satisfy van Mechelren's curiosity.

'Loadings now,' Pieter was saying as he entered. 'Humeral max?'

'Nine five kilos. Dextral emphasis sixty-forty.'

Van Mechelren tapped a stylus against his teeth. 'Good, good girl . . . femoral?'

'Two fifty by two.'

'Main sphincters?'

'A hundred kilos rated max.'

'Pieter,' said Richard, leaning over him. 'You and I have troubles.'

The Dutchman flicked a sheet of his notes. 'You look after de humans, my son, tak' all your time. I got my problems here. . . .' He mumbled. 'Lumbar configuration twelve by twelve, ah-hah. . . . Ganglia dee-fourteen-nines, lymphatics low-pressure. . . . Reaction to prim'ry stimulus . . . one over fifty, tolerance zero zero five. . . .' Still tapping, he contrived to grin. 'She's a tough li'l girl, Richard. A' tell you what, a' tak' care an' never argue wit' her.'

Megan smiled at him.

The counsel lit a cigarette, sourly. He sat on the desk edge and crossed his long legs. 'She'll be a dead li'l girl if we don't watch points. You scared to die, Meg?'

'No.'

'But you do want to live?'

'Yes,' said the Synth. 'Yes.'

Van Mechelren exploded suddenly. 'What's this bloody rot, my son?'

Richard blew smoke. 'Second we lose this case the opposition'll take out an injunction against her. Destruct or modify.'

'*What?*'

'You heard,' said Richard. Then, insultingly, '*My son.* . . .'

Pieter swore, hugely. 'You can' modify a stable brain matrix, you know that bloody well. Go back to first principles——'

'I know. They know.'

'Then what in hell——'

'Destruct. There's a precedent. Limber *v.* Cassidy, Manhattan '63. Synth flipped its lid, chucked a couple of guys through an apartment window. Turned out it was a tall apartment. They got a destruct order and blew it apart on the spot. Owner tried for costs. He lost out.'

'Well damme, that's pleasant.' The Dutchman smacked

angrily at the table. 'The thing got knocked off skentre. It had a clout, something. I was on dat case.'

'Yes, but they'll still get an order on the strength of it. Claim felonious conduct. Citizens' Protection Act, World Legislative Council '65. I checked it through. The Limber Synth blew a pretty big scare, they wrapped it up but good. Meg could get a one-way ticket for spitting on the sidewalk. If she could spit. We lose this one and Ira D's got her cold.'

'That bloody woman,' brooded Pieter, 'could well use a kick up th' ass. Who tol' you this?'

'Little legal sparrow.'

The President of InterNatMech glowered at his protégée, then at Richard. 'So why you worryin', my friend? Meg ain't paying you.'

Richard slapped his cigarette on the desk and leaned forward. 'Listen,' he said, 'it so happens I'm still trying to get Henry Aloysius off the hook. The fact that my revered client is a creepy little bastard has nothing to do with the deal. If Meg loses, he loses. Only Henry merely gets bled white paying alimony. Megan . . . *kkkkssss.*' He drew a finger across his throat and leered.

Van Mechelren grunted. 'You think we lose?'

'It's tied up with cast-iron string. Martensson's got the case; so far all I've done's make pretty patterns round the edges. Somebody has to crack. Nobody has. If nobody does . . .' He shrugged, and left the rest unsaid.

'There be bloody good row first,' said the Dutchman ominously.

'So. There be bloody good row. Meg still loses.' He turned to the Synth. 'Megan, I'm going to try and get you in the hotbox this afternoon. I may be rough. If I'm not, our friends will be rougher. O.K.?'

She nodded gravely. He squeezed her knee, trying to remember she wasn't human. 'Keep the flag waving then. I think you're taking old Hayward's fancy.'

Pieter's eyes were narrowed thoughtfully. 'You reckon he let you get away with this, Rich?'

'I can try it. He's a crusty old devil but there's a chance I can swing him.'

The Dutchman shrugged largely. 'Better you than me, son. . . .'

'That's O.K.' Richard smiled like a wolf. 'That's what Davenport's paying me for. . . .'

The bell rang for the opening of the session. Pieter, his equanimity restored, rose and stowed the notebook in his voluminous jacket. He followed the others into the corridor. As he walked, he whistled pensively. The ancient tune had once had a title: *Tulips from Amsterdam*. The Dutchman was nothing if not a patriot.

'M'Lord,' said Richard carefully. 'I would like to call the Synth, Megan Wingrove, to the stand. . . .'

A minor hubbub from the public gallery, and an instantaneous objection from Martensson. Judge Hayward rapped irritably. 'Mr. Blakeley,' he said, 'you are as aware as the rest of this court that legal precedents preclude the evidence of a Synthetic. Your request is disallowed.'

An interruption from the foreman of the jury. 'On a point of information, M'Lord. . . .'

'Yes?'

The man shuffled uncomfortably. 'For many years evidence by trivvy, film, wire, tape, any mechanical means, has been permitted. Would you explain the distinction in the . . . er . . . present case?'

'The distinction,' said the Lord Chief Justice cuttingly, 'seems to me to be self-explanatory. The employment of a method of mechanical reproduction in no way signifies that the evidence of the machine is accepted as is the evidence of a witness. The machine does not originate the evidence; it is the means of its production, and as such is in itself irrelevant. A machine cannot take an oath; neither, for the same reasons, may a Synthetic. Unsworn evidence is of little positive value.'

Richard waited. 'M'Lord,' he said finally. 'May I then be allowed to interrogate an exhibit?'

'What exhibit is that, Mr. Blakeney?'

'The Synth, Megan Wingrove.'

Extraordinarily, the Lord Chief Justice smiled. 'I see no objection, counsel. You may proceed. . . .'

When Megan was installed in the witness box the Judge unexpectedly intervened. 'In many respects,' he said to the court in general, 'this hearing has already proved itself unique; and the present circumstance is certainly without precedent.' He peered at Megan. 'Before counsel starts his examination,' he said gently, 'I'm sure the court would like to hear in your own words some account of your . . . ah . . . manufacture, and subsequent experiences. Have you an objection, Mr. Blakeney?'

'Naturally not, M'Lord,' said Richard uneasily. The Synth, undirected, could hang herself higher than the walls.

Megan smiled apologetically. 'I'm afraid you'll be a little disappointed, My Lord,' she said. 'I can't remember much more of my . . . manufacture than a human remembers of her birth.'

'That,' said the Judge, 'is understood. Simply tell us what you can.'

Megan closed her eyes, thinking deeply. For a time there was silence. Then she looked up again. 'I was born,' she said, 'I'm sorry My Lord, but among ourselves we think of our . . . making as a birth. . . . I was born three years ago, in Birmingham. I don't remember much of the actual . . . process at all.' She paused again. 'There was a . . . darkness,' she said slowly. 'And a . . . coldness and hotness combined, the first Sensation. I can't adequately describe it. It seemed I was . . . floating, in some void, while round me a world was created. It was as if . . . things, objects, the warmth and coldness at first, came into being round me. As if I had always been there. If you can understand what I mean. . . .

'There were . . . voices in the void. They went on and on,

saying over strings of figures, readings, pressures. . . . Only I didn't know, then, that they were readings. I didn't know they were voices. Sound was like warmth and cold to me, something . . . not-void. That's the only way I can describe it. Sometimes the voices were very distant. At others they were loud. When they came too close they turned to a sort of roaring that stopped, and then there was the void again. Nothingness. And it would start all over. I was being tested, of course. I realised that later when I . . . understood.

'Then I could see. But there was nothing at first except a sort of greyness. Like a fog. The . . . things, the objects, seemed to make themselves from it, and float back into it again. They had no meaning for me; sometimes they were like a . . . trivvy picture out of tune, they turned to lapping patterns of colour that had no . . . sense, no "up" and "down". In between them the voices were still threading about like other colours. There was no feeling of scale. I might have been a million miles tall or smaller than an electron. I still had no . . . understanding.

'I don't know when I started to be taught. Until then I could have no existence. I was the total of no experience, a sort of sum of zeros. But I . . . remember first lying on a bed. There was a . . . room. It was small and white, and there was a noise. A humming. I could see; and I knew "up" was above me, and "down" was beneath. I think . . . yes, I could move my head. Because I turned it, and beside me was a machine. It was very big, and grey. Lights shone across it, in lines across its facias. Blue lights, and red, and green. It was very big, it seemed to tower over the bed. There were little discs turning and spools, and the whole thing was singing. That was the noise I could hear.

'I was joined to the machine by a thick loom of cable. It went into my neck just below the jaw. I could have reached up and pulled it away, but I didn't. I didn't move my hands. I didn't know I had "hands".

'I lay watching the lights, and seeing the discs turn; and it seemed the machine spoke to me. I could understand "speak"

8

now, and "silence". "You are awake," it said. "I am a machine." That was all, for a very long time. "You are awake. I am a machine.". . .

'After that I found . . . things beside the bed. There was always something new there. I could pick the things up and handle them. The machine would tell me what they were. "These are flowers," it would say. "This is a book. This is a shoe.". . . Sometimes I didn't understand; then the discs would stop, and the lights would wobble and change, and something would happen inside me and the machine would start again. "This is a book. This is a shoe." It was very . . . patient.

'It told me other things too, when I was ready for them. "Beyond you is a window. Through the window is the sky. The sky is blue."

' "This is a city." . . .

' "It's name is Birmingham." . . .

' "You are a Synth." . . .

' "*This is a man*." . . .'

'How long,' asked Judge Hayward, 'did you remain linked to your machine?'

'The . . . indoctrination lasted two months. The other machine, the one they called a man, would disconnect the wires in little batches, carefully. By then I could speak. "Man," I'd say, "Man." . . . It sounded right to me—I knew "right" by then—but he'd laugh at me, and say "Man . . . *Man*." . . . I got it right in the end; but it took a long time.

'I was sorry when they took the machine away. They said I was finished with it then, they needed it for another like me. They taught me to walk. I was taught . . . properly, by a human. She gave me crutches to use and put me in a sort of tripod thing till I understood about balance. It held me round the waist and if I slipped the legs shot out to stop me falling. I couldn't understand why I had to walk. I just did as I was told.

'They taught me to wear clothes and wash and comb my hair . . . oh, hundreds of things. And of course each day I was going to school. That was easy. There was another machine.

I could . . . connect myself to it, there were flexes and they'd left a little socket under my jaw. InSems, they called the lessons. Inducted Seminaries. . . . I could choose, after a time, what I wanted to learn. If a . . . fact didn't fit in an established matrix I could research it, get a cross-reference. If the machine couldn't answer I could ask a human tutor. But that didn't happen very often.

'Sometimes they let me see the new figure they were making. She looked very pretty lying on her bed watching the machine, the little discs spinning and turning and the lights. She was coloured, they'd made her a sort of coffee brown. I remember I used to joke with them and say I wanted to be coloured too and I was jealous, but they wouldn't change me. I went back to my Seminaries. They said I had to be smarter than the rest, my owner would be a very particular man.'

'And that owner,' said the Judge, 'was Mr. Davenport?'

'Yes, sir. I met him the first time a few weeks before I was due for release. I remember he was very pleased with me. He made me turn round and stand up and walk. Then he said, "Get her some shoes. Heels. Show her height off. Otherwise, great." . . .' Megan smiled. 'So I had to learn to walk in high heels. It was the one thing they hadn't taught me.

'A short while after that I went out for the first time. Out of the Institute. It was strictly before I was allowed to. There was some trouble over it; Mr. Maskell the Director was very annoyed.'

'Because you left without permission?'

'Yes. I was trying something out, sir. Something I'd been studying. I wanted to see how well I could pass for a human.'

'And was the experiment successful?'

'Oh, yes.' Megan smiled again at a memory. 'I found a shopping level. I bought myself a hat and a dress and a pair of shoes. With heels. I wanted to please Mr. Davenport. . . . I was certain I'd be found out but I wasn't. It made me feel . . . good. An assistant wrapped the things and another—a human —held the door for me. I was very proud of myself.'

'How did you . . . ah . . . come by the money for this spree?'

'I stole it,' said Megan winningly. 'I calculated with the profit they were making on me they could afford that at least. In any case the clothes could be refunded. But they let me keep them. I think they were pleased too.'

Van Mechelren, sitting in the body of the court, smiled to himself, leaned back, and clasped his hands.

'A little while after that, after my final Seminars, Mr. Davenport came again. That time he brought his wife. She finally chose my name from a shortlist. It had to be an "M", I was in an M batch.'

'How was your second name determined?' asked Judge Hayward.

'By Random Selection apparatus,' said the Synth. 'It has no significance.'

'And after that, you were taken to Mr. Davenport's home?'

'I delivered myself. I was given the address, and an advance on my first month's salary.'

'I see. And . . . ah . . . if I may ask; what was the cost of your manufacture, Miss Wingrove?'

Megan smiled. 'Just over two million dollars.'

'Thank you,' said the Judge. 'And thank you for a most interesting . . . ah . . . exposition. Mr. Blakeney, if you would like to carry on. . . .'

'Thank you, M'Lord.' Richard walked forward to the box. 'Megan, will you tell us, once more in your own way, what happened after you joined the Davenport household?'

'Of course. For some time, some months, I was shown off to everybody. Mr. Davenport used to give a lot of parties. Some of them went on all night. All his friends wanted to see me, and I suppose he was naturally rather proud of me. He bought me a lot of things, clothes and dresses. Oh, and I learned to dance. That was very easy.'

'I see. So things ran smoothly for a time.'

'Yes.'

'What did Mrs. Davenport think of your arrival?'

'She was very pleased. It meant a lot to her, the . . . social distinction and all that. She told me once I was a walking, talking stat-symbol that beat all her friends down flat.'

An angry sound from the opposition desk. Martensson looked momentarily like interrupting, and thought better of it. In the court, van Mechelren grinned broadly.

'But after that,' said Richard, 'things took a turn for the worse?'

Martensson made his objection, noisily. 'Counsel is leading the w——' He stopped, realising the trap into which he'd fallen. Judge Hayward regarded him clinically. 'You wish to register an objection, Mr. Martensson?'

'No,' said the counsel for the plaintiff huffily. 'Not at this time. . . .'

'You'd better sit down then. Proceed, Mr. Blakeney.'

'Thank you, M'Lord.' Richard turned back to Megan. 'After that?' he prompted.

'Mrs. Davenport became . . . difficult. There were scenes. She said Mr. Davenport had no right setting me up to . . . make a laughing stock of her. It was over the dresses he'd bought, she didn't want me to have them. She said he didn't under- stand her and he didn't care about her. She wanted to send me back. He said I'd cost him two million, and he was going to get his use from me.'

'And after that?'

'She got . . . vindictive. She used to keep me up working till all hours. She tried to get me to do things that would damage me. Once she made me use a cleaning fluid that burned my hands. I had to go back to the Institute for grafting.'

'A charming preoccupation,' said Richard. 'But things didn't stay like that, did they?'

'No. They became much worse.'

'In what way?'

Megan hesitated. 'The . . . scenes became more violent. Once Mr. Davenport said he was sorry he'd ever married her. He said he'd sooner . . . sooner be married to a Synth, any day

of the week, than a human. I think that was what first put the
idea in his mind.'

'What idea?'

'Of teaching me poetry. He'd . . . take me driving, up on
Top Level. There were birds and flowers and trees. . . . It was
very beautiful. He'd take me to . . . cafeterias, and sit and talk.
Nobody ever knew I wasn't . . . real.'

'And why do you think he was doing all this?'

'To get away from his wife. He told me once if it wasn't
for me he'd . . . shoot himself.'

'Did he often become depressed? Speak of taking his life?'

'Yes. He was very . . . sensitive about his work. He used to
say whenever he sold a portrait, it was one more nail in the
coffin of Art. He wanted to . . . paint as he felt, not what the
sitters expected to see. He painted me once.'

'Clothed?'

'Yes.'

'Did Mrs. Davenport see the portrait?'

'Yes. She wasn't supposed to. There was another row.'

'And what happened?'

'She had it burned.'

'I see. Who destroyed it?'

'She made me do it.'

'Was it a good portrait?'

'Yes,' said Megan gently. 'It was the best work he'd done.'

Richard let a few seconds elapse. Then, 'And all this time
you were learning poetry? At the request of Mr. Davenport?'

'Not just poetry. I was reading a great deal. Mostly from the
Old Masters.'

'Was this also at Mr. Davenport's instigation?'

'Partly. Partly for my own interest.' Megan smiled. 'I
have a programmed bias to independent research.'

'Did Mrs. Davenport ever read?'

'Yes.'

'What type of material?'

'The fashion glossies.'

'Nothing else?'

'No.'

'Did she ever discuss Mr. Davenport's work with him?'

'She used to complain his prices weren't high enough.'

'Was that her sole interest in his calling?'

'Yes.'

'I can understand his preoccupation with suicide,' said Richard. 'Now can we move forward to the night of July fourteenth, when the incident we've heard described is alleged to have taken place?'

Megan waited.

'Describe it, please, in your own words.'

'Mr. Davenport had been . . . drinking heavily. His wife was away. He'd taken to drinking quite a lot. He called me several times through the day and talked. Once he asked me to go out and fetch him some more Scotch. He'd just about run through what was in the house.'

'What happened then?'

'He . . . drank it,' said the Synth unsteadily. 'Most all of it anyway. I asked him if he needed anything else. He said no, I was to go to bed. He said I was a . . . good girl, nobody else understood him.'

'And then?'

'I did as I was told. While I was . . . undressing, he came to the door. I let him in. He said there was . . . something he'd missed out on. He said he believed a man could fall in love with me.'

'And?'

'He kissed me,' said Megan quietly.

The court was silent; in the stillness the purring of the trivvyrigs was clearly audible. Van Mechelren, eyes narrowed, was watching like a hawk.

'What happened then?'

'He made me unbutton my blouse and lie on the bed with him. He . . . kissed my breasts, and said I was a goddess, and had ichor in my veins instead of blood. He said I was . . . warm, and lovely, and it was the first time he'd ever been happy. He started to cry.'

'And then?'

'He went to sleep.' Megan paused fractionally. 'He was very drunk. . . .'

From somewhere, a titter. Judge Hayward rapped angrily.

'I see. And that was all that took place between you?'

'Yes.'

'Tell me. . . .' The counsel leaned on the box. 'During this time, when Mr. Davenport lay asleep in your arms, were you conscious of doing wrong?'

The Synth frowned. 'I was conscious,' she said finally, 'of an unhappy situation. But I was not a free agent.'

'In what respect were you not free?'

'I was programmed to obey Mr. Davenport. He was my owner.'

'Thank you,' said Richard. 'Thank you very much.' He turned to the court. 'A great deal has been inferred,' he said, 'about the events that took place in the Davenport home prior to the separation which is the cause of our present proceedings. You have now heard, from an incontrovertible source, the truth of the affair; and a very innocent truth it seems to be. Mrs. Davenport lived for many months in a withdrawn and vicious world of her own, a prey to jealousy and insecurity, a drain on her husband's patience and emotions. That she and not the defendant instituted a campaign of mental torture is surely in no doubt. Ladies and gentlemen, a man of the calibre of Mr. Davenport needs understanding above all else. That understanding, that reassurance, was deliberately withheld. And Mr. Davenport, hungry for some comfort, resorted to the only person he knew who would exercise a compassion, a *humanity* towards him. That that person was a synthetic product, a thing not of flesh and blood but of plastic and steel, is a sad reflection on ourselves. But resort he did; and innocently, like a child afraid of the dark. For this, he has surely been punished enough already.'

He smiled at Megan. 'Thank you, Miss Wingrove. I have no more questions for you.'

'One moment. . . .'

Judge Hayward inclined his head. 'Mr. Martensson?'

'Permission to cross-examine, M'Lord?'

Richard shrugged mentally. If he'd thought Martensson would miss out on this one, the hope had been wild and wilful.

The counsel for the plaintiff took his time about approaching the box. When he finally addressed Megan, his first question was explosive. 'Miss Wingrove,' he said quietly. '*Were you in love with your owner?*'

'Objection!' Richard bobbed agitatedly. 'The question is semantically confusing. The phrase doesn't allow of a precise definition; Miss Wingrove is therefore unequipped to answer.'

'None the less,' said Judge Hayward after a pause, 'I feel in the interests of fairness an answer should be attempted.'

'*Objection!*'

The Lord Chief Justice looked, and was, annoyed. 'Mr. Blakeney?'

'Is Your Lordship aware,' said Richard quickly, 'that a finding for the plaintiff would in all probability result in the destruction of the Synthetic personage known as Megan Wingrove?'

A ripple of interest. Van Mechelren, watching carefully, pursed his lips and elevated his eyebrows.

'Mr. Blakeney,' said Judge Hayward with some asperity, 'the court is not unsympathetic to the problems involved here. But I must stress that such a supposition can hardly be our concern at the present time. It must certainly not be allowed to influence these proceedings.'

'M'Lord,' said Richard, 'Miss Wingrove must not be compelled to make a statement inherently damaging to herself.'

'You do appreciate,' said the Judge, 'that the . . . ah . . . witness is not under oath?'

'I do, M'Lord. My objection stands.'

Judge Hayward considered long and carefully. Then,

'Upheld,' he said. 'Mr. Martensson, will you rephrase your question?'

'M'Lord.' The counsel turned back to Megan. 'In your previous testimony you referred on several occasions to your private feelings. Of pride, pleasure, unhappiness, etcetera. What feelings did you have towards Mr. Davenport?'

Silence, while Megan considered.

'Were your feelings towards him friendly, or otherwise?'

'Friendly, I think. I . . . find it difficult to answer.'

'Why?'

'I was programmed to obey him,' said Megan simply. 'He was my owner. . . .'

Martensson was too old a hand to force an inconclusive issue. He bowed briefly to the bench. 'No more questions, M'Lord.'

Richard rose quietly. 'Permission to re-examine, M'Lord?'

'Granted.'

Counsel studied the jury carefully. 'Megan Wingrove, by her own testimony, is incapable of abetting even indirectly the infliction of mental pain. Her purpose, her only purpose, is to serve the race that conceived her and gave her birth. *She is a machine. . . .*'

He paused, significantly. 'No further proof should be needed of the absurdity of any allegation of misconduct. Yet my colleague appears unconvinced. If there exists in the mind of anyone here present the least shadow of doubt, it is my duty to dispel it. The Synth, Megan Wingrove, lay down with her owner. Because he ordered her to. That we make no attempt to deny. But she also burned the flesh from her hands by dipping them into a caustic cleaning fluid. *Because she was ordered to.* Because that is her function and her purpose. *To obey.* Now, Megan . . .'

The Synth raised her head.

'You obeyed your owner,' said Richard. 'And your owner's wife. Will you obey any human-originated order not damaging to another human?'

Meg nodded slowly. 'That is the purpose for which I was designed.'

'Will you obey me?'

A pause. Then, 'Yes. . . .'

From his pocket the counsel took a knife. A touch on the handle and the blade slid into place with an audible hard snap. He walked across the court to lay the weapon on the edge of the witness box, and returned to his place. 'Megan,' he said, 'in front of you is a knife. It's very sharp. Pick it up, please.'

The Synth hesitantly did as she was told.

Richard took a deep breath. 'Now,' he said, 'listen carefully. I want you to cut off your left hand, at the wrist. Do you understand?'

Megan stared blankly, lips parted. Van Mechelren leaned forward again intently. There was total silence.

Richard's voice crackled suddenly. 'You heard me, Megan. *Sever your wrist. . . .*'

The Synth started slightly, then lifted an arm to the edge of the witness box. Above her a trivvyrig swooped, predatory and sudden. The knifeblade touched flesh, trembled, started to saw. A trickle of some lubricant splashed her dress, ran golden across one knee; tendons showed, pinpoints of brightness.

'*Stop!*'

Richard walked forward, fingers clasped behind him. 'You will not cut off your hand,' he said. 'Instead, you will behead yourself.'

The knife moved in an uncertain arc to the girl's jaw.

'*Stop!*'

This time the interruption came from the Lord Chief Justice himself. 'Mr. Blakeney,' he said acidly, 'must the court endure this unpleasant and pointless exhibition?'

The counsel bowed. 'The point, M'Lord,' he said, 'has I believe been made; and the exhibition is finished.' Then to Megan, 'You may put the knife down now. I shall not ask you to destroy yourself.'

She relinquished the blade, trembling with reaction. Van

Mechelren sat back, giving a flicker of a smile. The thing had been nicely timed; another few seconds and Meg's inbuilt defence systems would have pulled the plug, throwing her into stasis. InterNatMech Synths were all conditioned against self-immolation, for obvious commercial reasons.

A quick glance at the faces of the jury showed Richard a mingling of pity with disgust. 'Ladies and gentlemen,' he said quietly. 'I put this to you as intelligent and responsible people. Could that creature'—he raised an arm at the Synth —'that thing devoid of will, of fear, insensible to pain, passionless . . . a machine, that could have been destroyed at any time by a gesture, a word . . . could *that* have broken a home, shattered lives? Is *that* the reason, the sole reason, why we are here in this court?

'I suggest most strongly that that is not the case. The reasons of this affair, the passions that culminated here, are no concern of the thing you see in front of you. I propose to show you, ladies and gentlemen, something of those passions. For that purpose, I recall Mrs. Ira Davenport to the stand. Thank you, Miss Wingrove, you may get down——'

'M'Lord. . . .' Martensson, on his feet, was smiling nastily. 'With the permission of the bench, I would like to re-cross . . .'

Judge Hayward looked enquiringly at Richard. The counsel bowed and sat down, hoping for the best and fearing the worst.

'We have heard,' said Martensson deliberately, 'the account of a machine. We have heard what it did, and said, and saw. We have seen, in this court, something of the nature of that machine; and we admit readily that the exhibition staged by my learned friend was both . . . ah . . . gory and convincing.'

He smiled at Richard. The counsel for the defendant scowled back.

Martensson took a pace up the courtroom and turned. 'Yet,' he said, 'surely there still remains some doubt. A machine . . .' He stared Megan up and down. 'A machine of great loveliness. A thing of incredibly delicate construction, a poised,

balanced, almost dare we say a *living* entity? . . . Machine?
The doubt, ladies and gentlemen, must remain.

'We have heard the testimony of one of the world's leading
experts on Synthetic humans. Yet there too a doubt remains;
for Mr. van Mechelren himself'—he stressed the 'Mr.' nastily—
'when pressed, owned himself not totally sure of his ground.
Machine? One wonders. . . .'

He took from his pocket a folded sheet of paper, turned to
Megan with it in his hand. 'My dear,' he said. 'I propose to
test a further aspect of your . . . ah . . . remarkable talents. It has
been given in evidence that Mr. Davenport is extremely fond
of poetry. Did he perhaps inculcate into your . . . ah . . . *circuits* some such similar feeling? Could a *machine* speak the
words of poetry, which so often are the words of love?'

Richard, sitting impassively, suppressed a desire to bury his
face in his hands. The pit yawned; it was black and it was deep,
and its bottom was hideously spiked.

'Six hundred years ago,' said the prosecutor, 'William
Shakespeare penned what has since come to be accepted as one
of the ultimate expressions of human love. I refer of course to
Romeo and Juliet. You are acquainted with the play? It did I
trust figure in your . . . ah . . . self-imposed course of studies?'

Quietly. 'Yes, sir.'

'Will you quote from it briefly, Miss Wingrove? Act
Three, scene two, line . . . nineteen, I think will serve. . . .'

Megan's lips moved. Her voice gained volume.

> '*Come, night! Come, Romeo! Come, thou day in night!*
> *For thou wilt lie upon the wings of night,*
> *Whiter than new snow on a raven's back.*
> *Come, gentle night; come, loving, black-brow'd night,*
> *Give me my Romeo; and when he shall die,*
> *Take him and cut him out in little stars,*
> *And he will make the face of heaven so fine*
> *That all the world will be in love with night,*
> *And pay no worship to the garish sun. . . .*'

'Thank you,' said the counsel for the plaintiff. 'Now did you also by any chance run across the twentieth-century playwright Dylan Thomas?'

The fierce, erotic beauty of the *Winter's Tale*; the bawdy lustiness of *Under Milk Wood*. The Synth's voice, husking and limping, seemed to have some spell to quieten the court and the long public galleries. Martensson conducted her neatly, through Shelley and Keats to Tennyson, Byron; John Donne completed the rot. The counsel silenced her finally, waving his hands for quiet. 'Beautiful words,' he said slowly, into the hush that remained. 'Beautiful, immortal words of passion and love; and beautifully spoken. *By a machine! . . .*'

He slammed his way to his desk, and sat down. Richard, rising to conclude his case, remembered an ancient gag. The punch line was, *Wait till you nod your head. . . .*

'Mrs. Davenport,' said Blakeney, 'I would like you, if you would, to tell the court a little about your early life.'

Ira opened her mouth uncertainly, and closed it again.

'You were born,' said Richard, consulting a sheaf of notes, 'on May the eighth, twenty-one thirty-seven, in Montreal, Canada. The youngest of four children. Am I correct?'

'Yes. . . .'

'Tell me about your early life.'

Again a silence.

'Come now,' said Richard encouragingly. 'Anything you remember.'

'Yes. My . . . father died when I was eight, and after that we came back to England. When I was——'

'One moment.' Richard held up his hand. 'What was your father's profession, Mrs. Davenport?'

'Objection!' Martensson glared at his adversary. 'I fail to see how an investigation into the past of the plaintiff can assist in any way.'

The Lord Chief Justice looked quizzically at Richard.

'M'Lord,' said the counsel for the defendant, 'my purpose

is to uncover and explain the motivation behind the charge levelled at Henry Davenport. Such motivation can only be understood in the light of a closer analysis of the past experiences of the plaintiff.'

'Objection overruled,' said the Judge. 'Proceed. . . .'

Martensson sat down, red-faced with annoyance.

Richard returned to the attack. 'Your father's profession, Mrs. Davenport?'

'He was a . . . steel erector. He worked on m-most of the big developments about that time. The tiering of Vancouver, Toronto . . . here and there, all over. . . .'

Richard nodded amiably. 'Steel erecting's a tough job I guess, Mrs. Davenport. Tough on the nerves, tough on the man. Wouldn't you agree?'

No answer.

'A lot of men just can't take it,' went on the counsel easily. 'The nerves go, after a time. But they still have to keep their families, don't they? They have to go on. . . .'

'I——'

'And your father was one of them, wasn't he, Mrs. Davenport? One of the guys that couldn't take it?'

'He was a . . . a good man,' she said. 'A good man, I won't hear bad talk about him. He was good to us, Pop was. Good to all the kids. He kept right on going, right to the end. He didn't give up——'

'Mrs. Davenport,' interrupted the counsel, 'your father died, at the early age of forty-nine, from alcoholic poisoning. Is this not correct?'

'*Objection!*'

'Mr. Martensson?'

'Counsel is needlessly maligning the witness.'

'The facts are on public record, M'Lord,' said Richard. 'That's where I got 'em from.'

'I must warn you,' said the Lord Chief Justice, 'the court does not approve of this method of approach. We deal in facts; in this instance the facts concerning and relating to the marriage of Mrs. Davenport to her husband. You must justify the relevance of your questions.'

Richard's best acts were frequently impromptu. He walked to the middle of the court; standing there, he tore the notes he carried into fragments and scattered them slowly and impressively round his feet. 'M'Lord,' he said, 'greater issues depend on this case than the alimony awarded, or not awarded, against a man called Henry Davenport. The bench is aware that a finding for the plaintiff would imply the destruction of Megan Wingrove——'

'We've been through all that before,' snapped Judge Hayward. 'The matter is totally irrelevant to the case in hand. I am not accustomed, sir,' he added bitingly, 'to repeating my rulings during an action.'

Richard felt on the point of explosion. The Muse was definitely with him. 'Once, M'Lord,' he said, 'many centuries ago in a little town called Athens, a woman was condemned to death. She was reprieved; because counsel tore her shift, and asked the people there, "*Can we kill this?* . . ." ' He turned to Megan; at a gesture, she stood up quietly. 'I wish,' he said, 'I could tear, not the shift, but the veil over a brain. A wonderful thing of gold and glass and steel, perhaps the most vital of its kind in the world. Beside this, against the fear I, all of us feel here for this . . . strange machine, anything is relevant. . . .'

The Lord Chief Justice coughed dryly. 'I find your reasoning obscure,' he said, 'and based on assumptions suspect in the extreme.' A pause. Then, 'You may continue, Mr. Blakeney. But carefully, carefully. . . .'

'Thank you, M'Lord. . . .' Richard turned back to Ira. 'After the death of your father your family fell on hard times. Money was scarce, jobs few and hard to get, none of the children really old enough to earn. So your mother supported her family'—he paused, significantly—'in the only way she was able. The only way she knew——'

'Objection! . . .'

'Mr. Martensson?'

'Pointless innuendo,' snarled counsel for the plaintiff. 'If my colleague intends to descend to mud-hurling . . .'

The first slip. Richard flung himself at his opponent. 'M'Lord, I am unable to understand the remarks of learned counsel. Mrs. Davenport's mother supported her family in the only way known to her; by continued hard work. Of course if counsel is in possession of facts unknown to me his reticence is understandable——'

'*My Lord!* . . .'

'Be quiet,' said the Judge. 'Both of you, you're wrangling like a pair of cats in an alley. Mr. Martensson, do you intend to press your objection?'

The counsel for the plaintiff looked as if he was swallowing cyanide. 'Objection withdrawn,' he said finally. 'Withdrawn. . . .'

Richard surveyed the court. 'In the only way known to her,' he said deliberately. Ira's old woman had been a whore all right; that made the point. He consolidated his triumph quickly. 'Mrs. Davenport, how many times in all have you been married?'

A long wait.

'Since you do not reply,' said Richard, 'I must acquaint the court myself. This is your third marriage, is it not?'

No answer.

'You do not deny that? Good. You were first married at the age of nineteen to a Mr. Aaron Shapeira of Maine, New England, a company director and a manufacturer of aqualung equipment and diving apparatus for the United States Department of Defense. An able, ambitious man whose luck unfortunately was not as good as it might have been. Shortly after your marriage Mr. Shapeira, encouraged possibly by you, began to expand his business. All went well for two years; then the loss of a major contract, the supplying of diving gear to the then-new Atlantic Project, America's first seabed town, left Mr. Shaperia as our friends across the water say "out on a limb". With the collapse of the company you obtained a divorce——'

'Objection——'

'Public record,' said Richard tiredly.

'Now don't start that again,' snapped the Lord Chief Justice. 'I have already warned you once, Mr. Blakeney. You must not draw unsubstantiated inferences.'

'I draw no inference, M'Lord, I merely allow the facts to speak for themselves.'

'*Hmmpph.* Proceed. . . .'

'Your reasons then as now were mental cruelty,' said Richard, 'coupled with a charge of adulterous conduct by Mr. Shapeira with a Puerto Rican woman; a charge which in fact was never substantiated. You next marriage was to a Monsieur Lefevre, a French businessman trading in England and the United States under the name of UniSupply, and closely associated with the CentSup distribution service. That lasted considerably longer; then finally there was unpleasantness. Condemned meat somehow got tangled with CentSup's supply; there were some minor outbreaks of food poisoning, a death or two——'

'That wasn't my f-fault! He was a . . . crook, a con-man. . . . How was I to know? . . .' Ira started to sniff, wadding a handkerchief in her fingers.

'Exactly, Mrs. Davenport: for once you yourself were taken for a ride. However, while your husband's case was pending you managed to meet in London one Henry Aloysius Davenport, an up-and-coming artist. A man of taste and distinction, a man with a future. . . .'

'He was good to me,' exploded Ira. 'I . . . didn't know what to do, where to t-turn. . . . I wanted to . . . kill myself. . . .'

'But you were saved your painful decision,' snarled Richard, 'by the timely intervention of your current husband, who one night in a Paris flat put into his mouth the muzzle of a point-three-eight automatic and succeeded in depressing the trigger. Just what sort of hell did you administer, Mrs. Davenport, to drive him to that?'

'*Objection!*'

'Question withdrawn,' said Richard instantly. He turned back to the witness. 'Mrs. Davenport, I suggest that many years ago a girl of poor family, ashamed of her background, of her father, of everything connected with her home, made a vow. That she would never again know loneliness, or hunger, or need. That she would move one day in the top circles of the land. That she would wear furs, Mrs. Davenport, and gold, and jewels. And I submit from that time on she dedicated herself, cold-bloodedly, to the realisation of her dream. But she found that as she grasped at them happiness and security eluded her, destroyed by the very things she had thought would secure them. Money, and influence, and social position. So that always she had to grasp higher and higher, reach for more and more. I suggest the history of that girl, your history, Mrs. Davenport, is a record of shameless and soulless social climbing. I suggest you discarded husbands one after the other, as they ceased to serve their purpose——'

'It wasn't like that! They didn't understand me, nobody understood me——'

'Until finally,' stormed Richard, 'you got what you wanted. What you thought was rightfully yours. A man of sensitivity, and culture, and wealth. And what happened, Mrs. Davenport? You found you couldn't keep him. Because you weren't his equal, madam, and you never will be. Not in a thousand years. You couldn't talk to him, Mrs. Davenport, you couldn't make him a home. You couldn't back him because you couldn't understand him. Maybe you never even tried. And you found in the end a machine was ousting you from his attentions; a thing not difficult to do, because for your husband you had nothing to offer. That was the final blow for you, wasn't it? That you lost out to a machine, that you were lower and less account than the Synth called Megan Wingrove. And you made another vow, didn't you?

That the machine must be destroyed. Regardless of misery, regardless of cost. A cheap revenge, Mrs. Davenport, but one that suits you very well. Because you are cheap, madam. You started from the gutter; *and at heart you never left it——*'

'*Objection!*'

'Mr. Blakeney . . .' The voice of the Lord Chief Justice cut through the noise from the public gallery. 'You have repeatedly been warned against the maligning of the present witness. I shall warn you no more. I instruct that your last remark be removed from the record of these proceedings; and I will have you understand, further and finally, that if you persist in your approach I shall hold you in contempt of court.'

Richard revolved slowly to survey his victim. 'Thank you, M'Lord,' he said finally. 'I have no more questions for the . . . witness.' He turned his back deliberately while Ira, snivelling well, was removed from the stand.

He stayed quiet so long, head down and brooding, that His Lordship was compelled to address him. 'Mr. Blakeney,' said Judge Hayward testily, 'are we to take it you have concluded the case for the defence?'

Richard looked up and smiled. 'Not quite, M'Lord,' he said. 'I wish to call Henry Aloysius Davenport.'

A rustle of curiosity as the artist took the stand. Richard let the interest build before he turned to address him. Even then he took his time. 'Mr. Davenport,' he said finally. 'I had intended to question you, draw from you the last fragments of truth concerning this unhappy affair. But this I find myself unable to do. You stand condemned, sir; you must realise, as I realise, that this case is lost. . . .'

Uproar in the court; a fluttering of consternation on the opposition desk. Martensson's jaw sagged with shock; his eyebrows retreated towards his hair. Henry Aloysius himself looked to be on the point of collapse. He stared at Richard dazedly as the counsel approached the box.

Blakeney had evidently taken complete leave of his senses.

'Mr. Davenport,' he said, as soon as he could make himself heard, 'believe me when I say I speak now not as counsel or as an officer of this court, but as a friend. And in that capacity I tell you, there is only one course for you to follow.' He turned back to the court. 'Through all the untold years that men have fought and dreamed and died on this planet we call Earth the thinkers among them, the philosophers and poets, the artists, have sought for one ideal. One illusion. The perfect woman, selfless, beautiful, ageless, her soul untainted by the evils of the flesh, unmarked by lust or greed. The ideal, the dream, shone from a million pairs of starry eyes; Circe and Venus Anadyomene, Helen of Troy, Bathsheba, Cleopatra . . . chimeras all, they beckoned, they promised, they lured. But the search, like the grim cause of Art itself, was doomed as is any striving for beauty, for truth. For the hands of woman are red with blood, her heart drowned in rapacity, her face padded on a laughing skull. You, Mr. Davenport, and all your breed of dreamers, will find no solace in the minds of your fellows: for there is none to be had. No solace and no comfort. *Comfort yourself,* as a poet once remarked; *what comfort is in me?'*

Henry's world seemed to be collapsing in a crashing tumult of bells. His eyes began to bulge, his face changed from white to a deepening crimson. He gripped the edge of the box, still unable to believe the evidence of his ears.

Richard's voice rose triumphantly. 'But after all that, the long ages of groping and needing and dying unfulfilled, an answer was made. Yes, made, Mr. Davenport, and made by men; by scientists and engineers.'

He pointed dramatically at Megan. 'There, after so many empty years, lies your salvation, your perfection. Your Venus, uncorrupted and incorruptible, the timeless Virgin, your *alter ego*, your *doppelganger*. There is your solace; the only solace to be had in an indifferent and brutalised world, a place chained and bound forever by the sins of the Parents of men. Mr. Davenport, ignore censure. Be damned to consequence, close your ears to the lowing of the herd. Take your salvation and be happy again; as you once were, all too briefly, before——'

A week of strain had left Henry's always precarious control in fragments. He whooped for breath, and it seemed suddenly the noise in his ears turned to laughter. Laughter that might spread across a country, across the world. He cracked; for a moment it looked as if he might begin to weep or just faint quietly away, then a more basic instinct gained the upper hand. He aimed at his persecutor's head a mighty blow; Richard prudently dropped flat, and instantly the court was a chaos of noise. Judge Hayward rose, glasses in hand and mouth ajar; Troopers, riotsticks swinging, scurried forward; Henry, pinned by spotlights and encircled by trivvyrigs, glared round wildly. His voice pierced the uproar in snatches, pitched on a thin high note of rage.

'*Don't laugh....*' He took another ineffectual swipe at a trivvyrig that surged back out of reach. He gripped his aching head, pulled at his hair. 'Venus,' he babbled. 'Helen of Troy....' His glazed glance caught Megan, standing shocked and still. He was out of the witness box with startling speed and scurrying across the floor. Blakeney, well placed to intercept him, made no move. 'What do you think you are?' squalled the artist. 'Did you think I wanted you? Were you laughing too? Nobody want's you. *Machine!* ...' A Trooper grappled with him; Henry reeled under the outstretched arms. He slapped at Megan, bringing her hair out of its grips. She rocked, making no attempt to avoid the blows. 'Did you think I couldn't do any better?' panted Henry. 'Was that it? Did you think I wanted you? I'll show you what you are. Where's your cogs, your gears? ... Why don't you ... blow apart, spill 'em out across the floor? ... Machine ... *machine, machine, machine....*'

Her blouse was ripped; trivvyrigs, swirling eagerly, obscured the details of the battle. Troopers grabbed the artist finally and pinned him, hauled him, legs kicking, from his victim. Megan squirmed from the fracas and ran, hands to her head. Twenty yards away she staggered. In her brain, inside the meshings of gold, the swirl and buzz of electrons, a breaker snapped apart. She dropped into stasis.

Van Mechelren, moving for all his bulk like well-greased lightning, caught her before she hit the floor.

On the opposition desk an anxious conference was taking place; Ira insistent, pounding on the grained wood with her fist, Martensson shaking his head and waving his arms. As order was restored he approached the bench of the Lord Chief Justice, talked agitatedly. Richard waited, leaning on his desk. A sharp question from Judge Hayward, an agonised nodding from the counsel for the plaintiff, and the Judge cleared his throat. 'I am given to understand,' he said frostily, 'that the plaintiff wishes to withdraw her case. *Is this correct?*'

Dead silence.

'Yes,' said Ira, exultantly. 'Yes. . . .'

Blakeney released pent-up breath in a long whistle of relief. It had had to work. Ira had seen her husband crawl, and the machine that had plagued her was dead. She wouldn't risk the Little Nell act again now, not if she could avoid it; she was getting just a little too long in the tooth. . . . Richard sat down to take the strain off his quivering knees. He grinned weakly, and caught a look from Martensson that was purest vitriol.

'My feelings,' said the Lord Chief Justice, 'at the wasting of the time of this court and its officers, in the prosecution of what I am compelled to describe as a personal vendetta, are probably best left unrecorded. However, under the circumstances forced on me I have no alternative but to assent.' He rapped sharply on the bench. '*Case dismissed. . . .*'

The court went wild again.

Counsel for the defendant overtook his client in the turmoil of the emptying public seats. Ira was hanging on to Henry's arm, crowing and posing for the trivvyrigs. The artist bared his teeth.

'Hank,' said Richard a little desperately, 'Hank, I'm sorry but . . . you wanted out, you're OUT. Look, Hank, I don't lose cases. Nobody'd crack, it just had to be you. . . ,'

Henry Aloysius swore blisteringly. 'Send me your bill,' he said, 'then keep out of my sight. I'll come to your funeral. Don't let it be too long. . . .' The mob, swirling, bore him and his wife away.

Van Mechelren paced slowly, down and back across the little room, one arm round Megan, her hand gripping his shoulder. His fingers, low on her hip, felt the electric trembling as she tried for control. 'Make it work, sweetie,' he said. 'Make it work . . . You ever come out the clips before?'

'No, I . . . I don't think so . . .'

'Make it work,' he said. 'There, is good . . . Gimme spherical volume formula now, quick . . .'

'Sphere equals . . . sphere equals four over three times, times phi, by radius cubed . . .'

'Value of phi?'

'Just a . . . a minute . . .'

'No. While you walk, please . . .'

'Like . . . patting my head and rubbing my stomach,' she said foggily. 'Phi is . . . oh hell . . . three point one five . . . no, one four . . . one four, one five nine . . . approximations twenty-two over seven, three five five over. . . over one one three . . .'

'Ach, good,' he said. '*Good.* You're O.K. You be all right.'

'Pieter,' she said. 'I was in love with him. God, *I was in love with him* . . .'

'I know,' he said. 'Here, you sit now.' He steered her to a chair, stood in front of her, hands on knees, frowning and shaking his head. 'How you do it?' he asked. 'You bloody mess o' plastic an' glass, how you make it happen?'

She shook her head dazedly. 'I don't know. I just wanted him . . .'

'Play it quiet,' said van Mechelren. 'You're off the hook now, tak' it quiet.'

He scratched an ear, pensively. 'In Amsterdam,' he said, 'is boats still, an' trees. Oh, pretty . . . not like this dump. It's nice, you like it there. But Christ, we got a lot to do. You first of a kind, you know that? We gotta see just how you tick. We gotta have a lot more tickin', just like you . . .' He put a finger under her chin and turned her face. 'O.K.?'

'Yes,' she said. 'Yes, O.K. . . .'

She 'felt' his hand on her shoulder.

The Pace That Kills

The car left the motorway with a prolonged shrieking of rubber on macadam and plunged down the thirty-odd feet of embankment shedding chunks of pink plastic padding as it rolled. Tinker swore violently and uselessly and steered his own vehicle onto the hard shoulder beside the twenty-foot gap in the barrier. He swung out and Johnny Morris followed, threshing his way from the cramped and illegal cockpit.

There was a bright, scorched smell. Way off down the grass the car had come to rest, lying on what was left of its roof. Three wheels thrust supplicatingly into the air; the fourth was two hundred yards away and still rolling, flashing back the sun, as brightly pink as a baby's fresh-scrubbed backside. Round the car too were scraps of pinkness, shreds torn from the safety cushioning. The ripped plastic was redder toward the centre, nastily organic. Smoke was drifting; Johnny saw the quick gout of an autoextinguisher. He leaned on the broken fencing and gulped, not wanting to move closer, seeing and hearing with the heightened perception of shock.

Tinker was already nearly at the wreck, half-running on the slope, turning back to wave and yell distantly. Johnny saw him stoop over the crumpled car and wave again. His own legs moved, pumping unwillingly, driving him forward and down across the grass. Behind him on the motorway the SafeTiPeds gurgled and bleated. The wreck was out of sight but the vehicle on the hard standing would raise a buzzing shoal of complaints once the Roadusers reached the nearest of the Tattleboxes. The whole thing was crazy; Johnny wanted out and knew he couldn't go.

The smell was worse where the slobbering of the extinguishers had killed the fire. A girl was lying in the wreck, seeming broken apart by the straps and bands of it that held her. Here a wrist, there an ankle; hair, and blood. The blood was startlingly bright against the grass. Tinker was pulling and swearing; there were metal cutters in the car they'd left, no time to go back. Another extinguisher blew, wetting Johnny's shoulder. He pulled at a wire that was tight round the victim's arm. Above on the road was the wailing of a siren.

Tinker was prising at a twisted subframe, shoulders flexing, the sweat standing on his forehead. The thing groaned, broke with a snap. Johnny unwound the wire, the throttle linkage, working wrist-deep in foam, the foam hindering now more than it helped. Some of the bubbles touched blood and reacted, frothing pinkly. He hauled at the victim, hands locked under her, forearms squashing her breasts. Her head hung limp, showing him a white parting on the scalp where the heavy hair fell forward. Tinker was swearing again; Johnny concentrated on dragging the girl twenty yards from the motor he knew now wouldn't burn. The SafeTiPed still foamed desultorily, a bright self-salted slug.

There was blood on the girl's forearm and a great swatch of it across her face. It ran down her neck as they turned her, wetting bright halfmoons in the collar of her blouse. The cut was curved on her forehead, darker and glittering. Johnny's hands made a pad of a kerchief, pressed it against her face; he was vaguely surprised at what he had done without thought.

There were two vehicles now on the hard shoulder. The bulging safety pads of the van were buttercup yellow, the colour of the long-disbanded A.A. The two men trotting across the grass wore black uniforms decorated on cuff and capband with the same sinister gold. The foremost Warden seemed pointlessly to be blowing a whistle. He carried in his hand his baton of office; from time to time he paused to whirl it round his head. He stopped twenty feet from Johnny, glaring and whooping for breath, a sallow-faced little man with a drooping moustache and faded pale blue eyes. '*My Sector,*' he said half-hysterically. '*In my bleedin' Sector . . .*'

Tink was staring, eyes narrowed. *The car,* thought Johnny, still crouching. *No trouble. Remember the car . . .* The second patrolman was already poking in the ruins of the SafeTiPed. The hankie was bright and soaked; Johnny felt panic starting again. He said as quietly as he could, 'Will you call an ambulance?' The girl twitched. *Please God, not to let her wake up . . .* 'She's very badly hurt,' he said. 'Will you call an ambulance?'

'Moira Alice Kelly, Mr. Bigge,' said the Warden. 'Address erased . . .

'I'm in charge 'ere,' said the little man. 'Don't you go tellin' me what to do . . .' Tink's wrist was gripping Johnny's arm. Way off the ambulance was coming anyway, whickering over the grass. The Warden pulled the wet pad away. The cut looked as if it had grown. '*My Sector . . .*' he said again faintly. His head, bent close under Johnny's nose, smelled of floral hair oil.

His mate straightened up grunting, the red governorbox of the SafeTiPed in his hands. He dropped it down on the grass. The official seals were cut and bent away; the lid gaped, mute testimony of sin. The Warden hissed between his teeth. Something jiggling at his waist Johnny had taken for a first-aid kit; it was nothing of the sort. He watched helplessly while a plastic bag was pushed over the victim's mouth and nose. 'Initial breath analysis impractical,' intoned the minion of the law. His companion inscribed the statement in a leatherbound notebook, consulted the chronometer on his wrist and added the time. 'Wind south-south-west,' said Johnny faintly. 'B-backing . . .' Tinker squeezed his arm.

The helicopter landed. At last there were white coats, a stretcher, efficiency. The girl was lifted; she rolled her head, moaning a little now. A handbag lay on the grass, contents spilled. The hospital folk would have taken it, but it was confiscated by the Warden. He straightened slowly, icechip eyes glinting unpleasantly, wiping his fingers on a bandanna handkerchief. 'I will now check you,' he said to Johnny, using the singsong intonation of unlettered officialdom. 'In accordance with the powers invested in me by the Road Traffic Act of nineteen sixty-nine. *Ahem*. And subsequent Acts . . .'

Johnny swallowed, and inclined his head. 'Speed Kills, Masterwarden,' he said dutifully. 'I am ready to co-operate . . .'

Johnny and Tink solemnly inflated the little plastic bags, and watched while reagents failed to turn their contents mauve.

The warehouse was situated in an old and disreputable part of the city. Over its doors was inscribed the faded legend ATLAS MANUFACTURING CO. Above were lines of roundtopped windows, the panes cracked and grey with dirt. Through them showed faintly the brown sides of old cardboard boxes. There was an air of dilapidation and ennui, a harsh Buffet quality about the pavements wet with rain.

The car turned cumbrously to point its padded nose at the doors. They grumbled open; the motor passed within, edging between tall stacks of crates. At the rear of the place ten feet of whitewashed and cobweb-hung wall made themselves silently and surprisingly scarce. Beyond was a fluoro-lit workspace. The walls were hung with fanbelts, head gaskets and valve lifters, all the paraphernalia of a garage; a long bench was scattered with tools, in a corner of the floor was a boarded pit. The car parked beside another, a low shape swathed with dustsheets. The wall section slid back into place with a hissing of hydraulics; Tinker writhed his way from the cab. Johnny followed him, patting the padded bonnet of the motor as he passed. The plastic squeaked and shifted under his hand.

In one wall of the workshop was a locked door. Tinker fingered the combination; the door swung open, revealing beyond itself a spiral stair. He clattered down it, Johnny following. The stair gave onto a passageway. The walls were of rough brick, whitewashed and lit at intervals by low-wattage lamps. Somewhere air-conditioning plant hummed steadily; the plenum effect brushed Johnny's face with a cool breeze.

A further door, metal-sheathed, opened onto a wide, low room. The two pushed through it, stood a moment while their eyes became used to the dimness. The study reflected the complicated personality of its owner. Opposite them an aquarium tank glowed softly, tetras flashing like short circuits among the weed. One end of the place was given over to shelves and cases; books and models, stacked in profusion, constituted a portable and highly individual motoring museum. Beside it was an unmade camp bed; at its head, on a Pembroke table, stood a tantalus with decanters of water and Scotch. Other ancient pieces of furniture, a Georgian console table, a yew wood secretaire, Sheraton style and Queen Anne chairs, were grouped in front of walls of whitened brick; a russet carpet tied the scheme together. In the far corner of the place a desk, topped with dark green leather, was lit by a slim Anglepoise lamp. At the desk a man was sitting, back turned to the newcomers. They waited, unhappily. He let silence deepen before he spoke. Then, 'You're a right pair of nits, are you not?' the voice was cultured, flat and softly unstressed.

'Hanssen, I—'

Peter Hanssen swung his chair abruptly, feet clear of the floor, braked with his heels on the carpet. 'What were you driving?' he asked. 'What had you got on the road?'

'The Elan,' said Johnny unhappily. 'Look, Hanssen, it was j—'

'Just one of those things. Johnny, there's a draught. Do something about it.'

Johnny obediently closed his mouth.

Hanssen stubbed his cigarette, selected another from a box on the desk, inserted it carefully into an amber holder. 'I will kill you,' he said pleasantly, 'fry you *à la Maryland*, and eat you piece by tiny disgusting piece, the very next time you display your more than monumental, your more than profound, your truly cosmic idiocy. Do I make myself quite clear? Do I leave within your microscopic brains the faintest shadow of doubt?'

Johnny shook his head unhappily. Useless to ask Hanssen how he knew; he made it his business to know everything.

'One question,' said the other wearily. 'Could you not simply have driven past?'

'I—'

'Who was in fact at the wheel?'

Tinker shuffled his feet. 'I was . . .'

'All,' said Hanssen, 'is explained. You oversized bomb-head; how long did it take you to become as stupid as you are?' He waved a hand. 'Don't bother with the estimate. Switch the tube on, will you, let's hear the end of this un-savoury affair . . .'

The incident naturally took first place in the bulletin, preceding an eyewitness report of the dropping of a small atomic bomb on Ghana. 'At a few minutes after twelve hundred hours this morning,' said the newscaster heavily, 'an Accident took place in Sector Twelve, Subsection Five, of the Western London Traffic Zone. Masterwarden Horace J. Bigge, first to arrive on the scene of the disaster—'

'Liar—'

'*Sharrap!*'

'—described the scene as gory and hideous. The Victim, Moira Alice Kelly, address unknown, was flown by police helicopter to the St. Martins Centre of Social Sciences, where she is still seriously ill. The governorbox of the

SafeTiPed had been tampered with and the vehicle was described by witnesses, some of whom are still being treated for shock, as easily exceeding forty miles an hour. Mr. Bigge, interviewed at our London news studio, said afterward, "I can but repeat a phrase that by now should be known to all; Speed Kills. I hope, with my colleagues, that this dreadful proof will be taken afresh to the hearts of every man, woman and child in this grand old country of ours." Presented with a personal message of congratulation from the King, Mr. Bigge said, "I only done my duty." Asked to comment further the Transport Ministrix, The Honourable Mrs. Agatha Gladstone-Hadley, said, "I can but endorse the sentiments expressed by our officer Mr. Bigge, and add my congratulations to those of His Majesty. We must redouble our efforts; the past two years have seen no less than three fatal accidents and seven cases of serious injury on the roads. This shocking, this dreadful toll can and must be checked; the evil of Speed must finally be stamped out from our midst. Scientists at the ten-million-pound Centre of Road Safety are already examining the means by which the governor of the vehicle was reset—" '

Hanssen rose impatiently and turned off the screen. 'I've got it made,' said Tinker, jigging with delight. 'Stick of dynamite and a detonator. Start prodding round with the box and *poomph*. Look, Daddy, no hands...'

'Get lost,' said Hanssen tiredly. 'As a special favour to me. For one morning, you've done more than enough. Go on, scat, the pair of you. I've got work to do...'

The armoured door closed silently. Hanssen sighed, lit his cigarette, stuck the holder in the corner of his mouth and sat staring at nothing in the dim-lit study. Then he turned back to the desk, clicked a switch and picked up a microphone. 'Transcription, Connie,' he said. 'Notes for the Western Sector quarter-annual.' He cleared his throat. 'My friends,' he said. 'The history of our Party, and of the war between the Drivers and the Peds that has so sadly handicapped this country, falls easily into two distinct parts. Prior to the mid-sixties the record of road transport in England was simply one of incompetence, inefficiency, inadequacy and Governmental dishonesty. Administrations vied each with the next in devising new and viciously unfair methods of taxation; for the motoring public was considered, when it was considered at all, as the natural milch-cow of the bureaucratic state. Needless to say little of the money levied annually in tax was ever employed in road improvement, despite the efforts of such visionaries as the Honourable John Scott-Montagu, afterward Lord Montagu of Beaulieu, who as early as 1903 was pleading for recognition of the problems that would one day beset us all. The Motoring Act of that year, although enfranchising those pioneers who hitherto had taken their vehicles on the highway only under threat of arrest, was badly mutilated by the opponents of villainous petroleum; in fact the motor car would seem even at that early date to have established itself as a *leit-motif* in the perpetual war between the haves and the have-nots.

'After the middle nineteen-sixties events took a new and more sinister turn. The well-advanced necrosis of the country's system of road communication interacted with the final victory of bureaucracy over intelligence to produce a state of affairs hitherto alien to patterns of British thought and later to British theories of justice. The relatively minor issue of road deaths had first been seized on by the aptly-named yellow press and inflated to mountainous proportions as a handy way of filling front pages between child murders, Royal scandals and the autobiographies of whores; but since no bureaucracy ever managed unaided to check any trend within itself, however dangerous or bizarre, the matter finally became a major factor in the shaping of governmental policies. Conservatism must bear the blame for the first genuinely retrogressive legislation but the banner was borne forward most enthusiastically by the Socialists, who found the belabouring of the discriminating motorist a cheap and convenient way of demonstrating their Love for the Masses while at the same

9

time increasing by fines and by taxation the income to the country's exchequer.

'Another critical factor in the *débâcle* of commonsense was of course the class hatred that sprang up with such virulence in the so-called classless society of the mid-twentieth century. The phenomenon, often remarked at the time but never satisfactorily explained, can now be seen in perspective as the end result of a process that had begun a century earlier in the dark days of the industrial revolution. The rise to power of trade unionism had resulted with comparative suddenness in the creation of a plebeian ruling class, a political occurrence unique in British history. The reversal of fortunes had some odd side effects, not the least of which was the traumatic urge of the new aristocracy, who now owned more collective power than singly they had ever desired, to return to the uterine insignificance that for centuries had been their lot. That urge, regrettably, could never be fulfilled; instead the rulers of our True Democracy attempted to close unlooked-for vistas of thought by supporting any and all legislation aimed at enforcing greater conformity to mass ideals. For make no mistake, my friends, intellectual and economic uniformity were the principles truly invoked in 1966 and the years that followed. But what neither highbrow nor lowbrow realised (and there were many of both, on both sides of the fence) was that they abetted not their own parties but the painful groping to the light, the fell self-seeking, of Bureaucracy; that long-legged Beastie that had stalked the twentieth century, that brainless, joyless, sexless entity that owns no creed, that has no *raison d'être*, no faith but the Power of the State and of itself. The Thing in fact against which the British had so often gone to war . . .

'However that might be, the country saw a succession of speed limits that declined from an initial seventy in 1965 to a national maximum ten years later of forty miles an hour. Statistics, produced in a steady stream, vindicated the restrictions; and although the White Paper of 1975, summing up the results of the first ten years of control as an overall reduction in *per capita* accident rate of forty-five per cent, was later proved to have been based solely on figures for the Rural District of Stoke and Oxshott, little outcry was made. Possibly a more accurate estimate was that prepared by the then newly constituted Ministry of Road Safety, whose investigators found that over the half decade the law could definitely claim the saving of the lives of thirteen humans, four dogs and the Transport Minister's Persian cat. This of course was at the cost of eighteen governmental suicides and the murder by stoning, hanging, garotting and dropping in the Thames of thirty-five Traffic Wardens; but these statistics were naturally played down in the interests of the greatest good.

'Meanwhile the ratification of the Road Traffic Act of 1974 had changed the basic concept of British law. The Warden organisation, by this time completely autonomous, was armed, and given powers over the ordinary citizen that virtually amounted to life and death. Motorists could be accosted at all times, and were in fact frequently dragged from their beds to undergo breathalyser tests and other examinations of a more fundamental nature. The results, friends, lie all about us today. We stand condemned, murderers from the cradle to the grave; and in fact it could be said that Socialism, via its attack on that section of society labouring under the criminal tag of Motorists, first formulated and applied the civic definition of Original Sin.

'The end of course could not be indefinitely delayed. The introduction of an allover speed limit of twenty miles an hour, coupled with the passing of the Act enabling the Wardens to enforce the fitting of governorboxes to all road vehicles, finally toppled the adminstration of 1980, returning the Conservative government of 1981. The collapse was largely brought about by mass voting swings engineered in desperation by the unions controlling the savagely battered motor industry. The new administration started well, with a daring increase of the national speed limit to thirty-five; but a singularly disastrous foreign policy led almost at once to the collapse of the pound, annoying intensely the then Sheikh of Bahrein. His Highness finally pulled the plug, halving at one stroke the British gold reserve; it was a blow from which the national economy never recovered.

'The government fell; and the Socialist régime of 1982, largely we must suppose from pique, instantly nationalised the motor industry. It was the final straw. Barricades appeared in the streets of Oxford, Birmingham and Coventry while the Cowley Commune declared a state of anarchy and marshalled its forces for a mass attack on Whitehall. Desperate measures were taken, including a last-ditch attempt to sway the electorate by knighting several pop singers and reducing the voting age to fourteen. All were of no avail. A new night, an economic dark age, descended on Great Britain; and although the reports of the trade in human flesh in Regent's Park must largely be discounted as exaggerations we did see an occupation by American and Canadian forces and the assassination of most of the members of the coalition Cabinet in the Downing Street Bomb Plot. From that blackest era of our history emerged the two great forces whose interplay has shaped the society in which we live. No longer Tory and Labour, no longer the Haves and the Have-Nots, but a division far simpler and more deadly. The Drivers, and the Peds.

'During the first Ped administration all motoring clubs and organisations, both national and local, were outlawed. Brands Hatch and Silverstone circuits, along with half a hundred private tracks scattered through the country, were ritually destroyed; and while the rest of the world tittered or stood aghast, a programme for the breeding of number-less horses was solemnly undertaken. The project, noble in conception, failed; we lived, despite the tenets of our leaders, in the twentieth century. The motor vehicle once more began to pervade our roads; but it was a motor vehicle with a difference. The SafeTiPed, that pink balloon, that unspeakable nexus, that Cloud Seven on which we all perforce must float. Rationalisation is complete, Pedestrianism triumphant. England at last is at peace with herself; the tranquil content of the cabbage patch reigns over all, the happy anonymity of the anthill. While the Individual withers, and the World is more and more . . .

'Friends, we of the Driving Party ask ourselves if these things truly must be. Have individualism and free will survived the onslaught of the Armada, the massing of the Grand Army, the terror of the *Wehrmacht*, only to sink beneath a self-created Bureaucracy? We feel the answer is no. We *know* there is another course; and we refuse, categorically, to fall down and worship before the Golden Calf of Normality. Hounded we may be and outlawed; but therein lies our strength. And we hope too, salvation; the salvation not only of ourselves but of all others who still might feel the stirrings of individuality. Who may in fact remember that once, long ago, they were British . . .'

Hanssen leaned back, blew a smoke ring and watched it float, paling and expanding, to the ceiling. 'All for now, Connie,' he said, briskly. 'Develop that into the Party Line, hard sell. Couple of hundred words should do it, you know the score. I'm going out for a drink; somehow I feel I could use it . . .'

The girl sat propped up on her pillows, face pale under the glaring lights. Her temple and cheek were still covered by heavy pads of gauze; her one visible eye moved restlessly, feverishly bright. Beside her a houseman checked her pulse, consulted his watch and nodded. 'Gentlemen,' he murmured, 'you may begin your investigation.' There would be no false answering; the patient was shot full to the ears with scopolamine.

Masterwarden Bigge glanced round at his colleagues and cleared his throat importantly. Public acclaim, if it had not physically increased his stature, had puffed his chest and given to his eyes the burning glow of the zealot. 'Your name,' he announced to the patient. 'You will tell us your name.' Beside him a camera dollied forward for a close-up; millions caught the flat whisper of the answer.

'Moira Alice Kelly . . .'

'Moira Kelly,' said Mr. Bigge, drumming his fingers on his black-uniformed knee, 'you stand accused of the gravest crime recognised by English law; the crime of Speeding. You stand accused of wanton Lust, of the naked will to murder. How do you make answer?'

Silence, while the girl seemed to puzzle over the words. Finally. 'I did not wish . . . to kill . . .' The syllables came limpingly, blurred by drugs and pain.

Mr. Bigge coughed again, crossed his booted legs and pulled at his moustache. Badly conducted, this interview could be disastrous; the watching masses could easily be swung to sympathy for the accused. 'Did you,' asked the Masterwarden finally, 'tamper, knowingly and with malice aforethought, with the governorbox of your ve-hicle?' He pronounced the last word carefully, giving full value to each of its syllables.

'Yes . . .'

'Were you aware at the time of your action that you were behaving contrary to the tried and established laws of this realm, that your behaviour was in fact malicious and selfish, that you were placing in mortal jeopardy the lives of your innocent fellow beings?'

'I was aware . . . that it was beyond the law.'

'When did your illegal act take place?'

'The morning . . . the morning . . .' The patient rolled her head miserably, seeming confused. 'Come,' said Mr. Bigge, 'I must insist that you reply.' A tear coursed instantly across Moira's cheek. The Masterwarden swore under his breath.

The houseman leaned forward quickly. 'The patient is suffering a deep trauma,' he said. 'Amnesia is commonly experienced in cases of this nature.'

The situation was saved. Mr. Bigge regarded the doctor icily. 'Of that,' he said, 'I was hin fact haware . . .' He turned back to the girl. 'It is the contention of the State and of this Tribunal,' he said roundly, 'that you have succumbed to that blackest of temptations, the Urge to Drive. That you are not in fact a Roaduser; that you have cut yourself orf, wantonly, from the innocent, decent mass of your fellow beings. That you have studied, in secret and alone, those black Disciplines long since proscribed and condemned, placed beyond the reach of rational men. I propose to establish this beyond doubt. You will answer what I ask; and you will answer truthfully. Do you understand?'

'Yes . . .'

The Masterwarden consulted a typewritten slip. 'What,' he asked, twisting his mouth at the unpleasantness of the question, 'was the largest vehicle ever to race at Brooklands?'

A pause; then, 'The Higham Special,' said Moira dreamily. 'Powered by a vee-twelve Liberty engine of twenty-seven litres.'

Mr. Bigge winced as though struck; then he rallied. 'I see. What do, or what did, the initials A.C. stand for?'

'Auto-Carrier. The firm was founded in 1904 to manufacture commercial vehicles.'

'I see. In what year was the first hill climb at Shelsley Walsh?'

'Nineteen . . . oh five . . .'

The questioning proceeded. The definition of the Treasury Rating; Bugatti's Christian name; the year of Zborowski's death; the date of Moss's retirement. Mr. Bigge's lips set in a whiter and harder line; his moustache bristled and quivered; his eyes snapped with their reforming zeal. And when at last he closed his black leather book, and drew over his nobbled hands his black leather gloves, the fate of Moira Alice Kelly was sealed.

A bright rectangle sailed back into blankness as Hanssen killed the videoscreen. He frowned, squeezed his lower lip into a vee, raised his eyebrows and shrugged. 'Well,' he said cheerfully, 'that, I take it, is that . . .'

Tinker, resting brawny forearms on the top of the telly-box, narrowed his eyes. 'Hanssen,' he said ominously, 'we're going to have to get her . . .'

'Out of the question, dear chap,' said Hanssen genially. He leaned back to examine faultlessly manicured nails. 'They'll have her tied up every way from Christmas. Special details, security guards . . . can't consider it.'

'Now listen here a minute, Hanss—'

'And you, listen to me,' Peter Hanssen sat up sharply, opening surprisingly brilliant light-green eyes. 'Tinker, you're a bloody fool. One day, now you just hear me through, you'll get yourself hung, and drawn, and quartered, and us along with you. No, don't yap back, I get tired of hearing you.' He fanned his hands impatiently. 'First that gag with the Elan. *Stopping* for a *shunt* . . .'

'Well what would you have done?'

'Driven past,' said Hanssen icily. 'Now listen. We're an extremist group, O.K. We believe in the Party, we want the Party to win. But we're not here, and this you know as well as I do, we're not here to start a private war. In just six months there'll be an election, you can take that from me. And the Drivers are going in, now that comes from the top. Anything we do to prejudice that—'

Tinker pulled from his head the old straw hat he habitually wore, slammed it onto the carpet. 'Hanssen,' he said. 'Oh, Hanssen, haven't you got a soul?' He pouted, pulling at the hem of his sweater. 'Owwwhh,' he said. 'She's a little peach, Hanssen. Didn't you see the freckles? And the little tear? Now you know what they're going to do with her, you worked it out? They'll shave all her hair. An' open her scalp, an' trepan her skull. And *bzz, bzz, bzz*, at the little white fibres . . .'

'Spare us,' said Hanssen wearily, 'the ghastly details . . .'

'I don't *wanna* spare 'em . . . !' Tinker howled, exasperated; the straw hat suffered again. 'Hanssen, I can't stand it. I gotta

do something; if you won't, I will. And I tell you you can't
stop me—'

'I could put a bullet through your vast thick head,' said
Hanssen cuttingly. 'Or maybe through something delicate.
Tinker, you've got more brains in the arse of your pants than
ever grew between your ears—'

'*The hell!*'

'SHARRAP!'

'Oh dear,' said Hanssen. 'I get so tired, I really do . . .' He
looked round at the others in the room, and back to Tinker's
glowering face. 'I take it the company is of a mind with our
. . . ah . . . colleague?'

Johnny Morris wagged his shoulders self-consciously. 'It's
murder, Hanssen,' he said. 'What they'll do to her. I reckon
m-maybe we ought to try. Can't do us any harm with the
Party. Good publicity.'

'Oh yes,' said Hanssen. 'It shall advantage more than do us
wrong. I've heard that line somewhere before. What about
the rest of you? Sue? Tony? Richard?'

Uncertain mumblings. Sue Mercer, sturdy and brown-
haired, fixed gorgeous eyes on Hanssen and rubbed her nose
reflectively. 'I think you're outvoted, Peter. After all we are
an Action Group.'

'*Einsatzgruppe*,' said Hanssen bitterly. 'You'll get all the
action you can handle out of this one. This is Trouble, I'll
tell you that for a start.'

'How do you know?'

'Divination by sieve and shears. The tealeaves looked ugly
too. Tinker, you maudlin great ape, have you worked out
how we can lift her?'

'Yeah.' Tinker heaved himself off the tellybox, unrolled
a wall map. At his touch a lighting trough flicked on, glaring
from the white paper with its cobweb-maze of streets. 'Now
then, here's the Social Centre. So. And here . . . Saint Paul's
Therapeutic. The State Home for the Bewildered. Here's
the only practicable route between the two.' He slashed in a

zigzag in coloured crayon. '*Here* . . . is where we pull the job.'

'A minute.' Hanssen was leaning back, fingers clasped round one knee. 'Why are we presuming the . . . ah . . . goods will be transferred to Saint Paul's?'

'Because they don't do laser leucotomy at the Social Centre. And Saint Paul's is a specialist hospital. Anyway I got it from the horse's mouth.' He smirked. 'Felicity Martin . . .'

'Ah yes, Felicity Jane,' said Hanssen reflectively. 'Nice little piece of crackling, as I remember. Still knocking it off with her neurosurgeon pal, I take it?'

'Aye.'

'What did you promise her in return for grassing? Or was it a simple case of animal magnetism?'

Tinker looked uncomfortable. 'Said she could have a run . . .'

'In what?'

'The . . . er . . . Speed Six.'

'You bastard,' said Hanssen evenly. 'Continue.'

Tinker bowed, gravely. The crayon became busy again, sketching in details.

Tinker waited nervously, fingers drumming a tattoo on the rim of the wheel. From time to time he drew violently on a cigarette; the flares of light showed up the illicit details of the cab. Beneath the moulded pink slabs of cushioning lurked an ancient Lotus Elan; the escape car. Across the road Johnny Morris lounged uneasily. Johnny had opted for the worst job of all; driving the ambulance, the red herring, through the maze of levels that lay behind the reconstructed Ludgate Hill. Fifty yards down the road a SafeTiPed was parked; Sue Mercer crouched beside it fiddling with a jack and one front wheel.

The plan was basically simple. A hundred yards away loomed the mouth of the Ludgate Underpass, from which at any moment the ambulance would emerge. Sue's task would be to ram it. Then would come the ticklish bit: disposing, with some rapidity, of the half dozen Wardens and police who could be expected to be travelling with the vehicle. Members of the Action Group, at present mingling innocently with the strollers-by, would perform that duty, losing themselves afterward in the back streets of the area. Johnny would drive the ambulance on at its highest speed while the 'goods'—one Moira Kelly, now officially slated for Personality Correction—were transferred to Tinker's care. The real escape route had been chosen for its unlikeliness; back past the Social Centre, out through the bright lights of the West End. If challenged, the Lotus would use its speed; and affairs would then be in the lap of the gods. Tink stroked the Saint Christopher medallion round his neck and offered up a brief and fervent prayer.

He stiffened. Across the street, moving purposefully, strode a small and black-clad figure, golden bands gleaming on hatbrim and cuffs. Past the muffled Elan, toward Sue and the SafeTiPed. Tinker held his breath. Another twenty yards, ten, five . . . the Warden was passing . . . and no. He stopped; Tink saw the girl straighten, slowly and unwillingly. He looked back at the underpass. Still quiet.

Sue opened the car door, lifted her handbag from the seat. Papers were exchanged; driving licence, insurance, certificates of physical and mental health, optician's report, psycho-chart, testimonials and referee-list, three-month test chit; all the paraphernalia of the twenty-first century Road-user. A torch flashed as the man began to scan the forms, reading with deliberate slowness.

'*Little bastard . . .*'

The words were jerked from Tinker, savagely. Sue smiled, clasping her hands; the torch shone into her eyes, checking pupil contraction. The papers were handed back; for a moment he thought she was clear, then the Warden produced from his satchel a bulky package. Some unidentifiable manœuvres, and a shoulder-high canvas screen began to erect itself on the sidewalk. Tinker groaned; beneath the underpass the glow of headlights showed distantly.

He opened the car door. Sue was shrugging and smiling, arguing with the patrolman while she cast desperate glances at the road behind her. Johnny had stepped forward uncertainly; a nod from Tink, a jerk of the head and he fell into step beside him. They converged on the SafeTiPed, the cosh already swinging in Tinker's hand. Twenty feet away, ten; and the Warden still unsuspecting, struggling with the mechanism of his screen. Tinker padded up behind him. 'T-trouble, Masterwarden?' asked Johnny pleasantly; and the man straightened to face him.

Thunk . . .

Twelve inches of loaded rubber hose flailed briefly. The yellow-banded hat tilted to one side, rolled along the pavement. Sue half-screamed; the body sagged, grunting, into Johnny's arms. No time for niceties; the patrolman was bundled out of sight in the shadows, Tink headed back for the Elan at a flat gallop.

Shouting somewhere; he slammed the car door, gunned her engine. The lights were very close; Sue turned the SafeTiPed out from the kerb barely in time. Tink heard a screech of brakes, a satisfying crunch. A hubcap bounded across the road; he pulled the stockinet mask down over his head, let in the clutch and guided the motor to the scene of disaster.

He saw the mistake almost instantly. The holdup had been anticipated; torches flashed as a dozen Wardens and police converged on the bloodwagon. Barked words of command and the mass of humanity struggling by the back doors parted unwillingly. Two Drivers already lay face down in the road, thumped by the coshes of the guards. Tink saw riotguns levelled, and swerved. A hammering; plastic chips flew from the bonnet, he felt a tyre blow. He ground to a stop and struggled out, arms held high above his head. It was useless; they were caught, fairly and squarely, in a trap of their own devising.

The noise of the helicopter battered back from the fronts of the buildings. The machine swung low, belly lamps glaring, flattening clothes and hair with the vertical gale from its vanes. Tink, staring, saw rope ladders sway against the brilliance. Beside him a Warden stood dazed, mouth ajar, gas grenade still poised to hurl.

Only one thing could pierce the din; the machine's loudhailer. '*Throw down your weapons,*' it boomed. '*On your faces, Wardens, in the name of Saint Christopher . . .*' Tinker's held breath escaped with a vast whooshing. Hanssen, typically, had made his own arrangements . . .

For a moment the patrolmen wavered; then gas bombs burst among them, lobbed in a circle from the machine. Soft thuddings, and the scene was obscured by whirling vapour. Tink wavered, caught on a fine edge of indecision; made his choice and began to fight his way, eyes streaming, through the mob. The disabled Lotus would have to be abandoned, the Warden was far more important. The little man had seen Sue unmasked, the others too maybe. If they left him, that was the end of an Action Group.

The patrolman was sitting up, holding his head with one hand and fumbling for his pistol with the other. Tink kicked him peremptorily across the jaw, stooped to swing him over his shoulder, shouted knowing nobody would hear. The chopper was already rising away. He howled again; a bad moment, then the hailer burst into curdling profanity. A ladder swung at his head; he gripped the rungs desperately, felt the ground snatched from under his feet. Seconds later he was high over Saint Paul's, hearing the wind rush in his ears, clinging to his burden while from below came the scattered plopping of carbine fire. The ladder shortened, winching him toward the cab.

Masterwarden Bigge sat nervously, still fingering his scalp, the focus of a blazing bank of lights. Behind the lamps the masked and shadowy figures watched impassively.

'I knows you,' said the Warden, kneading his hands. 'I knows you all. You'll not get away wi' this. Oh, no . . .'

'Nasty little man,' said Sue. 'Tried to make me pee into a bottle . . . what shall we do with him, people?'

'Hang him!'

'The garotte!'

'No! Something slow!'

'Death of a thousand cuts!'

'Choke him with exhaust fumes!'

'Tie him between two fenders! Tug o' war!'

'Poetic!'

'Hurrah!'

'*No . . .*' Hanssen held up his arms for quiet. He approached the sweating patrolman and leaned to stare at him, hands gripping the back of a chair, eyes glittering horribly through his mask. 'What tales of ghastliness,' he asked, 'could this man tell? What houndings, what atrocities has he not committed in the name of Bureaucracy? Of the State? How many hapless drivers has he condemned to the ranks of the Peds? How many rot in jail on his account? How many breathalyser bags have been filled at his request, how many innocent virgins has he forced to wee into his horrid little bottles? What fate can we devise for him, what punishment truly worse than death?' His voice dropped to a throaty murmur. 'You are in the hands of the Driving Party, little man,' he whispered. '*Expect no mercy . . .*'

Masterwarden Bigge began to twitch, puppet-fashion. 'I've done nothink,' he said. 'No, nothink. 'Cept my *duty* . . .' He swallowed convulsively, Adam's apple prominent against his thin neck. 'I'll . . . I'll tell you what I'll do,' he said desperately. 'I won't say nothink, see? Nothink. I won't talk, I won't give yer away. I *promise* . . .'

'What are promises,' asked Hanssen monrnfully, 'to us outcasts? To we people of the shadows? It cannot be . . .' He reached forward to grip the sleeve of Mr. Bigge. The Warden jerked away, terrified. 'See this man,' said Hanssen. 'This little man who has always Done his Duty. Mark him well, my brothers . . .' He turned the Warden's cuff. 'See these dainty hands. These fingers never steeped themselves in mortal sin; never gripped the wheel of a car, never sullied themselves with her oil. These tiny feet have never caressed throttle or brake. *Have they?*'

Mr. Bigge attempted to draw himself up. 'No,' he said faintly. 'No, I do not drive, I am a Masterwarden, driving is for my underlings . . .'

'No,' said Hanssen, 'he does not drive. The Warden, the guardian of decent wholesome living, the gourmet of temporal sin, would not so sully his palate, destroy that fine nose of his that so often has scented Crime. Brothers, the direction of our punishment is clear. Is it not?'

A rising murmur of excitement. Hanssen's voice rode above it. 'Masterwarden Bigge,' he boomed triumphantly, 'we, the Drivers, thus pass on you collective sentence. *You shall be deflowered . . .*'

Mr. Bigge, sensing at last the horror prepared for him, began to scream and writhe. His efforts were of no avail; the masked figures swirled, dragging him to the centre of the room. '*The Bible,*' intoned Hanssen, in a voice of doom. Mr. Bigge's hands were pinioned; and a great book was banged down on his knees. 'See the faces of depravity,' hissed Peter Hanssen. 'See the killers, the murderers, the viceroys of sin . . .' The Warden writhed again, arching his back; but his eyes were drawn down, with horrid fascination, to the pages that were turned for him.

They were all there; Chapman and Honda, Enzo Ferrari and the brothers Maserati, Bentley and Rolls and Le Compte de Dion, glaring up from their ancient spotty prints: Bouton and Pomeroy, Lanchester, Bugatti, Rudd; and the drivers, Lancia and Rosemeyer, Fangio, Gonzalez, Carraciola; Count Varzi and Nuvolari, Castellotti and Hawthorn and Clarke; and Moss, greatest and nearly last. Mr. Bigge gobbled; his eyes bulged; a sheen of saliva showed on his chin.

The ordeal ended finally; but worse was to come. 'Bring me,' cried Hanssen, 'the sacred vials . . .' The bottles,

unstoppered, were tilted; the Warden felt their contents run
gummily on his forehead, mingle with his thinning hair. Oil
from a Maserati; rad water from a Bugatti; brake-juice from
an XKE. He writhed, half unconscious now, and dimly felt
himself lifted.

They forced him into the Bentley, arranged his feet on
her pedals, curled his fingers on the rim of her wheel. He
smelled the ancient smell of her, the stink of leather and oil;
her bonnet vibrated as she was swung up and fired. Her
exhaust boomed in his ears; his head lolled; he was barely
aware of the flashbulbs that blazed, recording the scene for all
time.

He was hauled from the motor. His legs, jellied, refused to
take his weight. Hanssen turned from the grovelling man,
leaned his hands against the wall. 'Let him go,' he said. His
voice was flat, all passion spent. 'Let him go, we need detain
him no more . . .'

Mr. Bigge staggered down an alley between dim, high-
walled buildings. The night wind soughed past him, lifting his
hair; to either side the warehouses jerked by, window sockets
black and accusing as the empty eyes of skulls. In his nostrils
fumes of petrol and oil still reeked; he touched his face to feel
the dread stickiness there. 'No,' he moaned. '*No* . . .' But it
was true; the nightmare was real. He fell to his knees, clawing
at the collar of his jacket. Sullied, befouled . . . no more could
he wear the proud black of a Warden, no more strut in the public
gaze in the knowledge of duty well and nobly done. They had
ruined him forever, those fiends from the Pit; never, never
again could he hold up his head.

His fingers, falling slack, touched the empty holster at his
hip, fumbled at the leather. He raised his eyes hopelessly.
Ahead of him, at the end of the alley, lights of scarlet and lights
of yellow spun and swam. The Road, once his proud domain,
that could be his no longer . . . His vision spangled with tears;
he rose staggering, unconscious of his actions, ran fast on
wobbling legs toward the brilliance.

Brakes squealed, hooters belched and gurgled; Mr. Bigge bounced screaming from safety pads, cannoned off springy rubber bumpers, was saved time and again by the devious laws of the realm. But no law, alas, can save men from themselves; and the motor car that finally came to rest on his chest, though diminutive and Safe to a degree, still interfered with his breathing effectively enough.

The study was wide and dim, lit by a single Anglepoise lamp above the leather-topped desk. At the desk a man was sitting, back turned to the room. The girl approached uncertainly, feet soundless on the carpet. Behind her the door whiffled silently closed.

He stayed still, seeming unconscious of her presence; but when she paused he spun the chair, braking with his heels. She stood tensed, staring. The lamplight left his eyes shadowed, glistened on his broad forehead. His hair, receding, was combed in flat soft wisps across his skull; his face was heavy, long in nose and jaw, the skin pulled taut and smooth across the cheekbones. There was about him something of the bland intentness of a bull terrier.

The pause lengthened; then he smiled, and the quality of silence was transformed. 'Miss Kelly,' he said, 'how very nice to meet you, my name's Hanssen. Tell me, how do you feel?'

'All right . . .' She crossed her arms, rubbing her shoulders and shivering. 'All right, I think . . . May I sit down?'

He fetched a chair, instantly attentive. 'I'm so sorry. Most thoughtless of me, this must all have been very distressing . . . Have our people looked after you?'

She nodded wanly. 'Yes . . .' She looked round her frowning. 'Please . . . where am I?'

He shrugged. 'The exact location isn't important. I assure you no harm will come to you, you're quite safe. This is the headquarters of an Action Group. As you've no doubt gathered, we are Drivers . . .'

She put her face in her hands, rubbing her forehead with her fingertips. 'Gosh I'm . . . so confused . . . Did it all really happen?'

'It did.'

'Please,' she said. 'The . . . little man, the Warden. What happened to him?'

He frowned, toying with the paperknife on the desk. 'He's dead,' he said. 'I'm sorry.'

'Dead?' She stared at him, wide-eyed and tousled. The word seemed to hang between them in the air, heavily.

'No one was to blame,' said Hanssen. 'Believe me, we did him no harm. In fact it could be said, he died of Principles.'

She pressed her knuckles against her mouth. 'Poor little man,' she said. 'Somehow I was so . . . sorry for him.'

'Yes,' said Hanssen, 'so were we. We hope, truly, he found a happy release.'

'What did you . . . do to him?'

'I told you. Nothing.'

Her voice was very low. 'What will you . . . do to me?'

'Nothing.'

'It's all sort of anticlimactic,' she said. 'I don't know how to talk to you, you see. What you want me to say. There's no real . . . starting point, is there?'

He crossed to the side table, poured a drink. She heard the decanter tinkle as he set it down. He handed her the glass. 'It's brandy,' he said. 'Don't worry, it isn't drugged or anything. Just sip it slowly. You'll be all right soon.'

She warmed the glass automatically between her palms, dipped her nose to the rim. 'I'm not panicky really,' she said. 'Just confused . . .'

He watched her from the desk, expressionlessly, fingers steepled under his chin. She drank, coughed slightly and blinked. Set the glass down on the desk top and accepted the cigarette he offered. The room was silent; in the quiet the buzz of the air-conditioning plant seemed very loud. 'There'll be a terrific fuss,' she said. 'You've got yourselves into dreadful trouble over me.' A long pause; then, 'Why are you looking like that?'

'It's nothing.'

'Please . . .'

'I was wondering,' he said broodingly.

'What?'

'We lost a fine motor car and two good men. I was wondering whether you were worth it.'

She shivered again. 'That's not very fair . . .'

'No,' he said. 'It isn't.' He continued to stare, touching his teeth with his fingernails. Then abruptly, 'Are you afraid of me?'

'N-no. Should I be?'

'No . . .'

Another wait. She flicked her hair selfconsciously; she smoothed it again at once, but not before he'd seen the red curving halfmoon of the scar. 'It's funny,' she said.

'What is?'

'I don't know really. All the years sort of dreaming and wondering, never expecting to meet anybody . . . well, like you. Not knowing whether you existed or not, wondering if the world was really nothing but Wardens and SafeTiPeds, stuffed all full of people who didn't . . . care.'

He stayed silent. Then, 'Do I exceed your expectations, or fall short?'

'I don't know yet,' she said frankly. She took another sip at the brandy. 'I suppose you want me to talk now,' she said. 'Tell you about how it happened and all that.'

'Do you want to talk?'

'That isn't an answer.'

'It wasn't supposed to be.'

'I see,' she said. She studied the tip of her cigarette. 'I'm sort of on trial, aren't I? You didn't do all this for nothing. You want something back.'

'It could be,' he said gently, 'that we have Principles too.'

'Yes,' she said. 'The world's all a mass of Principles, isn't it? They grind up against each other and conflict, and nobody ever knows really where they are.'

No answer.

'It . . . started with my father,' she said. 'He was middle-aged when I was born, when he died he was quite old. He remembered when things were . . . different. He told me once, when he was young he saw Moss drive.'

Hanssen seemed to relax fractionally. 'Did your father teach you about motor cars?'

'No. Well, not at first. He had a lot of books. That was years ago, before you could get into trouble for being anti-social if you had too many. Some of them were always kept locked away. They were in a big old chest. I'd never seen it open. One day I found the key. I was quite small. All the books were about cars. There were models too. Like yours. I'd never seen anything like them, they were so beautiful. They made me cry.

'Father was furious when he found out. He said he was going to beat me for what I'd done, then he said . . . he couldn't beat a child of his for wanting to live and run about, and use air without counting the breaths. He often said things like that, he was a . . . strange man. After that he let me see the books as much as I wanted. I nearly wore them out looking at them. I can still remember them almost word for word.'

'What happened to them?'

'I've still got them. They're hidden. You can have them if you want. I think I'd like you to.'

Hanssen shook his head. 'We'll talk about it another time, just now would be dangerous. When did you learn to drive?'

'Father taught me, just before he died. On a SafeTiPed. The things he called it, you never would believe them. They were appalling . . . After he died I . . . kept it. The Wardens weren't very happy about it. They kept checking me nearly every day but I was careful never to drink anything so I was all right. I was frightened once, I ate a chocolate and there was rum in it and I didn't know. But they let me off. The bag didn't go quite the right colour. I suppose in their way they're fair.'

'Was that the motor you . . . er . . . ?'

She bit her lip. 'Yes. I . . . don't know what happened to me quite. It was just one day I . . . felt I couldn't go on any more not knowing. I had to feel what it was like to drive really fast just once. I felt if I didn't I'd burst.'

'How did you rig the governor?'

'It wasn't clever at all really. The lock number's on the bottom of the casting, you can see it with a compact mirror. I was a comptometer operator in a big garage near Slough. I just stole a key.'

'But you didn't know that in the interests of Road Safety, a Ped's steering assembly is built to fly apart at fifty?'

'No,' she said quietly. 'I didn't know that.'

He stood up. 'Well, I think that's quite enough for one night. I'm sorry I've kept you so long, you look very tired.'

She smiled faintly. 'I feel dead.'

'Yes,' he said. 'Yes, of course.' He opened the study door for her. 'Now I'm afraid we've got a slight problem,' he said. 'You'll have to stay in the flat for a time, and there's nobody else here except me. The gang's had to split up, you see, they're all indulging in diversionary operations because there's rather a large-scale search going on. Tinker's driving a Healey Silverstone down the Great West Road, Sue's dropping thunderflashes in all the Tattleboxes she can find, all sorts of funny things are happening. I have to stop here to co-ordinate everything, but you'll be perfectly all right.' He opened a door leading off the corridor. 'I think you'll find everything you want; and there's a bolt on the inside if it makes you feel better.' He smiled. 'Goodnight, Moira. See you in the morning.'

She stood watching him walk away, with no expression on her face.

Hanssen fell off the bed, sat up swearing. 'What in the name of ten thousand bloody devils . . .' He got up, fumbled for the switch and smacked on the roomlights. A short quilted gown hung across a chairback; he shrugged himself into it, yanking the sash round his waist. He scurried to the door; the second scream hit him in the face as he opened it, seeming solidly to fill the air of the corridor.

'*Moira . . .!*'

A sobbing, dimly audible. He banged at her door. 'Moira, what is it? Can I come in?' He turned the latch without waiting for an answer. The door opened; he clicked the switch of the bedside lamp, saw a terrified white face. She clung to him miserably, trying to keep the counterpane under her chin. 'They were all killed,' she said, 'because of me . . .'

'What *are* you talking about . . . ?' He rocked her, squatting on the bed. 'It's all right,' he said. 'It's all right . . . It's dawn; the cars are in their garages, the dead back in their graves . . .' Her hair was across his face; he rubbed her back, kissing her forehead, feeling with his lips the faint mark of the scar. 'Here,' he said, pulling at the blankets. 'You'll catch your death . . .'

'I was . . . dreaming . . .' She shuddered against his shoulder. 'In the . . . ambulance, when the bump came. I . . . remembered. The fence breaking and the . . . car going across the grass and seeing the wheel run away and . . . knowing I was crashing and there was n-nothing I could do, I couldn't . . . stop . . . And the . . . bang, the terrible bang . . .' She gripped him convulsively. 'In the dream,' she said. 'I wasn't . . . knocked out. I was . . . running and the blood was all coming and I was s-screaming and nobody would help . . .'

'Don't,' he said, frowning. 'You're all right now, now don't don't don't. Moira, *stop it*, do you hear?'

She shivered and clung tighter. 'Don't be . . . angry. Peter, don't go away . . .'

He was quiet, enjoying holding her. Her arms were wide at the tops and brownly strong. He sat a long time while sobbing turned to sniffs. Then, 'Sometimes you lose,' he said, smiling over her shoulder. 'Other times, you win . . .'

'W-what?' Not looking up.

'Hmm . . . Nothing. Forget it. Talking to myself.'

'Talk to me,' she said. 'Please . . .'

'What?'

'Anything. Just talk.'

Humorously. 'What about?'

'Anything. Anything at all. Please . . .'

He frowned. 'The medieval Saints,' he said finally, 'took a very dim view of marriage. Its only real advantage was, it generated fresh virgins.'

'*What?*'

'I was explaining an Attitude,' he said gently. He stroked her hair. 'It's a sort of riddle. In two halves.'

'What's the . . . rest?'

'The other half is an epigram. "There can be no romantic love in a country that lacks the bidet".'

'I don't . . . understand . . .'

'You're sleepy,' he said. 'Try and rest.'

'*No* . . .' Frightened again. 'Tell me about . . . about yourselves . . .'

'What, about ourselves?'

'Everything. Everything there is.'

'Everything isn't very much,' he said quietly.

'Please . . . .'

'Well,' he said. 'We break the law. In all sorts of ways, but mostly with our motor cars. We drive them very fast at night, and the Wardens get cross and chase us about. Sometimes they catch us but not very often. There isn't anything else to know.'

She was quiet again awhile. Then, 'You are a strange man.'

'Why?'

'I don't know. Because you are. You don't . . . care really, do you? About the Drivers and the Peds and all . . .'

'You must go back to sleep.' He was tracing patterns on her shoulder with a fingertip. 'It's very early yet. Only just after dawn.'

'No . . .'

'You'll get a chill.'

'I shan't. Please tell me.'

'About whether I care?'

She waited.

'Well, I do care,' he said. 'Of course I do. But being a Driver or a Ped doesn't really matter. That's only part of it.'

'Of what?'

'Of being one of us. One of His Majesty's Opposition.'

'I th-thought the Driving was the important thing . . .'

'No,' he said soothingly. Still stroking. 'It's what they used to call a *casus belli*, that's all. It annoys the Peds. It's very good for them to be annoyed actually. It helps keep them well.'

'I don't . . . understand.'

'Well,' he said, 'it's like this. When you live in an over-crowded little place like England, and the people keep getting more, and more, and more and more and more till they're standing on each other's heads for room and still more coming, there's two things you can do. You can become a part of the Great Universal Zero, and think everything that everybody else thinks, and do everything that everybody else does; or you can fight it all. Like we do. Do all the things the Peds just hate. Be an anti-Benthamite, a maggot in the big juicy apple of Bureaucracy.' He twirled a strand of her hair round his finger. 'We're all little non-conformists in our own special ways,' he said. 'Tinker writes poetry for instance, when he gets a spare few minutes. Some of it's very good too, though you'd never believe it to hear him boast. And Johnny sculpts and paints, Richard makes pottery. Sue breeds dragon-flies . . .'

'What?'

'Dragonflies. They're extinct now, like Bentleys. Except for the ones she keeps. Each year, when they've laid their eggs, she lets them fly away over all the factory roofs. They always die of course.'

'I'm scared again now,' she said unhappily. 'Somehow it's so terrible, knowing you can't ever win. That nobody cares.

Father used to say, in the old days a lot of the Drivers weren't any better than the Peds. They didn't care either. It was only one or two like you. You can't beat the Peds, not now. Nothing will ever beat them again.'

'Oh I don't know,' he said reflectively. 'One day England will sink back under the sea. That'll puzzle 'em a bit.'

'Peter . . .'

'You've got altogether the wrong idea,' he said gently. 'Winning's a bore. None of us really want to *win*. All the fun's in the fighting.'

'Peter,' she said, 'there's something I want to tell you.'

'Not now.'

'It won't wait.'

He pushed her away to arm's length, held her shoulders and looked into her eyes. 'You shouldn't try to hide the scar,' he said. 'You're very pretty, and it really doesn't matter.' He paused. 'Anything can wait,' he said. 'I mean that. *Anything.*'

She watched back miserably; then from along the corridor came a moaning wail. It rose rapidly in pitch and volume, becoming a howling, an eldritch shriek. It was succeeded by the imperious banging of a gong. She gripped her throat, eyes wide with shock; and Hanssen laughed. 'No,' he said, it isn't the Wardens. Or the Flight of the Valkyrie.' His voice sank conspiratorially. 'It's *my autovalet.*'

'*What?*'

'Autovalet. It's a splendid machine. Tinker made it.'

'But what does it *do?*'

'Well,' he said, 'it's like this. It gets up very early, and switches the rest of itself on, and makes a pot of tea. It's very clever, it has all sorts of little arms and things for measuring. Then it wakes me up . . .'

She began to giggle. 'With *that?*'

'It can get much crosser than that. It gets louder if I don't go to it.'

The sound rose again, sank at last to a mechanical muttering. 'It's in a real temper now,' said Hanssen. 'Stamping all its little

tin feet and swearing to itself. It'll go into the sulks soon; then
it'll switch itself off until tomorrow.'

'Peter,' she said solemnly, 'you're mad . . .'

He looked modest. 'It runs in the family,' he said. 'I really
can't claim any credit . . .'

She twined her arms round him again. 'Don't go,' she said.
'Not for a long, long time. Promise?'

He frowned at her thoughtfully, suddenly far away.

'I'll tell you what,' she said, nuzzling him. 'If you promise,
I'll tell you what I'll do. I'll make your tea myself, later on . . .'

'It was marvellous,' said Tinker cheerfully. 'Really terribly
funny. When I tore by they all jumped in the air like Keystone
Cops . . . Hanssen?'

No answer.

'*Hanssen!*'

He threw open the door, and stopped in his tracks. 'Oh, I
say,' he said. 'Oh, you randy old bastard. Oh, *well done* . . .'

A trilby hat, one size too small and perched centrally on
Peter Hanssen's broad skull, gave to his silhouette the decent
semblance of a Roaduser; spectacles, plain-glassed and owlishly
framed, completed the transformation. Moira, sitting beside
him on the front seat of the SafeTiPed, wore a drab frock
several inches too long to be fashionable; behind her Sue was
similarly veiled, and Tink had forsaken his traditional boater
for a vast cap of black and white checks.

The car turned into the forecourt of a large showroom.
Through the plate glass windows its identical brothers glowed
pinkly, prim in their neatly spaced lines. 'The finest place to
hide a pebble,' said Hanssen cheerfully, 'is undoubtedly on the
beach . . .' He glanced sidelong at Moira. 'You know,' he
said, 'I didn't go for it at first; but now I'm nearly certain I
prefer you blonde.' She smiled nervously, touching her forehead. The scar had almost vanished now; prosthetic make-up
took care of what traces remained.

The SafeTiPed crossed the forecourt, nosed into a covered driveway and floundered to a halt in a plain, fluoro-lit parking area. The hooter bleated thrice; typically, a portion of wall slid to one side. Hanssen drove through, parked and climbed out of the vehicle. 'Well,' he said, 'feel a thrill, m'dear? You're standing on the Central Museum.'

Moira sniffed. 'First you said it was under Buckingham Palace, then that you got to it through the Albert Memorial. I'm just not going to believe you any more . . .'

Hanssen grinned. 'As you like . . .' He skimmed the trilby gratefully into a corner, took her arm and guided her through a door. The others followed, closing it carefully behind them. Moira shivered slightly; the air struck cool and damp. A short passageway led to a flight of steps. 'Old wine cellars,' said Hanssen, ducking under a round brick arch. 'Very deep . . .'

A white-painted wall section lifted grumblingly to reveal yet more stairs. 'Steady,' said Hansen. 'Some of the treads are a bit dodgy . . .' Moira felt her heart begin to pound. She climbed down cautiously into blackness. A torch flashed; hands gripped her elbows. She pulled back momentarily. 'It's all right,' said Hanssen. 'Come on . . .'

The sloping tunnel beyond was like nothing she had ever seen. Completely circular, constructed of joined rings of concrete, its queer acoustics caught the echoes of their footsteps and echoes of the echoes, flinging them forward and back; strange winds owl-called through unseen vents, dry and vagrant breezes brushed her face. 'Peter,' she whispered. 'Where are we . . .?'

Hanssen laughed. 'In the days of the Grand *Débâcle*,' he said, 'some Transport Minister or other, I forget which, dreamed up the idea of tube railways. Must have had interests in cement and tunnelling gear. They didn't get very far with them of course and the plans of the bits they did build have been most artistically lost.' He chuckled again. 'Amazing what can be done,' he said, 'with a well-found tube railway.'

Moira spoke very quietly. 'How far does this one run?'

'About thirty miles. It's got dozens of entries and exits. It isn't one of the biggest of course, there are plenty longer.'

'I see. No wonder the Wardens can't ever catch you.'

'No wonder,' he said non-committally.

The tunnel ended. They crossed a hall dimly lit by pilot bulbs. Moira saw festoons of old cable, torn warning notices about smoking and being Aware of the Ramp. Sue and Tinker followed close behind; the echoes of their footsteps ran shrill across the curving roof.

Another door, at which a password was exchanged; Moira was ushered through and found herself once more in near darkness. Hanssen's fingers touched her wrist; she followed him timidly, setting her feet down with care. Again she seemed to be moving down a slope; the breezes blew stronger and cool, from round about came susurrations and whisperings, snatches of laughter and half-heard speech. Lights gleamed, vague and illusory, floating from distance to vanish again in the dark. Once a strange figure glided past. It wore the racing whites of an old-time driver; over its shoulders was draped a scapular chequered in white and black, and as it turned its helmeted head she saw it wore the startlingly lifelike mask of a skull. She caught her breath and the darkness was back, clinging and absolute. From it came booms and chuggings, the rising snarl of high-powered engines. She was startled again until she realised she was hearing a recording.

The atmosphere of mystery was well maintained. When Hanssen finally stopped she felt disoriented and bemused. A heavy grinding, as of a steel shutter swinging back before her face; she was urged forward gently, stopped to hear the metal clang behind her. She made to speak, felt Hanssen press two fingers lightly against her mouth. Darkness and silence were absolute; it seemed she could hear the thumping of her heart.

Somewhere ahead of her a light began to glow, colourless and swimming. With it came a noise, half musical, a single chord pitched on the low threshold of audibility. Her hand went automatically to her throat, subsonics triggering panic-responses. The note throbbed, faded with the strengthening of the light; and she gasped, a short hissing sound of sheer surprise.

She stood in a great square hall; and before her, dark grey against the brighter greyness of light, were the Cars. Brooding hulks they were at first before the light, still richening, gave splendour to their paintwork, gleamed from leather and glass, struck spindle-shaped reflections from headlamps and bonnets and wings, from radiators of brass and radiators of steel. They were all there, Fraser-Nash and Rolls, AC and Jaguar and Delage, Bugatti and Lagonda, Maserati and MG; but she had eyes for only one. It stood in front of her, raised on a plinth so its initialled bonnet was higher than her head; a mighty Speed Six, gleaming and perfect, complete to the last detail.

She walked forward helplessly. The thing that had loomed from so many pictures, studied and pored over till her head had spun; the great ghost, here in its complete steel, so big, so much vaster than she had dreamed. Aloud she whispered, '*I wasn't worth it . . .*'

Hanssen had moved in front of her. He stood with his head lowered, hands gripping reverently the cockpit side of the Bentley. She walked to him, silently, stooped fiddling with her dress, showing leg. She straightened, and pressed the nose of the little automatic against his neck just behind the ear. 'I'm sorry,' she said, small-voiced. 'Please don't try to move . . .'

He stayed still, eyes watching ahead, feeling the trembling of her arm transmitted to the gun. Tinker and Sue had stopped, frozen, halfway to the door. Hanssen inclined his head slowly. 'Very good,' he said. 'Nicely timed. I must compliment you, *Warden Kelly* . . .'

She jerked as though slapped. Then, 'How long have you known?' The voice was flat, expressionless.

He flexed his fingers slowly on the door of the car. 'All the time,' he said.

She glanced sharply to her right. 'No closer, Tink,' she said, 'or I shall kill him. Get down, both of you. Flat on the floor.'

They obeyed silently.

'How did you know?' she asked. 'No, don't turn round.'

'It was quite simple,' said Hanssen quietly. 'The drug scene wasn't faked, you used your proper name. I knew we were supposed to pick you up, it was to be made easy for us. Only Masterwarden Bigge and his little gang weren't in on the deal, they nearly spoiled it for everybody.' He paused fractionally. 'He isn't dead by the way,' he said. 'He's in hospital, we only found out this morning.' He moistened his lips. 'Well, Moira. What are you going to do?'

'It's done,' she said. Her voice was brittle as glass. 'You're all in the can, every one of you. By now the rest will have been taken away. Any moment they'll break through the door.'

He moved his head slightly from side to side. 'I don't think so.'

'I'm sorry,' she said. 'But I'm a walking radio beacon, they've been tailing me ever since you took me away. Every garage you've used, every house you've been to. It's finished, Peter. You're through.'

Flatly. 'Radio beacon?'

'Yes. I'm bugged, Peter. I wanted to tell you once. I nearly did, but you wouldn't listen. Now it's too late.'

He smiled. 'If you mean that mess of shoulderstrap circuitry we picked apart the night you joined us,' he said, 'I'm afraid you'll have to think again, m'dear. You see we're not quite as clueless as we look . . .'

He heard the little intake of breath; the gun wavered then pressed again firmly. 'I'm afraid,' he said, 'it's all up to you.' He swallowed. 'I'm sorry it wasn't for real,' he said. 'But while it lasted, it was very nice . . .'

A tear started suddenly, trickled to her lip. 'No soft talk, Peter,' she said. 'All that's done.' She brushed at her face with the back of her free hand. 'When I tell you, step down. Walk very slowly to the door.'

He shook his head again. 'It's no good,' he said. 'You're going to have to kill us, Moira. Because if you don't one or other of us will jump you.' He waited a moment. 'There's a pit over there,' he said. 'Best shoot us on that. The boards will stop the ricochets.'

'You're . . . mad,' she said unsteadily. 'You want to die. All of you . . .'

'No. We want very much to live.'

'Why, Peter,' she said bitterly. 'Why did you do it? Why did it have to be me . . .?'

'There's another little story,' he said gently. 'Moira, you know what it's like to be afraid. You nearly died once yourself, for the State, you're a very brave little girl . . . Well, there was a driver once years ago who vomited on the track every time he got into his car. Because he was so afraid. *But he always got in.*' His hands clenched on the cockpit edge. 'This is the real Inner Mystery,' he said. 'The thing the Peds will never understand. Because they shut it away in the dark, and won't look at it. That way they think they're safe from it. We're all afraid, every one of us, nearly all the time. That's what we pit ourselves against, over and over. We have to test ourselves against our own fear. That's what fear is for.'

He waited. The silence was intense.

'Ideas have to be tested too,' he said. 'Because if we're wrong, if the Peds really have inherited the earth and things are as they should be, then it's time we were dead anyway. We're anachronisms, wailing little ghosts that aren't important any more. That's why we let you go on. We showed you how we lived, what we were trying to do. We believed you had a brain that could think and choose. We were testing ourselves. *Against you . . .*'

She seemed to be panting. '*Shut up,*' she said. '*Just move . . .*' The gun jabbed at his neck.

He ignored her. 'More than us will die,' he said, 'when you pull that trigger. Look at the cars, Moira. Look at them. Can't you see a Shape? A Shape that runs somehow through every one, something that repeats and repeats all the way down the years? It's the Shape of speed, and blood, and fear, and loneliness. The Shape of the Spirit of Man. Look at them, Moira. Don't you think a little of somebody's soul went into making each one? Just a tiny bit? Can you really say, they're just old pieces of rubber, and glass, and iron? That they don't matter at all? These are all that are left, Moira, all in the whole wide world. Just these few, just one of each. All the rest are broken, and rotted, and burned.' He lowered his voice. 'It will be *Gotterdammerung*, little girl,' he said. 'The end of an epoch. The true Twilight of the Gods . . .'

A long, long wait; then, quickly, the pressure was released from his neck. He stayed still, not breathing, and heard the tiny click as the gun was set on the floor. Moira sat down quietly, head back against the rear tyre of the Bentley, and began to cry. The tears fell silently, unwiped, wetting her chin.

Sue crossed to her quickly, squatted beside her and put an arm round her. 'She'll be all right,' she said. 'Just leave us alone a little while. She'll be all right . . .'

Hanssen moved at last; stepped from beside the plinth, turned to feast his eyes on the great green car. He dropped his hand on Tinker's shoulder, smiling slightly, steering Tink ahead of him as he walked. Their footsteps receded, overlapping and confused, till in time the last faint echo died completely away.